Praise for the New York Confidential series
by *New York Times* bestselling author
Heather Graham

"This intricately plotted mystery...[is] especially enjoyable."
—*AudioFile Magazine* on *A Lethal Legacy*

"Immediately entertaining and engrossing."
—*Publishers Weekly* on *A Dangerous Game*

"A thrilling, suspenseful plot that starts on the very first
page and keeps you guessing until the very end! Kieran and
Craig are an amazing crime-solving couple written with keen
intelligence and sharp instincts. They demonstrate what a
romantic partnership should be."
—*RT Book Reviews* on *A Dangerous Game*

"An intriguing mix of mystery, romance and history. You will
find yourself drawn into the characters and atmosphere from
the first word."
—*Fresh Fiction* on *A Perfect Obsession*

"The vivid details throughout the story are conveyed with
precision and planning, from the gruesome elements
of murder to the beautiful descriptions of New York
architecture. Graham has an amazing way of bringing her
worlds to life, and the inclusion of historical lore emphasizes
the already exceptional writing."
—*RT Book Reviews* on *A Perfect Obsession*

"Intricate, fast-paced, and intense, this riveting thriller blends
romance and suspense in perfect combination and keeps
readers guessing and the tension taut until the very end."
—*Library Journal* on *Flawless*

HEATHER GRAHAM

A LETHAL LEGACY

mira

Recycling programs
for this product may
not exist in your area.

ISBN-13: 978-0-7783-0936-9

A Lethal Legacy

Mira
22 Adelaide St. West, 40th Floor
Toronto, Ontario M5H 4E3, Canada
www.Harlequin.com

Printed in U.S.A.

This one is especially for my niece-in-law,
Franci Naulin Davant, for loving books—
and for being the most incredible mom to
Graham, Noah, and Liam, and wife
to my incredible nephew, D.J. Davant.

A LETHAL
LEGACY

PROLOGUE

He'd found it! Good heavens, thank God above. He'd found it.

Frank Landon couldn't believe his luck. The cave wall was littered with strange symbols, and the little low archway in it had to mean that a hiding place was near.

He moved forward, sliding first to his knees and then down flat. The arch, which he figured must be an entry, was a good fifteen feet ahead of him down the narrow, low tunnel. People had probably stashed all kinds of goods in the caves since the beginning of modern history, but this had to be what he was looking for.

He started, nearly bumping his head against the hard stone, when he heard a shuffling down the length of the cave. For a moment, he froze.

How could he explain his current position to Finn?

He listened—there was nothing. He was probably being an idiot. Finn hadn't followed him, and there was no one else on the island. Except for Finn's new girl-friend, Elayne, and Frank's own fiancée, Margie.

Margie hated exploring anything; she would be sunning by the house, on the one little spit of beach the island offered.

And Finn and Elayne…were still in bed. They spent a lot of time there.

There were bound to be creatures in the cave. Rats, at the very least. That was probably it.

Rodents notwithstanding, it was all so amazing.

Just minutes ago, he had been standing on the highest point of the island, looking around. He could see the panorama of the great skyscrapers of New York City off in the distance—modern man's great pyramids to the sky, reaching almost to the heavens above. Now, he was deep in the earth.

The day was hidden; it was pitch dark except for the narrow stream of light from his lantern. Above, the day was a field of sunlight and blue.

Little-known Douglas Island was a tiny bit of granite and poor earth and dirt out in the water, far from the madding crowd, the bustle of ants. Close enough—but the mainland was obtainable only by boat. It was like an afterthought, or a crumb, left over when the continents split and shifted.

And it belonged to Finn's dad, Jamie Douglas.

A room! He felt another surge of excitement. Just beyond the archway and the sunken-in wall, there was an open space. A tunnel leading down to…treasure. He was certain.

Frank inched forward, army crawling on his belly.

Of course, Jamie Douglas had no idea that his son

and Frank were out on the island. To him, it was a dangerous place where pranksters came to die.

And that was because of myth and legend, Frank thought. Superstition. There were so many stories about the island. Frank didn't really know or understand them all. But the biggest rumor to include the island was about the Ark of the Covenant—that fabulous box crafted from wood and covered in gold, created to hold the Commandments and whatever else. The Ark had begun life in ancient Hebrew times in the Middle East. And supposedly according to the top scholars, the Ark was still somewhere hidden deep within a tunnel where a temple had been. The Israelis didn't allow people to mess with it because it was now a Muslim holy place.

However, legend also had it that the Ark had been seized by some unbelievers in a battle, then had been rescued by the Knights Templar, moved to a church in Scotland, and then *supposedly* brought over to the New World when the Vikings visited North America long before Columbus sailed the ocean blue. There had been rumors throughout modern history that it had been secreted on a Canadian spot of earth—Oak Island. Some even said that the Patriots had stolen it from Redcoats during the American Revolution, or that it had been hidden when a Confederate general/professor had sent spies to find it.

But recently a scholar by the name of John Smith had written an article that suggested Oak Island as the landing spot for the Ark was wrong from the get-go, that it had in fact been brought to Douglas Island by Scottish Vikings, descendants of Templars.

It was a small article about that rumor that had gotten Finn going. Finn didn't want to look for treasure. Finn was a businessman. He wanted to build a world-class resort. The island was rumored to be cursed, but what self-respecting island wasn't? Finn saw dollar signs. He was a good guy; a hard worker. Frank saw dollar signs, too. Just differently.

Frank didn't believe in curses or legends; he didn't even believe the Ark existed—religious artifacts were not his thing.

Although, as far as curses went, he'd admit that through time, many people had died here. It could be a rough world. Indigenous tribes had perished. Pirates had perished. Settlers had perished.

All that death was something he shouldn't be thinking about as he once again heard a weird shuffling sound down the cavern, from somewhere near the entrance.

Squirrels, rats, creepy crawlies—there were all kinds of creatures that might make those noises.

But the only people on the island right now were him and Finn and their significant others. Finn had gotten the old seventeenth-century house wired and set with private electricity and water, but the contractors who had done that work were long gone, and more workers weren't due out until tomorrow. So for now, it was just the four of them. And there was nothing to be worried about except for the rats. Or maybe bats. Or worms. Not even stray dogs lived on the island.

The last people to die here had been a pair of armed robbers. When they had been found, their stash of stolen gold and jewels had not. They must have gotten into some horrible fight with other robbers or drug runners, maybe. Their broken bones and decomposing flesh had been found out on the eastern rocks, just below the great stone cliff that faced the sea; they'd died painfully from the fall they had taken.

How two men had managed to fall like that to their deaths was beyond Frank. But he could still remember the media sensation when they had been discovered. The incident had occupied the pages of local and national papers for days. Douglas Island, previously unknown to most New Yorkers, had received its fair share of TV time.

Frank believed that somewhere on this island was enough "booty" to let him live to a ripe old age in absolute splendor—even if he turned it all in. The reward—still offered almost a decade later—was generous.

The police had searched. And Jamie Douglas had stepped in as well, but nothing had been found. And while Jamie had never wanted to sell the family inheritance, he also didn't really want to do anything with it. Nor did he want strangers prowling over his land. There were stern warning signs about trespassers being strongly prosecuted if caught.

Douglas Island was littered with caves. And it had been years and years since they had really been explored.

But Frank had discovered this labyrinth in the system. Just yesterday. Someone had been there before, of course. Maybe several someones. But it had been a while.

He'd explored and charted—all while Finn had thought that he was hiking and making notes. Because Finn had no interest in buried treasure, just his resort—a private getaway for wealthy New Yorkers. Somewhere they could get to quickly—twenty to thirty minutes by boat—but that was entirely different from the stone, steel and concrete jungle of the city itself.

Finn would make it happen, Frank knew. It wouldn't

hurt, though, if they could discover the cache of missing modern treasure that had seemed to have disappeared as cleanly as whoever had done in the bank robbers.

The sound came again—an odd shuffling sound. This time, Frank didn't think that it was rats. It sounded as if something was being…dragged, as if someone— or *something*—moved or walked while dragging half their body.

He grabbed his lantern and shot the light back down the passageway. Nothing.

But…yes. He heard the shuffling again.

"Finn? Are you fooling around with me? Come on!"

But there was no answer from Finn. Just that sound again.

He moved forward and the tunnel widened above him, providing him enough space to crawl on his hands and knees again. Then a riveting, blinding light suddenly shone in his eyes.

The light disappeared. And then he saw…

What? What the hell was he seeing? A face, not a face, eyes…eyes that seemed alive like fire in the brutal light.

"What the hell?" he managed to shriek.

Then he felt the first pain. Something hard and sharp against his temple. Then another, against his thigh, and another…hard against his arm.

He heard bone break, and he screamed in shock and pain.

There were more and more projectiles coming at him. Rocks, one after another.

And then he knew how the stupid bank robbers had managed to die. They hadn't fallen.

They'd been stoned.

Stoned…to death.

CHAPTER
ONE

Waves rocked the coast guard cutter gently against the rickety dock.

"I'm good! Thank you," Kieran Finnegan said, releasing the hand of the man who had helped her off the boat.

"No problem. Special Agent Frasier has been around for us plenty of times," the young man assured her.

Craig had friends everywhere, Kieran thought dryly. They'd had no problem getting out here after he'd received the phone call from Finn Douglas.

They'd easily hitched a ride with Captain Ernst of the coast guard, one of his old friends, a man with whom he'd worked at one time when a body had been found floating in the East River, or so Craig had explained to her.

So now she was on the dock, on Douglas Island.

Although, to call the thing she stepped out on a *dock* was an act of kindness—the tiny planks of ancient wood that stretched out to accept arrivals was crooked and uneven at best, but thankfully it seemed to be sound. She really didn't feel like crashing through faulty lumber into the salt water below, banged and bruised.

Especially since they were here today because a man had died—horribly mangled and brutally broken.

Craig watched her eyeing the questionable dock. He shook his head. "Honestly, I told you that you didn't have to come with me."

"I'm fine, just fine, and I want to be with you."

It should have been a matter for the police—one accidental death on an island off New York that she barely knew about herself—and only because she'd seen news back in school about two shiftless bank robbers who had met a mysterious end here.

Douglas Island. A private island. She'd thought it deserted.

Except that they were out here because Craig was a second or third cousin or a slightly removed cousin or something like that of Finn Douglas—son of the island's aging owner. Finn had called Craig, sounding shattered and desperate, and so here they were, on a Saturday evening when they should have been celebrating at the pub. They had a team who had been involved in a run for the elephants at the zoo. Kieran wasn't much of a runner, but the cause had been right. While she wasn't first over the finish line, she'd made it, and to her, that was worth celebrating "Finnegan's Pub Team."

Craig had assured her that coming here might not be as much fun, but it would be good for the elephants. Finn Douglas would donate to the cause, and do so generously.

"You're sure you're okay?" Craig asked her, taking her hand as she moved carefully down the dock.

She smiled. Pain-in-the-ass protective though he might be at times, she loved him. And seeing the concern in his eyes and maybe just his face—handsomely sculpted, and yet ruggedly so—made her realize that she was an incredibly lucky woman, madly in love with him.

And if this was about family—no matter how convoluted—she was all in. God knew he had dealt with her zany family at their wild Irish pub often enough.

"Of course. I'm fine."

"There are a few planks missing—take care."

"You know that this is solid?"

The look he gave her was one of reproach. "That's why I got off the boat first."

"When's the last time you were out here?" she asked him.

"Oddly enough, not that long ago. Mike and I were working a case when a pleasure yacht was stranded not far from here—with drug smugglers aboard. Used the island to hold a few people until the police boat could arrive to collect them all." He gave her a grim smile and added, "I was out here a few times when I was a kid. When Deedee—my mom's cousin—was still alive. Jamie Douglas was thinking of doing something with the place back then, but he decided against it, I guess. Watch your footing."

"I'll watch for the missing planks," she assured him.

But she almost missed a step, because she found that she was looking at the island.

It was small, no larger than one of the little spits of isle off the Florida Keys, but it offered towering rocks with a few scraggly trees and rugged underbrush. There was a large house before them, built, she assumed, in the later Colonial period, or perhaps early Victorian. It offered great columns and wraparound porches on the ground and second level. One cupola rose from the center of the house.

The paint was peeling. There were a few chunks missing from the columns, and in all, if she had come upon it at night, Kieran would have thought it a fantastic entry for a Halloween horror house. Of course, dusk was falling. That added to the look.

"Nice place your cousin keeps," she said lightly.

"Jamie Douglas hates this place. It's been associated with all kinds of bad stuff—the Native Americans didn't even want anything to do with the island, from what I understand. Finn is my cousin. Deedee was my mom's relative. Once... I was close to Finn. But that was before his mom died, and that was a long time ago now. Anyway, at no time in history has anyone ever wanted to do anything with the place—not the Native Americans, not the Dutch and not the British."

"Maybe it didn't work for farming," Kieran suggested. "You couldn't eke out much of a living here—not at a time when you'd need to supply your own food."

He glanced her way with a smile. "I'm going to assume that would be the main reason. The real reason, anyway."

"And the other reason?"

"I'll let Finn explain," he told her, indicating the house.

A man had come to the front porch; he was tall, like Craig, and had the same dark burnished hair. At a distance, she might have even thought that he was Craig. His build was similar.

He had seen them, and he was waving madly.

Kieran knew that Finn was Jamie Douglas's only

son, heir to a tremendous fortune. But Craig had told her Jamie was no easy taskmaster. Finn was expected to work, and work hard. Jamie had inherited his money, but the family was a long line that had believed wealth brought great responsibility; while he didn't publicize his deeds, Jamie Douglas was well known in certain circles as a great philanthropist.

Quiet seemed to suit the family. Kieran hadn't known about Jamie and Finn until that morning when the call had come and their plans for the day had changed so drastically.

The dock led off to scruffy sand and grass. They crossed over it to a place where a gate remained— though most of the picket fence around it was broken or gone. The gate led to an old tile path and up to the house.

Finn Douglas came down the steps hurriedly to meet them.

Finn was a few years younger than Craig, Kieran figured. His jaw wasn't quite as squared. Right now, his expression was anxious. And the man had been crying.

"Craig, thank you!" he said, clasping Craig's hand in a frantic shake. "Thank you... I know this is unusual... I mean, the cops came. And Frank was down on the rocks...and that fall...well, he could have bounced his way down, but Craig...it was exactly the same as it was years ago...as legend has others...and, oh, God, he was my friend!"

"Hey, I'm here. We'll find out what happened," Craig told him.

Finn was looking at Kieran.

"I'm so sorry. You must be Kieran. I'm Finn... Finn Douglas. I guess you know that. I'm sorry, I'm sorry,

I had to call. I can't... Come in, come in, please." He caught her hand, holding it before him. It wasn't a general invitation; he was asking her to become part of what had happened.

"Of course," she murmured.

He released her hand and spoke as they started to the house. "I've got electric and water set up, and with satellites, well, you know we have phone service. No landline, of course, but cell phones do work better here than in Brooklyn, sometimes. The house is solid. I had a contractor and workmen out here. Nothing going yesterday or today. We got the power on and the water set up prior to that, and next week, I was going to start meetings and bring some help back out here, but right now...now that the cops and the forensic people have gone...it's just me and Elayne and Margie. Margie... Oh, my God, she's a mess. They gave her something... some paramedic or whatever... The medics didn't believe me when I said that Frank was...that it was impossible that he could still be alive."

The porch was broad and handsome. Heavy double doors—in serious need of sanding and varnishing— opened to a foyer. A stairway to the right as they entered led up to a hallway. The foyer, and the great room it entered, had remarkably high ceilings. The great room offered a massive hearth and long banquet-sized table, with high-backed wooden chairs surrounding it.

Whoever had built the place way back when had been wealthy; the hearth would have been the only way to heat the place when winter came, and it surely did so here with a vengeance.

"They're in the white parlor, this way," Finn said.

As they passed through a doorway to the left of the

entry, Kieran saw why Finn had called it the white parlor. It was. White walls, white furniture…everything.

The Victorian furniture was covered in what appeared to be fine white velvet and linen. The side tables by the loveseats and wingback chairs were painted white. There was art on the walls: a painting of a white buffalo, and one of a musician playing a harp—and wearing a long sweeping white dress.

The only bit of real color seemed to be in the dresses worn by the two young women who rose when Finn led Craig and Kieran into the room.

Both had been crying. One was tall and dark-haired with a lean face, large dark eyes and a generous mouth. Her face was tear-stained, but her makeup hadn't budged. The other was a tiny blonde, every bit as attractive. Her makeup had run, and black smudges rimmed her eyes.

"This is Elayne, my girlfriend," Finn explained quickly, introducing the blonde. "Elayne Anderson. And this is Margie Appleby. Margie was…here with Frank."

"We're so sorry for your loss," Kieran said, gently shaking hands with each.

"He was a wonderful man, a great friend," Elayne said.

"I loved him," Margie whispered.

"I told you," Finn said to her. "Craig will find out what happened. He will get to the truth." He turned and looked at Craig. "The cops are idiots."

"Hey, I know some good cops," Craig said quietly. "I work with a lot of the guys on the city force."

"Yeah, well these guys…they think that Frank walked over the stone cliffs! Frank wasn't a drinker. He wasn't a fool. And he knew all the old stories that went with this place. He wasn't an idiot. He wouldn't have been walking that close to the cliff edge."

"He might have been," Margie said softly. "He... he..."

She started to sob softly, head lowered, hands to her face.

"Let's all sit, shall we?" Finn asked.

Kieran watched Craig; he waited until the women were seated and then chose one of the wingback chairs, sitting toward the edge, his hands lightly folded, elbows resting on his knees.

"What were you going to say, Margie?" he asked her.

She shook her head softly. She looked up and over at Finn. "He was here for you, of course. He is...was... brilliant with plans and ideas and he wanted your resort to be a great success. But he told me that he was looking for the gold." She was quiet just a minute and then added, "From the time we met, he was obsessed with the idea. In fact, it was part of one of our first conversations." She went on sadly, "I guess telling me was his way of sounding adventurous and intelligent...and exciting, having the possibility of making a tremendous discovery—finding the gold."

"The gold?" Craig pressed, a slight edge to his voice.

"About ten years ago," Margie said softly, frowning as if surprised that he didn't know, "there was a robbery. Safety-deposit boxes at a very exclusive bank. And the thieves were found on the cliffs, and they were found with nothing. They supposedly fell, too. But nothing was ever found of their haul." Her voice took on a bitter edge. "So, the two bank robbers hid their stash— and fell over the cliff. Or another theory was that they were killed by other bank robbers. But none of the stolen bills or the jewelry ever showed up anywhere, and Frank thought it was still here. And there's that ridiculous theory about the Ark of the Covenant going from the Holy Land to Europe and up to Scotland—and then across the ocean, ending up here. But Frank didn't believe that the Ark existed—much less that it could have made its way to Douglas Island. The best thing about the legend, he always said, was the movie with Indiana Jones."

"So he was searching out caves," Craig asked.

"But he was found dead at the bottom of cliffs?" Kieran interjected.

"I didn't know he was searching in the caves," Finn said. "I wouldn't have cared. I mean, my father owns the island, but he hates it. He said if I could make anything out of it, more power to me. I have carte blanche here—Frank could have told me."

"I think he wanted to surprise you," Margie said.

Elayne looked at Margie sadly.

"What would it matter if he was or wasn't in the caves?" she asked Craig. "He was found…at the bottom of the cliffs."

Craig sat back, glancing at Kieran.

"Finn doesn't believe that Frank just fell," he said. "And what he was actually doing might make all the difference."

Margie shook her head, tears filling her eyes again. "Again, I ask—what difference does it make? Frank is dead. I don't care what he'd been doing. And no matter what you do…you can't bring him back."

"No, I can't bring him back," Craig said.

And Kieran spoke up. "But he can give him justice."

"Maybe the place is cursed, really cursed," Elayne

said. "I mean… I saw this thing on Egyptians and they cursed everyone. Maybe that stupid box was in Egypt before the Israelites fled their bondage and it was cursed…like, I mean, King Tut's tomb had a curse on it, you know. And then there was something about the Templars!"

"The Knights Templar," Kieran murmured, as Craig stared at her with a look that questioned the direction this was going and suggested that she jump in. "Many historians and armchair historians believed that the Knights Templar managed to save the Ark of the Covenant. They were persecuted, and Jacques de Molay and at least a hundred others were tortured and burned at the stake. Some think the knights had become too powerful—and far too rich—and some thought that the king of France at the time—and the pope—were horribly corrupt and afraid of losing power. Anyway, they supposedly saved the Ark, and there is an element that thinks it just might have come to the New World. But most historians believe that the Ark—if it does exist—is still in the Middle East. And… Craig was involved with a case involving an Egyptian discovery complete with curses…except it proved to be that someone very human was doing the evil deeds. No curse involved at all."

Craig looked at Margie. "You said that Frank didn't believe in any of the rumors about the Ark—or curses of any kind, I imagine."

"He didn't. But that doesn't mean that this wretched island isn't cursed!" Margie said.

"I'm sorry. I'm so sorry that I made you come here," Finn said.

"I don't believe in curses, and Margie, you're hurting, but you can't really believe in them, either. That area of the island is dangerous—it's a horrible great cliff, with all kinds of jagged rock beneath. That's the curse, if there really is one." Elayne looked at Kieran and then Craig. "I don't know how well you know this place. I don't know it that well, but I looked it up when Finn planned on coming out here. I mean, it is a great spot. And a private island. But probably—and mainly because of the location—it's hosted all kinds of vagabonds and thieves. Bad things happened in the very early days, from tribal battles through the various wars and pirates and…that's why Finn's dad hates the place. He would never sell it, but he wanted nothing to do with it." She glanced at Finn. "Even Jamie says that curses are just ridiculous. And Margie is…horribly upset, of course."

"I need a few facts," Craig said. "Who found Frank?"

"I did," Finn said dully. "We realized this morning that he hadn't come back last night."

"You didn't realize it last night?" Craig asked, frowning—his look for Margie.

"He roamed the island late at night—and then, sometimes, Frank and Finn would be up all night, drawing plans," Margie said. "I—I fell asleep. And when I woke up, I knew that he hadn't been in bed."

"She rushed out… Finn and I were at breakfast," Elayne added.

"I got right up and started looking. There's a large hill in the center of the island, but I thought that I'd try walking the perimeter first," Frank said. "And then I found him, half in the water, half out, and caught between a few rocks on the shore there. I… I called the police right away."

"And they came out this morning," Craig said.

"They came right out. They were here for hours. And

they…" Finn said, and then paused, shaking his head. "The medical examiner has the body, for an autopsy. But everyone thought he had ventured too close to the edge of the cliff. Frank didn't just fall."

"They brought out a forensic team, right?" Craig asked.

Finn nodded solemnly.

"Three boats—the medical examiner, the forensic team and four cops," Elayne said.

"He's gone! He's really gone!" Margie sobbed softly. "Maybe we should just leave it. What does it matter in the end how he died?"

"She needs to mourn, Finn," Elayne said. "This is so fresh."

"Yes, it is. And you loved him, but he was my friend since we were kids," Finn said. "I owe him this… I owe him everything I can give him, everything I can do for him." He looked at Craig. "You can investigate, right?"

Craig winced. "Well, jurisdiction on this is really the NYPD. But I can ask my boss for help, and if the police on it are decent guys, they won't think I'm wedging myself in on it. I'll get the report, and I'll reach out to some people."

"Can you stay tonight?" Elayne asked anxiously. "Just tonight? Tomorrow, some of Finn's household staff will be arriving. It won't be so lonely."

Craig was obviously startled. He looked over at Kieran. "We didn't really bring anything…"

"Who cares what you're wearing?" Margie asked. "And Finn has toothbrushes and toothpaste, brushes, soap…and we have anything you could need… Elayne, right?"

Craig was looking at Kieran. She knew that it was her call.

"I'm so scared!" Margie said.

"There are no curses!" Finn said firmly.

"Please, we need a professional on the island. Finn can hire some security tomorrow. Just tonight," Margie said.

"It's already dark," Elayne whispered.

"We can stay tonight. Finn says cell phones work. I'll just call the pub and let them know that we will be out here. Excuse me," Kieran said.

"I'm going to have to get back first thing in the morning," Craig said.

"Sunday?" Margie asked softly.

"If Frank was brought in tonight, the autopsy will be tomorrow. Every forensic office in the country does its best to autopsy the next day," Craig explained. "And... I need to know just what happened to Frank."

They were all silent for a minute.

Then Margie started to cry.

Kieran walked out to make her call. She left the *very white* White Room and headed out to the great hall area. She dialed Finnegan's. Her brother Danny—the youngest in their family of four siblings—answered the phone.

She could hear the band playing and people laughing in the background on the other side of the telephone line.

"Finnegan's," Danny said cheerfully.

"Hey, it's me."

"Cool. Are you headed here? What was Craig's emergency? It wasn't FBI—Egan and Mike and some other guys from his office are here."

"No, long story, we're on an island that belongs to a

distant cousin of his, Finn Douglas. A friend of Finn's died this morning."

"What?" Danny asked. "My God—you're out on Douglas Island?"

"Yes, I am."

"Oh, you've got to get away from that place. It's cursed."

"Danny, you know that curses aren't anything real. And the place has to have the most convoluted curse I've ever heard about."

"Convoluted or not—people die on that rock like... like popcorn! Don't you know all the history?"

"I know a lot of screwed-up stuff happened here, but Danny, what's going on now is that Finn's family—"

"Craig is related to the Douglas family that owns that island?"

"I didn't know it either until today. Danny, we're staying the night."

"Don't."

"Oh, come on. I'm with Craig. We'll be back first thing in the morning."

"Let me guess. His friend is broken to bits—and he was found on the eastern shore off the rock cliff."

Kieran was silent for a minute, frowning. But of course, everyone knew about the bank robbers who had died.

"Yes, actually."

"You'd better be in to see me first thing in the morning. I'll tell you all about that island."

Danny had spent some time being a bit of a wild thing through high school and even college—but a few years back, he'd become a city guide. He was charming and personable and the perfect person for such a job. He'd also immersed himself in the history of the city with a vengeance.

"I'll see you before opening," she promised. "Meet at the pub?"

"I'll be praying for you all night," he promised.

"Danny, stop it. Curses don't exist."

"Okay, but call me again, before you even head in, okay? Better yet…"

"What?"

"I'm going to come to you. I'll be out in an hour and a half." He was quiet a second. "I'm going to bring you some of the stuff I have on the island. I even have copies of old maps."

"It *is* an island, Danny—there's no subway out here, no ferry—"

"See you," he said, and hung up.

Kieran stood in the great hall, staring at what looked very much like a medieval hearth and the long table that might have seated a noble court. The place was so…big. Maybe it wasn't going to be such a bad thing to have Danny out here, too. And he seemed to know so much about the place.

She headed back into the parlor. Finn and Craig were standing.

"We're taking a quick walk," Craig told her.

"Oh?" She arched a brow at him.

"Just around to the eastern shore. Thirty minutes there—thirty back. This island isn't much more than a piece of rock, you know," he said.

"The shore area is fine. Way too rocky for beaches, and then, in some areas, you have the sheer drop-offs. But it's perfectly safe to walk around at sea level," Finn said earnestly. "You just crawl over a few rocks and get through a bit of bracken."

"It's almost dark," Kieran noted.

"Full moon tonight," Craig told her. "And Finn has powerful lanterns."

"Really powerful. They were all that we had when Frank—when Frank and I first came out here about a month ago to assess what we needed to get up and going."

Margie sobbed again.

Elayne set her arm around the other woman and held her closely.

Craig looked at Kieran, aware that she was unhappy and yet, she knew that look.

Please stay here, watch these two and let me get started. Maybe you can help them, he seemed to plead with his eyes.

She was a psychologist, and she knew well that Margie had just started on the first stages of grief. She needed a good sleeping medication, and then, perhaps, therapy. At the moment, having her friend Elayne by her side was the best help she could receive.

"Okay," Kieran said, "so you're figuring about an hour and a half. Also, my brother is coming out. Do you want me to see what I can do about creating an evening meal?" she asked.

"Yes, please!" Elayne said. "We haven't thought about food."

"Your brother is coming out?" Craig asked, frowning.

"Danny. He could be a big help. You know how much research he's done on NYC."

"And my island?" Finn asked hopefully.

"And your island. Danny is a city tour guide," Kieran explained.

"Excellent," Finn said. He looked at Craig, and she thought again that the two were oddly similar. Finn looked the best he had since they had arrived; going into action was clearly what he needed. He was going to do something. And that was Craig, too. In any situation, do something—move forward. Get on it.

"Get going then," Kieran said.

The two men started for the door. Craig paused, turning to Kieran. "How is Danny going to get out here?"

"I don't know. I guess he has friends, too," she said.

Craig shrugged and he and Finn headed out, Finn telling him they'd just stop in the shed to get the lanterns and then they'd be on their way.

"Can you cook?" Elayne asked hopefully.

Kieran smiled. "More or less. My family owns a pub. It will depend on what's in the kitchen. Where is the kitchen by the way?"

"Through that door there's the small dining room on the left, and through the west door of the small dining room, there's a kitchen," Elayne told her. "The kitchen has doors that lead to the great porch, and then out to the night. And if you go the other way, across the great hall, you find the music room and behind it, the library, and beyond the library, a really cool old office. But kitchen—that way. Do you need help?"

Elayne still had her arm around Margie. Kieran shook her head. "You stay here. I'll find something," she assured her.

Kieran left them. One doorway and one turn, and she was already mixed up. To hell with the island. She really needed a map just to get through the house.

* * *

The island, while being a truly rugged patch of rock and bracken, was beautiful in a wild and majestic way. The level by the house was low; the spit of actual beach wasn't far from the entry to the old house, and then, bit by bit, there were more rocks on the shore, and bigger than those protruding from the water just beyond.

The full moon was a big help that night, casting a blue glow over the landscape as they walked.

Finn glanced over at Craig. "Thank you for coming. I know that we haven't talked in forever."

"It's all right. You weren't even in the country until recently, were you?" Craig asked. He had to admit that he'd been quick to come out here because he hadn't made enough of an effort to contact Finn since Deedee had died. In truth, he'd almost forgotten the relationship; he'd been busy with work, with life, and...with Kieran. Come to think of it, his work and his life had been inextricably bound up with Kieran from the moment he'd met her.

He loved her—and he was *in love* with her. But in all honesty, he knew that their relationship was solid because they worked so well when they did become involved in criminal investigations—sometimes because of happenstance, and sometimes on purpose. It was a fine line. She was excellent at what she did, and she worked with two of the best psychiatrists in the field, Drs. Fuller and Miro, who had supported FBI and police investigations in the city for years—long before he'd met Kieran.

At the moment, he was feeling guilty. For losing touch with Finn—and guilty for dragging Kieran out here when they should have been at a great party at her family's pub.

"You're right, I was in the Bahamas for several years. It's just as much my fault about us being out of contact. I knew how you felt about my dad, but… I should have called you. The last three years, though, I was down near Nassau. I bought some land—with partners—guys who already had a few resorts. We started up a couples-only retreat. It's going nicely. That's what made me think of this place again. A different kind of resort. I mean, I love New York. With a passion. But it's busy, and it's hectic and it's concrete. I see something that's wild and fun. Fix up the pool, get some stables—mules, Frank told me. Not horses. Mules are surer of foot. Even donkeys, but…that's so far in the future. You can have hiking trails—not for really serious hikers, but just for people who need to get away from the city. Frank said…"

He fell silent.

"It was a good plan, Finn."

"Thank you. I mean, thank you for coming. Like you said, we haven't talked since…"

"Hey, it was what it was. I'm glad to be out here now if I can help you."

"Thanks, Craig, really. I don't want to harp on things with Margie being such a basket case—which I understand, of course—but Frank was my best friend. And I can't let this go."

Craig paused. The moonlight was now pouring over the great rise above them; they'd come to the massive cliffs that fronted the eastern side of the island. The rocks appeared white in the glow of the orb above them.

Outcroppings and shrubbery broke the sheer face

here and there. If a man fell, he would bounce upon jagged rock after jagged rock until he reached the bottom and hit either watery sand or more rocks.

"Where did you find... Frank?" Craig asked. He'd almost said "the body." But Finn had just lost a good friend.

Finn didn't appear to want to go any closer. He pointed. "Right there, in the sand between those two boulders. I saw him, I rushed over... He was all twisted up as no human being should ever be twisted. I knew... even as I ran over. Craig, his eyes were still open. As if he was witnessing some unspeakable horror. I was screaming and wanting to touch him and not wanting— to go away, to close my eyes, to pretend I wasn't seeing him...there. As he was. But his eyes were open. I went over. I called his name—stupidly."

Craig was surprised that crime scene tape hadn't been left at the site. But then, if he understood what had happened, the police had already determined that the death had been an accident—on a private island. Forensics had come and gone.

"There," Finn said, lifting his lantern and pointing ahead and a bit closer to the rock.

Moving carefully, Craig stepped over rocks and skirted a larger one.

There was a stretch of dry pebbly sand near the base of the towering cliff that fronted the sea. He could see scuffing—where people had walked. He could see something of the impression of the body—like a distorted "angel in the snow" imprint.

He raised his lantern, spreading the light over the area. He wasn't sure what he'd been expecting to find; except that—if Finn was right, and Frank hadn't just fallen—there just might be something there that no one had thought to look for.

Including him. He searched the area, knowing that the scene had already been compromised. Police, technicians, Finn himself.

There were no rocks nearby that were of a size to be used as a weapon—certainly not to be used to batter a man into pieces, as Frank's body had been described.

Looking up, it definitely seemed possible that a man, bouncing down on the rocks, might indeed have been so broken.

But what would a man be doing at the edge of the cliff? Frank knew the island; he'd already been there with Finn and he'd been exploring for several days.

He moved the lantern, and as he did so, the light caught on indentations that would have been right around where Frank's hand might have lain.

Craig moved the lantern, casting the light in different directions.

Then he carefully stepped over the position where the body would have lain.

Hunkering down, he moved the light, and moved it again.

It took him a minute.

But it appeared…

It appeared that Frank hadn't been dead when he had first hit the sand. It seemed that…

Craig tried to picture the scene as Finn had come upon it. The body…faceup, if Finn had seen the man's eyes. Arm outstretched perhaps, fingers…writing backward?

He studied the sand, moved his face closer and studied it again.

The man had been trying to write something!

But what? Written backward, maybe letters, or strange signs.

"Craig?" Finn called to him. "What is it?"

"Nothing…nothing really," Craig said.

It had to be nothing. Because what the dying man had written, so it appeared, was a single word.

Aliens.

CHAPTER
TWO

Kieran had found some ground beef in the freezer and a box of instant mashed potatoes in the cupboard—good enough. There was enough to feed their group. She wasn't really much of a chef, though she had pretty much grown up in an Irish pub.

And, actually, her favorite chef at Finnegan's was from Puerto Rico.

At least her skill level was competent. She dug around in the cabinets some more and saw that while there wasn't much in the way of offerings that might be considered "fresh," there were plenty of canned goods.

Everyone liked their shepherd's pie differently; she had no idea of how this crew would like it or if they'd like it at all. Crawling up on the counter to reach some of the higher cabinets, she shrugged. She'd throw some peas and corn right in.

She crawled down and tried another cabinet, just curious as to what else she might find. To her surprise, the goods in the lower cabinet next to the refrigerator were all construction supplies. There were ropes and pulleys and other such paraphernalia. Workers were coming in the morning.

Odd, though, she thought, it had been when none of the workers were present that Frank had met his death.

Odd, maybe, but probably much easier for the police when they were questioning people. Then again, the island was full of granite cliffs—as if a whimsical hand at work when the massive continent Pangea had split up had decided to toss down a giant and curious piece of rock, like the dotting on an *i*.

There could have been others there, unknown by those who were in the great old house by the docks.

She closed the cabinet, wondering about Craig's family. There must have been some falling out at some time.

She figured that when he was ready, he'd tell her about it.

She had just managed to put together her very large creation and get it into the oven—having no real idea of how it was going to come out—when Elayne Anderson came through the kitchen door.

The woman was attractive by any standard, with fragile features and huge blue eyes to go with a diminutive height and petite but very shapely body.

"Hey, how's it going in here?" Elayne asked. "And thank you, really, thank you for this."

"Don't thank me until you've eaten."

"Food—anything—is going to be delicious," Elayne assured her. "It's not that I can't cook—okay, I'm really bad, but that wouldn't matter—it's just that Margie is so upset. I'm doing my best. She adored Frank. I think she's in shock. We probably should have insisted that she go into a hospital and be medicated or something. Anyway, I'm here looking for booze."

"That cabinet," Kieran said, pointing. She'd discovered an ample collection of top-shelf alcohol while searching for ingredients.

"I don't think she drinks too much," Elayne said. "But once, Finn told me that good Scotch whiskey is a cure-all."

"Hmm. In my house, it was Irish whiskey," Kieran murmured. "Anyway, right there."

Elayne walked over to the cabinet. She paused; it was high.

"Giants must have lived here. I thought people— other than me—in general, I should say, were getting taller. These cabinets are...old!"

"Let me help you." Kieran reached up into the cabinet and handed the bottle to Elayne.

"I guess you haven't had much time to explore the house," Kieran inquired.

"Oh," Elayne said, waving a hand in the air, "I've seen some of the house. But when no one else is around, Finn is a decent cook and handles the kitchen. I don't know where he keeps things."

"Ah," Kieran murmured. The blonde still stood there. She smiled. "So, have you been seeing Finn a long time?"

"Just a few months, really," Elayne said.

"Where did you meet?"

Elayne laughed. "Margie set us up. Finn was working in the Bahamas, and she was already seeing Frank, so she'd met Finn. I went down to join her for a vacation." She shrugged. "I guess Frank and Margie must have thought that we would hit if off—she made a point to introduce us, and Finn was so sweet and earnest and good-looking. How could I not fall for him?"

"Well, that's nice," Kieran murmured. "I've just met Finn, but he seems to be an extremely caring and responsible man."

Had Elayne been impressed by "caring" and "responsible"? Finn was a fine-looking man—but again, Kieran couldn't help but remember that he was also an incredibly rich man. She was quite certain that the beautiful people flocked to him.

Stop! She told herself. *Don't judge without knowing...* She had barely met Elayne. It wasn't really that the woman seemed less than honest—Kieran had a naturally suspicious mind.

She wasn't sure where else to go with the conversation, which made her feel awkward, since she worked as a therapist. But Elayne most probably didn't want counseling.

She was, however, possibly a witness in a criminal investigation.

"Imagine," Kieran murmured. "You've just been seeing one another a few months…and here you are, in this tragic situation."

Elayne poured a drink, then paused over a second glass.

"Want one?" she asked Kieran.

"No, I'm fine. With my luck, I'd forget the shepherd's pie. Anyway…are you coping okay? Did you get to know Frank well?"

"Frank was adorable. He seemed to love Finn. Such a good friend. But I have to admit, I was afraid for him. I mean, I'm not the type who believes in curses or anything, but man, he was inquisitive! This place has a bad reputation. We warned him to be careful…obviously, Margie would kiss him each time he was going out—she was so anxious! As if she knew…as if she had a foreboding or something." Elayne paused and shivered. "I don't mean that. The world is as it is. But I do know about those bank robbers…and, supposedly, Viking bones and Indian bones and…well, it has to be the terrain, of course. We warned him. And," she paused, looking back at the kitchen door, but it remained closed—no one was listening, "I think he fell. I think he just fell. Like the bank robbers. Finn can't accept it, and Margie can't accept it. But I'm delighted you're here, anyway. This place is a bit creepy—with just a few of us here!"

"Well, my brother is coming out, too, so…we'll be seven," Kieran said.

"Your brother? Really?" Elayne appeared confused.

"I was supposed to see him at the pub tonight, but he's just coming here instead. He's sweet and fun. You'll like him."

"Oh, I'm sure I will."

"And then tomorrow, well, you have lots of household staff coming out, right?"

"Yes, thankfully," Elayne said. "A cook, a housekeeper…an engineer, I think. And workers. It's maybe a bit odd to come from Manhattan to this, but then, that's what has Finn so excited. He thinks that he can do something great—and affordable."

"Seems like Finn is really a wonderful person," Kieran said.

"You've just met? How long have you been seeing Craig?"

"Several years with Craig," Kieran said. "But you know, life, people's schedules… I've just met Finn."

"Well, it's great that Craig could come now. To be honest, I didn't know anything about him, either, until Finn found… Frank." She paused, taking a deep breath. "I'd best get this out to Margie," Elayne said, lifting a glass.

"Of course," Kieran said. "Hey, by the way, what do you do in Manhattan?"

"Oh, I'm a model," Elayne said.

Kieran hoped her smile didn't falter; Elayne was certainly lovely enough to be a model; she was just… short. Tiny.

Elayne grinned. "I don't do runway, I do hands and feet," she said.

"Oh." Kieran tried not to stare at Elayne's toes.

"Believe it or not, there are lots of opportunities for hands and feet," Elayne said. With that, she gave Kieran a conspiratorial smile—as if they were both best friends who knew their current situation was tragic but ridiculous—and swept on out.

Was there any way that little Elayne could be a murderer? Kieran wondered.

Certainly, petite or not, anyone could be a murderer.

Kieran didn't think that Frank had been a little man. And how could such a tiny creature overpower even a small man? And what possible motive would she have?

She had no answers, and in truth, she was totally lost here.

She really hoped that Craig would be willing to explain his relationship to Finn tonight, along with what the hell he thought was really going on here.

Night was falling in earnest, but the moon was spectacular, the glow all but blotting out the stars.

Craig subtly took a picture with his phone; what he'd discovered on the sand wasn't going to be something he'd discuss until he'd had a chance to do more investigating.

The moon showed the cliffs—and that made Craig wonder what on earth anyone would be doing close enough to the edge to take the kind of fall that had apparently killed Frank.

"Have you ever walked up there?" he asked Finn.

"Me? Out on the cliff—hell, no." He shook his head. "That's just it. I know I sound like a broken record, but Frank wasn't a fool or an idiot. Yes, he was an explorer—he was so excited about this island. I didn't pay attention to him half the time. But seriously, he told me about all kinds of things that happened on the island or were rumored to have happened on the island. I guess he thought all kinds of things might be found somewhere here—I just didn't know he was looking for them. Oh, believe me, please, he wasn't a moocher—honestly. He was a friend. A good one. We'd worked together before." Finn fell silent a moment. Then, "Frank had great plans. He'd already charted out where we could have horseback riding, except, like I said, he suggested mules or donkeys and paths that would allow people to ride safely, far away from the cliffs. He had the best plan for stables and paddocks. We both agreed that the place should have a spa and a gym, and the kinds of things you'd expect in a high-end place, a little bit elegant. Frank grew up in a small apartment in Brooklyn. He was big on telling me how we could do all these things—and make it affordable."

"Sounds like he cared about people," Craig said.

"He did. So, you see why I can't let it rest, right?"

Finn asked hopefully. "I mean, I don't know what could have happened. When he supposedly fell, we were—to the best of my knowledge—the only ones on the island. But while the docks are right in front of us, someone could have taken a small boat around to another landing. Yes, it's surrounded by rocks, but in the right craft…"

"I'm sorry to ask you to go over and over this—you just said, *as far as you knew*, it was just you, Frank, Margie and Elayne."

Finn nodded. "You'd have to be a drunk or a fool to go out on the cliffs and fall over," he said softly. "And like I said, Frank was simply neither."

"All right," Craig said softly.

"You don't believe me."

"I do believe you," Craig told him.

"But the cops don't."

"That's okay."

"You really think that you can do something?"

"I can try."

"Will the local cops be pissed at FBI interference? I don't want to call you out of the blue with this huge favor and make your life hard."

"Finn, this is what I do."

"Yes, that's the point. I probably shouldn't have called you."

"It's all right. My boss has a way with people."

"And you have a way with your boss?"

"I do," Craig said. "I'm a good agent, and he knows it. My workweek is never just forty hours. He trusts me. I don't have to be official—and whether I am or not, I can call for help when I need company resources." He grinned. "Kieran works well with him, too."

"Kieran?"

"Kieran is a psychologist—she works with convicted criminals and victims. She and Egan are good at trusting one another, too. Speaking of Kieran, let's head back for now. I'm not letting anything go. I'll follow this. I'll do some exploring myself."

"Thank you. I—I know how you feel about my father."

Craig waved a hand in the air. "I don't like what your father did, or the way he acted."

"I don't like what he did or how he acted either," Finn said. "It was my mother who died, you know."

Craig nodded, looking up at the moonlit cliffs again. "Tell me...were the rest of you together when Frank died?"

"That is a problem to answer," Finn said.

"Why is that?"

"He went out Friday. I think it was still daytime. Yes, it was day. But then, he also often worked late. Margie and Elayne had been at the beach, and came in without seeing him. Margie fell asleep, thinking he'd come up whenever he got back. I went to bed, exhausted. None of us knew he was missing until the morning."

"And Elayne was with you?"

He nodded. "Yeah. I think we went up at the same time. I know that I slept well—like I said, I was exhausted. I'd been on the phone all day with the contractor and architects. I know it may not sound like much..."

"Desk work can get you," Craig said. It probably was exhausting—having that kind of money and trying to manage it all. But then again, Finn had never acted like a rich kid.

Finn's mom was Craig's mother's cousin. And she had been sweet and beautiful and down to earth.

He felt the bitterness well up in him; anger over what was—and what could have been.

He swallowed the gall.

Finn hadn't been at fault.

"The island... I want to make it something good, Craig. I want the rumors about it being cursed and all to end. And I want criminals and murderers to stop making it a playground."

"A noble plan. And I believe you—believe in you. Let's get back now, huh?"

Craig shone his light on the path to return to the house.

Finn followed behind him, silent for a minute.

"Oh, hell, Craig!" he said suddenly. "You don't think... I sure as hell didn't do this. And Elayne is... She couldn't push a cat off a ledge. Margie adored Frank!"

"I don't think anything yet, Finn," Craig told him. "Thing is, that's the way we work. Eliminate all that you can as impossible."

He kept walking.

Finn caught his arm. "But you don't think that one of us having done something is impossible?"

"I don't think anything yet," Craig told him, sighing and praying for patience. "Hey, you asked me here. I have to ask questions, okay?"

"Of course, of course."

He fell into step.

"Can Kieran cook?" he asked.

"More or less," Craig said. "Yeah, yeah, she's fine. And right now, edible will do!"

Kieran was pulling the shepherd's pie out of the oven when her brother Danny arrived.

He was brought into the kitchen by a curious, flustered Elayne.

Danny was, in Kieran's mind, charming and handsome enough to fluster anyone—he was well over six feet, had the reddest hair in the family and a smile that could charm dead men. He had, at times, been an absolute thorn in her side as well, but for the most part, those days were over.

Danny had never done anything illegal on purpose—only when someone down and out had been threatened. She and Craig had met in the middle of a diamond heist—because she'd been trying to put back a diamond Danny had taken to cause trouble for a man being incredibly cruel in the middle of a divorce.

His intentions had been good; he hadn't thought out his actions.

But now, Danny had a great job as a tour director with the city. He could spin a tale—even a factual one—like few others. If the Irish really had any kind of a gift for eloquence, in her family, it had settled in Danny.

He was also extremely bright—and knew history well because it was a passion for him. Especially history when it came to New York City.

"Sis!" he said, striding toward her, giving her a big hug.

She hugged him back, but looked at him skeptically. The greeting felt over-the-top. She'd seen him that morning.

"Great to see you, Danny," she said.

"Oh, you do look just like siblings!" Elayne said. "And the kitchen smells divine."

Danny looked at Kieran and quirked a brow. "You've been cooking?" he asked.

"Yes, and you're going to love it," she assured him flatly.

"Obviously," Danny said.

"I think that Craig and Finn should be back any min-ute," Kieran said. She hoped so, at least. It was dark out now. "I found paper plates," she said. "Elayne, would you mind grabbing them and that plastic silverware?"

"I'll get right to it!" Elayne said.

"Plastic and paper for a gourmet meal?" Danny asked.

Kieran somehow refrained from kicking him.

"Grab the big pan—with potholders. It's hot. I'll get something to put on the table."

"Ouch! Got it," he said, doing as instructed.

"And behave," she whispered to him. "A man was killed. These people are grieving."

"Hey," he protested, frowning. "I know how to be-have at a wake. We're Irish."

"It's not a wake—and that's what scares me," she told him. "There's nothing normal about this situation and no one knows who did what, who is in pain—and who might be a killer."

She started for the dining room. He set the pot down and caught her by an elbow. He was dead serious and very intense. "Kieran, I intend to be circumspect, but there's something about this place. It's not cursed as in hoodoo voodoo or anything like that—it's cursed because men have seen it too many times as a place where evil can be practiced. I'm not talking about it with anyone but you and Craig first, but you need to know the history."

"It's an island," she protested. "Rock and shrub and beach and trees. The whole point is—it's not about the property, it's about who would kill Frank."

"Agreed," he said softly.

She felt her edge waning. "Danny... I never expected

any of this when we started out this morning. And you…
you could have been enjoying the band and the day…"

He smiled. "No, my dear big sis. You've come to the
front for me so many times. You know, you don't have
to be here, either." He cleared his throat. "Cooking."

She glared at him.

"I do have to be here," she told him.

"Ah, love!"

She swatted him. "Yes! That's what partners do. Help
each other."

"The point is, we both have to be here. Okay?"

She nodded. "Thank you."

"Of course. And I'm going to love your cooking."

He turned to retrieve the casserole dish. Kieran
grabbed a mat to place on what she was certain was an
antique and very expensive table.

Kieran heard Craig's and Finn's voices drifting in
from the front hall. Margie was anxiously asking Craig
what he thought as they entered the dining room.

"Margie, I don't know. I've just begun looking into
all this," Craig said, glancing over at Kieran and Danny
quickly. "It takes time," he added very gently.

Margie nodded. Then she looked around the room.
"You're all so wonderful to have come to help, and I'm
grateful," she said. "Will you forgive me if I take a plate
and go up to my room?"

"Of course!" Finn said. "Whatever you need to do."

"I think I just need to be alone now," she said.

"Margie, you go on up. I'll bring you a plate. And
water? Soda? What would you like to drink?" Finn
asked, concern in his voice.

"More of that whiskey," she said. "And a glass of
water. Thank you, Finn."

Margie started out of the room.

"I'll fix a plate," Kieran said.

"I'll get the whiskey," Elayne volunteered.

Kieran scooped out the first serving of her creation for Margie. Elayne hurried into the kitchen. She came back with a glass of water and a good serving of whiskey in a second, smaller cup, on a tray. "Put the plate right here, Kieran. I'll run this up to her and be right back."

Kieran did as she was bidden.

"I'll take the tray," Finn said. "You all...go ahead. Sit down, please."

He took the tray and followed in Margie's wake.

"Ladies? Please?" Craig said politely, drawing out a chair for Elayne.

"It's really nice of you to come out here," Elayne told Danny as he handed her the first serving. "I admit, the more the merrier tonight. Is that okay to say on a day like this? We're all so saddened and so terribly unnerved. I mean, if it was an accident, it would be tragic, and we'd all be horribly stricken, but wondering if it was an accident or maybe not, and then wondering if... someone else could have been here..."

"I don't think we need to wonder if someone could have been here—that's a definite possibility," Craig told her. "But...we have to figure out, if so, how, when and who."

Finn walked back into the dining room. He looked incredibly worn and tired.

"I should have stayed in the Bahamas."

"Finn," Elayne said softly, touching his arm with what appeared to be very real affection and concern. "If we'd been in the Bahamas, something could have happened there, too. A boating accident, a mugging, a—a shark."

Finn shook his head. "Margie is… I suppose I could insist she get off the island. Maybe it would be better for her."

"She doesn't want to go home?" Kieran asked.

Danny passed Finn a plate of food and Finn thanked him. Then he said, "No. I thought at first that she did. Then, I thought that the police would give us all one of those 'don't leave town' speeches. But…as I told you, they *immediately* chalked it up to a sad accident—one that has happened before, even if that was to crooks and Frank was—wasn't a crook, was a good man. Good man, bad man, a fall is a fall and death isn't choosey. But they didn't tell us we had to leave the island, or not to leave the island. And when I asked Margie, she said she needed to be here, she couldn't get it together enough to leave, and being here made her feel a little closer to Frank."

"But she does seem to think it was an accident—and nothing more," Craig said.

Finn shrugged. "I wish I could have said yes, it was just a tragedy. I just can't."

"And you shouldn't," Kieran told him.

He smiled at her. A smile that was a lot like Craig's.

"Thanks—thanks for the belief in me."

"But you people work with bad things all the time," Elayne said. "Do you sometimes think that makes you a little jaded—suspicious of everything? I mean, I admit, when Finn told me about you, Craig, I was afraid that… that he was a little unhinged by what had happened. It didn't occur to me that it could have been anything but a fall."

"But it did occur to Finn?" Craig said.

Finn shrugged. "I knew him. It feels wrong."

"I'm curious," Elayne said. "How could you prove it was anything but a fall?"

"There are ways," Craig said simply. "I'll bring my partner out here after the autopsy tomorrow. We'll see what we can find."

Finn looked at Kieran. "Thank you for dinner. This is far more than just edible!"

Kieran turned and glared at Craig. He visibly winced. "Sorry!"

"It actually is really good," Danny said.

"Thanks so much for the confidence!" Kieran said.

"I had confidence all along," Elayne assured her. Then she gasped. "Oh, dear, we didn't think about getting rooms ready. I hope I can find sheets... I'm not even sure which rooms to use, which are in the best repair."

"The attic is all set up," Finn said. He looked at Craig, Kieran and Danny and said apologetically, "The attic was once servants' quarters. Naturally, we don't have servants anymore, but we do have employees. Those were set up because of staff coming in. I know that the attic has at least five rooms that have been cleaned and set up with linens and all."

"Oh, Finn. The attic?" Elayne said.

"I love attics," Kieran said.

"We've all been known to sleep anywhere," Craig assured Finn. "The attic will be just fine for us."

"It's been a long day," Elayne said, rising—and taking her paper plate. "Forgive me, but I have to call it quits, too."

She looked at Finn.

He rose quickly.

Being gallant? Or was she calling the shots? Kieran wondered.

"I guess we all need to call it quits," Craig said.

"I'll do cleanup," Finn said.

"No, no, you two go get some rest," Danny said. "We're good at this, and we even make Craig help bus tables at Finnegan's now and then."

"It's not right, you are guests," Finn said.

"No. I'm your cousin," Craig reminded him.

Finn looked at Craig a long moment, and then smiled. "Thank you," he said. "Shall we?" He took Elayne's arm, and started to lead her from the room.

"Good night" echoed around.

Danny started collecting plates.

"I am glad you opted for paper," he told Kieran.

"Easy," Craig said, collecting the casserole pan. He hesitated. "It was really good, Kieran. All gone. I'm sorry. You are a wonderful cook."

"I'm not, and neither of you has to suck up because you were caught insulting me," she informed them. "Danny, I want to know what you think you know."

He brought a finger to his lips. "Upstairs," he told them.

Kieran frowned. "You think there is someone else in this house?"

"No," Danny said. "Maybe on the island, but not in the house."

"Then?"

Danny lowered his voice. "It's obvious to me that you're suspicious. Either that, or you don't trust other women."

"I'm the psychologist, and I trust other women just fine," Kieran said.

"Kids, settle down," Craig put in, his voice hushed as well. "According to Finn, there were only the three of them on the island. That makes suspicion a natural thing."

"So, we'll talk upstairs," Danny said. "I rest my point."

Kieran let out a sound of aggravation and hurried into the kitchen. In quick order they threw away the paper plates, washed the glasses and casserole dish and had the kitchen back in order.

"Let's find the attic," Craig said.

They walked through the great hall, which was dimly lit and looking more like something that belonged in a Gothic novel than ever. They took the stairs to the second floor, Craig leading the way. The stairway to the attic was at the end of a long hall that passed by numerous doors, and once they had gone up, they found that the attic was very large—and appeared small only from the outside in comparison with the house.

The cupola was dead center; there were two doors on one side, and three doors on the other.

"Pick a place, I guess," Craig said.

"I'm staying close," Danny told him. "You pick, and I'll take whatever is next to you."

"Danny, are you scared?" Kieran asked him.

"No, I just believe that on a cave-filled island in the middle of the sea, it's good to be next to the FBI agent with the big gun."

"Go for it," Craig told Kieran.

She shrugged and opened the door next to the cupola.

The rooms might have been servants' quarters at one time and planned for employees now, but they had been remodeled very nicely. They weren't overly large—perhaps ten by twelve feet—but the room Kieran entered had a queen-sized bed, a handsome dresser with a thirty-two-inch television on it and pretty little maple tables on either side of the bed. There were two wooden chairs by the one window. A wardrobe stood in one corner, and bottles of water had been left on the dresser. There was a door in the room and it led to a bathroom, be it a small one, but adequate with a sink, toilet and shower.

"Finn does seem to be a good guy, Craig," Kieran said. "He wants his employees to be comfortable. That's more than many a man would do."

"Finn is a good guy, yes," Craig said. He didn't offer any more about his family, but turned to Danny. "Ready to talk?"

Danny looked around the room and pulled one of the chairs up by the bed, straddling it backward and leaning upon the curved back. "Wanna sit?" he asked.

Kieran and Craig perched at the end of the bed, close to him, waiting.

"You know about the bank robbers, right?" Danny asked.

"Yes, we both know. Two of them. Found dead—like Frank, right about where Frank was found," Craig said.

"Well, before that, it was three Redcoats."

"What?" Kieran said.

"Redcoats—British! Three of them. During the American Revolution."

"There was a battle on the island?" Kieran asked skeptically.

Danny cast her a dry glare. "No, they had deserted— they were after the pirate treasure. And that's because of the dead pirates."

"Dead pirates," Craig said.

"The Golden Age of Piracy!" Danny said. "An early New York governor, Colonel Benjamin Fletcher, was very corrupt—and very friendly with many pirates, as was many a man before 1700. Fletcher was removed in 1698, and by 1720, Navigation Acts changed things around, and it wasn't so great to rail against pirates by day—and buy their goods in alleys by night. Supply and demand, entrepreneurs. Anyway, the pirate captain Reginald Grey was at work in the city, but apparently, he was causing problems for those in power in 1720. He was known to hide out on the east side of the island—in caves beneath the cliffs. He was found dead there—along with seven of his men—in 1728. Some people think that he buried a vast treasure on the island. But here's the wild thing—"

"No. You're not going to tell us about the Ark of the Covenant," Kieran said.

"Nope—I don't believe it's here, though I do believe the story that goes with it," Danny said.

"What?" Kieran demanded.

Danny sighed, as if he were a teacher truly disturbed to have a student who was so sadly lacking in knowledge.

"Okay, the Biblical Ark of the Covenant disappeared. It was carried in battle, lost, regained and lost to the Babylonians, 587 BC. Some people believe it was spirited away before the battle—others believe that it was taken to Babylon. There is a claim that it's now in Ethiopia, but scholars dispute that as well. Some say that it's hidden in the Chartres Cathedral, or other locations in France. A group is fighting now for the right to dig in Ireland. It could be in Rome, or…it could have been found by the Knights Templar, spirited up to Scotland, and from there—made its way to the USA."

"I know the Viking stories, but the first Viking raid was at Lindisfarne, off the northeast coast of England, and those raids were supposed to have died out by the eleventh century, especially since the King of Denmark was a king in northern England as well," Kieran said. "Which leaves me to wonder—"

"How," Danny broke in, "the Knights Templar—after Jacques de Molay's death, March 18, 1314—wound up getting anything the Templars had to Vikings. Well, the Norsemen weren't really attacking anyone, but they were trading. Okay, let me go way back. A band of Massapequa—part of the Lenape Tribe—came here long, long before the Europeans of any kind arrived. They were rumored to have fought a battle with an unknown rival group—another tribe from the area—and when they lost, the survivors were thrown off the cliffs that faced the eastern shore. That was right before the possible Viking exploration soon after—in the year 1000 or so, Leif Erikson arrived in North America, landing on what is now Newfoundland. In the years after, other Norse and Icelandic explorers knew about the North American continent, the Native inhabitants and so on. They found bones here, and didn't settle the island, but many scholars believe, made use of it. So, you see, it's not that farfetched that if the Knights Templar were holding any kind of treasure, by the 1300s—with the Christianization of most of Scandinavia, a Norseman might have brought some kind of treasure to the North American continent, a Christian *Viking*, if you will, trading here across the Atlantic, might have brought a treasure for a friend who was a Knight Templar."

Kieran stared at her brother. "All right, this isn't a history I know particularly well, but the way I always saw it, Philip IV of France was an extremely clever, conniving and manipulative man. And deeply in debt to the Templars. I believe that the pope was afraid of his power. It wasn't just Jacques de Molay who was arrested and tortured—Knights Templar everywhere were hunted down and in the end, Philip condemned dozens to burn at the stake."

Danny made a dismissive gesture. "Thing is, people have been dying on this island forever. Gianni Verrazano supposedly saw the island, and discovered more bones. When the Dutch came and began their settlement in the early sixteen hundreds, they found bones, and from there, pirates came, and then Revolutionaries and Patriots, and there is even a story that Confederates came, heading home from London with a shipment of gold, and managed to go off the cliffs as well."

"And does any of this have to do with Frank Landon dying on the island *now*?" Craig asked, frowning. "Assuming that any part of it did happen."

Kieran was looking at Danny. "What we believe can be more important than what's real," she said softly.

"Well, it might be real," Danny said.

"You mean that people might have been killing people here for hundreds of years because of a belief that an ancient treasure might be buried here?" Craig asked. He shook his head. "Bank robbers had nothing to do with the Knights Templar or Norse traders—if the Norse did come this far south. We are a bit of a ways from Newfoundland."

"Ah, but the Norse were magnificent seamen," Danny said. "Which, of course, is beside the point. What's true is that people might believe it. Many people, maybe like Frank, do believe that there is some kind of a treasure on this island. There have been many historical documents regarding treasure brought to the new world, and there's no reason to discount those documents and manifests."

"Which means...the bank robbers might well have been killed by someone who was searching for treasure a decade ago, who wants to be sure they're the one who finds it," Kieran said.

Craig was quiet a minute, looking at them. Then he nodded. "That same person from ten years ago could well still be active. He or she—or they—might have been searching since." He shrugged. "Part-time, maybe. Maybe *they* manage to hold down a full-time job and take weekends and holidays to treasure search."

"And to kill," Kieran added softly. She looked over at Craig. "Then it is possible. The same person who murdered years ago might well have murdered Frank Landon now."

"Or we have a new killer on our hands," Craig said. "I'll also call in and get our research team looking into Frank's past. At the moment, I don't know of any business enemies the man might have had, but I will get my office checking to make sure. Then again, with all we know, Frank might have stumbled onto something. Or disrupted someone. Someone who watched Frank. Afraid he was getting too close. Afraid he was a danger."

"Someone who just had to send Frank over the cliffs as well," Kieran said softly.

CHAPTER
THREE

Craig sat at the foot of the bed. He had chosen the FBI; he had chosen a life that exposed him to some of the worst humanity had to offer. He was trained, he knew what he was doing.

He couldn't help but be bothered by their current situation.

Three people known to be on the island—just three—other than the dead man.

Though it was absolutely possible that someone else had been there—was there even *now*. Either way, they might be stuck on an island with a killer.

"Okay." Kieran had popped her head back out from the bathroom. "Your cousin didn't lie—this room is set up. Soap, shampoo, razors…and, most importantly, toothbrushes and toothpaste. We'll just have to wear dirty clothes in the morning."

"You can borrow something from Elayne," he suggested.

She stared at him, frowning. "Elayne is—at best—
five foot one. I have her by seven or eight inches!"

"Ah, then Margie."

Kieran grimaced. "I'm not so sure I want to ask Margie for anything. She's just stepping into her first stages
of grief. The world will be harder for her before it gets
better."

"How long do you think she'd been seeing Frank?"

"Longer than Elayne has been seeing Finn," she told
him, taking a seat by him. She was watching him in-
tently. He knew he owed her an explanation.

And she was waiting. Patiently…

"So, I'm not related to Jamie Douglas—just Finn,"
he said.

"You're related through his mom," she said. "Deedee."

He nodded. "Delores McCloud Douglas. Jamie
Douglas has been married three times—he just divorced
his third wife, I believe. I hadn't really paid much attention in a long time."

"And Deedee was his first wife?" Kieran asked.

"Yes."

"Three marriages. But Finn is his only child?" Kieran asked.

"He is. My mother and Finn's mom were very close.
They were the same age, and grew up with each other.
They stayed almost like sisters and so I grew up around
Finn. I'm three years older, and, back then, he was like
the little kid who followed me around, and, of course,
I was the hotshot, teaching him the ropes. Then," he
said, reflective, and paused for a moment, "about a de-
cade ago, Deedee was diagnosed with breast cancer.
Doctors said that her best chance was a double mastec-
tomy. Jamie Douglas didn't stay by his wife's side, car-

ing for her—he filed for a divorce. The cancer spread. Deedee didn't survive. She died surrounded by people who loved her, but heartsick at the desertion of the man she'd assumed to be the one who loved her most." He paused again. "I could never stomach Jamie Douglas after that. I don't care how much he gave to charity, what other good works he did. Finn hated his father for abandoning his mother, but… I'm sure Jamie told him that they had been falling apart already or some such thing. And…well, I guess he eventually forgave him. I never could. And so Finn and I drifted apart."

"Craig, I'm so sorry," she said, slipping her arm around him and leaning against his shoulder. "I guess all I knew about Jamie Douglas was how generous he was to local charities. It's really a shame that he has the financial power that he does…and yet can behave in such a cruel manner to family. But… I'm glad you're willing to give Finn a chance."

He nodded. "I never meant to lose Finn."

"Obviously, he very much believes in you—and you're here for him now."

Craig rose and caught Kieran's hands and pulled her to her feet, into his arms. He held her there for a moment, feeling his own heartbeat, feeling hers.

He could never, ever lose her.

She had become his life, his breath and his soul.

He pulled away, smiling as he looked down into her eyes.

"Wanna fool around in the servants' quarters?"

"I need a shower."

"We can shower together."

"Actually, no, we can't. Evidently, servants weren't supposed to mess around together. There isn't room in that shower for two," Kieran told him. "It is very, very small. But… I will be right out!"

She turned and headed to the shower, casting off clothing as she did so. Finn doffed his jacket, shoes, socks and holster, and followed her.

But she wasn't lying. The shower was seriously tiny, wedged into a space that might have traditionally had just a wash basin. Determined, he stepped in, and Kieran laughed because there wasn't room to move their arms, and they were literally flush against one another.

It felt very, very good, but was absolutely frustrating, since movement was quite impossible.

"I had actually planned on using soap," Kieran told him, her hand on his chest as they crushed together.

He laughed, and said, "Okay, fine. You, and then me."

With a towel wrapped around his waist, he walked out to the one window in the attic room. From it, he could look out toward the great cliff that dominated the island, with the jagged edges that fell to the rocky shoreline below.

The moon was full—high over the cliffs, it sent down a strange glow that created a massive and ominous darkness where the cliffs cast shadows over the landscape. Maybe it was that darkness and the crippling danger of the rocks that had created a haven here for criminal activity.

"Your turn," Kieran called, heading out in her towel.

He didn't linger long, soaping down and rinsing quickly in the tiny space. When he emerged, Kieran was waiting, stretched out in a movie diva pose, grinning, on the bed.

He made an exaggerated leap and crashed down next to her.

Her skin was warm and damp from the shower, with a sweet lingering scent of soap. She pulled him in for a deep kiss as he ran his hands in a liquid journey over the curves and perfect angles of her body. He was fully aroused in seconds, and soon they eased together, breathing in gasps, hearts beating hard.

After, with her in his arms, he slept.

Kieran didn't know what awakened her. It was still late—or early. Glancing over at the clock on the side table, she saw that it was about 3:00 a.m.

Craig seemed to be deeply asleep at her side. He woke easily, and for long moments she lay still, not wanting to disturb him. But then she rose, and headed to the window. Looking out, she saw the moon glow over the cliffs. It was a strange scene, both haunting and ethereal, and natural as well. Beautiful, if it weren't for the evil it all seemed to encompass.

She blinked. She didn't know what the source was—but some kind of light burst briefly out of the shadow. Then it was gone just as suddenly.

There were no storms plaguing the area; no lightning was bursting down from the night sky.

Had she imagined the lights? She couldn't see anything now.

"Aliens."

She almost jumped. No matter how quiet she had been, she had wakened Craig. She turned to see that he was staring out the window, just as she had been doing.

"Aliens?" she asked him.

"I'll show you," he said, picking up his jeans from

where they lay by the bed and digging in the pocket for his phone.

"It's been bugging me. I don't know if I saw it right, but I took a picture. I think that Frank wrote the word in the sand, there on the beach. Maybe while he was dying. I don't think that Frank did fall. I think he was... beaten, broken, first—and then dragged out so that it would look like he had fallen off the cliff. The autopsy will tell me if I'm right."

"Craig, you don't really think that...aliens have anything to do with this?"

He stared at her with aggravated patience.

"No...no, I don't believe that alien life forms came to Earth and murdered Frank. The thing is, I'm pretty sure that he wrote the word in the sand."

He brought his phone over to her, keying up his picture gallery.

She stared at the picture.

At first, she saw nothing but sand and scratches in the sand. And then, the word did seem to appear. It hadn't been sketched out in cursive...rather painfully set forth in awkward angles and disjointed letters.

It might have been a random selection of lines.

Or, it might have been the word *aliens*.

"Aliens," she repeated again.

"You see it?"

"I do."

"Or, did I suggest it?"

"Yes, you suggested it. But I see it. So, neither of us believes that UFOs visit us—"

"But people do believe it. There are all kinds of theories, and supposed eyewitness testimonials. It's all a matter of conviction. And I can't begin to imagine what might have happened... Did Frank think that he was being attacked by aliens?"

Kieran shrugged, handing the phone back. "I don't know."

He set the phone on the dresser, turned and took her into his arms. "Maybe you should come back into the city with me when I head to the autopsy tomorrow."

"Because...you're afraid aliens will get me?" she asked skeptically.

"Funny, no. Remember, perception is nine-tenths of the law, or something like that."

"Pretend aliens might be on the island."

"Kieran...three people we know about were here—other than Frank. I do believe that Frank was murdered. I don't like you being here without me."

"Danny is here."

"Danny—who admits he likes being next to the FBI guy with the gun."

Kieran hesitated a moment. "Craig, you're going to go to an autopsy. Then you're going to have to ask Egan to support you and maybe Mike to work with you, too. I think you're going to be extremely busy, and if I'm here, on the island, I can watch the three people who are probably the main suspects. Nothing is going to happen tomorrow. Finn wants you here—Margie and Elayne both want to believe that Frank did fall. We'll be fine."

"Others are coming in tomorrow," he reminded her.

"Workers—who weren't here when Frank died."

"Not that we know about."

"Craig, it will be okay. I promise. And, seriously, you know it."

He was quiet, and then he pulled her against him.

"No exploring," he said.

"That's hard to promise—it's an exploration to get from the dining room to the kitchen."

"Not funny. No delving into caves without me."

"No spelunking without you. Danny has maps. We'll do all our exploring with them just to get some idea of the structure of the island and where to go. Where Frank might have been. Okay?"

He nodded after a moment.

"Think we ought to get some sleep?" she asked softly.

He nodded again. He suddenly lifted her up and laid her back down, sliding into bed beside her. She curled against him.

Then she pushed up so suddenly that she startled him.

"What?" he asked.

"The lights! Craig, I could swear I saw weird lights out there—on the cliffs."

"Like alien spacecraft?" he asked.

She punched his shoulder lightly. "No," she said softly. "Like someone out at night who shouldn't be."

"Maybe," he said quietly. "Kieran, we just discussed—"

"I've got it, honestly. Stick close to Danny. No exploring in the caves. Be careful. I know the drill, Craig, come on, please."

"You always seem to manage to get yourself into trouble."

"And so do you!"

"I'm supposed to get into trouble," he protested.

"Well, I won't get into trouble tomorrow, I promise."

"Famous last words," he murmured.

She decided to let it go. Curling against him, she

closed her eyes again. She tried to sleep, and she wasn't at all uncomfortable. She was fine, wherever she was, in his arms.

Still, she couldn't help but imagine saucer-shaped spacecraft flying around the island.

But in her mind, they weren't occupied by little green men. They were filled with the ghosts of the Knights Templar, seeking a place to hide the Ark of the Covenant.

"You're calling me on a Sunday. Party or dinner invite?" Richard Egan asked Craig dryly.

"Well, you always have a dinner invite," Craig said. He hesitated. Egan was one of the best directors in the FBI, as far as he was concerned. He ran his agents from his desk, but he had decades of experience, and he wasn't against becoming hands-on when necessary.

He also listened to his agents, and when they came to him with cases that might go well with federal assistance, he always at least gave it thought.

"Yes, thanks. Easy enough when you're involved with a family who happen to own a pub," Egan said. "Let me guess. You're out on Douglas Island."

Technically, Craig was no longer on Douglas Island. A boat had come in to drop off a number of Finn's new employees and workers. He'd hitched a ride back in to Brooklyn, where Mike would be waiting to pick him up.

"You heard about the death on Douglas Island?" Craig asked.

"A fall." He could hear Egan sigh. "Except you don't believe it's a fall. And you're related to the Douglas family."

"I'm related to Finn Douglas. But I don't think that I ever told you—"

"Please. I've been with the FBI for decades." Even over the phone, Egan sounded pleased with himself.

"Anyway, you're all set. The NYPD detective on this is Teddy Brice. Nice guy. He says that it's pretty clear that Frank Landon took a fall, but if you want to investigate further, he's happy to have you take lead. He's also on the murder of a drug lord out in Brooklyn, and it's taking up his attention."

"Great."

"You're heading to the autopsy? Keep me up to date."

"Will do."

"Maybe you can find the bank robbers' stash. Or something else." Egan was quiet for a minute; Craig almost thought that he'd hung up. "Maybe you'll solve a cold case, too."

"Thanks, Egan," Craig told him. The director did hang up.

Twenty minutes later, he was on shore—and Mike Dalton, Craig's partner agent, was waiting right at the dock. He was dressed for work in his blue suit. Craig was still in a polo shirt and jeans, but at least he had a leather jacket.

Mike was about a decade older than Craig, and usually looked like he'd seen it all before and wasn't impressed by any of it.

"Leave it to you to find a way to work on a Sunday," Mike said.

"Sorry."

"Not a problem. You were missed at Finnegan's last night. Declan hired a kick-ass band. Gaelic rock. Pretty cool."

"Yeah, I figured."

"Kieran's still out there?"

"Danny is with her—and the boat that picked me up delivered a bunch of people—housekeeper, workers… In truth, my cousin is a good guy."

"Didn't murder his friend, huh?"

Craig glared at him.

"Hey, you know we've got to ask the question."

Craig nodded.

"Well, I don't get out on private islands owned by the über-rich that often."

They reached the car. Mike tossed Craig the keys. They'd been partners a long time—Mike knew Craig preferred to drive, and he didn't care in the least.

As they drove, Craig caught Mike up on what he knew—and what he didn't know.

He tossed him his phone so that he could see what had appeared to him to be the word *aliens* scratched into the sand.

"He was killed by aliens?" Mike said doubtfully. "That would be a new one—bizarre. Even for New York City."

"I don't think he was killed by aliens—but it does make me wonder who else has been on the island."

"How could uninvited guests get out there without being seen?"

"It's only recently that anyone has actually been on the island for any extended amount of time. At first, I guess the Douglas family saw the island as a possible home—they built the big old house. But bad things happened. Family tragedy, that kind of thing. Finn's father hates the place—and that's probably why he gave it to Finn with carte blanche to do with it as he would. Finn is a good businessman—he can be trusted. But do I think that people have a colony living out there—

no. But I do think that they know how to come and go.
I thought it was really important to get to the autopsy
first—find out exactly how he died. Then, we can head
back out to the island. Oh, I have to stop by Kieran's
apartment. Get some things. We hadn't intended to stay
out there."

"Whatever. Do I get to pack, too?"

"You want to stay out there?"

"Hell, yes!"

Craig was grateful it was a Sunday as they maneu-
vered the streets from Brooklyn into Manhattan. Of
course, it was New York; there was traffic, but not the
kind to be found on a weekday. Mike warned him there
was an Italian parade scheduled for certain areas and
Craig gratefully avoided them. In twenty minutes they
arrived at the downtown morgue.

They were known there, and quickly ushered in. The
autopsy was already well under way. The medical examiner that day was Dr. Griffin Hodges. Craig knew
him—and liked him. He worked with facts, and would
also explain what those facts could mean, helpful to law
enforcement without trying to play Sherlock Holmes.

"Poor fellow, hell of a mess," Hodges told them. "I've
never seen so many broken bones."

Frank Landon lay on a stainless steel table, looking
nothing like a human being. The Y incision had already
been made; Hodges had been in the middle of weighing the heart when they arrived.

Frank looked like a child's rag doll that had been
painted red and put through a wringer. Blood had been
washed away, but his many gaping wounds and slashes
were an ugly shade of crimson.

Detective Teddy Brice arrived as Hodges continued his examination.

Brice was about forty, medium in height and stature, with dark brown, close-cropped hair and a lean face, worn for his years. He greeted Craig and Mike with a grim smile. "This guy really took a physical beating. But I hear you were out there already—you're related to the Douglas family?"

"Finn is a cousin," Craig said briefly.

"He was really broken up about it, too. I'm sorry. My guys went up the cliffs. We did what we could. I would have closed this as an accidental death, but…from my point of view, it's all yours." He hesitated. "But naturally, keep me informed if you do find something."

"Absolutely," Craig promised him.

The autopsy went on.

"His injuries are consistent with a fall from a great height, right?" Brice asked.

"Could be," Hodges said.

"But?" Craig asked.

Hodges glanced at his assistant. "Would you close him up, please?" he asked. "This was a relatively young man in perfect health—great heart, liver, all organs. Didn't abuse drugs or alcohol, ate well—and kept fit. But he was truly broken to bits. Let's move over to the X-rays."

They followed him to the wall near the body where screens showed X-rays of the body in several positions. "Head bashed, limbs…well, you can see. They're broken everywhere."

"Which could have resulted from a fall," Brice said.

Craig offered, "Otherwise someone being severely beaten?"

Hodges hesitated. "Yes," he said. "The way the bones are broken…"

"Maybe someone used a bat," Mike suggested.

"I've ordered some tests, but the only residue on the body was rock and sand," Hodges said. "From what I understand, the body was found on the rocky shore at the base of the cliffs."

"Or," Craig said, "he could have been beaten to death with a large rock."

Hodges gave that some thought. "Yes, I would say that's a possibility."

"Smith. John Smith," Kieran said.

"Sounds like a made-up name," Danny said. He grinned. "The kind a guy would use when he was checking into a hotel with a mystery woman, huh?"

"Danny, it's a very common name, and has been, I imagine, since the colonies were begun. Remember, John Smith and Pocahontas?"

"I do, of course. Knew them well," Danny teased. "She didn't marry John Smith, you know. She married John Rolfe. And had their son, Thomas Rolfe."

"But she did save John Smith."

"So the legend goes."

"The point is that it is a legitimate name. The man probably really is John Smith."

"Still sounds made-up to me!"

Kieran sighed softly.

She'd slept late. Craig was long gone into the city and she hadn't even been downstairs yet. She'd showered again and dressed in the same clothing she'd been wearing the day before—very uncomfortable, but then again, she had no choice.

Danny had already been downstairs. People were milling in. Finn's housekeeper had come.

Breakfast had been very good, he assured her.

She forgave him for any implication that it had been better than last night's dinner because he'd brought her a huge cup of steaming coffee.

"Sure," Danny said, reflecting on the name. "And the Smith who wrote the article on the Ark of the Covenant possibly coming to Douglas Island is supposed to be some kind of a scholar, so I guess you couldn't go changing your name through years of university and all that. You want to see him?"

"I do."

"Let's go."

"You make everything sound so easy. We just show up on his doorstep?"

"It's better to act and ask forgiveness sometimes."

"Um. That's been your motto a few times too many."

"And it's worked most of them." He grinned at her. "Actually, there's a fellow who works part-time as a tour guide because he just loves it. In real life he's a professor at Columbia. He knows John Smith. I already contacted him. You want to go?"

She stared at him, stunned. "Wow. Your finagling charm and curiosity about everyone you come in contact with seems to finally be paying off. Do you have a plan for finding out where Smith lives and getting to him as well?"

"Indeed, I do!" Danny said. "I talked to Finn this morning. He's got a boat and a captain at our disposal. Smith lives on the Upper East Side, close to the Museum of Natural History. The boat pops us over to Brooklyn, and there…"

"There?"

"Taxi or subway, your choice. At that junction, I'm out of friends."

Kieran grinned and gave him a big hug.

"Let's go on down," she said. In Kieran's mind, everything seemed changed from the night before, with the sunshine and the arrival of new people. A woman was crossing the great hall floor when they reached the bottom of the stairs, and she smiled pleasantly.

"Good morning!" She extended a hand. "I'm Evie. Evie Summers. I've been with Finn…well, a long time. I was in his dad's household and when Finn moved on up and out…" She paused, shrugging. "Anyway, pleased to have you, Kieran."

Kieran shook her hand. Evie was small, maybe five-three. She was probably in her early fifties. She didn't color her hair—it was a steel gray held firmly in control by a bun at the back of her neck. Kieran had a feeling most things she could keep in control were held just as firmly.

"I know all about you," Evie said.

"Oh?"

"Danny was the only one down for breakfast," Evie said. "We had a lovely chat."

"Oh. And where are the others now?" Kieran asked, not sure if she should give her brother a kick or a thank-you.

"I brought Margie a tray earlier," Evie said. "Finn and Elayne are in their room."

"I see," Kieran murmured.

"But I—along with Victor Eider, the groundskeeper I guess you'd call him—are always at your disposal.

We're so grateful you're out here to support Finn. Anyway, can I get you anything?"

Kieran should have said yes. She should have been starving. But she'd had the coffee Danny had brought up, and more than anything, she wanted to go meet John Smith.

Lunch later would do.

"I'm fine, thank you. Danny brought me coffee. He and I are leaving the island for a bit, but we'll be back."

"I'll see that your rooms are refreshed."

Kieran didn't think that she personally did the "refreshing." The actual housekeepers who did the cleaning part were still on the way.

"Lovely meeting you, Evie," Danny said brightly, and they headed out.

"What do you think of her? She was more friendly over breakfast. Think she likes me better?" Danny asked, laughing as they went down to the dock.

"Hmm. If I had to analyze her, I'd say she sees other women as a threat. Wonder how she's managing with Elayne?" Kieran said.

"Interesting. The plot thickens."

Kieran shook her head. "That would be melodrama. We're in the middle of a murder mystery."

"Or sci-fi."

"You saw Craig this morning?"

"Briefly. He still doesn't want to share the picture that might say the word *aliens* that might have been etched in the sand by Frank Landon before he died." He looked at Kieran curiously. "You don't think that aliens did it, right?"

"Danny, what in your years of knowing me would lead you to think that I believe in little green men?"

"They don't have to be green."

"Of course not. I do believe there is other life in the universe, though not necessarily sentient. Some kind of bacteria probably exists on Mars. I do not believe that Frank Landon was killed by bacteria."

Danny was silent as they approached the waiting boat.

"Danny?"

"I don't believe in little green men. But there are many, many people who do believe that maybe ancient aliens did come to Earth. Educated people."

"I know that."

"If anything, someone could be playing upon those beliefs, on the legends surrounding the island."

"Anything is possible," Kieran agreed. "Let's go see your friend's friend—the mysterious man who goes by the terribly unusual name of John Smith."

CHAPTER
FOUR

"I'm on my way into the city," Kieran told Craig over the phone.

"I'm on my way back out to the island," he replied.

"You're done at autopsy?"

"Yes," Craig told her.

"And?"

"Well, it's possible that Frank Landon fell from a cliff. He's battered badly, as if he managed to hit every possible obstacle on the way down. Or as if he was beaten by rocks."

"That's strange, or maybe not. I mean, if you fall from a great height, you would be broken to bits. Especially if you crashed along the way."

"True. But it's as if the blows landed everywhere." He was silent a moment, and then said, as if testing the sound of it to his own ears, "The way his injuries are all over... I think... it's possible that he was stoned to death."

"Stoned to death—as in the Biblical style of execution?"

"Exactly. Anyway, why are you going into the city? You're with Danny, right?" He wasn't sure why that should reassurc him. Declan, her oldest brother, was as steady as a rock. Kevin, her twin, was very responsible. Danny was a bit of a wild card—although always with the best intentions. Then again, since he had started a regular job, he'd become far steadier.

"I'm with Danny, and he's proven to be a great asset—he has friends who have friends who fixed us up with a man who wrote an article about the Ark of the Covenant possibly coming to the New World."

"Sounds like a bit of a stretch to me."

"Follow all leads—that's what you tell me," Kieran answered.

"Okay, sounds good. I'm going to do some cave exploring."

When she was quiet for a minute, he prompted her, "Kieran?"

"Be careful," she whispered.

"I won't be alone. Mike is with me. And there's a special agent who will be joining us in the next few days. Bracken Silverheels. His grandfather was a Mohawk steelworker—helped build a lot of the skyscrapers in the city. He's an expert on rappelling, digging, caves, shoring them up...anyway, he's a good man to have on our team here."

"So—we're going to stay on the island."

"Yes, but let's meet in the city first. Finnegan's at 8:00 p.m. Then, we'll go back to Douglas Island together for the night. What about Danny? Is he coming back, too?"

"Do you think we'll get him to stay off the island now if we're there?"

Craig ended the call. Mike was watching him.

"You know," Mike said, "there is still the possibility that Frank Landon just fell accidentally."

"Yep."

"We're going to have some serious egg on our faces if we can't find anything."

"We will find something."

"Yeah, I agree with you. Just thought I needed to throw the possibilities out there."

Soon they were thanking their coast guard transport and stepping off on Douglas Island. Gulls cried, and there was a cool breeze and a scent of salt in the air.

Mike paused, staring at the house.

"Man, I can't believe your family owns this place, and you live in your girlfriend's apartment."

"Not exactly my family. My cousin's father's side," Craig said.

Mike nodded, not pressing the point. Craig climbed the winding wooden steps toward the house. The front door opened before they got there.

Finn stood on the porch, anxiously watching them arrive.

Craig performed the introductions. "Thank you for coming," Finn said to Mike.

"I'm glad to be here."

"I wish it was under different circumstances," Finn said. "I meant to change the bad reputation of the island. Instead, I made Frank become a part of it."

"You didn't make anything happen," Craig told him.

"We'll find out what's going on here," Mike assured Finn.

"Well, let's get moving, shall we?" Craig asked. "Mike and I want to get out on the island, if that's all right with you."

"Of course. So the autopsy showed…"

"That Frank was broken," Craig said. "We still don't know anything conclusive. We have to investigate the geography here and so much more."

Finn nodded. "Go ahead. Please," he added softly.

"We will," Craig told him. "As soon as we put some stuff down, if that's all right."

"Of course. I create and run resorts, and I totally suck as a host!" Finn said. "Come in, please!"

He led them in. There was no sign of Elayne or Margie, but Evie was there, ready to greet Mike. He smiled. "So I get a room in the attic?"

Evie bristled. "We've now brought in a handful of workers, and they've done more setting up. You can have a room on the second floor if you like. Mr. Frasier, you and Kieran and Danny can move down. I mean, you are staying around for a bit?"

"We're fine in the attic," Craig said.

"I'll take a room anywhere," Mike said.

Evie escorted the group to a room on the second floor—it was spacious, with access to the balcony and a shower that allowed a man to move his arms.

"You can move down to this level," Finn reminded Craig.

He thought about the attic room—and the high window that allowed them to see out over the island.

"We're fine," he said. Other than the shower, of course.

"And now," he added, "Mike, let's get going."

"Anything you need…there's a little shed out back by the pool. It was…it was Frank's place for ropes and what have you. Though you probably shouldn't be fooling around with ropes," Finn said. "God help us, we don't need another accident—or whatever."

"'Whatever' won't happen," Mike assured him. "Craig and I have been watching one another's backs for a good long time."

Finn nodded. "Still…"

"Finn, we're not going over any cliffs, I promise you," Craig said.

"Yeah, we have a special agent coming in for that," Mike said, but his effort to make Finn smile fell flat.

"A special cliff agent?" Finn asked.

"Special Agent Bracken Silverheels is coming in. He's an expert on cliffs, caves and spelunking, actually, along with rappelling," Craig said.

Reassured, Finn went back downstairs, but Craig stopped Mike before his partner could follow his cousin.

"Just a minute. Danny left me some maps."

"Maps?"

"Copies of old maps—I don't know where or how he got them. With Danny, I don't always ask. Anyway, he texted me this morning. He left them in a sleeve between the mattress and the bed."

"Why?"

"Why? Because the maps may help us."

"No, why did he hide them between his mattress and the bedsprings or whatever?"

"Because he doesn't trust anyone."

"Good thinking on his part," Mike said. "Get them. I'll guard the passage."

Craig shook his head and ran up the attic stairs.

In Danny's room he paused for a minute, wondering if there was any way to find out if someone else had been in the room since Danny had left it.

But obviously, the housekeeping staff had been in it. The bed had been made—and Craig didn't think Danny was much on making beds. There was also a fresh flower sitting on the windowsill in a pretty little vase.

But had anyone else been in, curious as to what Danny might be doing there?

They hadn't had any belongings with them, so a search would have done no good. Still, he looked at the one dresser in the little room. It appeared that one of the drawers had been closed, a little off-kilter. Had someone tried to see if Danny had stuffed anything into a drawer?

Craig shook his head. To know for sure, he'd need to lift fingerprints and have them analyzed, and even if he did, all the prints from any of the house inhabitants would be easily explained away.

He moved to the bed and lifted the mattress. At first, he saw nothing. He shoved it farther up. There were the maps, complete with a plastic protective cover. He reached for them, and, with some difficulty, pulled them out.

Five minutes later, Mike and Craig were in the little shed. The shed was, in context, a fairly new structure, Craig thought, perhaps built thirty years ago or so, when he figured that the pool must have been added. It sat to the far right of the property, as one looked out from the back of the house. Old, cracked concrete surrounded the pool as a deck, and the shed was built of heavy unfinished lumber. Craig was pretty sure that his cousin would want to refurbish the entire area eventually.

But the shed was crafted with shelves and hooks, and was still filled with equipment. They easily found high-powered flashlights, ropes, hooks and all kinds of paraphernalia for cave exploration.

"How do you get from a cave underground to the top of a cliff?" Mike wondered aloud.

"You don't. I think that Finn is right. I think that Frank was murdered. What I'm wondering now is if we're dealing with something related to the island, maybe treasure seekers who were worried that Frank would get to it first, or if it was something personal to do with Frank, and the island was just a convenient means."

"Glad you've narrowed it all down," Mike said. "Let's go see what we can see."

He hesitated and then reached for a long coil of rope.

"We'll wait for the expert before dropping into giant holes," Craig said.

"I was a Boy Scout. I want to be prepared in case you fall in," Mike told him.

"Start around the east side—where Frank's body was found. I'll show you what I saw, if it's still there at all, what with the wind and the sea."

"That's right," Mike said. "Let no clue be unfollowed. Let's just hope that the aliens don't have advanced weapons that instantly destroy good FBI-issue Glocks!"

John Smith lived in a handsome apartment in a six-story building off Central Park. As they arrived in a rather posh entry with a security desk, Kieran whispered to Danny, "I thought that scholars were poor and bookish."

"He's written textbooks," Danny said, and shrugged.

"The kind that are bought by students around the country every year. It's a great gig—if you can get it."

Whoever Danny's friends of friends were, they had definitely stepped up for him. John Smith was expecting them. They signed in at the desk and were instructed to take the elevator to the top floor.

The elevator brought them up to a hallway with just two doors, and, as the elevator opened, so did one door.

Kieran thought that she might have been expecting a stereotype—a slightly crazed-looking older man with wild white hair and a bow tie.

John Smith was nothing like that. He was tall and well built, perhaps forty-five, and his hair was dark and neatly cropped. He was dressed in a polo shirt and jeans, obviously spent some time in the gym as well as with his books, and had an easy smile that lit up his eyes.

"Hello! Danny Finnegan—and Miss Finnegan?"

"Yes, hello, and thank you so much for seeing us," Danny said.

"I'm Kieran," she said, offering her hand.

"Good to meet you. Please call me John. And come on in. Coffee? I was just having some myself."

The apartment was tasteful and yet leaned heavily toward the academic—the walls were covered with framed prints, many of them antiques or copies of ancient maps. Imitation Egyptian statues adorned little pedestals around the large living room, and there were dark wood bookshelves from floor to ceiling on two walls, full of handsomely covered hardcover books. A grouping of leather chairs and settees was arranged around a coffee table that faced a large marble hearth. A silver coffee service had already been set out.

"I understand that you're somehow related to Douglas Island—in a roundabout way," he said, escorting them over to take seats and then pouring coffee for them.

"A very good friend of ours is a cousin of Finn Douglas," Danny explained.

"And an FBI agent," Kieran said.

"He's an FBI agent—working a fall from the cliff?" Smith asked. "Seems a waste of taxpayer money."

"Mr. Douglas doesn't believe that his friend fell. We're trying to find out just what Frank Landon might have been looking for," Kieran explained. "And your article came to mind."

"Ah! Yes, well, many people think that I'm a mad professor, or something like that, looking for the oddities in life because I live alone in a dusty old house somewhere," Smith told them, smiling. "I assure you, there is solid evidence for all of my theories."

"We're sure that your research is impeccable," Danny said.

"That's why we're here," Kieran said. "Growing up here, I'd heard about Douglas Island now and then, but I thought that much of what I'd heard was just fantasy built upon campfire stories."

"It's the position of the island that's led to its reputation," Smith said. "Easy access from the mainland. First stop if you were coming down the coast. We know that Norse and Icelandic explorers did arrive on the North American continent. There are some instances of verifiable proof—such as the Norse houses that have been found at L'anse Aux Meadows in Newfoundland—and areas of supposition, such as stone towers, runes on cliff…that kind of thing. While settlements might not have been permanent, the Norse most probably did trade with Indigenous populations along the North American coastline for hundreds of years."

"There's the rumor that the Ark of the Covenant made its way to Oak Island—the possibility inspired all kinds of great stories," Danny said.

John Smith poured himself more coffee. "Yes, the Ark inspires many tales. But if you look into Douglas Island, you'll discover that one thing proves that many, many things have gone on there. The proof is in the bones. For every time anyone from the Vikings through to the twenty-first century bank robbers visits, there are reports of human remains discovered on the island. The thing is that people have been either using or searching for something on that island as long as we have recorded history for it. Do you know how it came to belong to the Douglases? I don't know how much of the family history you know—you say your friend is a cousin?"

"Yes, but we don't know much family history. Different branch of the family," Kieran said.

"Their ancestor James Douglas was a Scot involved in the Jacobite Uprising of 1745. That, as you may know, was put down fiercely, but Douglas was one of those allowed to come to the Colonies as long as he served the British Navy. He was to serve with the British against the Americans when the Revolution rolled around. But he had no true love for the people who had basically enslaved him, and he became a spy. Well, most of the signers of the Declaration of Independence died broke. But Douglas was to be offered a boon. The island was granted to him for his service to the Patriots. It was just there…a spit of land plagued by death and destiny. It was a poor offering, but Douglas made it a base. He was an excellent carpenter and had many other talents. He managed to make money as a furniture maker at first, and then he began to invest... He did well as a trader. As you know, the family fortune grew throughout the generations. But sadly, once they moved off the island, they began to believe that the place was cursed. I think it was just the legends about the place—and the brutality of life—that caused the notion of a curse to continue. A baby died in infancy—not unusual back then, but possibly attributable to a curse. One of Finn's ancestors went insane at the age of ninety, something we might see as an aging disease now. And there were other deaths that no one wanted to accept as age, infection and so on. Anyway, the family never did anything with the island."

"I think Finn Douglas plans on changing that," Kieran said. "And I'm not sure he believes anything about Egyptian curses, Hebrew relics or Viking visits."

"Whether he believes it or not, if the Ark of the Covenant did make its way to the New World, it certainly would have brought protection with it—be it a mystic curse or otherwise. Some scholars see the reigns of various Egyptian pharaohs differently—depending on whether the astrologers then were taking their observations from Memphis or Thebes. In movies, you'll always see that Ramses II was the ruler when Moses brought the Israelites from Egypt to the Sinai, but... that's open to debate. What's true is that the Israelites were enslaved by the Egyptians, and that Moses did lead them to the Sinai. But that is where it all gets very interesting where the Ark of the Covenant is involved," John said, beaming.

"Because the Ark resembles similar structures found in Tutankhamen's tomb?" Kieran asked.

"The Ark described in the Bible is very much like such objects found in Egyptian tombs. And the Bible, like any other religious tome, was written by man. Not to detract from religion—it may be the word of God transcribed by Moses. The thing is, Moses was born a slave in Egypt. The Ark might have been taken from Egypt, or Moses might have ordered it to be built in the manner of many other such items found in Ancient Egypt."

Kieran smiled. "Okay, we don't doubt that Moses knew things Egyptian. But then…"

"Then—the Philistines. The Ark was lost in a great battle to the Philistines and they kept it for about seven months. But horrible misfortunes occurred wherever it went—and so they returned it."

"Then the Babylonians," Danny said.

"In 585 BC, the Babylonians destroyed Jerusalem and Solomon's Temple. And after that, everything is speculation. Some say the Babylonians have it, and the Ethiopians claim they still have it, that it was hidden there. Fast-forward, and you get to the Knights Templar, circa eleventh century to the early fourteenth century, sworn to celibacy and their dedication to Christ. Many believe that in their travels and their great battles against the Arab world, they came into possession of the Ark. We all know about their downfall—or do we?"

He looked at Kieran and she smiled.

"I know a bit about the Knights Templar," she said.

"Well, while King Philip was busy seeing that Jacques de Molay was prosecuted and finally executed, he was also hunting down every man he could find who had belonged to the Templars. They fled—and many fled to northern Scotland. By then, Norse conquests had come and many people—lords and ladies and royalty included—had both Norse and Scottish blood. There would have been many people with friends and relatives and other contacts in Scandinavia and Iceland, and they were still trading with people in what would become North America. A true Templar might well have wanted the Ark out of Europe—where Philip might still reach, where the pope might have sway… It's theory, yes, but theory based on the fact that we know these things to be true. Surviving Templars did flee to Scotland. The Scots and the Norse had connections, and, the Norse were still sailing to North America."

"But why Douglas Island?" Kieran asked.

"Look at the cliffs! The caves," Smith said. "The ease with which these traders might have reached the island. I don't believe that after the tribal battles that took place on the island it was used as a settlement by anyone. But I do believe—because of its proximity to the mainland—that they came here."

"Did the first James Douglas think that his island was cursed?" Danny asked.

"Apparently not. He lived and worked there. He was mocked, and he was a curiosity at first. Tall tales didn't start with our present generation, you know—they've been around forever," Smith said.

"But do you honestly believe that the Ark—or some other treasure—is buried somewhere in the caves on the island?" Kieran asked.

"I think it's more than possible that something is there—including the Ark of the Covenant or perhaps other holy relics that the Templars had held dear."

"Fascinating," Danny said.

"Hey, is Smith your real name?"

"Danny," Kieran murmured.

Smith laughed. "It is. John Smith. I'm not even a junior, but the name has been in my family since the days of our first English settlements."

As he spoke, a young brunette woman suddenly emerged from a hallway that probably led to the bedrooms. She appeared to be in her early thirties, medium in height, slim and dressed in jeans and a tailored blouse.

"Hi," she murmured awkwardly.

Smith rose and Danny quickly did the same. "Annie, I wondered when you were coming out. Danny Finnegan, Kieran Finnegan, meet Miss Annie Green, my research assistant, and one of the finest to be found."

"A pleasure," Annie said, shaking hands and joining them. She looked at them with curiosity.

"Sister and brother, not husband and wife," Smith quickly explained.

"Oh, sorry! I didn't mean to be staring."

She was pretty, with a quick smile.

Danny grinned in return. "You weren't staring. It's fine. Did you work on the article that John just posted?"

"I did," Annie said happily. Then her smile faded. "I'm just... Well, I was so sad to hear about the man dying out there. And, I can't but think that if we hadn't published that piece, the poor man might still be alive."

"Oh, that's not true at all, you mustn't think that way," Danny said.

Her brother was flirting. Kieran sighed inwardly, but went on to agree with him. "Finn Douglas wants to make a getaway for New Yorkers out there, a resort.

Frank was working with him, and even before the article, all the rumors about pirate treasure, Confederate gold, bank robbers and whatever else were circulating. I didn't know Frank, but he was a bright man with an inquiring mind. He would have been exploring anyway."

"The news said he fell from the cliffs, right?" Annie asked.

"I don't think our visitors believe that Mr. Landon fell," Smith said.

"Oh? Oh!" Annie said.

"Well, if you're able… I'd love to see the island," Smith said.

"Me, too," Annie told them. "The place has such an intriguing reputation."

"We can see what we can do," Kieran said.

"Oh, yeah—even those people who believe in ancient aliens think that something is up out there—you know, the aliens who came and built the pyramids and then traveled about the world creating other pyramids and other such structures," Smith said, waving a dismissive hand in the air. "You wouldn't believe the foolery that goes on—and what excuses people can give for believing such nonsense."

"John," Annie said. "They're allowed to have their theories, too—even if they're a bit on the farfetched side. Some people believe that ancient aliens did come to Egypt, even creating the age of Akhenaten, who worshipped the sun god, Aten. They say that Egyptians sculptors were supposed to create lifelike images, and if you see art created at the time, the artists gave the pharaoh Akhenaten a very long, angular, expanded face—kind of like we imagine aliens might have. Then, there are those who think that the aliens came long, long before Ramses the Great, and even Seti, his father, and they believe that the Ark might be a kind of communication system for those aliens. They associate mummy curses and the things that happen supposedly because of those curses with a power left behind by the aliens—the Ark itself might have been Egyptian, created by aliens, and taken with Moses when he set his people free." She laughed. "John, be nice. Allow everyone their theories."

Aliens! Kieran thought. *Did anyone really believe such a thing?*

"Ridiculous!" John Smith all but snorted the word.

"I agree," Annie said. "But that's not the point."

Kieran stood, and Danny—a little unwillingly, she thought—did the same. "We can't thank you enough for your time, Mr. Smith," she said. "And you, too, of course, Miss Green," she said.

"Oh, you can thank me. Get me an invite out there," Smith said.

"We'll try," Kieran promised. "Finn is a truly gracious man. I'm sure we can make it happen. Maybe not right away..."

"I wouldn't want to impose. I'm a patient man," Smith said cheerfully.

"Bye—and don't forget me in that invite!" Annie said.

"We wouldn't forget you, I promise," Danny said.

Smith led them to the entry. There, he lingered a moment. He looked straight at Kieran. "Do you have dinner plans, Miss Finnegan?"

She was startled. "I—I—yes, I'm afraid I do," she said quickly. She was stunned enough to blush—she'd been with Craig several years now and everyone in their customary circles knew it.

Maybe he wasn't asking for a date; maybe he just wanted to talk more.

"I…"

"She's dating the FBI guy," Danny said.

"Ah, forgive me, then," Smith said. "You are simply a fascinating young woman. I would have enjoyed more time. Anyway, do keep in touch."

The door closed. Danny laughed.

"Kieran, the seductress!" he said, laughing.

"Me?" she stepped into the elevator. "You were flirting."

"So? Annie is lovely."

"We're working here, supposedly."

"Yeah? And didn't you meet Craig in the middle of a heist?"

"Because I was putting back a diamond that *you* had borrowed!"

"Okay, okay. Still, you met in the back of a van being driven by thieves!"

Kieran let out a groan of aggravation. "Let's get to Finnegan's. After tonight, you can call Annie Green on your own time."

"We'll get them an invitation out to the island," Danny said.

"Finn is grieving."

"But Smith probably knows much, much more than he told us. If I show him some of the old maps I have, he may see something in them."

"Maybe, but Craig said they have a man coming out trained in cave exploration. Let's let them work it, huh?"

"I left Craig my maps—who knows what they'll find today. Still, I got you out to see Smith. The man took the time to see us." He grinned. "And you could have had dinner with him."

"Yep, could have."

"Odd that he invited you."

"Thanks."

"No, I didn't mean it that way. I meant that I... Yes, I thought Annie Green was a charming little cutie. But I also thought...well, she came out of the bedrooms. I thought that maybe they were a couple."

"Maybe his office is back there. Or a research library. Computers and all that," Kieran said.

"And, maybe she sleeps with him...sometimes. You know, maybe it's a kinky, open relationship," Danny speculated.

Kieran groaned. "Danny, their sleeping arrangements are none of our business, right from the get-go."

He laughed. "They are if I'm going to wind up sleeping with her."

"Danny—you know what? Forget it," Kieran said. "Taxi or subway?"

He shrugged. "Either." He glanced at his watch. "It's still early. But I am starving. Anyway, I'm willing to bet that Craig will be late."

"Why?"

"He went back out to explore the island."

"He'll be doing a quick assessment of where they should go with the cave guy."

"He might do more."

"Oh? Why do you say that?"

Danny grinned. "Like I said, I left him a stash of maps. And he may just not be able to resist temptation."

Kieran was quiet for a minute.

"What?" Danny asked her.

"Aliens."

"Aliens among us?" Danny asked.

"No, no, they were talking about ancient alien theorists."

"And Craig thinks that Frank Landon wrote the word *aliens* in the sand before he died."

"Kieran…"

"Danny, the point is that perception can be stronger than any truth. What if some people believe that the Ark was created by ancient aliens and then brought out of Egypt with Moses?" Kieran wondered.

"There are so many ifs! If the Templars had the Ark, if they had Norse trading friends. If they happened to land on Douglas Island, if…"

"Perception, Danny, perception. If someone truly, fervently believed all that, they might believe in a Biblical treasure. And if so…"

"If so?"

"It might be a treasure they see as being well worth killing to find."

"There!" Craig said.

"Where?"

Craig had barely seen the outline of the cave entry himself; it was a hole in a wall of rock, it reached only up to a man's waist and it was largely hidden by the thick shrub that grew in front of it.

"I see!" Mike said.

"It lines up with the map—it should lead to tunnels that stretch across the island," Craig said.

Mike looked over his shoulder at the map. "With spidery-webby tunnels leading out from all angles. We really need Silverheels for this."

"Yes, we do, and yes, he'll get here. But…"

"You're going in now."

"I'll just scope it out—then we'll know where we're going when he gets here."

"It might be a drop. Now, aren't you glad I brought rope?"

Craig stepped behind the bush and hunkered down, using his flashlight to try to ascertain the depth. It looked like a drop of no more than five feet or so.

"Hold this," he told Mike.

Mike complied. "You're going to break a leg."

"Hey, old man, I'm not that uncoordinated."

"Insolent pup," Mike said.

Craig grinned, flattened himself to the ground and wriggled backward into the cave. It was an easy drop.

"Give me the flashlights—come on down."

"If I break a body part—"

"You'll wind up on another great leave."

"I hate leave."

"At least it won't be a shot in the buttocks this time," Craig told him.

Mike cursed him, but handed him the lights and situated himself. A second later, he had easily dropped down as well. Craig handed him one of the flashlights back.

Mike was really in excellent shape—and not that old. Just in his forties to Craig's thirties. He was already moving forward.

Craig crouched to study the floor. It was dirt and rock—to be expected.

"Mike."

"Yeah."

"Come back."

Mike returned and hunkered down next to Craig. "Look…nothing clear, but these could be footprints."

"And drag marks," Mike said.

"What would someone have been dragging?"

"A body?" Mike suggested.

Craig thought about it a moment and then shook his head. "I don't think so—Frank Landon's body was found on the east side of the island—below the cliffs. The house faces almost perfectly to the west. Right now, we're on the north side of the island."

"Which wouldn't be that far from the rocks and sand beneath the cliff."

"You might be right. That would mean that Frank could have been killed by someone in these cliffs, then dragged through the tunnel to the east shore to be left."

"We'll have to take a good look at the foliage out there."

"Might be blood specks—somewhere."

"Specks? We could find a puddle."

Craig rose while Mike was still inspecting the floor. He shone his light over the walls. There were scratches on them—possibly gouged out of stone by stone. He moved closer.

"I think this is writing," he said.

Mike joined him again. "If it is writing, I don't get it."

Craig pulled out his phone and took pictures. "I'll get these sent to Egan, see if he can find the right linguist for us."

Mike moved farther into the cave while Craig documented the walls and uploaded the pictures into an email to Egan.

"Craig."

"Yeah."

"Over here."

Craig went to see what Mike was looking at.

It was a skeleton. The bones were obviously very old. No sign of flesh or tissue remained. Disarticulated, the skull to the side, but the body seemed set up as if it had purposely been put where it was.

Like a warning.

A way of saying, enter here and die.

CHAPTER
FIVE

Sunday night

"Kieran, dear, thank you for waiting on us. I see that the place is well staffed, but I always love it when we have an actual Finnegan with us! Oh, of course, we'll be having the roast," Melanie Rayburn said. She was the owner of a boutique dress shop in Lower Manhattan. She redecorated her shop windows every weekend and finished her day by coming to the special roast dinner at Finnegan's that was always held on Sunday. Tonight, she'd brought her window-dresser, June, and the store's manager, Gloria, with her.

"I'm just getting you started, but don't worry, one way or the other, I'll be around tonight."

Kieran didn't need to be working on the floor that night. Declan, her oldest brother, was a perfect owner/operator of Finnegan's on Broadway.

The pub belonged to all the siblings, and while they

might have squabbled as children, as all children tend to do, they had become the best of friends as adults. They'd lost their mom before they were really grown up, but with the loss of their father, they had managed to band together. They had always wanted to keep Finnegan's going in the best possible way—they'd all agreed that Declan made the best manager, and so he had the final decision on everything. The rest of them all had "day" jobs: Kevin—Kieran's twin—was an actor, Danny was a tour guide, and Kieran worked as a criminal psychologist with Drs. Fuller and Miro—two psychiatrists who consulted for law enforcement. She'd been with them for ages, and it just worked out well that she and Craig could collaborate on the strange cases they often found themselves on.

"That handsome young man of yours is coming in, I take it?" Melanie asked.

"He is," Kieran said.

"Lovely man!" Melanie said. "Strong man, everyone notices when he walks into a room."

"You've been with him quite some time," June remarked. "And he's FBI! Applaudable!"

"A very long time now," Gloria said. "Is there a wedding in the future?"

"Maybe somewhere along the line," Kieran said. "Let me get—"

"You know, dear," Gloria said, leaning toward Kieran and speaking softly, "the farmer doesn't have to buy the cow when the milk is plentiful!"

Kieran tried very hard not to laugh outright; she felt as if she had just been waiting on the three witches from *Macbeth*. In truth, of course, they were charming middle-aged women, well aware that her mother had passed away when she'd been in her teens, and certain that she just might need some advice.

"I will bear that in mind," she said seriously. "Let me get your order in. And if you don't see me around and you need something, just grab anyone."

She headed to the bar. Both Declan and Kevin were working. Sunday was always busy.

Declan took her order. "We have plenty of staff on the floor tonight, you know."

"I know. But I'm restless. I think well when I'm working here."

"Douglas Island, huh?" Declan asked.

"I think that the man was murdered. Thing is, there isn't just one motive, really—there are hundreds of years of motives," Kieran said.

"You're going back out there. So is Danny—he told me so. He says you might find the Ark of the Covenant. I told him that he was taking Indiana Jones movies far too seriously."

"Declan, logically, I believe in history that *most* scholars deem to be true—I think there was an 'ark' or trunk or container that contained relics that were considered to be holy by the ancient Hebrews. It might or might not have been associated with Ancient Egypt. But what's also true is that people die on that island. Tribal battles, pirate feuds, war—all those might bring about death. They also lead to people believing that treasure is on that island somewhere. I think Frank Landon was looking for it, and I sincerely believe he was murdered. That could mean a real person—or persons—also believes the legends, and is willing to kill to get the treasure."

Declan set an icy glass on her tray to join the two

drafts of Guinness he had perfectly poured from the taps.

He leaned his hands on the bar. He shook his head, perplexed. "Kieran, I'll never get used to this. It's bad enough when we're somehow connected to a crime…" He paused, wincing. "But this…"

"This time, Declan, it's Craig investigating," she reminded him. "I'll be hanging out with armed FBI agents."

"Yeah," he said quietly. Suddenly he pointed a finger at her, very much the older brother. "All right, but you and Danny keep in contact, yeah?"

"I promise," she told him.

She smiled. She was lucky—she had siblings who cared.

As she delivered the drinks, she saw Richard Egan walk in.

She really admired Craig's boss. He was in charge of several groups of agents who worked the criminal division out of the New York office. He had a way about him that kept agents, police, marshals and other law enforcement working easily together when such occasions arose. He wasn't the kind who demanded that his office take over anything—he was careful to keep information moving and he could state his case eloquently when needed. He had several teams working at any given moment, but he always knew the particulars of each case. Kieran had been in their offices often enough to know that yes, agents were incredibly well trained and worked like a well-oiled machine, but they were also *human*. They teased one another; they played practical jokes. They had families; they formed friendships.

Craig had told her once that Egan, unfortunately, had

a couple of failed marriages. A silence had followed, as if he worried about anyone as dedicated to the job as Egan was—or perhaps as he himself was—really being able to form a long-term, binding relationship.

But then Craig had turned to her. "Thank God you're you! You...you understand. We fit."

"Kieran!" Egan called from the entry. Egan was tall, lean and still very fit, with close-cropped gray hair.

He was in a suit, despite the fact it was the weekend. She didn't think she'd ever seen him in anything but a suit.

She walked over to him, taking his hands, giving him a kiss on the cheek. "I have a table over here all set up," she said.

"Mike and Craig will be late. Craig said he called you, but you didn't pick up your cell." Egan always seemed to know everything.

"I was rushing around here. Why are they running late?"

"Bones."

"A body?"

"Not anymore. Just very, very old bones. They have a forensic anthropologist coming out. Finn Douglas wants them taken and kept at a museum to be studied. Anyway, they'll just be a little late. Craig wants the crew that's collecting the bones off the island before he leaves it himself."

"Oh, I see."

"I'm starving," Egan told her, eyes twinkling. "To hell with those late people. Will you order me a plate?"

"You got it."

Kieran ran to the kitchen, set orders in motion and

came back out. Danny was already seated with Richard Egan; he'd brought them all a pitcher of tea and glasses.

She'd chosen one of the booths they often used at Finnegan's—between the front door and the bar, enclosed with panels of pine, making them a comfortable, private little alcove. Taking her seat, she told Egan that his food would be right out.

"So, I hear you were visiting a scholar," Egan said.

"It was interesting. I'm not sure we gleaned anything that we didn't know already," Danny said. "Except that Professor John Smith wants to come to the island."

"I'm sure you could arrange that," Egan said.

"Yes," Kieran said. "But I thought it polite that we ask Craig and Finn first. Okay, if I thought it would have really helped anything, I wouldn't have worried about polite. The thing is… I am now curious about ancient-alien theorists."

"You think aliens did this?" Egan asked. She knew damned well that he was entirely skeptical; years of training in interrogation allowed him to keep his voice even and curious.

"No, sir, I do not. But—"

"I've seen the writing in the sand—the picture of the writing in the sand," Egan said. "Which might lead one to believe that Frank thought he was being killed by aliens."

Kieran hesitated and then plunged in. "Okay, here's a working theory. There's a person or people who believe in the theory that aliens visited Earth in ancient times. This particular group believes that the Ark of the Covenant and other Biblical treasures did come to the island. And they're either searching for them, or feel they have to protect the artifacts. They may have been

at work there for years and years—killing the bank robbers, first. And, now, Frank Landon."

Egan nodded slowly. Danny stared at her.

"You got that from a scholar who thinks alien theorists are ridiculous?"

Kieran sighed deeply. "Anyway, I'm going to ask my
docs if I can have a few days off—I want to find some
of these people."

"Don't engage alone," Egan warned, frowning.

"I don't even know if I can find anyone who will
engage with me. It's a long shot, but it's something to
work on," Kieran said.

"Ah, the troops have arrived!" Danny murmured.

Kieran looked to the door; Craig and Mike had just
walked in. Danny waved and they came toward the
table. Craig looked tense and worn.

But then, he had looked that way since the whole
thing had started. She understood, of course.

He loved his cousin. He seriously disliked his cousin's father.

"Hey!" Craig said. Reaching the table, he paused
to kiss her quickly, and then slid onto the bench in the
alcove.

Mike took the chair that rounded out the table.

"Bones?" Kieran asked.

"An old, old skeleton. Our forensic anthropologist
had reasons to believe that the remains are from the
1700s," Craig said.

"One day—just one day—and you found bones."
Danny's eyebrows went up.

"Bones that really don't seem to help us any," Craig
replied.

"Not true—they prove that a lot of the legend and lore about the place is true," Mike piped up.

"Right, but here's the thing. I don't think that modern-day pirates are looking for ancient treasure," Craig said. He looked at Egan, and took a deep breath. "What I'd like to do is dig up the bank robbers," he added.

"What?"

"The guys who robbed the bank ten years ago. I have a theory that the people who killed Frank also killed the bank robbers. I think it's more than one person—they've been working the island for a long time. That makes me believe that we may be looking at a cult, or a crime family. They know something or think they know something. They are willing to take time—years. They keep looking *extremely* carefully for the most part—Jamie Douglas has always disliked the island and been determined to keep trespassers off. I don't know if he believes it's cursed...or what. He's been in Europe for the last year or so, and has had nothing to do with the island. But it's been easy enough until now for people to come and go. The bank robbers might have disrupted what was going on."

Egan looked at him and groaned. "And you want to exhume the bank robbers? You know, it was never proved in a court of law that they were the perpetrators of that crime."

"Yes, sir."

"And, even if it had been proven that they were criminals, they still have rights. As do their families."

"Yes, sir."

"And you want to dig them up."

"I do. I want Dr. Hodges—who just did the autopsy on Frank Landon—to reexamine their bodies."

"Because Frank Landon might have been stoned to death. Biblically."

"Yes, sir." Craig leaned forward, earnest as he spoke. "Frank Landon didn't just fall. I'm entirely convinced of that. In an investigation, if we suspect murder, then, yes, he might have been pushed. The bank robbers might have been pushed. But if we can establish that they were all killed by the same means, and if that means was stoning, we might have an idea of what we're looking for."

"Mike?" Egan asked.

"I agree," Mike told him. "You can't imagine the caves and tunnels on that island. They are endless. It's going to take time, but I honestly believe the more information we have about the deaths, the better we'll be able to put the pieces together."

Egan nodded. "All right. Kieran, you're going after the alien believers. And Craig, we're digging up the dead."

"Alien believers?" Craig asked, looking at Kieran. "That's what you got from the scholar, John Smith?"

"Danny, let's go get the dinners. Then we can explain again," Kieran said.

"Sure." Danny rose to help her. He looked at Craig. "Hey, don't blame me. That one is her idea, not mine!"

It was midnight before they returned to the house on Douglas Island. Craig was tired and thoughtful. But still curious once they were alone.

"What was your real impression of John Smith—and how did that get you going on aliens? Does he believe that aliens built the pyramids?"

"Not at all," Kieran told him. "Actually, he was really anti such an idea. Thinks it's ridiculous."

"Well, time-wise it is. That kind of space travel, even with tremendous technology. Although there is string theory, and the concept of worm holes and all that."

"Yes, well, the point is, doesn't matter whether they're real or not. But I do want to look into it, and yes, I will be safe. I promised Declan."

They'd stopped at her apartment to do a bit of packing before heading back, and now she was setting a few of her things in the top drawer of the dresser.

He pulled her down on the bed, holding her close. "It's admirable that you promise your older brother. You can promise me, too, you know."

"I always promise you. You know—you'd better watch out. Some of our favorite regulars gave me a lecture tonight. About cows. Give the milk for free, and you know the rest."

He laughed, rolling to press a kiss against her throat and collarbone.

"Damn. They're right. I never should have just given you my body without marriage! You've just been using me over and over again."

She laughed in return, curling into his arms.

"I'm a terrible person. I'm after nothing but your body and your sexual prowess."

"You hussy."

"Just appalling, huh?"

For a moment, he paused. "Should we at least get engagement rings? I think we both believe we're forever, but…"

"I know I love you!" she said softly. "I know that I will love you forever. But I also know that we'll do everything on our own time, when we're ready. And right now… Craig, let's solve this thing! I know how much you care about Finn. Actually, you could probably use some therapy over this family rift."

"You are a psychologist."

"Right—but you should never work with those closest to you."

"Okay, marriage and therapy, for the back burner. Right now, I'm ready."

"For?"

"For you to use my body, just come after me for sex," he told her, very seriously.

She laughed softly. "Then you'd best get ready because…"

"Yes?"

"I'm going to use you like you've never been used before."

"Oh, my love, do get to it…"

It was much later when Kieran woke and rose again. She stared out the attic window at the island, the dark shadow of the cliffs spreading out, the moon still casting a strange and eerie glow over it all.

Then, for a second, just a split second, she thought she saw light again. A flash of light—as if someone had moved from a point of cover to a point of cover, and been unable to hide the light in between.

Craig was behind her.

"I saw a light again. I swear I saw it, but each time you get here…"

"It's gone."

"Am I seeing things?"

"You think that someone is out on the island now?"

"There's plenty of places to hide."

"We would need a full task force to really watch this place. Egan has talked to friends with the coast guard and the police. Maybe we'll get some help. Thing is, we are facing the Atlantic. The rocks prevent anything big from coming in, but a knowledgeable person with a small boat could probably maneuver in... Except we haven't found any boats around."

"I know this is wild speculation, but what about a little port in the caves somewhere?"

"Possible," he said. In the moonlight, she glanced up at his face. His features were knit with tension.

"And if there is, we will find it," he swore softly.

Something about the rugged determination in his words made her shiver. She slipped into his arms.

"We will find it," she agreed softly. "We will find out what's going on."

Monday morning

Kieran was restless through the remainder of the night. Craig was aware of her up and working from the very early hours of the morning.

When he crawled out of bed and looked over her shoulder, he saw that she was reading articles on ancient aliens.

"Aliens?" he said.

"Hey, you're the one who took the picture in the sand of what Frank Landon wrote as he was dying."

"You know, Dr. Hodges—the medical examiner—did say that the injuries could have resulted from a fall," he said. "Or from repeated trauma, like being *stoned* to death. I can't help but think that stoning might make

more sense—if Frank was able to draw in the sand before he died."

"Well, he could have fallen without dying instantly.
But…"

"Or…ancient aliens have really been living on this
island for about a thousand years. And any time anyone gets close to the Ark—which is here and is some
kind of alien communication device—they kill them.
Aliens killed the Native tribes, the Vikings, the pirates,
Rebels and Confederates—and the bank robbers and
then Frank."

She cast him an exasperated glance. "I'm just reading up on it," she told him. "There's a site run by a man
named Jay Harding. He calls himself an expert in alien
interaction with human beings on Earth. He draws all
kinds of conclusions while studying world architecture
and history."

"Interesting."

"I'm planning to see him," she said.

"Please make it in a public place—I'm not so sure
you and Danny should have gone to an apartment alone
yesterday. Danny is pretty wily, but…"

"I'm pretty wily!"

"Yes, you are, but…"

"Public place. With Danny," she assured him. "I've
sent him an email," she said.

"All right. I'm going to get back into the caves with
Mike today. I don't believe that Frank Landon knew
about the entry Mike and I found yesterday—he was
getting into the cave system a different way. But I want
to keep following that path."

"I'm coming with you."

"I thought you were chasing aliens."

"I have to wait for Jay Harding to get back to me."

"All right, then." He wasn't sure he was happy about her exploring in the caves.

"Oh! By the way. I don't think we got around to mentioning this yesterday. John Smith would like an invite out to the island. With his assistant."

"Assistant?"

"Who may or may not be sleeping with him. Danny was flirting with her. She was flirting back."

Craig shrugged. "I'm not sure we need some wild-eyed scholar out here right now."

"He's not a wild-eyed scholar. He was very reasonable. And he looks like he could be a bouncer in a city club."

"Let me talk to Finn. We're working here, Danny and Mike are here...but I don't own the place."

There was a tap at the door. They looked at one another in surprise. Kieran was already in a robe; Craig quickly donned his.

It was Evie Summers at the door. "Breakfast in twenty minutes," she said. "Finn is hoping that you will join the household."

"Sure," Craig told her. "We'll be right down."

He closed the door.

"Almost ready," Kieran said, leaping up. "Let me dress for cave exploration. Jeans, of course...and a sweater? Is it cold in the caves?"

He shrugged. "A little, I guess. Jeans and a sweater— sounds okay to me. Then again, I don't crawl around caves that often."

She laughed. "Just abandoned subways in the city," she said lightly. "Give me ten minutes!"

Kieran could be ready to do just about anything in five minutes—something else that he loved about her.

Finn, Elayne and Margie were at the table when they came down; Danny was helping himself to coffee from the buffet.

Finn rose politely. "Thanks for coming down," he said.

"Thank you for breakfast—you and Evie and your staff, of course," Craig said. Kieran had headed over to help herself to coffee as well. He waited for the two of them to come to the table.

"Morning!" Elayne said brightly.

Margie, dull eyed, tried a weak smile.

"Morning," Kieran said.

Mike made his way to the table, and they went through the greeting ritual again. When they were all seated, Finn turned to Craig.

"Anything new?" he asked hopefully.

"Finn," Craig told his cousin, his tone as gentle as he could manage, "we're investigating. Investigating takes time."

"It doesn't matter," Margie said. "He's dead—the rest just doesn't matter. Nothing will bring him back. But he does need a decent burial. Or interment. He was the last of his family, but there's a place for him. Calvary Cemetery, in Queens. He belongs in his family's vault. He wasn't sure what he believed, but his family was Catholic."

"I'm sure his friends will want to pay their respects," Kieran told her, and Kieran's voice, of course was very kind and soft. "I'm sure you want to write his obituary and get it to the paper, and make sure there is time for his friends to arrange to be at a service."

"How do you plan if people are still ripping his body up?" Margie asked with a little sob.

"I'm sure his body will be released soon," Craig said.

"Do you know what funeral home you'd like to use?" Danny asked. "When you've made the arrangements—"

He didn't finish. Margie sobbed and leaped up from the table, fled the room and raced up the stairs.

They were all silent at the table for a moment.

"I'm sorry. I meant to be helpful," Danny said.

"It's not you," Finn assured him. "It's… Margie is just having a really hard time with this. I suggested that she leave the island again. She said she isn't going anywhere until she can see that Frank is given a proper send-off."

"I'll speak with the medical examiner. See if they can hurry things along," Craig told him.

"Have you discovered anything interesting at all?" Elayne asked.

"We've confirmed pretty much what we already know—it's a fascinating island with an incredibly rich history. We're going exploring again," Craig said.

"Maybe you'll find yet another body," Finn said.

"Finn!" Elayne placed a hand on his. "Finn, those bones were so old…whoever they belonged to—they've been gone a long, long time!"

"True." Finn sighed.

"The anthropologist was thrilled that you found them," Elayne reminded him dryly. "She believes she'll find fascinating information through them. It was a creepy discovery!" she said, shuddering. "But good for science."

"Right. Are you going back to the same area?" Finn asked.

"We plan to follow the tunnels farther," Craig said.

"Bones!" Danny said. "And a forensic anthropologist. All that happening while we were sitting there with a pile of books," he added, looking over at his sister.

"But maybe you'll find another skeleton today," Elayne said brightly.

"Elayne," Finn groaned.

"Sorry. But they're old bones. No matter what, the bones belonged to a man who would have been dead several hundred years," Elayne told him. She turned to Kieran. "We could go into the city and have a spa day if you like."

"A spa day sounds incredible," Kieran said politely. "But I'm going to go with Mike and Craig and Danny."

"As you wish," Elayne said. "A creepy old tunnel—or a lovely spa with champagne and all good things."

"Maybe you could get Margie to go in with you. That might be good for her," Kieran suggested.

"She won't leave the island."

"Finn, maybe a couples' day for you would be fun," Mike Dalton suggested, clearing his throat and speaking up. "You're going to be setting up a resort—with a spa, I'm assuming. It would be a bit of respite—and a bit of research."

But Finn shook his head. "I'll be working with the contractor and meeting with the engineers," he said. Then he turned to Elayne. "I'm sorry."

"It's all right, my love. I'll try to get Margie out to at least sit on the beach with me."

"There's a plan," Danny said.

Evie Summers swept into the dining room, followed by a tall, brawny man in his late forties or early fifties, a big fellow with the kind of mustache and beard that made Craig think of a lumberjack.

"Excuse me, I hope the breakfast buffet is satisfactory?" She frowned. "You haven't even opened the chafing dishes yet. It's not good to live on coffee alone!" she chastised.

"We're going to eat, Evie, I promise," Finn said.

"You must!" Evie told him. "I wanted your friends to meet Victor, as well."

"Apologies," Finn said quickly. "I wasn't thinking." He stood. "Craig, Mike, Danny, Kieran—this is Victor Eider. He's been with me for years. He's my assistant."

The man introduced as Victor laughed. "I'm a glorified handyman," he told them, smiling. "But I do try to assist in all things. If you need something you can't find, if something isn't working, if you need any kind of help, please just let me know."

Kieran thanked him, and her words were echoed by the others.

"I'm going to be working on the pool, if you're looking for me... Nice to meet you all," Victor said, and he exited the dining room.

"Good Lord, are you going to make your plates, or do you need me to do it for you?" Evie asked.

"No, no, we can do it, Evie," Finn promised. And they all stood, as if they were children who had properly been scolded and were now going to behave.

Craig saw Kieran looking at him, slightly amused. He gave her a shrug and a smile in return.

They could at least start off the day with a good breakfast.

While they ate, Kieran made a point of turning the conversation away from the island, old bones and

Frank's death. She asked Finn about the Bahamas, told him about her own experiences enjoying those tropical islands and asked about his work there.

Finn enthusiastically talked about opening resorts. "I swear, I don't do things for the rich and famous. I love creating something that's an affordable fantasy. Sure, we have things that may appeal to the bigger budget, but the real thrill is giving something special to those who might not be able to afford the high-priced places. I remember my mom…"

His voice trailed for a minute.

Craig decided to take the high road. "Your mom thought vacations were needed most by those who worked the hardest. She would be thrilled with what you're doing."

Finn cast him an appreciative smile. "I'm going to name it after her," he said softly.

After they finished eating and cleared up, Mike led Kieran, Craig and Danny back to the storage shed. Mike again insisted they have rope and picks and other paraphernalia. Kieran packed them bottles of water and a handful of snacks.

Then they headed out over the cliffs. When they reached the shrub-covered opening to the cave and tunnel, Craig hesitated.

"It's a drop," he told Kieran.

She looked at him, arching a brow. "And what would make you think I've suddenly become terribly uncoordinated?"

"What would make him think that you had suddenly become coordinated at all?" Danny teased.

She socked him in the arm.

"No cause for violence!" Mike said.

Craig groaned aloud. "I'll go first. Give me the lanterns. Kieran, I'll catch you. Danny—I'll catch you, too."

They were all quickly down; with four of them wielding high-powered flashlights, they were able to illuminate a good section of the cave's entry. Still, the tunnel before them stretched out into darkness, with small shafts that led off in many directions.

"Wow!" Danny said.

"Where was the skeleton discovered?" Kieran asked.

"A few feet down, there, on the boulder. The skull had fallen, but the way that the man had been set up—as if sitting guard—the rest of the bones didn't crumble," Craig told her. "We called in right away. Egan found our anthropologist and she came out with a representative from the medical examiner's office. Authority over the bones was given to the anthropologist."

"Did you all dig around in the area?" Danny asked.

"No," Craig said.

"We didn't get very far," Mike said. "Once we found the remains...we had to call it in."

"Don't you think we should go farther?" Craig asked.

"You have the maps, right?" Danny asked. "The third in the series that I gave you is a supposed pirate map— made by a Captain Nathaniel Argus. He found bodies and, in his log, swears that he and his crew did not kill those that they found. I wonder if your bones might well prove to be those of the dead pirates he found. Argus believes that he and his men survived the island because they sought the treasure and left quickly. They did not explore all the tunnels—he didn't like it. Gut feeling—he wanted him and his men off the island as quickly as possible. He believed it was a cursed place."

"So—he left one of the dead men to guard the entrance?" Kieran asked.

"So it seems," said Danny dramatically.

"I think we need to go farther," Craig told them.

"Why don't you and Danny go ahead?" Kieran asked him. "I'd love to look here. Mike can stay with me. If you don't mind, Mike?"

"I'm here to explore as directed," Mike assured her. She smiled.

It was good that Kieran and his partner got along so well, Craig thought. He was a lucky man.

But he was anxious to move forward, and it seemed that Danny was equally ready to see what lay ahead.

"All right—just watch out. None of us knows what is really going on here," he said.

He and Danny started walking down the tunnel, raising their lanterns high to see to each side. He'd given Danny the map he'd requested.

"Stop, hey, just a second. There should be a shaft off to our left," Danny said.

Craig stopped, raising his light. It seemed that there had been some kind of a rockfall—the wall there wasn't sheer as it had been.

"Closed over now, so it looks," Craig said. But then, perhaps because of the way he'd discovered the entry the day before, he dropped down.

"Danny."

"Yeah?"

"There's an opening. The only way through, though, would be to get flat and crawl through it."

"Maybe the entry was always this way." Danny sounded excited. "Maybe that's where the pirates hid their gold."

"I don't know, Danny. This map was made by the survivors. According to what you read, the pirate captain hated the island and wanted to get off it as quickly as possible. Why would he have hidden treasure instead of taking it?"

"Ah, come on, Craig! It's a mysterious tunnel!"

He grinned. Danny was right. How did you ignore a mysterious tunnel?

"All right, Danny, but we need to let Kieran and Mike know what we found. We'll start back to tell them—"

"Hey!"

The yell came from the entrance.

Craig hurried back, Danny on his heels.

He stopped, seeing Mike on the path ahead of him.

"Is everything all right?" he called.

"Come see what Kieran found."

Craig frowned, walking back.

He and Mike and the anthropologist and the medical examiner and two other assistants from the mainland had spent several hours looking over that area.

How the hell had Kieran found something?

He moved along and lifted his flashlight. And there was Kieran, her face smudged and dirty, smiling.

"You found the pirate treasure?" he asked her.

"Better," she said softly.

"Better?"

"Two things," she told him. "This…"

She raised her hand, and he studied the little piece of trash she had raised.

It was a candy wrapper.

"A historic candy wrapper?" he asked.

She shook her head. "Craig, there were a bunch of rocks that looked to me as if they'd been moved to where they were, specifically. And yet, whoever had set them up didn't want it to appear that they'd been set there on purpose. I moved the rocks—they were heavy, by the way—and I found this! But, Craig, it means that someone else was here. And if Frank never found this opening, it means that someone was definitely here other than Frank or Finn or someone who had a right to be here!"

"Right," he said softly.

"Oh, and a few inches down in the dirt under the rocks, I found this!" she said.

She lifted a second, small dirt-encrusted object. The light from his lantern caught on it. It appeared to be nothing more than a small piece of metal.

"Pirate...gold?" he asked.

She shook her head.

Danny answered, "Oh, my God! It's a bracteate!"

"A *what*?" Craig asked.

She nodded happily. "A bracteate—a piece of jewelry. At least, I think so. We need to get it cleaned up."

"What the hell is a bractite—or whatever you said?" Mike asked.

"A medal. Bracteate," Kieran said. "An ornament or amulet. And if so... Craig, it would mean that John Smith was right. Well, maybe not about the Ark, but it would mean that the Vikings had definitely been here. We'll have to find an expert, but... Craig, it could mean that some of the legends about this place are real, and if this is here, and if the bones found dated from the pirate days... Craig, it's just more than likely that someone has been out here, hiding out here, and searching for treasure—someone who is more than willing to kill. Who knows what else we'll find if we keep going!"

CHAPTER
SIX

From a very exciting start, Kieran thought, it became a long and grueling day that basically yielded nothing else.

Craig and Danny had found a side tunnel. It was intriguing to say the least, but after they had entered the tunnel—lying flat on their backs and rolling to make the entry—they found nothing. Nothing but stretch after stretch of tunnels that led ever deeper into the rock cliffs.

"There have to be more access points to this," Danny said, as they hit sheer wall at last. "I mean, a tunnel this long, this size...we missed something."

"Time plays havoc with geography," Craig reminded Danny.

"Maybe we should have stayed on the main path," Mike said. "And maybe this is going to take a long time."

"According to this supposed pirate map I have, there are entrances, but it seems that...that they aren't here. Maybe the map is no good," Danny said.

"What about going back to the main tunnel?" Kieran asked. "There are all kinds of smaller ones snaking out of it."

"It is going to be a long haul," Craig said. "But our cave expert should arrive tonight. We'll start again in the morning."

Mike agreed.

"We did find something—something that might prove to be incredibly important," Kieran said. "We could show it to John Smith and see what he has to say."

Craig was silent a moment. "I want to meet Smith. We should get him and his assistant out here. But I don't think I want to share any of our discoveries with anyone yet. I'm not even telling Finn anything—except on a need-to-know basis. I think I'll talk to Egan. He'll know someone who can authenticate your find, Kieran. As for now..."

"I need a shower," Mike said. "There's a great shower in the room I have. New-fangled head that has a pulse... just phenomenal."

"Maybe we should have changed rooms," Craig murmured. He looked at Kieran.

"We're fine," she said, smiling.

"And if you move, I have to move," Danny said. "I don't want to be by myself in the attic."

"Okay, let's just get back," Craig said.

Going down into the tunnel had been easy enough, but it took them another forty minutes to climb out. For Kieran, it was okay getting back up out of the opening—Craig just lifted her.

He stayed until the end, giving the others a boost. Then he crawled out himself, emerging completely dredged in cave dust and dirt.

Craig pulled out his phone. He looked over at Mike. "Bracken Silverheels wants to meet off the island first. Finnegan's, seven thirty—we should have time to make that."

"We're going to go back to the city again?" Kieran asked.

"Yeah, I have some Coast Guard friends coming by. You don't have to come," Craig told her.

"Oh no, I'll come," she said. She was looking at her own phone then.

Jay Harding—the ancient-alien theorist—had gotten back to her. He was extremely eager to meet with her; he was always happy to expound on his realm of knowledge.

"It's Jay Harding—the alien guy," she said.

"And?" Craig demanded.

"He's excited to meet me. I'm going to set it up—" She smiled at Craig. "I'll meet him at Finnegan's, too— we'll get tables far enough away so that you can look as if you're just getting together with an old FBI buddy. And I'll be safe in case he's a weirdo."

As they walked back around the island to the house, Kieran moved ahead with Danny.

"So," Danny murmured. "It's amazing. I mean, it's gotten to be fairly common knowledge—taught in history classes, I'm pretty sure—that the Vikings came to North America long before Columbus. But this is… proof! I mean, they came here—Vikings came here! Oak Island is like a thousand miles away, something like that. Of course, there's supposition that they did trade much farther south, and many places in New England may have artifacts that *suggest* Vikings might have been there… Wow!"

"Were there still Vikings by the time all this would have happened?" Kieran asked.

"Vikings, Norse. By any name, they were fantastic sailors and explorers!"

Kieran had her phone out and was busy looking up information. "Okay, so, it went in this order—Denmark was Christianized, or established its own archdiocese in 1104. Norway was second, establishing an archdiocese in 1154, and then Sweden, in 1164. The great age of the Vikings is considered to be the late eighth century to the mid-eleventh century."

"Yes, but that's the whole point, isn't it?" Danny asked her. "Robbing, raiding and pillaging had ended by the time many of the Templars ran to Scotland. The Norse were traders—and they had a settlement in Greenland for years, too. So they came from Scandinavia, Iceland and Greenland—and maybe from Scotland—still having contact with local Natives and trading for lumber and all that kind of good stuff. And...friends! We all do a lot for friends. This is just incredible."

"If it's real," Kieran reminded him. "We have to have this little piece authenticated."

"Maybe we should have dug more right where those bones were discovered," Danny said.

Kieran paused, smiling at her brother. "I knew you were really up on your New York history. I didn't know you had expanded it so far."

"One thing leads to another. How the hell did you know that you'd dug up a bracteate?"

Kieran laughed. "Mom."

"Mom?"

"She had all those books from Ireland. And Dublin

was founded when an *ard-ri*, or high king, of Ireland married his daughter to a Viking, Olaf the White. I think it was a doomed romance, but the city of Dublin was founded. I used to pour through all of her books."

"Wish I had."

Kieran smiled. "They still exist. I have them. I'll get them to you."

As they neared the house, Kieran saw Finn Douglas on the porch, as if knowing they were coming back—or anxious to see them when they arrived.

Darkness was falling.

He had to have expected that they would be returning soon. They'd barely stepped up on the porch when Finn asked, "Did you find anything?"

"Time, Finn, we need a little time," Craig told him.

"Yeah, I know, I know. You were gone pretty much all day. I just... I feel like I'm in limbo, you know? I meet with people, I work on my plans...and I feel like I'm just going through the motions, you know?"

"Maybe you need to get off the island for a few days," Craig told him.

"I should. But I can't."

"We have another man coming in tonight—a man who knows caves," Craig told him. "We're heading into the city shortly."

"In fact, I'll hop in my wonderful shower!" Mike said.

Danny laughed. "I'll hop into my adequate shower," he said.

"A good shower would be nice," Craig said, trying to brush some of the dirt off his sleeves. "If we only had a decent one."

"Any shower will be nice," Kieran told him. "A 'decent' shower would take too much time." She smiled. "And right now time is something that we don't seem to have much of, if we've got to catch a boat to the mainland."

Finn was looking at Craig; he needed more info, it seemed. Kieran decided she could get in and out of the shower before the two finished their conversation.

"I'll run up," she told Craig. "Be out in a flash."

She hurried upstairs, leaving Craig to talk to Finn. She shed her clothing in the tiny bathroom.

The shower was small, but the water was deliciously hot. She scrubbed quickly and rinsed. She turned the taps off—knowing she couldn't stay as long as she wanted.

As she did so, she heard something.

A click.

Like a door clicking open or shut?

She opened the bathroom door, wondering why she felt so on edge. She was expecting the door to open from the hallway—Craig should be on his way up.

"Craig?"

No answer. She wrapped herself in a towel and stepped out quickly, but Craig still wasn't there. Diving into the little bag she had brought, she found a knit dress and quickly slipped into bra, panties and the dress. Then she paused, looking around the room.

Had someone been in the room? If so, why?

To go through her clothing—find out if there was anything in her pockets?

Even if she had undressed in the bedroom instead of the tiny bath, nothing could have been found. Craig had both the candy wrapper and what she believed to be a bracteate.

She was still staring around the room, trying to decipher if anything was out of place, when the door opened.

"What's the matter?" Craig asked.

"Nothing." Then she asked him, "Did you see anyone on the stairs?"

"No, why?"

"The shower was going. I thought I'd heard you come in."

"Danny?" he asked.

"Maybe. I'll ask him when you're ready. Hey, how are we getting in to the city?"

"Our inestimable friend and my director, Mr. Richard Egan, is sending a boat. It'll be out there any minute, so…" He grimaced, lifting his arms.

"You do look like a wet dog that has been rolling in the dirt," she told him.

"Thanks."

"Get cracking!" she told him.

He walked into the bathroom and immediately walked back out. For Craig, disrobing in the tiny space would be a difficulty.

As he shed his clothing, Kieran sat at the foot of the bed, scrolling through her phone contacts.

Craig hesitated, looking down at his dirty body. "Don't feel like making use of this cow at the moment, huh?"

She laughed. "My dear, I think you'd be the bull, even though a bull doesn't give milk, does it? I would make use of you any way at all! But we have no time. Get that pile of dirty temptation into the shower!" she commanded.

He sighed with mock sorrow. "You just don't really know how to use a man," he told her.

Once he was in the shower with the door closed, Kieran dialed Jay Harding. A pleasant voice answered.

"Harding here. How may I help you?"

"Hi, Jay, this is Kieran Finnegan. I'm the one who emailed you through your site and you left me your number."

"Hey! Glad you called."

"I was hoping you could see me tonight."

"Tonight?"

"I know…it's probably impossible, but…"

"No, no, it's fine. I'm in the Village. Did you want to come here?"

"I was hoping you wouldn't mind going downtown. My family owns a pub. I can promise you a lovely dinner."

"Sure—are you thinking of joining the society?"

The society?

Yes, yes, of course, his web page talked about the society.

Believers…it was called.

"I'm interested," she told him.

"Where's the pub?"

"It's on Broadway, downtown. Finnegan's."

"I've heard of the place. I'll be there. When?"

"Seven thirty."

"How do I find you?"

"Ask anyone!" she told him.

Her plans were set by the time Craig stepped out of the shower.

"Wow," she told him. "Now, you're really tempting. I'm going to run next door—Danny should be ready.

We'll meet you downstairs." She planted a quick kiss on his cheek and went out.

It wasn't until she knocked on Danny's door that she remembered she thought she'd heard a click. When Danny let her in, she asked him, "Did you come into our room?"

"No. I wouldn't do that without knocking. God knows, I do *not* want to take the two of you by surprise." He spoke lightly, but then he frowned. "Why?"

"I don't know. I thought I heard someone up here."

"I think we're still the only people in the attic. The staff—housekeepers under Evie Summers—apparently come by day and go home by night."

"Maybe I imagined it. Power of suggestion—I was expecting Craig. Anyway, he should be ready in a minute. I called Jay Harding—the alien guy. He wanted to know if I was interested in joining his society."

"Oh? Are we joining his society?"

"I don't know, Danny. Are you ready to believe in aliens?"

Richard Egan was already seated at their favorite booth when they arrived at Finnegan's.

"Thanks for being here, sir," Craig told him.

Egan waved a hand in the air. "We have a few missing persons, possible kidnappings we should be investigating, some possible gang-related murders growing cold, but…hey." He grinned and then grew serious. "This could be something—solving a cold case that has been on our books and on that of the NYPD for years now."

"The bank robbers," Mike said. "Well, we did find a candy wrapper."

Craig had both the little piece of metal—the bracteate—and the candy wrapper Kieran had found in evidence bags. He discreetly handed them over to Egan.
"We could use analysis on both of these."

Mike went on to explain that Kieran and Danny believed that the one piece proved that Norsemen had
come down as far as New York.

"Well, there's a find for you, then," Egan said. "No
gold or jewelry from the bank heist?"

"Candy wrapper," Mike said.

"Maybe Frank Landon had a sweet tooth."

"We don't believe that Frank was ever in the cave
where we found this," Craig told him.

"Interesting," Egan murmured. Then he noted,
"There's our man, Special Agent Silverheels."

Craig swirled around to see the newcomer approaching their table. He was a tall man with long black hair
worn in a queue at the back of his neck. His high cheek-
bones and facial structure were evidence of a Native
American heritage while the man's eyes, pale green
against his bronze features, seemed to shout of Northern
Europe. While he was tall, he was lean, evidently fit.

He wasn't wearing a blue suit.

The man was in jeans, a T-shirt and a denim jacket.

Egan kept his seat at the back of the booth; Craig
and Mike stood to greet the newcomer. Silverheels offered them sound handshakes before taking his seat,
observing Craig and Mike—just as they observed him.

He suddenly smiled. "Sorry to take so long. I was
winding up in DC."

"Not a problem—we're grateful you could come,"
Craig told him.

"You have excellent reputations as agents," Silverheels said, grinning slightly. "And who could resist Douglas Island—especially when being assigned there."

"Well, we like to think we're decent agents," Craig told him. "And, as Kieran pointed out to me, we're good with underground deserted subway stations."

"Then again, true, what we don't know about caves..." Mike's voice trailed. "Well, it could fill a library of tomes on the subject."

"Silverheels's great-grandfather worked on the Chrysler Building," Egan said.

"That's up—not down," Mike said.

Silverheels laughed. "I come from a long line of Mohawk ironworkers," he said, shrugging. "I'm not sure how, but that made me love caves and cliffs and exploring just about anything that had to be ascended or descended. I grew up in New York City, but old legends and old traditions die hard. My dad was an ironworker, but one of his best friends was a cop, and some of his friends were FBI..." He paused. "Well, we try to use all our talents in this game, right?"

"Right—and as I said," Craig told him, "I'm grateful as all hell. So—" he looked from Egan to Silverheels "—we'll get you both up-to-date on everything we have."

"I gathered you're a little worried about the walls at the house having ears. That's why I suggested this meeting first," Silverheels said.

"You never know," Craig said.

"No, you never know. Egan also told me you found a bracteate today," Silverheels said.

"You mean, you know what one is, too?" Mike asked, shaking his head.

Silverheels simply smiled.

"We think we found one. Egan will have it authenticated. First thing tomorrow, we'll take to the caves," Craig said. "For now, I'll do my best to draw a verbal picture of it all." He briefly explained his family connection, and as he was about to describe his initial sweep of the site, he saw a young man with long shaggy hair and wearing a T-shirt that advertised a metal band walk in. He was looking around, as though trying to locate someone. Danny Finnegan walked up to him, smiled, shook his hand and directed him to a booth on the other side of the room.

"Craig?" Egan asked.

"Sorry." He glanced across the table at Silverheels. "Kieran and Danny are meeting with a society who believe aliens visited ancient Earth. I believe that's the group's head."

Silverheels raised his eyebrows. "What's the lead there?"

"You saw the picture of what Frank Landon wrote in the sand," Craig said.

"You think people with far-out beliefs are the killers?" Silverheels asked.

"No. I think that people with far-out beliefs are like any other people. Some are fine and good and hardworking. And some may be criminals. Just as in anything else."

Silverheels nodded. "Egan has sent me a brief on the case. I just need your take on the people involved." He hesitated. "You know, you can't let the fact that a man is a relative cloud your judgment."

"And I will not," Craig promised him.

Kieran had come out from around the bar and was joining Danny and the newcomer at the table.

Jay Harding looked as mild mannered as possible;

he looked very much like a bright but socially awkward...nerd.

Craig wished he could be at both tables. He forced himself to focus on Egan, Silverheels and Mike.

"My cousin, of course, is Finn Douglas. He's spent his life being decent and hardworking—and generous to a fault. He's incredibly rich, and a man for the people, and if he weren't my relative, just because I do know him, I wouldn't think him possible of murder. Also, he called the cops immediately, and then called me. His girlfriend is Elayne Anderson. I don't know her well. Nor did I know Frank, or his girlfriend, Margie Appleby, who is still on the island. Because of the nature of the crime, we know it wasn't random, nor is it the kind of murder that would likely be attributed to someone not connected to the island in one way or another. As to other players, they're just coming into the fold. My cousin's housekeeper is Evie Summer. His assistant-slash-handyman is a man named Victor Eider. We've just met, but our offices have run background checks for all of them." He kept talking, answering the questions Silverheels asked.

Only now and then did he glance over at Kieran, Danny and Jay Harding. The young man was speaking. He seemed passionate.

Aliens. It seemed out of the realm of possibility.

Aliens.

Written in the sand by a dying man.

"Trust me," Jay Harding said, "most people think I've lost my grip on reality. But lots of scientists believe that there is life elsewhere in the universe, though many posit that that life would be, perhaps, one-or two-celled organisms. Thing is, theories on worm holes and folding time have been around just about as long as we've known the world wasn't flat!"

He paused, smiling at Kieran as if they shared a great joke.

He leaned back. "So, did you read my book? My articles...what?"

"I read some articles," Kieran said. "And I was completely rapt."

"It is fascinating," Danny chimed in enthusiastically.

Kieran glanced at her brother. Kevin might be the actor among their brood, but Danny was great at talking to people. Gift of gab—yes, her brother *had* kissed the Blarney Stone.

"Fascinating," she echoed. "I loved the explanation of Akhenaten's statues."

"Where else did the Egyptians come up with such advanced building methods? Slave labor does not account for the incredible feats accomplished—such as the pyramids."

"But the pyramids—the Great Pyramids at Giza, at any rate," Danny said, "are way older than the time of Akhenaten. Khufu's pyramid, I believe was built about 2500 BC."

"Between 2580 and 2560 BC, so they estimate," Jay said, clearly impressed that Danny seemed to be up on his history.

"And Akhenaten died around 1336 BC—we're talking a lot of time there," Danny said.

Kieran had to admit, she was glad she'd brought her brother. Not long ago, another of Craig's cousins had been involved in a murder case at a new Egyptian museum in the city—Danny had obviously been paying attention to the exhibits. Then again, she did know a few things herself because she had helped with some research while Craig had been working on the case.

But Egyptians had not come to Douglas Island. Still, Jay Harding had picked up on John Smith's article—and explained how Moses might have had the Ark of the Covenant with him when he'd left Egypt.

"Here's the thing. My group believes strongly that aliens have been among us. Not once or twice, but many times. Compare the artifacts on Easter Island, the pyramids that could be found among the Mayans and the Aztec civilizations. You can even see small stone carvings created by many different peoples that appear to be men—of some kind or another—in space suits." Jay Harding stopped speaking and took another bite of the corned beef and cabbage dish he had chosen. "Delicious," he said. Then he smiled and looked at Kieran. "So, are you really interested? Or does this have to do with you being out on Douglas Island?"

She tried to show mild curiosity and not surprise.

"Oh, we're interested!" Danny said.

"And, we do have a connection to Douglas Island," Kieran said. "But how did you know?"

"Ah, Miss Finnegan! I know that you looked me up on the internet. I simply did the same with you. You're involved with the FBI."

"I'm not an agent."

"No," he said seriously. "But I do see that you are quite constantly in the company of a particular agent, Special Agent Craig Frasier. The tall dark-haired brick sitting over there with his fellows, huh?"

"Yes, and we are a couple," she said simply. "Our work often coincides."

"His cousin is a Douglas."

"Yes," she said again.

"It's okay," Jay said, grinning. "I'm flattered that you thought to talk to me. I'll try to give you my theory in a nutshell. The Ark isn't just an Ark. It's very special. The Ark was given to the Egyptians in history long before Ramses the Great. It was left by the aliens. It is like a super-duper cell phone. I think that's been the cause of many a curse—you know when Tut's tomb was opened, bad things happened. Very bad things. And there was a similar ark found in the tomb. I believe that the extra-terrestrials are the 'gods' we believe in. The Ark was in Egypt when Moses was there, and it left with him. I sincerely believe in that whole theory that it came into the keeping of the Knights Templar. When Philip began his money-grubbing to destroy the Templars and confiscate their riches, a number of them took the Ark with them to Scotland, entrusted it to Norse traders who brought it to the New World to hide. Except that I don't believe it went to Oak Island, I sincerely believe that it is more than possible that they came to their southern-most trading station—Douglas Island. Just as the Ark defended itself against ancient invaders, it has caused death and destruction on Douglas Island. Trust me, this is possible. And when the aliens are ready—and believe we're ready—they will come again."

Both Kieran and Danny were silent when he finished his speech.

Jay Harding laughed. "You think I'm crazy. Just like Mr. Scholar, John Smith, thinks I'm crazy—and writes all kinds of things to deliberately mock me and other believers. But you tell me—what religion out there isn't a matter of stories of magic and belief? And, you tell me it's not true that, once upon a time, any intelligent and rational man believed that the world was flat."

"I don't think you're crazy," Kieran said. "You're as entitled to your beliefs as any man."

He smiled at that and then leaned forward, looking from Danny to Kieran. "Think about it—whether you believe that the Ark was created by aliens or not, isn't it a fabulous idea to think that it might be there—right across the water—on Douglas Island?"

"Beyond awesome," Danny said, nodding.

"So!" Harding sat back. "Can you get me on the island?"

"What?" Kieran said.

"I could go ask the FBI guy," he said, shrugging.

Kieran shrugged as well. "He is right over there. Feel free—go ask him."

Harding sighed and frowned. "Ah, come on. He isn't going to like me. FBI. All logic and 'get the bad guy.' But if you were to ask him…"

"Everyone wants out to that island. Hope it still goes that way if Finn does get his resort up and running."

"A resort? On an island that's all but holy!" Harding said. "I've been contemplating my ways of getting out there, of asking Finn Douglas if I might have his permission—or even if I could just go without permission! But, now, of course, if I could get there first…"

"Mr. Harding—" Kieran began.

"Jay, please. Do I look like a guy who likes to be called *mister*?"

"Jay, there are endless caves and tunnels on the island. People could actually search a lifetime and not find what they were looking for. And Finn Douglas isn't going to let a group in to dig up his property. I can find out if he'd be willing to let you come out and see the island, but…"

"At the moment, it's still a crime scene," Danny said.

"Right," Kieran said.

"The entire island?" Harding asked.

"The police and the FBI aren't going to allow anyone other than law enforcement on the island," Kieran said. "Not to dig things up."

"Crime scene? I thought a guy fell," Harding said, looking perplexed.

"They want to check it out," Kieran said. "There have been a lot of deaths out there."

"Ah-ha! You see!" Harding said triumphantly.

"You could possibly see the island—maybe Finn would let you in the house. But I'm really afraid that you couldn't explore or dig or anything like that," Kieran said firmly.

"Would you try to get me an invite?"

Danny cleared his throat. "You could, Kieran, right?" he asked.

"Whether you do or don't, you are welcome to join the Believers," Harding told them.

"What do you do?" Kieran asked him. "Are you a club?"

Danny laughed. "Car washes to raise funds? Community projects?"

"You're making fun of me," Harding said.

"Honestly, I'm not. If your group wanted to be recognized, raising money for charity is one way," Danny told him.

"We don't need to be recognized. People who believe

find us. We meet to discuss whatever research members have done. New theories. We draw comparisons in history," Harding said. "You'd be amazed at similarities among events and structures worldwide when different people were yet to move around the globe. John Smith be damned—we're rigorous scholars."

"Sounds like it," Kieran said.

"We meet Wednesday night. You want to show your interest—you're welcome to join. Seven o'clock, at the coffee shop on the left side of the Grecian Spa Boutique Hotel, down in the Village. Do you know it?" Harding asked.

"I do," Kieran said. Her apartment was in the village—the hotel wasn't far. She even knew the coffee shop.

She'd just never known that ancient-alien theorists met there.

Harding folded his napkin and sighed. "This was a delicious meal. Thank you for having me. Have to go—beauty rest, you know. Come for a meeting."

He stood and Danny rose politely as well.

"Thank you. Thank you for seeing us," Kieran told him.

"An absolute pleasure," Harding said. Hands in his pockets, he headed on out of the pub.

Danny sat. "He's a total nutcase!"

"Maybe. Maybe worse," Kieran said.

"Worse?"

"Someone has been out on the island," Kieran said. "Maybe some of his 'Believers.' He may not need an invitation—he might have been out there already—time and time again."

"Because they...believe?" Danny asked.

"Maybe. And maybe they pretend to believe. That

way, they find out anything that's going on at the island."

"And they're not bad at finding things out," Danny said.

"You think?" Kieran asked him.

Danny sat back, drumming his fingers on the table as he stared at her. "He sure as hell found out a lot of details about you, didn't he?"

"It wouldn't be that hard," she said softly.

"He knew about you and Craig—and knew Craig was Finn's cousin."

"But we're not secretive. All you have to do is check certain social media accounts to see who was with who when and where. Of course, Craig doesn't keep pages, but Danny does, my other brothers do—and we have a page for the pub. Easy enough. He looked up information on me. I looked up information on him."

"Ah, but I'm willing to bet—he had more on you. Anyway, who knows? Maybe he is just a minor nutcase."

"And we may have to find some faith ourselves if we're going to discover what the Believers really think."

CHAPTER
SEVEN

"Now you want to have a UFO conspiracy group come out to the island? A guy who looks like a leftover from a '60s commune?" Craig asked Kieran.

"You're the one who found the word *aliens* written in the sand," she reminded him.

"Yes, but…"

"I do believe we should start this way, though. Danny and I go to their meeting and we find out what is going on."

He was lying in bed. She straddled him. "It makes sense. Stoning—something done in the Biblical sense. This man—Harding—definitely believes that aliens have been among us. And they have a communication device—the Ark—and because of that, bad things happen here. We're not ready for the aliens to come again, or they're not ready for us. So, if a group was protecting the Ark, they might well stone those who interfered, acting on behalf of the aliens—making bad things happen."

"Good theory," Craig said. "*Or*…a killer used stones as a weapon to make it appear that the victim had fallen from the cliffs."

"Ah, but no clue goes unfollowed, right?" she asked.

He grinned. "Too bad you're already using the hell out of me. You could bribe me."

"Maybe bribery would work anyway?" she said.

"Maybe. You could always give it a try."

"Hmm…tempting…"

"Let me tempt you a little bit more!"

He switched their positions, rolling over her.

He loved her eyes when she looked up at him with pure laughter and mischief.

And he loved the taste of her lips, and that of her flesh.

They made love, and then he lay by her, feeling so very lucky to be taking a moment with the love of his life…and then eventually allowing his mind to turn back to the case at hand.

"What are you thinking?" she asked him.

"That I have one incredible job. I'm working a case, and lying next to you, and all I have to do is turn and take you into my arms again, and…"

"Did the bribery work?"

He laughed softly. "There's one thing I've realized since we've been together. You're going to do what you're going to do."

"So this group meets at a coffee shop not far from the apartment."

"May be interesting. Maybe I'll go with you. We'll see what's going on." He was serious. "I think we'll move much more quickly now that we have Silverheels."

She crawled out of bed and walked over to the window. He watched her move, loving the sight of her, like an ancient Aphrodite, sleek and beautifully formed, dark red hair tumbling down her back and over her shoulders.

He rose to join her at the window.

"You're looking for that light again, aren't you? It could be some kind of a reflection," he said.

She turned in to him. "It could be. And I know that you always look at everything from all sides. But Craig, tell me you don't think that something has been going on here, that people have been coming here—strictly for riches, or because of some arcane belief."

"Yeah, it's possible. But something bugs me. I can't help but think that someone here knows more than they're saying."

"Who? Finn? I know you don't believe Finn is in on it. Margie? She's completely honestly distraught. That leaves Elayne. She might break a nail if she tried to dig."

"Point taken. How about Evie? She's a bit creepy."

"Creepy?"

"Something about her. Too nice. Like a cross between…a surrogate mother and a dictator."

Kieran laughed at that. Then she gasped. "There, Craig—there!"

He looked. There was nothing. Nothing but the moon playing over the dark rise of the cliffs.

"I missed it again," he said.

"I'm not imagining it!"

"I would never suggest such a thing."

"We need to get out there, Craig. Not just in the daytime. By night."

He was quiet a minute.

"It would be interesting to find out if others go out

at night—Finn, Margie, Elayne or creepy housekeeper Evie," he said.

"We could go knocking on doors," Kieran said.

"And we could find ourselves booted off the island," Craig said. "But you're right."

He turned away and headed for the foot of the bed, finding his jeans.

"What are you doing?"

"I'm going to prowl the house at night."

"Craig, I just saw the light. If someone is about—they're out there."

"I'll still just take a walk around," he told her.

"Wait, Craig. There's another player. Victor Eider. Handyman extraordinaire. Finn is dedicated to him and to Evie. I think he's staying somewhere in the house now, too."

"Yes. He's here somewhere. And, yes, both Victor and Evie have been with Finn a long time. I won't be long—I'm just going to take a walk around. Oh, lock the door."

She nodded. "Okay, but…"

He reached for a shirt and then his holster and gun. "Don't worry—I'm not going unarmed."

She smiled. "Don't be long!"

"I won't be," he promised. He realized that she didn't want him to go.

He left the room, pausing on the attic landing. All was silent.

He descended to the second floor. No one was stirring there, either.

On the ground floor, he stood in the great hall for a moment. And then he heard noise.

It was coming through the kitchen.

He walked through the White Room and the dining room and pushed open the kitchen door. He found Elayne Anderson there, busy fixing a tray with two glasses of what appeared to be milk.

"You, too, huh?" she asked.

"Pardon?"

"I don't know what it is about the night. Finn can't seem to sleep. Thought we'd try milk—and a few cookies. Funny, isn't it? We grow up, and we still like our comfort foods."

"Yes, I guess we do," he said.

"Want me to get you something?"

"Ah, I was just coming for water," Craig said. "Thank you. Let me get the door for you, with you carrying that tray."

"Well, thank you, sir. A true gentleman."

"I do try," he said lightly.

She took down a bag of cookies and added it to the tray, and then collected it and swept by him.

There was more than milk in the glasses, he thought. She'd laced the milk with alcohol. Whiskey in tea— old-time Irish cure for sleeplessness, or so it seemed in Kieran's family.

He held the door for her.

When she was gone, he wondered.

Had someone here had something to do with Frank Landon's death?

The police were leaning toward the theory that it had been an accident, because it might well be impossible to prove that it had been anything else. However, he knew how the police worked; they were undoubtedly checking backgrounds of those here.

Too often, this kind of crime was committed by

someone with an impeccable background. Because this kind of murder was specific—committed by someone with a specific agenda.

Someone here or someone close. Very close.

Finn slept each night with Elayne Anderson. But then… Once he was out, just how deeply did Finn sleep?

Tuesday morning

The household had wound up downstairs for breakfast. Evie had seen to it that they had a spread that included eggs, pancakes, toast, fruit, bacon, ham and just about anything that could be desired. They also discovered that now a boat was coming every morning at 5:30 a.m., bringing in staff for the day. The boat left again every night at four thirty, taking the daytime maids and workers back to the mainland. There were five maids who were preparing the rooms and common areas of the house and two groundskeepers who were working to restore the pool and patio area. It seemed Finn was still moving toward his dream of a resort on the island. "We really don't need service in our rooms," Kieran told Finn on learning that they could now have maid service. "Craig and I can make our own bed."

"We prefer no one clean our room," Craig had said firmly.

"As you wish," Finn assured them.

Agent Silverheels was introduced to the gathered group, with a brief rundown of his area of expertise.

"So, were your people here, on this island, originally?" Elayne asked.

"Not that I know about. There were Mohawks in New York State, part of the Iroquois Confederacy, but to the best of my knowledge, my dad's family were always in what's now Canada. They were never part of the battles that went on between tribes in this area," he told them.

"But there were Native Americans here, right?" Margie asked.

"Many. Seneca, Oneida and Cayuga, to name a few."

"Craig says that you're down in the DC area now," Finn said.

"I'm with the DC office."

"And they call on you when caves are involved?" Elayne asked, apparently enthralled.

Bracken shrugged. "And heights."

"Nice," Margie murmured absently. For some reason, that caused a silence at the table. She seemed to realize that she was being watched. "I'm sorry. So sorry. It's just... Frank is dead. He'll be dead no matter what you find out. Forgive me."

"It's all right, Margie," Finn said. "Please, understand. I have to do this."

"And, please, understand," Craig said, "that the FBI has opened an official investigation. Neither Finn nor I could stop it if we chose."

Margie nodded. "Excuse me," she said. "I'll just tell Evie that breakfast was great... Oh, well, I don't see her now. Will you tell her for me?" she asked.

And she stood, smiled weakly and left the room.

"Maybe you should go after her," Finn told Elayne.

"I've tried, Finn!" Elayne said.

"I'll go," Kieran volunteered. She rose and hurried after Margie. She caught up with her on the second floor—and made a point of noting which room she was heading to.

"Margie, is there anything any of us can do?" Kieran asked her.

"That's kind of you. I—I didn't sleep much last night. I'm going to try to go back to bed for a while. Be a more social person tonight."

"You don't have to be social."

"No, but… I have to learn to start living again, right?"

"At your own pace," Kieran said.

Margie thanked her again, then turned and went into her room.

Kieran started to head back down the stairs, but then paused, not at all sure why.

Instead of going down the stairs, she went up. The door to the room she and Craig were using was slightly ajar.

She walked to the door and pressed it inward.

Evie was standing by the bed—plumping the pillows.

"Ah, hello, dear. Breakfast okay?" she asked.

"Breakfast was great, thank you," Kieran said. "Evie, I don't mean to sound ungrateful, but Craig and I like our privacy. We don't need our room cleaned."

"Oh…well, I'm sorry. I just run a very tight ship," Evie said. "I like things clean and neat."

"Craig and I are clean and neat," Kieran said.

"I didn't mean to imply…well, all right, then. I'll leave you all to your own devices."

Evie left the room. Kieran watched her go.

She couldn't help the way she felt about the woman.

Had Evie been in the room the day before when Kieran had been in the shower, hoping maybe that Kieran had left her clothing outside and that there might have been something in her pockets?

Her handbag and computer and other belongings were also in the room.

Or had she just imagined that her door had opened and closed?

She needed to talk to Craig; she didn't want to haul a computer and everything else with her every time they left the room. There had to be a way to lock the door when they were gone.

Kieran heard humming from Danny's room. She went out to the hall then peeked in. A young woman was busy making Danny's bed.

"Hello!" the maid said cheerfully. "May I help you—you need something?"

Kieran smiled. Danny was a slob—but he was careful to give anything of importance to Craig. It was fine if his room was being cleaned. For the best, really.

"No, no, thank you," Kieran said.

"De nada!"

With a wave, Kieran left her, hurrying downstairs. She was glad she wasn't trying to sneak around; she had worn boots for their day of cave exploration and she thought that she'd be able to hear herself coming from a mile away.

"Trowels—definitely," Bracken Silverheels said.

Mike, Bracken and Craig were out by the storage shed with Finn, supplying themselves for the day's work. High-powered flashlights, rope, hooks and trowels. Bracken had brought harnesses and other climbing gear.

"I should go with you," Finn said. "I should...but there's so much going on here. And, honestly, I can't

seem to bring myself to want to become involved with…
whatever happened."

"Frank was your friend. Let us do the work," Craig
told him.

"Maybe the island is cursed," Finn said.

"To me, most of the time, something being 'cursed'
has to do with people doing very bad things," Bracken
said.

"It's just that so many bad things seem to have happened here. Sad, isn't it? I can't even be surprised if you
find more bodies. Or bones. I guess bones aren't really
a body anymore. Remains," Finn said.

Victor Eider, who had been carrying out large buckets of chemicals for the pool set them down, then waved
and walked over.

"Do you need help? I'm another able-bodied man, if
you do," Victor offered.

"I think we're good for now," Craig said. "Thanks
for the offer. But I know Finn wants to get moving on
finishing up the resort."

"Whatever *you* want, Finn," Victor said cheerfully.

His voice was easy.

Still, he meant for them to know that he worked for
Finn Douglas—and not any of them. And, if Finn had
wanted it, he'd be there whether they needed him or not.

Finn seemed oblivious. "Thanks, Victor," he said.
"I guess I do want to keep moving forward. Here. At
the house."

"I'll get back to it, then," Victor said. With another
jaunty wave, Victor went back to work.

"I'll get Kieran," Danny said.

He went back into the house while Craig and Bracken
sorted the supplies.

Craig, slipping loops of rope over his shoulder, saw Victor Eider out of the corner of his eye.

Victor had gone back to his buckets at the edge of the pool. He was hunched down, seeming to fiddle with a tool. But his eyes were up on Craig. Watching.

Bracken laid the map down on the dirt floor of the cave entrance while Danny held the light right over it.

"All right, I'm going to say that the first people making use of this island did so because it offered a natural profusion of caves," Bracken said. "Then, throughout history, different areas have been dug through and shored up. This tunnel that we're in, for one. I'm going to have to see more, but I believe, at some point, someone joined it—here, at this odd juncture of webs— with natural caves on the other side. Without heavy equipment—the kind we use today on coal digs and the like—it would have been laborious and taken some time. But if—as suggested in many theories—Norse traders were using the island as a far south trading post, they might well have created the passages. Or pirates, centuries later. Then again, who knows? Where did you find the bracteate?" he asked Kieran. She appreciated his straightforward manner, and how he seemed comfortable in the cave.

She showed him where she had been digging the day before, in a little niche in the cave just behind the rock where the bones had been.

"Interesting," he said. "Someone could keep digging. I have a feeling, though, that whatever else might have been found here has already been taken. Your bracteate might have been dropped, forgotten or gone undiscovered by whoever had the candy wrapper."

"They could find DNA on the candy wrapper, right? Or fingerprints?" Danny asked hopefully.

"Maybe. Or the diggers might have been wearing gloves," Bracken said.

"And the thing about DNA is that you have to have comparisons," Craig said. "Then again," he added softly, "if anyone in the house is involved, it will be easy enough to get hold of some DNA."

"I'll look here," Danny said. "We brought the trowels today, right?"

"Yes, we brought the trowels," Bracken said. "Listen to the ground as well. Tap it—you can hear a difference between hollow ground and solid rock beneath you."

"I'll stay with Danny—no splitting up, okay?" Mike asked.

"Onward, then," Bracken said. The tunnel was a broad expanse—a natural cave, Bracken assured them—and their lights shone on the ground before them as they walked.

They paused for Craig to show Bracken the hole they had gone through before—one that had led them to a tunnel that had simply gone on to sheer wall.

"There should be more entrances here," Bracken said. "This one map Danny discovered…it shows a man-made tunnel, one that may have led off from the area you were in before. But whatever you find, let me go ahead…to make sure that we're not facing any kind of cave-in."

Kieran watched as Bracken tapped on the walls of the cave. "Listen," he said. "Hear that? Solid. It will be different if there's space behind what you see."

They kept moving forward, pausing now and then to

check the walls. Where the light didn't hit, it was solid black around them.

Kieran heard a scampering and paused, swallowing.

"Rat," Bracken said. "You all right?"

"Oh, yeah. I've known a few rats in my day," she assured him.

"I didn't mean people," Bracken said lightly.

"I didn't either—though I have known people who might have been considered rats," she replied. "I have boots on—the real kind won't be running over my feet or anything."

"Watch where you put your hands as well," Bracken warned.

He had just spoken when she leaned against the wall and it suddenly seemed to come to life with a flapping of wings.

Somehow, she kept from screaming.

"Bats," Craig said. "I guess we could come across a lot of them down here."

The bats had taken off in a flurry. Once they were gone, the cave tunnel seemed to be silent again.

Craig paused as they walked along.

"Bracken, what do you make of this?" he asked.

Kieran followed Bracken over to where Craig stood, his lantern high as he frowned, studying the wall.

There were some kind of markings gouged into the stone.

"They don't look like Indigenous petroglyphs," she said. And then she murmured, "Runic? Is it an ancient Norse inscription of some kind?"

"I don't think so," Bracken said.

"I think it means something," Craig murmured.

"Maybe it's some kind of notation of place? A map, or…"

"I wish I knew. I really don't. And it's not like I'm all that familiar with ancient Norse," Bracken said. "I was in Italy once, certain that I'd made a great discovery. It was an ancient Roman stone with writing, but it basically said, 'Park horse here.'"

"But this really could mean something," Kieran said.

"Of course."

"I'll send it in," Craig said, handing his light over to Bracken. He pulled out his phone and began to take a series of pictures.

Kieran kept studying the lines cut into the stone.

Suddenly, she gasped.

"What?" Craig and Bracken said in unison.

"If you rearranged the lines a little bit…"

"I'm not seeing what you're talking about," Craig told her.

"Think of printing—in English!" she said. "That line—part of an *A*. Then a dash, and another slanted line. A shorter line and a strange curly symbol. Then three slanted lines. And then…then, I'm not sure, but if you look at the beginning, it could be the word *Alien*."

Both men were silent, studying the lines again.

"It could say *Alien*," Bracken said.

"Or, we could be looking for the words *alien* or *aliens*, because of what we believe Frank Landon was trying to write," Craig said. "Sorry, devil's advocate here—we can't really be sure. And if that is the word *alien*, what the hell does the rest say?"

"We could stare at this a really long time," Bracken said.

"Or keep moving," Craig agreed. "I say I send this

in to the office and see what they can come up with—
we have linguists who can figure out just about anything. And code breakers, if it's some kind of a code."
He turned back to his phone, loading pictures of the
wall carving to send into headquarters as soon as they
were aboveground.

"Aliens," Bracken murmured as they moved along.
Their steps were slow; they checked the wall, the floor,
everything around them. "What did you make of Mr.
Harding, Kieran?"

She thought about the question. "He believes what
he says—I think."

"You're a psychologist, right?"

"Yes, and I believe it helps me sometimes, but...peo-
ple can hide their true selves pretty efficiently, when
they choose. He's a bright man—once I wrote to him,
he apparently investigated me."

"And there is information about you online?"

"I've been involved in a few things that have happened in the city," Kieran said dryly. "And, of course,
Craig is a federal agent, so..."

"Sometimes, too much information might be public knowledge," Bracken said. "So, Jay Harding is re-
sourceful. And he believes aliens visited the earth in
ancient times."

"I think that many educated people are open to the
possibility. Because we're just discovering our own galaxy and the fact that the universe stretches far beyond
what we know..." Kieran shrugged and let her voice
trail. She was busy tapping on the stone wall of the cave.

She had barely finished speaking when something
in the wall gave. She wasn't sure what she did, or how
she managed to make it happen.

She'd hit the wall at shoulder height—what happened was down by her feet. Suddenly her footing was gone.

She screamed, sliding down, down...and farther down. It was as if she had hit a slide. Rocks and dust rained all around her.

"Kieran!"

She heard Craig call her name in alarm. She hit bottom.

She was stunned and terrified herself, but she couldn't let him know that.

"I'm fine, I'm fine! I just came down some kind of a...shaft," she shouted.

Her flashlight had fallen some distance from her. It was shining on more cave wall. She scrambled into a crawling position, making sure she was all right.

She really was fine—her fall had been at such an angle that she didn't even think that she'd gotten a bruise.

"We're coming down. Damn, but that hole is little!" Craig called. "How the hell..."

"It was probably bigger. Time has played a number on it," Bracken said. "Craig, if you can't get down, I can dig a bigger opening and set a spike so that we can create a rope pulley—we will be wanting to get back up."

Crawling to her flashlight, Kieran listened to the two men talking.

She could hear the shuffling at the strange little opening as the two of them worked together.

She found her flashlight and grabbed it, sitting back—just as a large beetle went scurrying away from her.

She shone her flashlight around her.

What she had come down was a rock chute—almost sheer, and at an angle.

Craig was trying to fit through the opening up above.

She cast her flashlight around.

Wall. Cave wall.

She turned.

And a scream froze in her throat.

She was staring at a corpse.

CHAPTER
EIGHT

"Kieran?"

Craig found her silence frightening.

He slid down the shaft—and found himself sitting next to Kieran.

Staring at the sight illuminated by her flashlight.

The corpse wasn't new.

Nor was it very old.

He couldn't tell much by staring at what remained of the flesh on the face, part of it dried out by time, as if the cavern had brought about mummification. But there were creatures in the cave—the eyes had been chewed out and some of the flesh had been consumed.

Like the bones above, it looked as if she had been seated—just leaned up against the wall. In this case, remnants of a cotton blouse remained, along with strips of denim here and there, covering bone and dried-out flesh.

"My God!" Kieran breathed at last.

"Hey!" Bracken called from above. "What the hell did you find?"

"Not what," Craig told him. "Who."

"More bones?" Bracken shouted down.

"Um, a little more than bones."

Craig slipped an arm around Kieran. "You're all right."

She nodded. "Craig…she's not…she wasn't recently killed, but…she wasn't a pirate, or a Viking, or…she's not that old! I mean, hasn't been here that long…"

He took a breath and swore softly. "What the hell has been going on around here?" he muttered. He pushed himself to his feet and looked up at Bracken, who was lying flat by the opening above.

"Call Egan," he said wearily. "I don't know how long she's been here. A while. Probably years, but I have no idea how many. A medical examiner is going to have to give an estimate."

"I'm sending down the rope," Bracken said.

Kieran was still just staring at the corpse as a coil of brightly colored nylon cord came tumbling down to them.

"Hey," Craig said softly.

She shivered, rising. "She looks like a mockery of… of life. And death," Kieran said softly.

"I'm getting you out of here," he said.

That seemed to wake her. "I'm assuming we both have to get out of here. This woman… I suppose she could have just come down here and been…stuck? Or…"

"Are you ready to go?" Craig asked Kieran.

"Craig… Can you imagine? She might have fallen down here! She might have screamed and screamed for help, and no one came!"

"We don't know anything yet."

"No. I was so stunned, I haven't had a good look. Did she have a flashlight? Is there a purse, a handbag, a backpack, anything?"

Kieran wasn't taking the rope; she was shining her flashlight around the cave. But no matter where her light bit through the darkness, there was nothing.

It was a small cell beneath the main floor of the cave.

And there was a dead woman decaying, and nothing else.

"Kieran, we'll get a team out. If there is anything to be found, they'll find it."

She accepted the rope at last, looping the solid lasso that Bracken had tied over her head and fixing it under her arms.

She gave the corpse a last glimpse.

He waited until she half walked and was half hauled back up the slope. Then he pulled out his camera to take pictures of the corpse.

The rope came back down. Going back up was no easy deal; getting out of the small hole was even more difficult.

"She was…small, I think. Hard to tell now," Kieran was telling Bracken. "She could have gotten down on her own, but…how? Why?"

Craig crawled through the hole and made it to his feet.

"Man, that wasn't easy," he murmured.

"Hey, you weigh a hell of lot more than she does!" Bracken said.

"Yeah, yeah. We're going to have to dig this out somehow, though. We'll never get a team down there if we don't."

"I'll talk to Egan as soon as we're out of the caves.

The team will bring pickaxes. And I assume you'd appreciate the same medical examiner on this."

Craig nodded.

"What did you see?" Bracken asked him.

Craig shook his head. "Hell, I don't know. It's hard to tell. The environment of the cave half preserved her—and yet…creatures down there were not kind to her at all."

"Five to ten years," Kieran said.

He looked at her. She shrugged. "When your cousin was here, involved with the case at the new Egyptian museum… I spent some time with her. She told me about natural mummification. That poor woman…she's partially mummified and I'm not an expert, but I think she's been down there five to ten years."

Craig looked at Bracken. "Egan is on the way?"

"He has people heading to a boat as we speak."

Craig nodded, looking at Kieran. "Exploration is over for the day," he said softly.

She nodded. She looked okay. Just a little pale. He was probably a little pale himself.

"We need to tell Danny and Mike," she said.

She started walking toward the opening to the caves. He glanced at Bracken.

"I won't move," Bracken promised.

"I'll send the pictures to you and Mike and Egan at the same time," Craig told him.

Bracken just nodded grimly.

When they reached the entrance, both Mike and Danny were down on the ground. They were covered in dirt, and working away with their trowels.

"Hey, you're back pretty quickly," Mike said, rising and trying to dust the dirt from himself. All he managed to do was just smudge it in.

"You found something?" he asked. "More of those brac—those medallion things?"

"Scratches on the wall—and a corpse," Kieran said.

"What?"

Danny leaped to his feet as well, staring at his sister.

"Bones?" Mike asked.

"No, a corpse. Not…" Kieran's voice trailed as she looked for the right word. "Fresh?" she said.

"Egan has people on the way," Craig said. "They'll be here within the hour, I imagine. You know Egan. When he says jump…"

"I thought we were just getting somewhere," Danny said. "Can we keep working until they get here?"

"Danny! We just found a woman's body!" Kieran said.

"Yes, you just found her. But it sounds as if she's been here a while. Kieran, there's something here, just below. I tapped the way that Bracken said to—when Mike and I started. And there's something…we heard it," Danny said.

"We have some time," Craig said.

Danny was already back on the ground. Craig didn't want to forget that they had found someone who had once been a living human being, and who had—one way or another—died alone and in misery.

But he took up a trowel himself.

And began to dig.

Before he knew it, Kieran was down beside him, and then Mike, as well.

"Careful, careful… I can feel it!" Craig said. "No more trowels. Brushes… I'm sure we brought brushes, hell, fingers! But don't…"

He didn't need to be giving any instructions. They were all being as careful as possible. Minutes passed.

And more minutes.

"There's something. There's definitely something. Maybe… Damn! Maybe a treasure chest," Mike said. "Or…"

His voice trailed.

Kieran had found a brush. She was working slowly. Painstakingly slowly.

The others sat back.

And something began to appear.

It wasn't a treasure chest.

It was a stone, buried under less than a foot of packed dirt. Mike shone the light on it.

They all stared.

It was covered in symbols that meant nothing to any of them.

"'Park horse here,'" Craig murmured softly. "Or…"

He stopped speaking, surprised to hear noises coming from beyond the cave. The forensic crew and perhaps the medical examiner had arrived. They had all become so engrossed in carefully completing their task that none of them had realized the passing of time. They had been at it longer than the half hour or so it took to reach the island from the mainland.

He made an instant decision. "Let's get it out and covered up," he said. "I don't want anyone else knowing what we found."

Tuesday night

While the forensic team was still down in the cave, Kieran, Danny and Mike sat with the household at the dinner table.

Craig and Bracken had remained behind, oversee-ing the work.

It was a late dinner. Finn had taken one look at them—all covered in dirt and grime—and put the meal on hold until they'd had a chance to clean up.

This time, Kieran had locked the door when she'd gone in to shower. And, as an added safeguard, she had taken her clothing with her. She wasn't sure why—there was nothing to be found in her pockets. And she didn't even really know if someone had been in her room the last time.

At the dinner table, only Mike really seemed to be eating.

Finn was glum, deeply disturbed about yet another death on the island. He'd been shocked to see the boat arriving filled with crime scene technicians.

Margie was quiet, withdrawn as usual.

Only Elayne tried to make conversation. "Here's the thing, Finn. You mustn't let this stop you. Your idea is a good one. Turn this island around. The body found today…well, one way or another, it's been there awhile. Whether a year or twenty years. We had nothing to do with it. Someone was using the island for bad things, and you're going to make it into something good. It was an old body, right, Kieran?"

"It had definitely been there awhile," Kieran said. "And, Finn, she's right—I don't know how long. I do know that it has been there quite some time. Elayne is right—none of this is your fault."

"Frank is my fault," Finn said. "He wouldn't have been here if it hadn't been for this ridiculous plan of my mine. A body a day," he said glumly. "So it seems. Maybe I should just give it all up."

"Finn, no," Elayne said.

"It is cursed—the island is cursed," Margie said. She looked around the table and said, "Oh, I am so sorry. I'm like a broken record, a voice of doom." She took a deep breath. "Finn, I don't know—I just don't know. On the one hand, I had felt that you shouldn't give up. Frank wouldn't have wanted you to give up. But now, and with my whole heart, I think you should stop. I'm wondering if there is really a curse—and if Frank's death wasn't a sign to stop what we're doing."

"Thank you, Margie," Finn said. "I appreciate that sentiment. And I know… I know that none of us are really thinking straight right now. Still…we haven't managed to accept the fact that Frank is gone, and all this…"

Mike cleared his throat. "Craig and I spoke briefly before Danny, Kieran and I walked back here. He believes we might discover that the dead woman was out here at the same time as the bank robbers. This young woman might have been with them."

Finn stood suddenly. "Forgive me. Please, enjoy dinner. I'm just not very social this evening."

Elayne started to rise as well. Finn set a hand on her shoulder. "No, sweetheart, stay here. Finish eating."

"I'm not very hungry, really," Elayne said.

"Forgive me, I need to be alone," he told her. He smiled tightly. "Please don't worry. I do appreciate you and how hard you're trying to help me—come up to the room in a bit."

Finn left the dining room. Kieran could have sworn that he didn't go upstairs; she was certain that she heard the front door open and close.

A moment later, Evie came into the room. "Where is Finn?"

"He, uh, needed a walk, I guess," Mike offered.

"Evie," Danny said. "You have done an outstanding job, as usual. But you'll have to excuse us, too. Kieran, I've got to put a call into Declan about the event at the pub. He's going to want to talk to you, as well."

"Of course," Kieran said, rising. "We'll call from my room. We have great reception there."

Mike arched a brow. He must have known they'd fill him in later.

On what, Kieran didn't know.

But Danny wanted her.

They fled the dining room and hurried up the stairs. Kieran followed Danny into his room, and he closed the door. "Someone was in my room," he said quietly. "While I was in the shower. I'm not being paranoid."

"And I thought someone was in mine…and I know Evie was up here earlier. Danny, I know you handed your maps over to Craig and Bracken, but is there anything else in here that someone would want?"

"My computer, but it's well protected," he said.

She pulled out her phone. "I'm texting Craig."

"Craig can't do anything right now. He's knee deep in…a half-mummified corpse!"

"I want him to know that Finn went out."

"Finn might just be in his room."

"I'm pretty sure that Finn went outside. That he's walking around the island. It may or may not be important, but I want Craig to know."

"I can't begin to tell you the factors involved in discovering a time of death for this woman," Dr. Hodges told Craig and Bracken.

They were the only ones down in the hole with him

at the moment, other than his assistant. The medical examiner was always supposed to have access to a corpse first—even before police or other law enforcement rifled through the pockets, searching for ID.

"You didn't touch her, right?" he asked Craig and Bracken.

"Nope. Didn't even fall into her. I just stared and took pictures," Craig said.

"And the young lady with you?"

Craig paused a moment. The last thing he could imagine was Kieran searching through the clothing of a corpse.

Especially this corpse.

"No one touched the body," he said.

Hodges, down on his knees, studying the remains of the woman, shook his head. "This is a hard one. Some of the skin has been dried and basically mummified. Soft tissue…eyes, lips…not sure what else…has been eaten. Bugs, small animals, and we're not looking at a new body, so the rate of consumption…never mind. I'm going to get her out of here—which will be no easy task either—and start tests at the morgue tomorrow." He was quiet a minute. "I will say this… I actually recognize the remnants of her jeans. They were extremely popular about a decade ago—I know that because they were by a designer who died a few years back. My daughter wanted a pair in the worst way. I wasn't about to invest hundreds of dollars in a pair of jeans. That's not scientific, but…"

"We thought she might have been with the bank robbers," Craig said.

Bracken walked over and looked up the shaft to the tunnel above. "How's the hoist going?" he asked.

"Done to your specifications, sir!" someone called from up top. "Ready to pull her up!"

A lightweight metal stretcher with a basket came down. Dr. Hodges watched as it lowered, and then turned to Craig and Bracken.

"Gentlemen, if you would give me a hand. I want to get this tarp beneath her first, and then we lift carefully and get her on the litter." He hesitated, trying to be careful with his words, and then shrugged. "She's probably very brittle, in part, at least, and I'd like to get X-rays before...well, before the corpse is injured."

They managed to get the corpse onto the gurney, and watched as it was carefully and slowly pulled on up. Craig was still helping to steady the pulley when he felt his phone buzz, but he had to wait.

When he pulled out his phone, he found that Kieran had sent him a message. Amazingly he'd had enough reception for it to come through.

"Finn is out walking somewhere on the island. He seemed distressed—told us he wanted to be alone. You might want to see if you can find him."

He glanced over at Bracken. "You still okay to hang in while the forensic crew comes down?"

"As long as you need," Bracken assured him.

A rope slid down to help hoist out Dr. Hodges. Craig stepped before him. "May I? Sorry, sir, I need to move here I think."

"Far be it from me to slow down a fed," Hodges said, stepping back. "She's been down here a fair amount of time, as we all can tell, but we'll still be getting her in tonight, and your boss seems to think we may be finding...something, so autopsy bright and early."

"Thank you. We'll be there," Craig said.

He headed on out to the main level of the tunnel within the caves. The forensic crew—five members—were seated on their own packs or the ground, waiting for their turn below. The tunnel was well lit—they had brought a high-powered work light along with individual headlamps on the helmets they were wearing.

Once outside, even though he moved quickly, he could find no sign of Finn. If he'd left the house and taken the "beach" path, he would have come in Craig's direction.

But he might have gone up the cliff path.

Almost running, Craig went past the house, heading toward the east side of the island. It was no longer a full moon that illuminated the sky, but it was still generous enough to light the way. Making his way uphill through scruff, rocks and brush, he finally came to the top of the cliff. The area where the cliff jutted high—and out over the rocky eastern shore beneath.

His cousin was standing dangerously close to the edge. Staring out at the darkness of the Atlantic beyond, like a forlorn hero out of a Gothic romance.

Craig jogged toward him.

A bird shrieked high overhead; something large, a hawk or a kite. It was most probably hunting some small creature on the cliff—a mouse perhaps. But it was careening straight toward Finn.

Finn looked up and staggered several steps, avoiding the dive of the bird.

He was almost on the dead edge of the cliff.

"Finn!"

Craig shouted his name and sprinted the last few steps. Leaping, he tackled Finn—and thrust them far from the edge of the cliff, sending them both rolling backward over bracken and rocks.

When they came to a stop, Craig pushed away, staring at Finn with incredulity and fury.

"What the bloody hell were you doing?" he demanded.

Finn looked shaken. "Just…just walking. I swear, Craig—I had no plans on being that close. I wasn't going to jump over—God help me! I'd never jump. I came… I came to see what might have happened to Frank. Man…"

Craig swore softly, coming to his feet, reaching a hand down to help Finn.

"Don't do that," Craig said.

"I'm sorry. I swear. I wasn't that close. The freaking bird…"

Craig set his hands on his knees, bending over, still catching his breath.

Finn shook his head and repeated softly, "I'm sorry. Um, are you okay?"

"Yeah—fine. Except for the ten years you scared off my life."

He was surprised to see his words almost brought a smile to his cousin's lips. "I have a feeling you deal with much worse."

"Can't be a hell of a lot worse than it being you," Craig told him.

Finn suddenly embraced him in a fierce hug. For a moment, Craig stood still, surprised.

Then he returned the hug, disentangled himself and stepped back.

"I think we should head back down. All the way down."

"The morgue guy is here?"

"Dr. Hodges is here, yes. He's taking the corpse... they have it up. Her up," he amended softly.

"Who was she, Craig? What was she doing?"

"I don't know. We'll find out tomorrow. Hopefully."

Finn lowered his head and nodded. "Maybe I should get massive bulldozers in here. Level the cliff over the caves, bury—forever—whatever else lies here."

Craig groaned. "Finn, come on. Let's get back to the house, take showers and get some sleep. Tomorrow maybe we'll get some answers that will help us make some sense of this."

Finn nodded. "Okay. I freaked out a little. You deal with corpses a lot—I don't. I lost a friend. But I called you because I want justice. Something is going on here. And, so help me, I'm not going to freak out anymore. I'm going to do whatever the hell you need me to do."

"First, I need you to stay off the damned cliff."

"I'll stay off it. I swear."

"Then...we may have to host a dinner."

"We have dinner every day. Evie has dinner for who-ever needs it."

"No, I want to have some people out for dinner."

"People?"

"John Smith—who claims to know how the Vikings brought the Ark here. And a guy named Jay Harding—who thinks that the Ark is here, too, only aliens brought it."

Finn just stared at him.

"Let's see what they have to say once they're here," Craig said.

Finn nodded. "Okay, Craig. It's your show—or,

sorry—investigation. You do whatever it is that you need to do, and I'm game. Just tell me what you need."

Craig set an arm around Finn's shoulders. "I need to see you back at the house. Then I need to see if the forensic team got anything, but I doubt it. Then sleep—and tomorrow, a trip back into the city."

Finn nodded. "I think I upset Elayne. I need to get back to her."

As they picked their way along the rocky path back, Finn pointed out some of the details he planned to add to his resort. A bit of excitement crept into his voice as he spoke.

When they reached the house, it was quiet. Finn ran up quickly, anxious to see Elayne.

Craig stood in the great hall for a minute, frustrated.

He'd been so certain that someone there had to be involved.

But now…he wasn't sure what to think.

He paused and put a call through to Bracken, letting him know that he was back at the house.

"Forensic team is still busy here."

"Are they finding anything?"

"Nothing. Nothing at all. But Craig, I think that little hole she was found in was created just to be a hole. Like a French oubliette. A place to drop someone—and forget about them."

"Dug out…but when?"

"Funny thing—the mechanics of it… I think it's been as it is for hundreds of years."

"But someone knew about it."

"You found it," Bracken said.

"Kieran found it." He was quiet for a minute. "And

I found the cave entrance there…strange, it's all really visible. If you look in the right place and see…"

"The forest for the trees," Bracken said.

"Yeah. I'll go in for the autopsy."

"Good. I'll sleep."

"A fair plan," Craig said, and hung up.

He thought about food. It wasn't appealing at the moment.

He'd rather go see Kieran. It was always better to talk to her than to himself.

He turned and hurried up the stairs.

Kieran woke, aware that darkness surrounded her other than a little glow from the window caused by the moon, waning now from its fullest form, but still granting a pool of gentle light. She was aware without moving that Craig had come in, and was beside her.

He was lying awake, staring up at the ceiling.

First, she was amazed that she had been able to sleep. And then she was a bit angry. She edged up on an elbow and stared down at him.

"Hey, sorry," he said softly. "I didn't mean to wake you."

"You didn't. But I should punch you. You didn't call me back! I'm assuming that you found Finn okay?"

He nodded. "He's back here. Safe in the arms of his Elayne."

"And you're still awake."

He shook his head. "I was so convinced that someone here was involved. The woman we found tonight… she was killed years ago."

Kieran murmured, "Bizarre, sad and—I admit—terrifying. At first. But…isn't it better somehow to find old bones and corpses than…"

"Fresh ones. Yeah," he said. "We're just not getting any closer to what happened to Frank. And if we've found bones and a half-mummified corpse…what will we find next?"

"Hey, you're the logical one. What we'll find out, possibly, is that people have been exploring and searching this island for years—and dying. Either naturally, by accident or because they've intruded upon someone else's exploration. We aren't finding anything we could have changed, or done anything about," Kieran said softly.

He turned to face her. "What is your take on Elayne? Does she love my cousin? What about Margie?"

"I don't know either of them very well. Margie retreats to her room. Elayne hangs on Finn."

He laughed. "I could have said that. You're a professional. You must have something more."

"All right, but…as a professional, I see people, I study their past and they sit down and talk to me. So I haven't really been able to form a professional opinion. I feel very bad for Margie. I think she was really in love with Frank. She should want to get off this island, be with people who love her and who she loves. She hasn't wanted to leave. So, I'm assuming Frank was her entire world. She doesn't go back because she has nothing to go back to."

"Elayne?" he asked.

"Gold digger," Kieran said.

"You don't think she loves Finn?"

"She may be in love with Finn. But I'm not sure she'd love him if he wasn't rich. Look at the two women. Both young and attractive. Margie barely brushes her hair every morning. Elayne has a cut that requires her to put some work into that sweep over her forehead. Her nails are perfectly manicured—fingers and toes are done. She's perfecting a tan on the beach. Her clothing is all designer. Margie has a nice figure, she shops well. But she certainly didn't bring anything fancy or expensive out to the island."

He stared at her and laughed suddenly. "You don't like Elayne."

"I don't dislike Elayne. The thing is, I don't see her exploring caves or digging in the dirt." She was reflective a minute. "Unless she knew untold riches were to be found."

"And Margie?"

"If Frank had asked her, she'd have probably done some digging."

"I don't think that we've talked to her nearly enough. Maybe you can get her off the island in the morning. I'll be going in for the autopsy."

"Is it...a regular autopsy?"

"Yeah. This case...if she was murdered, the murderer might still be out there—and might be the murderer we're looking for now."

"You know, we can find out if people are leaving the house at night," she reminded him.

"How?"

"Fire alarm? Screaming in the middle of the night?" He gazed at her, smiling. "You have a plan?"

CHAPTER
NINE

Wee hours, Wednesday morning

In the middle of the great hall, Kieran stood alone. And she screamed.

It was a damned good scream—it was loud, shrill and sounded of desperate terror.

Craig was ready at the attic stairs. He and Danny paused, though—they had to see what would happen.

He heard footsteps.

First one running down the stairs, his cousin Finn. Not trained in any kind of self-defense, but a man who would run, by nature, to the defense of anyone in trouble.

Evie Summers came running in from the direction of the White Room. A second later, handyman Victor Eider was rushing in. Then, Elayne—but she came from the opposite side of the house, where the library and office could be found.

Margie made an appearance on the second-floor landing, slow as she moved down the stairs.

Bracken and Mike went racing down.

And then Craig.

"Kieran!" he cried. "What, what happened?"

Finn was already by her, an arm around her shoulder. He was looking around wildly.

"What? What?"

Kieran shook. She pointed toward the door of the house. "Someone…someone… I didn't see. They were here, and then they were gone. But…for a minute…"

"Bracken and I are on it—we'll search," Mike said, and he and Bracken ducked out the door. Their silhouettes could be seen passing the front windows.

"What did you see?" Finn cried. "Please, Kieran, can you tell us anything more?"

"It was a shadow…of a man. Or a woman. It was someone trying to get in. They saw me…maybe I scared them as much as they scared me," Kieran said.

"Or—you came downstairs in a dark house and imagined that someone was at the door," Elayne said drily, yawning.

"I didn't imagine it!" Kieran whispered.

Her voice was shaking.

"What…what were you doing downstairs?" Finn asked.

Craig stepped in to answer for her. "Milk. I hear you have a glass of milk when you don't sleep. I thought I'd try it—Kieran offered to get it for me."

"I'll get you some milk, Special Agent Frasier," Evie offered. "As soon as…"

"Come on, we'll go through to the kitchen," Craig told her.

"I'll do a window and door check," Victor Eider said

grimly. "No one will be coming in here, taking us by surprise."

"Finn," Craig began.

"I'll stay right here with Kieran, Margie and Elayne until Mike and Bracken are back."

Craig headed into the kitchen with Evie. "Evie, were you down here already, in the kitchen, when Kieran screamed?"

"I was. Something about this place—I couldn't sleep either. Thought I'd pick up the rest of the dinner dishes. Frankly, I like being the housekeeper-manager. I'm older now. Been around a long time. Been with Finn a long time. But I can't see having anyone else out here, not until we're up and going." She sighed. "Another corpse. I won't leave Finn. But I wish he didn't have his heart set on this island. His father left the place alone for good reason, and his father before him."

"Don't you think it's best to find out why—and, of course, most importantly, to find out what happened to Frank?"

Evie shrugged. "Frank fell. Have you been up on those cliffs? It's easy to think 'What an amazing view!' And then you might well move too close to that ridiculous edge." She shook her head. "And then you tell me—wouldn't it be better to believe that Frank fell—than to have someone else die?"

"Evie, no one else has died. We found victims of long ago crimes."

"So far!" Evie said dourly.

Victor came into the kitchen.

"I'm going to go through and check on the back."

"I'll come with you," Craig said.

Victor nodded. Craig followed him through the kitchen door.

The back room there had originally been an open porch, Craig thought. At some time, it had been enclosed, mainly with glass windows that stretched almost from floor to ceiling. French doors led out to the patio and pool, complete with loungers and umbrella-covered tables.

"These doors...the bottom is locked, but no one swung the bolt," Victor said, shaking his head. "Doesn't look like anyone tried to come through here."

"No, it doesn't," Craig agreed. "I guess Elayne is the only one using the pool."

"No, Finn came out... I came through here today. Even Margie came out. Might as well be depressed in the sun as well as in a bedroom, huh?"

"She came out during the day?"

"Yeah. We haven't had a night pool party in...well, actually, we've never had a night pool party. The air is too cold by night, huh?"

"I guess," Craig agreed. "But Finn hasn't been out here that long, really. Maybe come summer. And, I'm assuming, he'll have it open by night once he has his resort going."

"The plans for the resort are exhausting, really. The house will stay—it's historic. But he's had people out already about the pool—it will double in size. And the wings for the building won't really attach, but they'll stretch out, east and west. See that little bit of flatland... well, you can't see it now! It's dark out there and the moon isn't making it through the trees. But out there, he'll have stables for people to go riding. A stable master of course, riding guide—make sure people stay on the shore and don't try heading up to the cliffs." Victor paused for a minute, studying Craig.

He stopped speaking.

"What is it?" Craig asked.

"We all want him to succeed. He can't go belly-up on this. He's just a great guy. All that family money he has! But he never holds himself above others. Like I said, when I'm not busy, I'm welcome to the pool. Come and go as I like. He knows I work my hardest at anything he needs. But I have never met a human being so capable of giving back, of having no…"

"No asshole traits?" Craig asked, smiling.

"Yeah. I've worked for some people—not even rich people—who think they're better than the rest of the human race."

"Having money doesn't make a person bad."

"No, but it can make them careless of others. Finn is never careless. So, I mean it—anything I can do to help. Anything."

"Thanks. You know the house—just make sure we're locked in tight."

"That, I can do," Victor said. He paused, looking at Craig. "You don't think that your…partner… Kieran. You don't think that maybe she just imagined that she saw someone?"

"Oh, I don't think so."

"She's not—trained like you."

"No, but she's been through a lot of cases. She works with psychiatrists who deal with the police and FBI and other law enforcement. She's bright."

"Helluva scream!" Victor said.

"Yes," Craig agreed politely. "Yes, it was!"

Danny was still in their room with Kieran when Craig finally made it back up.

"Anything?" Kieran asked anxiously.

"Maybe, maybe not," he told her, but he smiled, taking her hands. "Kevin may be the actor in your family, but that was one hell of a performance."

"Yeah. It just cost us all a lot of sleep," Danny said.

She elbowed her brother.

"Bracken and Mike were pretty good, too. They came back into the great hall and announced that they might have seen footprints—too hard to tell on the rocky ground and in the dark. But the ploy was a good thing, maybe. If someone else is on the island, we need to batten down," she told Craig.

"They probably enjoyed it," Craig said. "Both of them are good agents—they know how to keep poker faces."

"What did you get?" Danny asked Craig.

"Evie was in the kitchen. Victor must have still been up, too. And Elayne. Margie seemed to come from her room," Craig said.

"No one came running in from outside," Danny said glumly. "And no one was a no-show. Did this get us anywhere?"

"Yes, I think so."

"Where?" Danny pressed.

"I don't know yet. But it was interesting to see the nocturnal activities of the household. So, Danny—go to bed," Craig said.

"Go to bed? You just cost me an entire night's sleep!"

"You can sleep late tomorrow," Craig told him.

"I can?"

"I'm going in for the autopsy. With Mike. Bracken will be on the island."

"We're going to that meeting tomorrow night," Kieran said.

"What?" Craig asked, frowning as he turned to look at her.

"Craig," she reminded him, "tomorrow night is the meeting of the ancient-alien theorists—the Believers. I think it's important that I go."

"We go," he said.

She shook her head. "An FBI agent working on a case? No. Just Danny and I should go."

He was quiet. She knew that he didn't want her and Danny going alone. "I'll be waiting for you. On the street. You understand? And if you don't show up right when you should, I'll drop in on that meeting."

She nodded. "Fine."

He turned to Danny again. "Go to bed!"

"You're the one who woke me up. But yeah I'm going, I'm going."

They heard Danny's door close. Craig turned to Kieran. "Ah, well, we've got two or three hours left."

"Great."

He grinned. She knew that his adrenaline was racing.

"I only need fifteen minutes of that."

"Fast draw. I could complain."

"But you won't. I promise," he told her.

Like a kid, he made a leap to the bed and patted the mattress at his side.

Kieran obligingly slid in.

In a few minutes, she was no longer thinking about sleep.

"Brain average weight, 1198 grams exactly," Dr. Hodges was saying to his recorder. "Despite strange state of decomposition. Heart weight, low, soft tissue decomposition…"

Craig and Mike stood back, watching the ME work.

They had arrived late. New York Police Department detective Brice had gotten there before them and they had taken their places next to him while Dr. Hodges worked on the corpse.

The woman, now cut open, looked even less human, as if she never could have lived and breathed and walked on the earth.

"You guys do find…very strange things," Brice murmured.

Craig felt guilty—he hadn't given the cop the least thought since they'd started exploring and seriously working on the case.

"Nothing new on Frank Landon, right?" Brice asked.

"No, nothing yet," Mike told him.

And that was true.

"Glad the FBI came in lead on this," Brice told them. "Me, I don't have a lot of time for people who've been dead hundreds of years—like your last body, the one they brought in an anthropologist for instead of the ME. But this…"

His voice trailed. Until Hodges finished, none of them would know just how long the woman might have been dead in the cave.

Hodges turned to them suddenly. "This one is a very strange mystery, indeed. The cave preserved the body. Wildlife did a number on it. So far, X-rays…bones…she was somewhere between thirty-five and forty years of age. She was most probably in good health."

"What killed her then?" Brice asked. "Knife…bullet…strangulation?"

"None of the above," Hodges said. "I still have tests

running at the lab. But if you want my educated guess at the moment…"

"We do," Craig told him.

"I believe she dehydrated. She was stuck down in that cave. She couldn't get herself back out. I don't know how she got there—you say your people found nothing, right? No backpack, no identification, no tools around her—nothing?"

"Not a thing," Craig said. "A forensic team worked all night, searching the cave and everywhere near it."

"Who knows how she got out there then," Hodges said, shrugging. "She got out to that island somehow— but who goes out hiking with nothing? We're using the process of rehydration in the fingers hoping to find a print match, somewhere in the system. We've also taken dental impressions to match with any available records," Hodges told them. "We'll be…sewing her back up. I'll keep in touch—with the FBI and the NYPD," he added.

They all thanked him and headed out.

"You're looking back at the bank robber case, right?" Mike asked Brice.

Brice studied him and nodded. "September, ten years ago. Mark Borden and Cary Templeton robbed the Euro-Savings Bank of New York. They took cash, and tons in jewels and gold—they managed to raid the vaults, you see. They'd obviously planned the heist for months. They involved a bank teller—who they shot and killed before leaving. We discovered the connection after the bodies were found out on Douglas Island. Their getaway driver was also found shot and killed on the docks. As we know, Borden and Templeton were found dead out on the island. And cops searched and searched for months—with permission, of course, from Jamie Douglas. Finally, the case went cold."

"You think this woman might have been with them?" Craig asked.

"If she's been there a decade, yeah. She might have had the getaway boat, except, it was gone, too, when Borden and Templeton were found. But with their record for taking care of all their accomplices and trying to make sure they split the booty with just one another, I think it's likely we'll find out that she might have been an accomplice."

"And they just threw her down the shaft, knowing that she'd die eventually," Craig said,

"Pretty cruel," Mike murmured, "but how sorry do we feel for anyone involved in that heist?"

"Well, she might have been a thief, but if she was just the getaway boat, she wouldn't have known about the way they killed the others," Craig said. "She might have been an accomplice to theft—but not a murderer."

"Question is, which I'm sure you're asking yourself, is just this—did the two of them fall? Or were they helped to their deaths? At the time, we had to give it up. Despite the fact that the money was not recovered. Because, of course, they zigzagged their way through the city, making a few stops. The department searched… but we still don't know. It's one of our most notorious cold cases. And," he added quietly, "we don't have the manpower for what you're doing. So, while you're investigating, please bear in mind—there might be about ten million in cash and goods out on that island somewhere. A tempting amount."

Brice hadn't made any accusations. Craig felt his jaw tightening anyway.

"You're suggesting that the FBI wouldn't turn over anything we found immediately."

"Hell, no," Brice said. He grinned. "You guys are well paid, right? Just like cops. I'm just saying there is a hell of a lot of reasons for someone to be searching and digging on that island."

"More than ten million," Mike murmured.

"I'll be taking a trip back out there myself," Brice told them.

"We'll show you where we've been—and how our search is progressing," Craig said.

Brice nodded. "It's just that…hell. We searched. Thoroughly, we thought. Just ten years ago. We didn't find this woman. If we had…"

Brice's tone was resentful. Craig realized that the cop thought that if they'd searched further, she might still be alive.

"The robbers weren't found for days. She was dead before you got there," Craig said.

"Yeah, I'd like to think so. I was pretty young, new at this, back then. Still…"

"We're not stopping," Craig said.

"Then you're lucky. You may have to give up, too, and spend the rest of your days—in quiet moments— wondering if your cousin's friend fell, or if someone has been out there, searching…and killing anyone in his way. Well," he murmured, "I have a dead gang member on my hands today, too. So, keep in touch. And I'll see you on the island."

"Let's go to the office. I want to see what we have on the bank robbery," Craig told Mike.

"I wasn't on it—but I do remember it," Mike said.

"What about the robbers? Did they have records? Known accomplices that we might shake down now?"

"Yeah—the two they killed," Mike said.

"Let's give the records a try anyway."

"Nowhere else to go at the moment."

"Except back to the island," Craig said. "But…" He paused, glancing at his watch. "We have to be in the Village by seven. I don't want Kieran and Danny at that meeting without us nearby."

"Do you think she's on to something?" Mike asked.

"I don't know," Craig said. "All I know is that our investigation must be pretty shaky if our main lead is a possible visit by aliens."

When Kieran woke again, she was amazed to see that it was past noon.

She jumped up, showered and dressed, choosing jeans and a knit pullover, thinking the outfit could work for a day in the caves—and for a meeting.

If she didn't wind up covered in dirt and grime again.

Dressed, she hurried out and knocked on Danny's door. There was no answer from the room, so she pulled out her phone and called him.

"Thought I'd spend the day out by the pool," he told her. "Chatting up friends," he said quietly.

"You're there with Margie? Elayne?"

"Both of them."

"Where's Bracken?"

"He's not doing any digging, but he is out on the island. Said he's going to go through the tunnel from where we were and make sure we're not looking at a cave-in," Danny said. "Ah, Evie," she heard him say, speaking to the housekeeper and not her. "Thank you—best lemonade ever!"

"Is it really that good?" she asked.

"Um, no. But come on down."

"Sure, I'm not going in the pool, but I'll meet you. We need to get to Manhattan, too, before rush hour."

"You think a slew of boats is suddenly going to be leaving the island?"

"I think we have to get to Manhattan from Brooklyn. If we go in a bit early, we can hang at my apartment and then just go to the coffee shop for seven."

"Okay. We have a few hours. Come on down. Really!" he said.

She wondered what was going on at the pool, but before going down, she called Craig.

He answered right away. He was back at the FBI field office.

"Mike and I are searching old records, trying to find anyone out there who might know something. We have an idea…we'll see. When are you coming in?"

"Soon. Danny's at the pool right now. With Elayne and Margie. I told him we needed to catch a ride in before it got too late."

"Don't go in to that meeting without calling me," he said.

"I won't. I promise."

"Mike and I will be nearby. Have you heard from Bracken?"

"Danny says he's checking to make sure the tunnels are sound before we go back in."

"Good man. All right. Call before the meeting."

"I will."

She finished the call, shoved her phone and wallet into her jeans pockets, and headed downstairs.

There was no sign of anyone in the great hall or the White Room. She walked through the dining room and kitchen. Evie was doing an inventory of the cabinets.

"Well, hello, sleepyhead!" Evie said. She smiled. And then she asked worriedly, "You are okay, right? I was concerned last night."

"I'm fine, thank you."

"You're sure... I mean, you don't sleepwalk or anything, do you?"

"No. I don't sleepwalk."

"Well...anyway. I guess we weren't worried enough before. I mean, this is an island, right? How could a stranger just be roaming around? But now, we will be more careful. So, what can I get you? There are little sandwiches and drinks out by the pool—Elayne does love that pool!"

"I guess she does."

"The pool and the beach," Evie said, sighing. "It's funny. I honestly didn't think that she would stay on the island."

"Oh? Why not?"

Evie waved a hand dismissively, as if the answer should be obvious. "Well, she's... Elayne. She loves dinner clubs, and shows, and shopping and...things you can't do on this island."

"Well, she loves Finn, too, I guess," Kieran said.

Evie gave her a weak smile. "It's not my place," Evie muttered. "It's just not my place."

"Well, I'll step outside and enjoy that pool for myself," Kieran said, smiling. She slipped by Evie.

Danny was in between the two women, stretched out

on a chaise lounge on the patio, wearing sunglasses, and just…basking.

"Hey!" Danny said, seeing her and sitting up.

"Hey, yourself."

She walked over and took a seat on the end of his lounger.

"You all right this morning? Or, I should say, afternoon?" Elayne asked her.

"I'm fine."

"You really saw something?"

"I did," she lied. It wasn't really a lie. After all, she'd seen *something*. Many things, actually.

"Oh, honey!" Margie said. "It's this island. I believe you think you saw something—I just don't believe that you did see what you think you saw."

"It's easy at night to get spooked. Took me a couple of days to get used to it. And then Finn…he can suffer from such sleeplessness! I'm always going down in the wee hours for milk for him. I had to get used to the old place. It creaks and moans all the time. Honestly! I don't see how this house is going to be the center of a resort."

"It's actually a beautiful old place, architecturally," Margie said.

"You like the old. Me, I like the new. Shiny and new—no bugs!"

"That's because…" Margie began. Then her voice trailed.

"Because I don't like old things!" Elayne snapped. She looked at Kieran and shivered. "Old things can… smell funny. And have bugs and spiders and things in them!"

Danny laughed. "New things can have bugs and spiders. Think about it. The bugs and spiders aren't old."

Elayne shuddered. "I'll be in the new section, any-time I stay!" she said.

Margie looked into the blue ripples of the pool. "I'll never come back," she said.

"Margie, we're all friends. When Finn has it up and running…"

"I'll never come back," Margie repeated flatly.

"That's understandable," Kieran said. There was a bit of an uncomfortable silence. "Um… I'm a bit hungry. Evie said there were sandwiches out here."

"Oh, yeah. She had one of the girls who comes in from Brooklyn make up sandwiches for us," Elayne said. She made a little noise. "You don't think she made them herself, do you? Honestly, Finn loves that woman, but I don't know why! She's a battle-ax!"

"Too old for you?" Margie asked her dryly.

"Yeah, well, she's that, too. She's a little dictator. Finn doesn't see it. Things were so much better when she wasn't on the island."

"Except none of us can cook," Margie reminded her.

"Ah, ladies! Such a glorious day!" Danny said. "No ice, no snow—spring has sprung here. And the sun is so beautiful."

"So it is," Margie murmured.

She lay back down.

Kieran really was starving—she hadn't eaten much the night before.

Whoever had made the sandwiches, they were very good. Cheese, turkey, salami, ham, roast beef—and combinations thereof—all cut up into little quarters so that one could enjoy a taste of each.

And there were pitchers of lemonade.

Kieran took a plate of food and sat down again at the foot of Danny's chair.

She tried to judge the women.

Profession be damned, it was hard. In therapy, she tried to get to truth, and to feelings—and to a person's real truth about events and their feelings.

Here...

Elayne could just be spoiled. Margie could just be miserable.

And one of them, either of them, or even *both* of them could be playing a game, acting out innocence when they were guilty as all hell.

When she was done eating, Kieran was restless. She wasn't going to learn anything more about Margie, Elayne or anyone else.

Not at the moment.

She stood up and said, "Well, enjoy the sun!"

"You're going in already?"

"I don't even have a bathing suit here," Kieran said. "And I need to go into the mainland tonight."

"Yeah, I should shower, and we should get going," Danny said.

"You have a boat?" Elayne asked.

"We'll hop something somehow," Danny said cheerfully. "Finn has a little get-around motorboat and through Craig, Kieran now knows half the Coast Guard."

"How nice!" Elayne said.

"Elayne wants off the island," Margie said.

"Not without Finn!" Elayne said. "And I can't seem to get him to leave."

"He'll leave," Margie said.

"When?"

"When we bury Frank," Margie said.

"Oh, Margie! I do have to get you off the island, too! You need to grieve. But you need to live again, too. Margie, you're still alive!"

For once, Elayne seemed truly concerned and caring.

"It will be good for you to be somewhere else," Kieran said.

Margie nodded.

"In time," she said.

She rolled over, letting the sun touch her back.

And ending the conversation.

Danny stood up. "Well, time to get ready."

"You're coming back tonight?" Elayne asked.

"Um, yes, I think so," Danny said.

Kieran told Elayne, "Craig is talking to Finn about having a couple of guests out. The conversation should be...interesting."

"Bye then, until later," Elayne said.

"Bye."

Margie rolled back over.

"Kieran," she said.

"Yes?"

"Stay in your room tonight, huh? We don't want any shadows jumping out at you. I'm sorry. I don't mean to be rude. But the rest of us need our sleep."

"Sure," Kieran murmured.

She turned away, walking back to the house, Danny behind her.

And she had to wonder—did Margie have a reason for wanting her to stay in her room?

A reason other than sleep?

CHAPTER
TEN

"Templeton did time for breaking and entering," Mike said. "He was caught almost immediately—the people had cameras on their house."

"It's the same with Borden—doing time, except that he wasn't caught so easily. He was arrested because a witness picked him out of a lineup. And this is sad. The witness wound up dead—hit and run—about two months later."

Craig and Mike each had their computers up as they researched, sitting across from each other in Craig's office at headquarters.

"They met in prison," Craig said, looking over at Mike. "They did two years together, and they were there together with Alphonse Cantorelli, the supposed genius Mafia don. They had a lot of learning from him."

"Like learning that witnesses couldn't be left behind," Mike said.

"Yes, I imagine, but we can't talk to Cantorelli—he died of a heart attack a few years ago."

"No help there," Mike said.

"Yes, but we can find out who else was in at the time. And if anyone who was with them might want some extra privileges. Let's keep looking."

They went back to work. A few minutes later, Egan walked into the office. "I've had your writing analyzed—the writing on the wall, and the writing on the stone tablet."

"And?" Craig asked.

Egan tossed printouts of the pictures Craig had taken onto his desk.

"The first—this writing on the wall? Five people looked at it—museum experts on ancient languages."

"And?" Mike said that time.

"The best they can figure is what you figured. *A-L-I-E-N.*"

"In that case, someone fooling around with alien beliefs has been there!" Mike said.

"And the other carvings? On the walls right at the entrance where we found the sitting skeleton?" Craig asked.

Egan sighed. "Again, what you might expect. The stone says, 'Enter unto death, ye who enter here.' Oh, and it's not written in Ancient Egyptian or Hebrew— it's a very elaborate old Gaelic."

"Gaelic?" Mike murmured.

"Ancient Scot's Gaelic," Craig murmured. "I guess that would mean that it's true—that, at least, the Scots of the time were friends with Norse traders of the time—and the Norse did carry objects for the Scots."

"Still, it's a stretch, in my mind, at least," Egan said,

"to imagine that the Ark did survive the Babylonian attack, fall into the hands of the Templars a few hundred years later, head up to Scotland—and wind up in New York."

"Truth is a matter of what is believed—we've all seen that over and over," Craig said. "And, I'm thinking, it didn't have to be the Ark of the Covenant that made it over here. Maybe something else considered precious."

"The Holy Grail?" Mike suggested.

"Not even, just something…a relic…anything. That would start the rumor, legend or myth about the island."

"Man has been battling man since time began," Egan said.

"True," Mike murmured.

"And does any of it matter—if the bank robbers were killed before their stash could be found?" Craig murmured. "This is what I'm seeing—someone is messing around out on that island. Whether they believe that the Ark of the Covenant—or a ten-million-dollar bank haul—is out there, it's important to know who we're searching for." He went on to show Egan what they had discovered.

"So, they were at the same time as Cantorelli," Egan murmured.

"Who is dead," Craig said.

"Yes, he is."

"But?" Craig asked. Egan was half smiling.

"I know his daughter. She goes by a different name. She loved her father, but she's a good kid—well, if you call thirty a kid. At my age, I do."

"Was she in contact with her father?"

"She was. She has a husband and three children now,

and keeps her distance from everything related to her father's activities."

"How well do you know her?" Mike asked.

Egan smiled. "I worked with some US Marshals. She didn't go into the program, but we managed to erase her history. She likes me. I think."

Mike looked at Craig and laughed. "What's not to like?"

"I'll give her a call," Egan said.

"Getting hold of her could take some time," Craig said. "I want to be in the Village within the next hour or so. Kieran and Danny are going to attend a meeting of the Believers."

"Well, you're in luck."

"How so?" Mike asked.

"Jenny Stratton is in an old brownstone, right off Christopher Street. I'll call her, and if she's willing, you can kill a couple of birds with one stone."

They wound up getting into the city later than Kieran had wanted. By the time Danny had changed and they were set to go, the boat had come to bring the day help back to Brooklyn.

They hitched a ride that way.

From the dock, they made their way to the subway. The streets at that time would have taken forever.

Danny was starving; Kieran was anxious. But they stopped for a quick bite of pizza.

"We're going to a coffee shop, you know," Kieran reminded her brother.

"And coffee and a pastry will be great after pizza," he said. "Come on! You're eating your pizza, too!"

She ate quickly as they moved through the crowds.

She put her call through to Craig as they exited the subway.

"I'm here—in the Village," he told her.

"Are you at the apartment? It's about a block and a half away."

"Closer than that," Craig said.

"Invite Harding to dinner tomorrow night."

"Will do. What about John Smith and Annie Green?"

"We'll call them."

"What if they have plans?"

"I have a feeling they won't."

They rang off. Kieran looked at Danny. "Let's meet the Believers!"

They entered the coffee shop. Danny walked up to the counter, getting in line behind a young couple.

Kieran looked for their group.

She saw Jay Harding. He was in the back of the shop where several tables had been pushed together; he must have had an arrangement with the owner. There were a few people already seated with coffee and pastries before them, and they seemed to be speaking casually before the rest of their group arrived.

Harding saw her and stood. "Hey, you came!"

"Danny and I just had to hear what you have to say," Kieran told him.

"Here, take these seats." He indicated the chairs on either side of him. She thanked him and sat. Harding began introductions. "Grace and Nick Tanaka, Ben Garcia, Rudy Stein and his wife, Judy. The 'young-uns' there—heading to the table with your brother and your coffee, are Dallas Berne and his girl, Valentina Tischenko. And down there at the end, are Priscilla and Ells Chapman."

Hellos and welcomes went around the table.

The "young-uns"—Dallas and Valentina—were in their early to midthirties. They were, however, the youngest in the group.

Jay began telling his gathered crew about Kieran and Danny.

"They're with the Finnegan family—of Finnegan's on Broadway," Jay said.

"Wow, cool place!" Dallas said. He looked similar to Jay, with long shaggy hair, bright eyes, a scruffy jaw, a Grateful Dead T-shirt.

"We've been there several times," his girlfriend, Valentina said. "Love the bands!"

"I'll tell my brother, Declan—he hires the performers," Kieran said.

"We used to go so often!" Priscilla Chapman said. "Ells and I love the place." She and her husband couldn't have been more different from Jay or Dallas and Sydney. He was in a suit; his white hair was close cropped, and his demeanor was refined. Priscilla was also in a suit, with a pencil skirt. She was slim and sleek and looked as if she spent her days in the business world as well.

"Thanks, so glad you all like it!"

"We're on the Upper East Side now," Ells said, as if explaining why they weren't good customers anymore. "We were only downtown for a bit when we first moved to the city. You know city traffic. Getting down sometimes..." He let his words trail. "One day," he added, "we can hold a special meeting at Finnegan's!"

"Great," Danny said.

"Ah, yeah. Super," Kieran agreed.

"Let's see what we've all been working on!" Jay said cheerfully.

"Ah, well, we've been having a great time," Priscilla said. "Looking at the Moai of Easter Island—we've compared pictures with dozens of accounts of alien abduction." She rose, handing out pages with sketched images shown alongside copies of pictures of giant statues on Easter Island.

"We did phone interviews with several of the people," Ells said proudly. "Not a fake among them—we talked to three store clerks, an auto mechanic, a teacher and an attorney!"

"Goes to show," Jay said. "An attorney," he said, looking at Kieran, "who has experienced an abduction."

Danny looked at Kieran. "Not a fake among them!" he said.

She managed a smile.

"I've been going back through documents that have made it through the ages—written by Viking explorers!" Sydney said.

"We've been going through them," Dallas corrected, clearing his throat.

"Yes, yes, of course," Sydney said, blushing. "Dallas had to work some overtime this week. I just meant that I was doing more of the reading." She also produced a number of copy sheets, passing them around. Kieran studied the pages before her.

The two had done some interesting research. The pages showed the old Norse, and they also showed the translations.

"Wow, these are great," Jay said. "Especially," he added, "since Kieran and Danny are staying out on Douglas Island."

"Man, really?" Dallas asked. "Lucky!"

Kieran smiled weakly.

Jay provided the facts.

"Kieran is with an FBI agent, who also happens to be a cousin of the owner of the island. And they're looking into the death of the man who died Friday night. His cousin's friend."

"I heard the man fell," Grace Tanaka said. "He was on a cliff, and he fell. Tragic, but…"

Grace and Nick were in their later forties or early fifties, an attractive and fit couple who were still in their jogging clothes.

"Grace," her husband said, "we can't make that judgment. If the Ark is out there, and if it is a communication device…"

"Then the Ark is protecting the island," Sydney said sagely.

"Protecting the island?" Kieran said.

Ben Garcia, a man of about forty with dark hair and a handsome face, leaned forward to explain.

"If you look at the ancient-alien theory, it's more than possible. Many think that the aliens visited Egypt long before Ramses II, before Seti, back to the time when the Great Pyramids were built, or even before. When historians see the unification of Egypt in dynasties…say, 3100 BC. They became the gods of Egypt. They were so technologically advanced over us—still way over what we have today—that they could set that technology into arks—trunks, if you will. If that's the case, there might have been many arks in Egypt. One very similar to what we think the Ark of the Covenant was, found in Tut's tomb—remarkable."

"And, you know about all the curses, right?" Judy

Stein asked excitedly. "Any person disturbing a mummy—be they a tomb robber or an archeologist—is cursed."

"Howard Carter's canary was found in the mouth of a cobra!" her husband, Rudy said. "A cobra—an animal used by the pharaohs in their headdresses. You must realize, events like that do show that there is more at work than meets the eye—so much more than most people accept."

"And we all know what happened to Lord Carnarvon. He died! Soon after the opening of Tutankhamen's tomb," Judy said, nodding almost triumphantly—as if her words absolutely proved a curse.

"He died of a disease," Kieran said. She smiled. They'd spent a lot of time at one of the city's new museums on antiquities when another of Craig's cousins, Harley Frasier, had become involved in a case of murder—one that supposedly had to do with curses, too.

"Mysterious disease!" Ben said.

"Bitten by a mosquito—right where the pharaoh Tut had an injury," Valentina told her.

"Do you really believe in curses?" Danny asked. He wasn't mocking anyone; he was serious.

"That's the whole point," Nick Tanaka put in. "No—curses aren't scientific."

"But aliens are," Judy said.

Jay explained, "The aliens would have left protection for the pharaohs—and those with whom they dealt. They knew to breed bacteria—to infect those who would interfere with the dead. And they might have, we believe, left devices that created sounds. Sounds that humans couldn't hear, but that might make a cobra hungry."

"Okay," Dallas said, "the cobra might have just been hungry. Cobras were common. That wasn't much of a surprise, I would think. A cobra eating a bird."

Jay smiled at Kieran. "Don't you see, that's the point! Douglas Island isn't cursed. Douglas Island might well hold the Ark of the Covenant. And if the Ark of the Covenant did come out of Ancient Egypt with Moses, and it was rescued at some point by the Templars and brought to Scotland—it might have made its way to the New World. And the bad things that happen on Douglas Island aren't because of a ridiculous curse at all—they are the workings of the alien-crafted Ark!"

He sat back, entirely triumphant, as if his words were so logical that no one could possibly argue them.

"Interesting," Danny said.

"Fascinating," Kieran agreed. She smiled, looking at Valentina. "And these Norse texts you've found and translated...do they mention Douglas Island?"

"Well," Valentina said patiently, "it wouldn't have been Douglas Island back then, so we can't be certain. Page two of the papers I gave you...it's from the journal of Sven Longbeard—a trader out of Iceland. He talks about trading with the Native people on the 'island of many bones.' The Natives traded on the island, because that's where they could meet the seafarers. But the island was bad—cursed! And so, none would live on it. Sounds like Douglas Island," she said, nodding.

"All—um, fascinating," Kieran murmured. She wished she could think of something else to say—other than they really had no *scientific* proof whatsoever for what they seemed to think had to be logical and scholarly.

She made a mental note to remember everyone at

the table. They needed to have Craig's office look into all these people.

Even the youngest—Valentina and Dallas—would have been in their early twenties when the bank robbers died out on the island.

"I was at the university this week," Rudy Stein piped up. "I found a fantastic article written back in the 1920s by a Harvard professor. He interpreted letters by a Knight Templar, Jon du Beauville, who wrote to his uncle—his mother's brother in England—while he was fleeing north."

He stood up to hand his sheets around.

"As you can see in the translation from the French, he wrote that he hoped to live to see him, and he prayed to escape the persecution of the Knights. He says here, and I quote, 'Dearest sir and mentor, I have faithfully followed my vows, and while I pray for escape and life, it is not so much for myself, for my faith is pure. But I pass this to the pilgrims returning north, hoping it will find its way to you. But I pray not so much for my life, but for the preservation of the precious relics I and my companions have sworn to give our lives to protect. If we can travel far enough north, we have willing friends to see that they are brought far from the grasping fists of His Most Greedy Highness, Philip of France.'"

"The letter is real?" Kieran asked.

"Kept in archives in London. The book I found at the university was written by a professor—Stanfield Adams. I trust in the veracity of a Harvard man," Rudy said.

"These are wonderful," Kieran said, and she spoke truthfully. "Thank you so much for including Danny and me in this meeting—and thank you for these."

"Maybe we can have a meeting at Finnegan's—and one on Douglas Island," Ben Garcia said.

Kieran smiled. "I don't own the island," she said simply.

"But you could tell us about it, right?" Valentina asked. "Danny?"

He looked at Kieran and grinned. "Oh, of course! There's a beautiful but very tiny beach, and a creaky old Victorian house. Rocks, of course—they surround the place. You'd have to have been a Viking or a Norse seaman to have made your way around the rocks before dredging and sonar and all that. The moon at night over the cliffs is spectacular!"

Danny went on.

Kieran was proud of him.

He talked and talked.

And didn't really say a damned thing at all.

Jenny Stratton was an attractive woman with light green eyes and soft brown hair. Her little boy was about five, with coloring as light as his mother's.

She was happy to meet with Craig and Mike, as long as they were willing to come to the park near Christopher Street.

She had a quick smile and a warm handshake. "I guess I should have hated my father," she said, watching as her little boy chased pigeons across the grass. "But he was my father. I guess I was a lucky kid—he kept me out of it all." She was quiet for a minute. "He killed—or had killed—a lot of people. Usually, however, just people in the same game. He had a lot of rivals. It's a miracle he lived to die of a heart attack."

"You were able to visit him—and maintain anonymity?" Craig asked her.

"I saw him in solitude," she said. "He started off in Chicago. My mother and I were in Chicago when most things were going down—and when he was arrested. When I visited him once... I told him I couldn't come back. I knew about the things he had done. And that's when he told me—and convinced me it was true!—that he only had people killed when they were killers themselves. I know for a fact he never went after anyone else's kids or family. And I guess...well, my name has been legally changed—my maiden name—and my history erased from any public records, new info put in, but...well, you know people. I think my father was telling the truth. I spend my days out with my kids and no one has ever come after me. I don't think they will. My husband knows the truth, naturally. He's an amazing man."

"Of course," Mike murmured.

"I don't see how I can help you."

"I'm just curious. Your dad was...well, he had a hell of a reputation," Craig said. "We know that he was in with a couple of guys who were amateur badasses. Templeton and Barton. They—"

"The bank robbers!" she said.

"Yes. You know about them?"

"Sure. Dad talked about them. He said they were two of the biggest idiots he'd ever met—and he wasn't surprised when they died on the island."

"Why was that?"

"They were always trying to make big plans. Oh, and, of course, they wanted to hear about him all the time, and they believed some crap about him never having left witnesses anywhere. My dad said that it definitely was crap—he never carried out any of the... executions he ordered. Others did. And his family had a code of honor. Sounds funny, but it's true. No women or children. Ever. Under any circumstances. So...but he called them idiots. He used to say, 'Mark my words. Those idiots will get themselves killed. If they don't kill themselves.'"

"So he wasn't surprised when they wound up dead."

"Not at all. I remember, because it was the talk going around. When I visited Dad back then—even the prison guards were talking about it."

"This is a long shot, but...did you happen to know who visited them, if they were friends with anyone other than your father?"

"I don't think my father considered them to be friends," Jenny said. She shrugged. "Tons of convicts find God, right? Well, my father didn't find him—he returned to him. He was a very good Catholic at the end, trying to help others. Believe it or not."

Craig smiled. "We have no problem believing you."

"And you don't think maybe I have criminal tendencies?"

"None of us is our parents. We have traits, and we learn from them. But we all take our lives and make of them what we will ourselves," Craig said.

Jenny's little boy—Alfie, she'd called him—giggled delightedly and sent a ball flying their way.

Craig caught the ball, and rolled it back. Alfie chased after it happily.

"Thanks for that," Jenny said. She sighed. "Honestly, I don't remember a lot, but my dad did write letters to me. I'd be happy to go through them, see if he ever talked about anyone else's visitors, or if they had prison buddies or anything relevant. It would be my pleasure to help you."

"That's good of you," Mike told her.

"Really. Thank you," Craig agreed.

"Mr. Egan—I don't know his title now—was so good to me when everything was going on, when the FBI was seeing Dad, and the Marshal's Service was trying to help me. I'm happy if there is something that I can do in return."

Craig produced a card and handed it to her.

The ball hit him again. He laughed, caught it up off the ground, and rolled it back.

Little Alfie giggled delightedly and tried to kick it back. Craig ran a few steps to catch it, and kicked it gently to the child.

"He's going to love you forever!" Jenny told him. "Alfie, you have to let the man go now, he's busy. You have to play with me!"

But the ball rolled back to Craig.

"Alfie…"

"It's okay," Mike told her, amused. "We have to hang around this area anyway. Craig used to play ball. Maybe he'll remember a little bit about the game!"

"Did they look like murderers?" Craig asked.

Kieran turned to glare at him. It wasn't a serious question—but he'd posed it anyway.

"And what does a murderer look like?" she asked him.

When they'd arrived back at the Douglas house, it had been quiet. Only Victor Eider had been up, waiting for their return. He'd let them in, greeted them pleasantly and gone off to bed, presumably.

Now, up in the room, they were alone. Danny had gone straight to his own room; he and Kieran and Craig and Mike had discussed what they had discovered—and not discovered—on the boat trip back.

"Well, you have a few looks in murderers," Craig said. "The wild-eyed Charles Manson look. Then, you have the guilty look. And there's also the pleased look. That comes from someone who is usually a psychopath or a sociopath, feels no remorse whatsoever, and is simply proud—nonchalantly proud—because they believe they've gotten away with murder."

"I gave you the list of everyone in attendance," Kieran said.

"I've already gotten it to Egan," Craig told her.

"They all looked…normal, I guess. They were an interesting crowd," Kieran said. "Jay and Dallas—long haired, casual, look like friendly guys. Valentina—Dallas's girlfriend, pretty, enthusiastic. There are the Steins—Rudy and Judy, older and more tailored. Ben Garcia—looks like he might have been military or a bodyguard. Grace and Nick Tanaka—nicely dressed in their jogging clothes, and Priscilla and Ells Chapman, the oldest in the group—a couple who look like they belong in a yacht club setting. No crazed eyes among them. They were all just excited about their research. They did come up with some interesting papers. When they meet, they show each other what they've been working on for the week. I have copies of everything. But it doesn't tell me anything about what's going on today."

"Egan will check out their names. At this point, we're

looking for any kind of link we can work with," Craig said as he shed his gun, holster and shirt. "If we can find someone who was associated somehow with the bank robbers, we might have a way to go."

"Oh—Jay Harding is delighted to come to dinner tomorrow night."

"I thought he would be."

"What about John Smith and Annie Green?"

"Yep, Mike called Mr. Smith and chatted and said that Finn would be delighted to have him out tomorrow night."

He was restless, pacing over to the window.

Kieran walked over to join him. She slipped her arms around his waist.

"And how are you doing?"

"I'm hoping we have an ID tomorrow on the woman we discovered," he said, turning to face her. "And we can have the Believers out here. With John Smith. If nothing else, between them, it will be lively dinner conversation."

He shifted slightly and as he did so, Kieran's view out the window was clear.

A light flashed out in the darkness.

And then it was gone.

"Craig, the light…"

He turned around. Naturally, the light did not flash again.

"We have to stay out there at night!" she said. "I swear to you—I just saw a light again!"

He smiled. "I never suspected that you were making it up. Well, other than last night, and that was a stellar performance."

"Craig, I think that someone is working out there,

and the light is usually hidden in the tunnel or the caves."

"Or," he said softly, "someone is sending a signal— and the flash of light means that it's safe to come in."

He stared out the window reflectively.

"What are you thinking?"

"Tomorrow night," he said softly.

"We're going out there, by night?"

"Bracken. Bracken and I will keep watch. After our guests have been sent back…we'll head out as soon as the house has grown quiet."

"I'll go with you."

He shook his head. "You and Mike and Danny stay here."

"Hey," she said softly. "Danny and I have been the ones finding—"

"Corpses."

"And ancient stones and wall scratchings."

"But we won't be searching for clues. We'll be searching for whoever may be out there…searching for Frank's killer. And I'll need Mike here, and you and Danny, to see who here just may be slipping out by moonlight, aiding and abetting that killer."

CHAPTER
ELEVEN

Thursday morning

Egan really was a force of nature when he got going. Craig received the call from him just after 7:00 a.m.

He'd arranged the paperwork. The bank robbers would be disinterred from their plots in the potter's field on Hart Island at 10:00 a.m. Detective Brice intended to be involved and a police cutter would be coming by for Craig in about thirty minutes.

Kieran stirred as Craig got up. He explained what was going on.

"You'll be out most of the day?" she asked him.

"Yeah, I'll be there for the disinterment, and I'll accompany the corpses to the morgue. Dr. Hodges will start on them tomorrow. I'll be back out here as soon as possible." He hesitated. "I'm going to ask Mike to stay behind. Bracken will be in the caves."

"And, I'll be…sunning at the pool?" she asked him.

He sat at the foot of the bed. "Yes—using your talents. Trying to see if you can get anything out of anyone here."

"Elayne is a spoiled brat, Margie is grieving and Finn works all day. Evie is creepy. Victor seems okay, but he is in good shape and could easily climb around caves."

"You know that you can get me more than that."

She smiled.

"What time is dinner? Do Finn, Evie and the others know?"

He nodded. "Finn is all for anything that could help. And Evie thinks that a dinner party would be a very good idea."

"Well, then. Have you spoken with Bracken yet?"

"No, right now, I'm going to wake Mike. Ask him if he'd mind staying around here. The closer we get to something, the more I worry about what goes on around here."

"But we haven't gotten close to anything."

"I beg to differ."

"Someone on the island is involved—and someone has been searching for treasure. That's what we've got," she said.

"But things will break soon. We'll get an ID on the woman you found in the caves. We'll make a connection somewhere."

"Of course," Kieran told him. She smiled. "You always do."

He loved her look. Especially in the morning. Hair tumbling all around her shoulders. Eyes bright and soft at the same time, covers falling from her naked flesh.

He stood quickly, kissed her on the forehead and hurried out.

He tapped lightly on Mike Dalton's door; his partner opened it immediately. Mike was already dressed.

Craig told him about Egan's call.

"And you want me to stay here?" he asked.

"We won't learn anything. I'll be the representative when Templeton and Borden are dug up—I'll be there when they're brought in."

"I am on guard," Mike told him. "I swear. Like the best German shepherd ever."

Craig grinned in return. "Tonight..."

"Dinner party with the wackos!"

"Hey, won't we all be surprised if those wackos are right, huh?"

Craig glanced at his watch—he had about five minutes left before the cutter would arrive at the docks.

He hurried downstairs to check in on Finn.

His cousin was seated behind his desk, studying plans on his computer.

"Hey!" Finn said, looking up at Craig.

"You're up early."

"I keep moving forward. I don't know what else to do." He brightened suddenly. "I love your setup for tonight, though. A scholar—and a guy with a...different belief!"

"Sparks may fly."

"I hope so," Finn said. He managed a smile. "Do you really think that a scholar could be involved—or even an ancient-alien theorist?"

"Someone is involved," Craig said. "Mike and Bracken are here. Kieran and Danny. I'm going to be out for several hours, but I'll be back in plenty of time for dinner."

That morning, once Craig had gone, Kieran couldn't sleep. She rose to make sure the door was locked. She curled back in bed, but sleep eluded her.

She rose, checked the door again and decided on what she hoped would be a long and invigorating shower.

She cranked up the water delightfully hot and just let it roll over her.

But then she thought she heard something.

The door to the room jiggling.

She stood still, listening. She heard nothing other than the water hitting the tiled floor.

Leaving the water running, she stepped out of the shower and cracked the door to her room.

She didn't know if she was imagining things—but she thought she heard another *click*.

There was no one there; nothing seemed to have changed. But... Was her robe right where she had left it? What about things on the dresser? Her handbag?

She checked the door—it remained locked. Stepping back in the tiny bathroom she turned the shower off.

She must be paranoid.

She and Craig had been out all day yesterday. If someone wanted to search the room, they could have done so easily then, without any fear of being discovered.

What was in the room that might not have been in there the day before?

Her papers! She thought.

The papers she had acquired last night at the meeting of the Believers.

She quickly checked her large handbag.

The papers remained. She couldn't be sure, but the things in her bag seemed messier than usual.

Doubting herself, she couldn't help but wonder if someone had been in there. Someone who lived in the house, who might have a master key.

But if the Believers were part and parcel of what was going on, why would they need to find papers? They would all have the same information.

It was the house, she thought. The island.

Kieran didn't believe in curses, and she didn't believe that aliens were commanding bad things to happen through an ancient communication device.

She did believe very much in the evil that could live in the hearts of men.

She dressed hurriedly and went downstairs. It wasn't quite 9:00 a.m.

Not that early—but she wished she was still sleeping.

It was going to be a very long day.

Hart Island was on the western end of Long Island Sound.

A man named Thomas Pell purchased the island from Native Americans in 1654. It was purchased from another man named Edward Hunter by the City of New York in 1868, but even before the city had officially owned the island, it had been making use of it. The very first "public" use had been at the end of the Civil War when it had been used as a training ground for the United States Color Troops in 1864. It had also served as a prison for Confederate troops—over three thousand had been held there; over two hundred of those had died. In 1870 it had been a place of quarantine for victims of a yellow fever epidemic. It had served as a psychiatric facility, a prison now and then, and was still under the jurisdiction of the Department of Corrections.

Soldiers had been buried there, from the North and South, Civil War and onward. Soldiers were separate from the potter's field.

More than a million dead were buried on the island. Many records had been destroyed due to fires through the years.

It was, to say the least, a depressing place. Not due to the number of the dead, but due to the fact that in the potter's field, there were so many dead buried in trenches, one atop of the other, no memorial to the fact that they had lived and died, nothing that spoke of humanity.

Because Templeton and Borden had not been claimed by relatives or loving friends, their bodies had been sent to Hart Island. Because their burials hadn't happened that long ago historically, the records were intact. When they had been buried no one had cared enough to make other arrangements, so no one cared now that they were being disinterred.

Craig stood next to Detective Teddy Brice, watching as the diggers and cranes went to work. The morning held a chill, and Craig kept his hands in his pockets. As the earth was moved, the air was redolent with old dirt and dampness.

Dr. Hodges had come out to supervise; with bodies such as these, chain of custody was important.

Detective Brice turned to Dr. Hodges. "You really think that Frank Landon might have been stoned to death?" he asked.

"There is that possibility," Hodges said, nodding.

"And these fellows might have been stoned to death," Brice murmured. "Interesting, and very sad—not because the pair were good people. They weren't. They were killers themselves. But..."

"That would mean that the killers took the bank haul?" Craig asked.

"It could. But stoning! Who the hell stones people to death? We're not in the Middle East."

"The ancient Hebrews were never quick to mete out the death penalty, but stoning was one of their methods," Craig said.

"You think a group of modern day Hebrews—"

"Nope. Not for a minute," Craig said, cutting him off. "I think that there may be a group interested in the island—though they hold very different beliefs, and might be using the method because it's ancient. Or because they can make it look as if the victims simply fell off the cliffs."

"Hodges, I can't remember," Brice said. "Who did the original autopsy on Templeton and Borden?"

"Dr. Lane Freely—who passed away about two years ago. But I do have all the original records from the initial autopsy. I'll be working with them."

The giant claw of the digger bit into the earth.

There was a crunching noise, and someone cursed; a coffin had been breached.

Workmen hustled to check on it. They were lucky—the damage hadn't been to one of the two coffins they were seeking.

In another hour, the plain boxes were out of the ground.

Brice turned to Craig. "If those two were killed, the bank haul could still be on the island. The killers could be out there now. They bided their time, and now they think they can pick up the booty. Not one of the numbered bills taken in the robbery has ever been recovered. Not a single numbered diamond has shown from the jewels taken from the vault. There's more than enough for someone to kill for." He hesitated a minute. "The

FBI was always in on the bank robbery. I'm glad you pursued this. Anything on the island?"

"The dead woman yesterday," Craig said dryly.

"But nothing more?"

"Indications of human presence through the centuries. But trust me, if I'd found the bank haul, you'd know."

"Yeah, I figured."

Craig heard his phone ringing. He excused himself and answered it.

Egan.

"We have an ID on the woman you found. Angie Tremaine. She went missing over ten years ago—about five months before the bank robbery."

"Did she do time? Any suggestion she might have known the bank robbers?"

"None that we can find. She was from Cleveland. Her parents—who reported her missing—died three years ago. She'd worked at a boutique that went belly-up—employers and friends have scattered across the country. We're still working it."

"She a scholar by any chance? Did she spend any time at a university?"

"Two years junior college. If she was a scholar, we haven't found anything on her yet. We'll keep digging. We're going to post her picture and ask for help. We were able to get a yearbook picture of her—she did get her associates of arts degree, back in Ohio."

"Thanks, Egan. Brice is here with me. I'll give him the news."

"I already informed the NYPD," Egan assured him.

And so he had. Brice was on the phone, too. Talking to his people.

"You heard?" Craig asked.

Brice nodded. "I'll work on that angle. You're heading back to the island? I hear you have some ace guy working out there with you, a specialist in caves and cliffs."

"Bracken Silverheels," Craig said.

"Maybe you need an army."

"The place is full of holes and twists and turns. One guy who knows what he's doing is better than an army. Too much weight anywhere, we could cave it all in."

"Yeah, and frankly, despite what we're looking for, the NYPD is pretty busy. We don't have an army. Anyway, I'll see what I can find on this dead woman."

"They'll be working from our offices, too, of course."

"The more the merrier," Brice said. "Hell, I'm not expecting any cave-ins on paperwork."

"I believe," Evie said softly, as if sharing a conspiracy with Kieran, "you should watch out for that woman."

Evie was by the sink, watching as a day maid rinsed plates to slide into the dishwasher.

Kieran had been passing through to the pool area. Bracken Silverheels was out by the supply shed, gathering up more spikes, which he'd told her he used when he needed to crawl up—or down. *"When you're climbing alone, you have to make sure you've got coverage to get back out. Or else you could wind up like the woman in that oubliette."*

"Makes sense to me," she'd told him. Now, she wanted to hang around with him—follow when he headed back to the cave entrance.

But Evie had stopped her.

"You don't mean the young lady washing the dishes?" Kieran couldn't help but ask, wide-eyed.

Evie sighed. "I'm speaking out of place. I know that. Finn is an adult. And, in most things, he's the most responsible man possible. But when it comes to Elayne, I'm worried. I know that Craig loves his cousin—maybe he can do something."

Was Elayne a gold digger? Or was Evie jealous? Maybe both were true.

But was one of them complicit in murder?

"Evie, I'm afraid I don't know Elayne well enough."

"She's after his money. She'll hurt him."

"But as you said, Finn has to make his own decisions."

"She's trying to get rid of me," Evie said. "But I'm not going anywhere. And I don't believe that Finn will turn on me. I mean, I hope not."

"Why do you think she's trying to get rid of you?"

"Ah, well, the things she does. First, she complains about everything. Her room isn't clean, I'm always around—she says I'm a snoop!"

"How do you know that?"

"I heard her telling him. Look, I know I shouldn't have spoken to you the way that I did, but like I said, I know that Finn loves and respects Craig, and I know that—despite Mr. Jamie's horrendous treatment of Deedee—Craig loves Finn. And a few words from him might make Finn see what…what she's really up to."

"What is she really up to?" Kieran asked.

"Marriage—with no prenup!" Evie said.

It might not be ethical, Kieran thought, but it wasn't criminal. She'd thought that maybe Evie had seen Elayne sneaking around the house, in or out.

"She's an outrageous flirt," Evie said. "You should see her with all the captains and boatmen. She loves to sit out on that beach in her teeny bikini and wave at the men when they come in. She's horrid."

"She may just like the way she feels in a teeny bikini," Kieran said.

Evie sighed. "I see you don't understand. You're right—you don't know her well enough. I'm sorry. I shouldn't have spoken."

Evie turned away, looking distressed.

A dish had gone into the dishwasher without being thoroughly rinsed. Evie snatched it out and ran it under the tap.

"Evie, please, don't worry. I won't say anything. I just don't think that Craig will interfere in his cousin's love life," Kieran said. "What do you mean by her… sneaking around?"

Evie nodded. "She's always in Finn's office—when he isn't there. And she's always quizzing Margie, wanting to know what Frank had done each day. She pretends she cares about Margie—she's all sweetness and condolence—but I think she knows there's a major-league treasure out here somewhere. I'd guarantee she's working on a way to get her hands on it."

"But no one has found it."

"She's plotting to do so. You mark my words," Evie said.

With a warning wag of her finger, Evie hurried over to the maid who had loaded the dishwasher. She liked to control things; she liked to supervise. But Kieran noticed she wasn't mean to the young woman. She just showed her how to rinse the dishes properly.

Kieran went on out to the porch and then beyond to the patio and pool.

Danny was in trunks again, between Margie and Elayne, soaking up the sun.

Lazy little brat! she thought.

But as he greeted her, she realized that he was, in his way, working. Kieran didn't know Elayne or Margie very well. Danny was doing his best to get to know them. He was so easy and casual with conversation. He was doing well.

"What are you up to, sister dear?" he called in a friendly manner.

"Hello, there," Elayne said.

"Just heading over to chat with Bracken," Kieran said. "It is a beautiful day. It seemed kind of chilly this morning, but now the sun is lovely."

"It is. A perfect day," Elayne said.

She was an attractive woman—and her bikini was teeny weeny. She stood, slender legs scissoring as she swung from her chair to walk over to the serving table to help herself to iced tea. "You should really join us," Elayne said. Her face wrinkled in a grimace. "It will make you stop thinking about awful corpses and bones and…"

Margie heard her words.

"Dead friends," she said softly.

"Margie," Elayne chastised. And she added, "Please, sweetie. We know how badly you're hurting. We're trying to make you feel better. The sun helps, right?"

"The sun helps," Margie said. She sat up and looked at Kieran and smiled. "And Danny is sharing some great stories about the city of New York."

"He's good," Kieran agreed.

Margie smiled and lay back down. Danny gave Kieran a shrugging look. Kieran was about to head on out to the shed when Elayne pulled her back and whispered, "That old bat has been talking to you, right?"

"Pardon?"

"Evie. The woman is a piece of work. She's so possessive of Finn, it's pathetic. I guess he's never been as serious about a woman before—as he is about me. She's a snoop!"

"Oh?" Kieran said.

It seemed the women had similar opinions of each other.

"She's horrible. I caught her in our room. Cleaning! Bah. She was going through my things. I know that she was. I mean, what the hell was she doing?"

"Maybe she really was making the bed," Kieran suggested.

"I told you—she never cleans. She just supervises. She's looking for something—I don't know what she thinks she's going to find!"

"Well, I imagine you two will get along eventually," Kieran said.

"Elayne!" Margie called suddenly.

Elayne turned to look at Margie.

"What is it, sweetie?" she asked.

"Quit whining about Evie. It's just going to backfire on you. The woman is an old battle-ax, but she's basically part of the family. Just let it go—drown her in sweetness."

Elayne grinned. "You may have a point there. I'll just be so charming she won't be able to stand it!" Elayne laughed softly. "She'll just want to vomit, I'll be so nauseatingly sweet."

"There you go," Kieran said. "That's a plan. Kill them with kindness."

Elayne grinned. "Will do," she promised.

Kieran hurried on to the storage shed. Bracken was explaining to Mike that he was bringing two-by-fours with them to shore up spaces that might be dangerous.

"Seems like that tunnel has been used. Strange, though, Frank was found all the way on the other side of the island. We found the one entry, but there has to be another," Bracken said.

"Another?" Kieran said. "There may be many! Those satellite maps that Danny managed to get—they show that the cliff is riddled with cave openings. There have to be more entrances."

"Bracken was thinking of walking up the cliff today—heading to the area where it was assumed Frank Landon went down…and where the bank robbers were found," Mike said. He looked toward the group by the pool to determine that they were out of earshot. "I just talked to Egan. They're taking the exhumed bodies back to the morgue."

"Good," she murmured. "If you're walking up the cliffs, I'll come with you," she told Bracken.

"I move fast."

"I'll keep up, I swear."

He studied her for a long moment. He was weighing the risks. She was certain that he knew she'd been involved in a number of cases Craig and Mike had worked.

Under his scrutiny, she felt extremely glad that she hadn't let her scream out the other day when she had found the corpse.

"Sure. I won't be going into the caves anywhere."

"I'd planned on staying here, watching over you and Danny," Mike said to Kieran.

"Watch over Danny—I'll go with Bracken."

Mike looked at her. He didn't speak aloud. His look was enough. *Not sure it's a good idea. Craig might not like it.*

"You got hiking boots on?" he asked.

"Trail sneakers," she told him.

"All right, let's go," Bracken said.

She nodded.

She paused to whisper to Mike. "Don't worry! Craig knows full well what I'm going to do. And I'm just walking. With an expert." She hesitated, smiling. "I'm leaving you with the dangerous people. Two vicious women. Take extreme care!"

Mike groaned.

Kieran hurried off after Bracken.

Craig was about to board the police patrol boat that would take him back to the island when his phone rang.

To his surprise, it was Jenny Stratton.

"Mrs. Stratton, thank you so much for calling," he said. He could only assume that she had found something that might be of importance.

"Of course, my pleasure. I'd told my husband what was going on, and he helped me go through my dad's letters. I have a couple that might be of some help to you," she said.

"Thank you."

"But I don't know how to get the letters to you."

Craig glanced at Detective Brice, who was watching him with curiosity. "Actually, I'm with the New

York City detective in charge of Frank Landon's case. I believe we can both see you now, if that's all right."

Brice nodded.

"Different direction, boys!" he told the officers on the boat.

He and Brice boarded. After a moment, as the boat pulled from the dock, Brice said, "Thank you."

"For?"

"For not pretending that no one was on the phone."

"It's a joint investigation," Craig said.

"I've worked with other law enforcement agencies when it doesn't go so well. So, thank you."

"Not a problem. We're both working toward the same goal, right?"

"Right," Brice said. He was quiet, watching the island grow small for a minute. Then he said, "No, not really. You care about the dead man. I want to know what the hell happened with the goods stolen during that bank robbery. Which, eventually, is the same thing—but honestly, we are coming at it from different directions."

Craig laughed. "That's all right. Hopefully we'll both get what we want in the end."

Despite police assistance, it was a trip getting from the island to Long Island, Brooklyn and then over to Manhattan. But this time Jenny Stratton and her husband, Roald—a tall, grave man a good two decades older than his wife—were waiting at their apartment.

It was a handsome place, well-appointed and large—certainly for New York City. Two children were there, the little boy Craig had already met, and an older girl of about six—who had been at her dance lessons the day before. A young nanny took the kids off to play.

Roald Stratton showed them to his office and invited

them to sit in a pair of chairs in front of his desk. Jenny perched on the edge of the hefty desk, while Roald took his own leather chair. Roald Stratton was apparently a corporate lawyer who did some of his business from home.

"We try not to live in the past," Roald Stratton said. "Jenny's history has basically been erased, and anyone looking her up for any reason only finds what the powers that be have created for her. She was never involved in any criminal activity."

"Neither was my mother," Jenny said. "She stayed away. My father conducted his business in New York."

"We understand that," Brice said. "We're here because we're hoping for help."

"You're here because we did find something." Roald passed a letter across the table. It was worn with folds.

"I used to read his letters over and over," Jenny explained. "I wanted to be grateful that I did have a father, and I wanted to believe, that underneath it all, he was a good man."

"In his way, sweetheart, he was," her husband assured her. He looked back at Craig. "I believe the man was terribly lonely, and while his daughter was young—in her early teens at the time—he poured out everything to her. I guess she was all that he had."

Craig didn't know enough to judge. He offered a quick smile and accepted the letter Jenny handed him.

Brice read over his shoulder.

Alphonse Cantorelli had apparently tried to amuse his daughter with his letters. He spoke about Templeton and Borden—in the next cell from his—as if they were a pair of dumb comedians. He referred to them as "Itch" and "Scratch." Cantorelli had written:

Bumbling idiots. Itch was almost hit with a shiv today; I figured I'd save the sorry bastard. My mistake—he and his cohort immediately began planning revenge, instead of kowtowing to the Brotherhood. But then again, they're out soon. Saw them making plans with a woman; she visited now and then. Poor thing. They both talk about her as if she were a pet dog—to be owned by two different owners. Thing I don't get is, I think she wants something out of them. They were talking about an island; that much I heard. Itch told me later that they were planning a major heist—and that it would go well, thanks to the fact that they'd known me. I told the little bastard he'd better not ever thank me for any horrendous foolhardy thing that he did. My ethics might be skewed, but I have them. All Itch did was laugh. "Old Man," he said, "you don't know. Them that can't do, they say, teach!" Thought about having the little bastard shivved myself, but I've been seeing my priest, and I'm on the Great Road to Heaven or Hell, so... I wanted to tell that poor girl not to trust them, but all I knew was that her name was Angel or Angela or something like that. Anyway, love you so much. Trust that I am seeing my priest, and that I am happy enough, loving your letters, seeing your beautiful pictures when you send them!

Dad

"I don't know if that helps you or not," Jenny said. "But Itch and Scratch were the bank robbers, he refers to them by their real names in another letter that just states they were the new men in the cell next to his."

Angela. Angie.

"I can't tell you how much you have helped us," Craig told her.

"Tremendously," Brice said quietly.

"Perhaps you can find this woman," Roald said.

Craig just nodded; Brice was waiting for him to speak. The news would be out soon enough—he decided to tell the truth.

"We already found her," he said softly.

"She's…she's in the morgue," Brice explained. "She was killed around the same time as the robbers."

"Oh, no!" Jenny said. "Well, oh dear. I thought this might help."

"It does help," Craig assured her.

"But…she's already dead."

"'He who lives by the sword, dies by the sword,'" her husband quoted softly.

Out on the street, Brice sighed. "So. We know our victim, and we know that she was involved with the robbers. They probably did throw her down that oubliette—before they met their own fate. Do you think it's possible that the idiots did bury their treasure and then just fall?"

"No."

Brice gave him a grudging smile. "Well, you are not iffy on that point."

"No, I'm not. Frank Landon was killed. Those bank robbers were killed. Someone has been out on that island, and I'm going to find out who and why."

"Good," Brice said.

"We'll be digging around again tomorrow," Craig told Brice. "Naturally, you are invited to join us."

"That I may," Brice told him. "For now, what can I do for you?"

"Get me back to Douglas Island," Craig said. "We're hosting a very strange dinner party tonight. I'm extremely anxious to see just how it goes. You're welcome to attend."

"Who else is coming?" Brice asked.

"John Smith, scholar, and Jay Harding, theorist on ancient aliens."

Brice waved a hand in the air. "I'm going to go back to my office to hit every record to see if I can find out more about Angie Tremaine. I'll let you handle that… interesting…dinner."

CHAPTER
TWELVE

Thursday afternoon

Kieran considered herself to be healthy and physically fit.

But keeping up with Agent Silverheels was no easy feat. She forced a smile every time he looked back to make sure she was okay.

When they reached the top of the cliffs, he stood there for a long moment. She didn't go to the absolute summit; only one person could safely fit—and *safe* was a term that only applied loosely when it came to the cliff.

Bracken walked back, shaking his head. "No way those people went off here and died the way they did. No way a body wouldn't have hit one of those big ledges. And Craig said that Frank wrote on the sand—impossible. He couldn't have survived this kind of a fall, even briefly. Didn't happen."

He paused.

"There are other entrances to that tunnel."

"In plain sight," she said softly.

"What?"

"The entrance...it's not even really hidden. It's just so low and the bracken covers it. Wherever the other entrances are, they're in plain sight."

"I think you're right," he said.

He looked around. "We're going to go back slowly," he said.

She wasn't going to argue that.

"Look at every bush, every tree...every fault in and off the path."

"Okay," Kieran agreed. Looking at the sky, she could see that the sun was falling.

"We'll make it back just about dark—in time for a later dinner."

Their descent was twice as slow as the ascent had been. Partially from caution, but also because they scanned the terrain as though they were looking for a lost earring in the rocks and brush. It was going to take some time.

The sun kept falling. Oddly enough, it was that which allowed Kieran to suddenly see. A ray of the dying sun, streaking through and shifting on the side of the cliff, fell upon something that caught the light— and glinted.

"Bracken?"

"Yes?"

"There's something...there. Just to the left, ahead."

"Pine trees."

"And brush. But behind..."

Bracken moved quickly. She followed him. He was already down on the ground, almost flat, looking into an opening. As she arrived, he asked her, "How the hell did you see this?"

"Something glinted."

"Pines don't glint."

"Then…there's something caught in a tree or a bush. Something lit up when a sun ray broke through. I'm not sure exactly where."

He hunkered halfway up again, staring at her. "It's an entrance. And when you look low enough, you can see that just below the opening, it's smooth. Someone has used this way in—recently. I'm willing to bet that it's the way Frank Landon was going in and out. It's too late now, but tomorrow, we'll get in here. There's got to be a way through the entire system. I know we can find it in a few days' time." He was still staring at her, as if he might be trying to figure out just what she was.

"You're pretty amazing—you have bloodhound in you?" he asked lightly.

"No, trust me. I really saw something glinting, and it seemed like there was a strange difference in the shadows… I think."

He smiled. "Don't mention anything to anyone but Craig and Mike."

"That goes without saying," she murmured.

"Then let's head back—time to hear about the aliens and the Ark of the Covenant."

When they returned to the house, they entered through the back garden. There was no sign of anyone by the pool. The rear door was locked, but when Bracken knocked, Victor Eider appeared to let them in.

"Trying to be careful—watching the place," Victor said.

"Good idea," Bracken said. "Well, I'm headed for the shower!"

"I'm going to freshen up, too," Kieran murmured.

Evie was in the kitchen, directing preparations. "Guests should be arriving soon," she said.

"Did Craig get back yet?" Kieran asked.

"Haven't seen him," Evie told her.

"Thanks."

Kieran followed Bracken on through the dining room—the table was already set, crystal shining, plates gleaming, flowers all around—and through the White Room. They reached the great hall and went up the stairs. "I'll be down in ten," Bracken said, reaching the second floor.

"See you then." Kieran hurried up to the attic.

She closed and locked the door to her room as soon as she was inside. All of her things were where she had left them, and yet, she couldn't help an uneasy feeling.

Her computer bag was at a slightly different angle. The robe she had left at the foot of the bed was just slightly askew. Her suitcase had moved, just a hair.

Or had her unease caused her imagination to go off?

She didn't know. But she wasn't taking any chances. She pulled out her phone and called her brother; she could hear his phone ringing in the next room. He answered it quickly.

"I need you to watch my door."

"What?"

"I'm going to take a shower. I need you to watch my door."

"You're kidding."

"No, I'm not. Please, just do it."

She heard his heavy sigh.

"All right. I'm on it."

"Thank you!"

She hung up and smiled. The feeling of security was exhilarating.

She showered…and showered. And, of course, remembered that Danny would just be standing in the hall.

She hopped out, dried quickly and dressed in a simple halter A-line piece and slipped on a pair of heeled sandals.

Then she headed out. Danny was there, leaning against the wall by her door.

She thought he would make fun of her.

He was frowning.

"What?"

"Someone was coming up the stairs…slowly. Quietly. I heard the stairs creaking," he said.

"Who was it?"

He shook his head. "I heard something, and I waited. Then I ran to the landing and…whoever it was, they were gone. Damn, Kieran, just what the hell is going on?"

Thursday evening

Professor John Smith hadn't come alone. He'd brought his assistant, Annie Green.

And Jay Harding hadn't come alone, either. He'd brought Ben Garcia.

Finn played the charming host, all were being very polite. He had put one member of his household between each of the guests—and the alien enthusiasts at one end of the table and the scholars at the other end.

They were quite a large dinner party, but the house's dining room could accommodate them easily—there was only one seat that had to be quickly added, and that was because Jay Harding had not informed them he was bringing Ben Garcia.

"Sorry about Ben! I hope it's all right. He was at my place when it was time to leave," Jay had explained, meeting Craig at the docks. Their separate boats had gotten in at about the same time.

"Not a problem," Craig had assured him. Finn was willing to do what Craig asked, and if that meant bringing in parties who might know something, however many didn't matter.

Because he'd gotten back to the island later than expected, Craig had no chance to have a conversation with anyone at the house before dinner started.

Now, they were all seated and the meal was underway.

"My group finds the most interesting bits of information," Jay Harding explained, passing a large bowl of broccoli au gratin down the table, and responding to a comment John Smith had made about the merits of serious research. "We meet once a week, though it's a come-as-you-can situation. But what we study are the events that have occurred around the globe. And by the way, Mr. Smith, a number of our people are highly educated. Priscilla and Ells Chapman were both professors of history at Midwest colleges for years before coming to New York City—they wanted to be closer to their grandchildren, who are here. They are some of the finest researchers I've ever met. And Rudy Stein taught in our school system, and so did his wife."

"Jay's group have found fascinating copies of letters—one translated from Norse—from a Sven Long-beard," Kieran said.

"And someone in your group gave us copies of an-other great letter," Danny said. "Translated from the French. A letter written by a fleeing Templar. I hope the guy made it!"

"You have a letter by a Templar?" John Smith asked, his tone doubtful and condescending.

Jay smiled, ignoring the tone. "Yes, the original letter had been authenticated by Samuel Nottingham in Eng-land—you've heard of the man, right?" he asked John, and he turned to Kieran and said, "We always check for the authenticity of the information we receive."

"A letter written by a Templar, one we might not have seen," Annie Green said. "Oh, I'd love to read it!"

"I can see that you do," Ben Garcia told her.

"You really think that something is on this island?" Margie asked.

"Yes," Jay Smith and John Harding said, almost in unison.

"And we'd like to extend our sympathies to you," Annie said. "We know you've suffered a recent loss."

"Yes, we did. And we plan on getting to the end of it," Finn said.

"Do you think your friend discovered the treasure?" Smith asked Finn.

"I don't think that he could have," Jay Harding said. He looked around the table. "I mean, if he'd found some-thing, he would have told one of you, right?"

Margie let out a little sound of distress.

"I'm sorry," Harding murmured.

"He didn't find a treasure," Margie whispered.

"Well, I hope you all realize there may not be any kind of a treasure at all," Elayne said.

"It's likely that there is something on the island," Craig said. "A pair of bank robbers died here following a sizeable heist—and we've recently discovered that a body we found was a young woman who was connected to them. So either they killed her, or she was exploring on her own and fell. We don't know. But it's more than possible they hid their haul on the island somewhere."

"Maybe," Ben Garcia said. "But that's not why they died."

"Then why did they die?" Craig asked.

"Because the Ark of the Covenant is here," Ben said. "We believe that."

"Ditto," John Smith murmured.

"And," Jay continued, "the Ark protects itself."

"Excuse me?" Craig asked, gazing down at Kieran. She glared back at him. He silently informed her, *these people are crazy.*

Her look back warned him to pay attention, and he knew she was right.

Crazy might well mean involved somehow.

"Hear me out, and try to stretch your imaginations," Jay Harding said. "Look at the tech we have now. Computer chips—information moves fast as lightning. A hundred years ago, no one would have begun to imagine us all with personal computers, smart phones—watches that received texts and through which we can speak to one another. Drones, satellites. It's our belief a superior alien race has visited Earth—and that their technology is far superior to the little bit we've attained today. In ways we can hardly conceive. That being the case, it's more than likely they built something into the Ark that protects it—and will keep it safe until this superior race of beings returns to us."

Craig, close to John Smith, thought that he heard the man mutter "Rubbish!" beneath his breath.

Very low, but audible.

But Smith smiled as he looked at Jay Harding. "Totally improbable and implausible. We know a great deal about our own galaxy. Space travel would take lifetimes. If life exists, it is not superior. Bacteria did not come to Earth to build the pyramids!"

"Oh, my friend. You just missed something. Sir Arthur Conan Doyle and his brilliant creation, Sherlock Holmes. I don't know the exact quote, but it is something like this, 'That which is not impossible, no matter how improbable, must be the truth!' Superior aliens may not come from this galaxy at all. The universe is huge. We are but pathetic little specks in the vastness of the universe. What ego we have to assume that we even begin to resemble intelligent life!"

"I do wonder about some of us," Annie Green murmured.

Jay and Ben looked at one another and laughed goodhumoredly.

"Dear Miss Annie," Jay said. "Not to worry—we do not offend easily. So, the thing is, there is a lot we agree on. Okay, in your mind, Mr. Smith, Moses had the Ark created according to the specifications given to him by God. In my mind, the Ark was already created—and when Moses fled, he brought the Ark with him. Events after that, we're pretty much in agreement. Knights Templar rescued the Ark. They brought it to Scotland. Norse trading friends of the good Scots and Templars brought the Ark to the New World. Many believe that it landed on Oak Island. We believe that it landed on Douglas Island."

Annie smiled. "I'm so sorry," she said. "I spoke too quickly, and too harshly. We should share our research."

"Yes, of course," John Smith said.

Craig was pretty sure that Smith would be glad to see the research the Believers had accumulated; he would likely not be so generous with his own.

"The Vikings—during the Golden Age of Vikings—when they were sailing to raid, plunder and murder, were quite remarkable," Jay Harding said. "Their helmets weren't horned, as we see in so many movies, but round, created to protect the head. To the best of my knowledge, there's only one full helmet still in existence. They left the history mainly with storytellers, but also, much was written down."

"They were an interesting society. A Viking wedding celebration could last a week," John Smith put in. "They did keep slaves, wrested from other communities most often during their raids."

"And they were part of the Viking trade as well," Harding added. "Say, a woman—a good, healthy female slave—might be the equivalent of a suit of chain mail or perhaps two cows or a cow and an ox."

"Charming," Elayne muttered.

"Ah, not to worry! A healthy male slave could be worth a horse or three cows," Danny put in.

"Equal opportunity," Mike muttered. "But if Norsemen brought something here from the Templars, it would have been years after that 'Golden Age.'"

"Right," Harding said. "Thing is, they were brutal, but it was a brutal age. Even in that 'Great Age,' many were looking for land. Rich land. Younger sons went off to find a place, and then, if you were going to take a place, you conquered it. Or if you didn't conquer a place, you might be looking for the riches that would allow you to rise within your own society. What we consider the first Viking raid was Lindisfarne, the Christian monastery there. They came with their bows, spears, axes, swords and knives—sending the monks running. There had been raids before—but nothing like what happened at Lindisfarne. The attack was, of course, completely out of the blue—and a scourge."

"Why did the Vikings die out?" Elayne asked. "Sounds like they were doing all right."

"In my mind," Danny said, clearing his throat, as if aware that John Smith would hardly consider him to be a scholar, "it was Haakon IV of Norway and Alexander III—when the raids began, you see, there were no actual kings of Scotland or Norway. Come around to about 1262 and Alexander II had already died of a fever, trying to sail against the Norse. They battled over the northern islands off Scotland. Anyway, Haakon raised a great navy that Alexander knew he couldn't beat—so he let the weather do it for them. After a storm broke up what was essentially Haakon's armada, Alexander went in and there was a slaughter—which still didn't solve anything. Haakon headed over to Orkney to wait out the winter—and he died. Anyway, the raids in general began to end after that. The Hebrides wound up belonging to Scotland and the Orkney Islands went to the Vikings—well, until way later when they became part of a dowry when Margaret, daughter of Christian I of Norway, married James III of Scotland. It was officially annexed by what was then the Kingdom of Scotland in 1472."

Everyone was silent for a moment. Craig saw that Kieran had lowered her head; she was smiling, proud of her brother for probably taking both John Smith and Jay Harding by surprise with his general knowledge of history.

"Um...cool," Elayne said after a minute.

"And, important, really, in any story relating to the Scots and the Norse," Kieran said pleasantly, looking up. "Jacques de Molay was burned at the stake in March of 1314. His followers would have been running to Scotland to escape Philip's purge in the years right before— de Molay was imprisoned for years before his execution was carried out—and right after."

"The Templars were dissolved by Philip in 1307," Ben Garcia said. "That's when anyone who could fled with what precious relics they had."

"Right," Kieran said. "And at that time, the battle between Haakon and Alexander was long over, and trade relations between Viking and Scot were growing strong. You also had large populations that were mixed. Easy to see that there might have been many friends between the two cultures."

"Yes! So, you see, there could be all kinds of things on this island," Annie Green put in.

"Or ten million in goods stolen by murdering bank robbers," Mike said dryly.

"What we need to do is see the island," John Smith said.

"Maybe, one day," Finn said.

"We could help now," Jay Harding told him.

"Not at this time, I'm afraid," Craig said. "The property is part of an official investigation."

"And," Bracken added, "at the moment, I'm still

doing my best to make sure that the caves and tunnels aren't dangerous. I believe that much of the system is natural. But over time, people dug tunnels to suit their needs. How sound they are, we just don't know yet."

"In this day and age," Kieran put in, "Finn also has the liability to think about."

"It's not impossible. Maybe one day," Finn said cheerfully.

"Better than the caves, the beach is so beautiful. And the pool," Elayne said. "We all need to look to the future—and the fantastic resort that will be here."

"We hope. If more people don't die," Margie said. She rose, without excusing herself, and left the room.

"She's still in a great deal of pain," Finn said. "So are Elayne and I. We lost a very dear friend."

"Under these circumstances, thank you for having us out here," John Smith said politely.

"Oh, yes, thank you!" Jay Harding agreed. "Perhaps… perhaps…well, the house provides light. Perhaps we could just have a look out front after dinner—at that beautiful beach Miss Anderson is speaking about."

"That we can do," Finn said, and he looked at Craig, seeking his approval.

"The full moon was a few nights back, but there's still lots of light," Craig said. "We have the floodlights from the house. I don't see why not."

But first they would have tea or coffee, which Evie and Victor had set up.

Everyone rose to help themselves, and they were able to mingle and chat. Ben Garcia spoke excitedly with Danny as they compared letters they had read at different times in their lives, suggesting that the Norse had come farther south than what was now Nova Scotia in their travels.

Annie Green joined their group. "Remember, we do need to refer to these traders as Norse, and not Vikings. Vikings really refers to the raiders who were out seeking riches in other lands—those who invaded, robbed, raped and killed—and sometimes stayed to found cities," she said. "The Norse were farmers, often looking for land. And, then, of course, when the Great Age of the Vikings was basically over, the Norse were still out there—sailing and trading!"

"Of course!" Danny agreed. "The Danes ruled in Northern England for years."

"And the Norse spread their seed here and there and everywhere— Rollo in Normandy, part of the Conquest!" John Harding said, joining their conversation.

"They were quite incredible," Danny said. "They went all over Europe and beyond, reaching the Ukraine, Russia—and even the Byzantine Empire."

Bracken approached Craig. "So, we found another entrance to the caves today."

"We?"

"Kieran was with me."

Craig wasn't surprised.

"We were walking back, late, and I don't really know how she spotted it, but I have a feeling it must be the entrance Frank found. I think, however, that the system all connects—unless there's been a cave-in somewhere along the line."

Craig lowered his voice. "So, when we go out tonight…"

"We're going through the entrance we've been working. Tomorrow, I'll check out this cave properly. With your approval—I can't condone any of us dying because of a rock fall."

"Agreed."

He turned to the gathered guests. "Hey—has everyone had their coffee?" he called out.

"We are ready for the great outdoors," Ben Garcia said.

"So, then, come along," Craig said.

He led them out through the White Room and the great hall.

He glanced back, and Evie was watching them go. She didn't look happy. Victor Eider appeared to be oblivious. He was taking the large coffee urn back into the kitchen.

They trailed out. As they made their way to the beach, he noticed Margie standing in the center of the small beach area. She'd worn a knit maxi dress that night, and the breeze was picking up the skirt, as it did her hair.

She looked strangely forlorn there.

She turned, startled when she saw that others were coming.

Jay Harding was right behind Craig. He walked past, addressing Margie.

"Miss Appleby. Not to intrude. I just have to tell you how beautiful you look there, on the sand, in the moonlight."

Margie turned, and actually smiled. "Thank you," she said softly.

John Smith and Annie Green moved by them, joining Margie and Jay where they stood.

"It's beautiful. Truly beautiful!" Annie said.

Elayne joined them next. "Ah, yes, but turn to the

west. There's that bastard cliff! Even when all else is beautiful, it looks treacherous and sinister."

"Only if you choose to see it so," Kieran said, stepping up.

"It's really a great maze of mystery," Jay Harding said.

"Well, every once in a while we agree," John Smith told him.

Harding laughed. "We agree on a lot, my friend, like I said."

"And so we do," John agreed.

"Oh, thank the Lord!" Annie exclaimed. "See, John? Jay is not a mindless crackpot."

"Did you call me a mindless crackpot?" Jay asked John, amused.

"So I did."

"That's all right," Ben Garcia said, joining the conversation. "Jay once told us all that you had the imagination of a stunted amoeba."

Everyone on the beach laughed. Craig looked around at the group. A lovely dinner party. Margie seeming to actually enjoy people. Elayne was now hugging Finn's arm. But there was Mike at a distance, watching, alongside Bracken.

A boat horn sounded.

"That's your ride," Finn said. "We'll keep in touch, I promise."

There were goodbyes all way round and Craig walked down the dock with Finn. "I forgot that you'd arranged the transport."

Finn looked at him and nodded. "I got 'em here, and I'm getting 'em out. And I assume you're with me to see that they do all get on the boat."

"That is true," Craig said, grinning.

"Could they be…involved?" Finn asked. "I mean, actually, they're all very bright…bookish. Nerdy!"

"You can never tell," Craig said.

He hurried forward, reaching out a hand to help Annie Green step over a spot where a plank was bad.

"Thank you, kind sir," she said, smiling.

She was lovely and cheerful—especially next to John Smith, who tended to be much more reserved and serious. Were they a couple? It hadn't appeared that they were. All night, Danny had been flirting with her.

Danny was a flirt.

John Smith paused to shake their hands. "Thank you so much! This was like a dream come true."

"So much so!" Jay Harding, boarding behind John, said.

"I'm so glad you enjoyed the evening," Finn said.

Then they were aboard the boat, and they were gone.

Kieran was still standing on the beach, right behind Margie.

And Evie Summers had come out; she was watching the boat leave.

The others had gone back in.

"Well, it has been a long day," Craig murmured.

Finn turned to him. "Are we any closer to solving Frank's death?" he asked a little desperately.

"I think so. We know that the woman we found in the cave was in contact with the bank robbers, and she was probably one of their accomplices. If so, they might have wanted to get rid of her—they apparently believed in the mantra that no one should leave witnesses. Borden and Tremaine were disinterred today. Autopsy tomorrow."

"But still…"

"We're getting there, Finn. We're getting closer to the truth. I promise you, we will not stop until we've found it."

His cousin nodded.

"Well, then, I for one am tired, and for bed."

Then he hurried off back to the house.

Craig followed more slowly; in just a little time, they'd start their night out.

And, hopefully, discover the source of the light Kieran continued to see...but which eluded him every time.

CHAPTER
THIRTEEN

Friday morning, 1:00 a.m.

By all appearances, the household was sleeping.

Kieran believed that someone had already slipped out, be it Evie, Victor, Elayne or Margie.

It might be hard to slip away from Finn—but then, they'd actually never asked Finn if Elayne was always with him when he woke at night.

They left via the back door; Bracken was careful to fix the lock.

"If anyone comes this way after us, won't they realize that the lock has been fixed so that we can get back in?"

He smiled at her. "Not the way I do it."

They made a strange little party, Bracken and Craig at the lead, Kieran and Danny behind and Mike bringing up the rear guard.

They trudged in silence for a while, eyes on the ground watching their steps in the dark, and finally reached the cave. "Flashlights, everyone," Bracken murmured.

"Wait!" Kieran said.

They all looked at her.

"I see light flashing at night—let's not make the same mistake. We'll get in the cave before we turn on our lights."

"I'll get down there first," Bracken said.

He easily slid into the entry and down, and called back up.

"Kieran," Craig murmured, and she slipped through, followed by Danny and then Mike, who complained that he was getting too old for cave exploration.

"You're in better shape that most twenty-year-olds I know," Bracken told him, shaking his head.

"Maybe. But age—the older you get, the more you like to whine," Mike said cheerfully.

In a few minutes, they were all inside.

Lights went on.

"Let's travel the length of what we know, at least," Bracken said.

It really wasn't that much different being in the cave by night than it was being in the cave by day; underneath the world, it was dark—no matter what time it was.

They went by the discoveries they had made.

"'Park horse here,'" Danny murmured.

"'Aliens,'" Mike murmured.

"We can search another fifty feet or so," Bracken told them. "After that, I'd like to go ahead of you all again. If these people came and saw to the safety of the caves, I don't believe they've done it recently. I've hauled all kinds of things out here, and it takes some doing."

Danny had stopped, hunkering down with his flashlight.

"Bracken?"

"Yeah?"

"Look here...doesn't the ground look a little different? It's subtle, but...it doesn't look as hard as the stone of the ground surrounding it."

Kieran bent down by her brother and studied the earth. "Danny, it's like at the front, where we started digging, right where we came into the cave."

Bracken had joined them. He looked up at Craig and Mike.

"I think she's right," he said. He stood and opened the canvas bag he'd brought and took out a pick, a shovel and some trowels.

"I'm into it," Craig said.

He grabbed the pick and Danny and Kieran moved back. He hit the earth—and it immediately gave way.

"Wow, shovels, gently!" Bracken said.

Craig and Mike took up the shovels.

Kieran heard a soft *clunk* and quickly cried out. "Stop...stop, there's something. I think it's another stone."

"Why would they bury the damned stones?" Danny asked irritably.

"Who knows, but..."

Kieran had already gone for the brushes that Bracken had carried in his bag. The others stood back while she painstakingly went to work. In a few minutes, she had uncovered another stone. There was writing on it. It looked like strange curly cues to her at first, but right when she realized what it was, Danny spoke.

"This is in French," he said.

"Templars?" Mike asked skeptically.

"I don't know, but..."

"What does it say, can any of us read it?"

"I can," Danny said.

"You really read French that well?" Kieran asked him.

"I've seen the exact writing before. It's in a catacomb in a small church in Paris," her brother murmured. He looked at her. "No, I haven't been there! I read about it."

"What does it say?" she demanded.

Danny paused, looking around at the others. "'Know ye that trespass upon Holy Relics,'" he said. "There was a program on one of the history channels recently—it was all about Christianity, the Crusades and holy relics. The little church in Paris believes it has pieces of the cross on which Christ was crucified. And that's why they have the same sign over their catacombs."

"So, something is here...somewhere," Bracken said. He looked at Craig. "These stones, what we're finding here...we may not be talking value, but they do belong in museums."

"Of course," Craig said. "But for now, until we know what we're looking at, we keep everything that we find a secret."

Kieran had barely heard him. Their flashlights had been laid on the floor, illuminating the area where they had been working and the stone they had uncovered.

But now she could see across the floor. And there was something wedged against the stone wall of the cave and the floor beneath it.

She rose and went to it.

"Kieran? Another historical find?" Bracken asked.

She looked back at them, shaking her head. "Not so historical. Bracken, did you lose a flashlight today?"

"I never lose gear," he said.

She reached out. By then, Craig was next to her. "No," he said softly, catching her arm.

He reached into his pocket for an evidence bag and used it to pick up the flashlight. He studied it for a minute, and then turned to the others. "Not historical at all—you can buy this in dozens upon dozens of stores in the city. It's a compact, high-beam light. They sell them any time winter is approaching. They're great when storms knock out electricity."

Kieran suddenly felt very cold. She swallowed.

"I've seen that—or one like it—before."

"Where?" Craig asked her.

"The first day we came. When they asked me to make dinner. I was prowling around the kitchen. There was one just like it in a drawer near the sink."

Craig carefully encompassed the little light in an evidence bag. He looked around the cave and tunnel where they stood.

"No openings," he said. "You didn't see that flashing light from here."

"No," she agreed.

"But," he added softly, "it does mean that someone from the house has been here."

"And maybe we'll get a fingerprint," Mike said. "Maybe."

"And maybe our culprit wears gloves—and, if it was in the house, it could have a print from anyone in there," Craig says. "Still…"

"And we need to quit for the night," Bracken said. "It's 3:30 a.m. Time to get back and to our rooms before the morning boat with hired help heads in, and before the household—the innocent and the guilty—begin to waken. I'm not sure what our timing will be, hiking out of here. A couple hours, at least, I think."

Kieran stood, dusting off her hand.

"Well, we didn't really get anywhere, did we?" she asked.

Craig set a finger beneath her chin and lifted her face so that he could meet her eyes. "You found that flashlight," he said, "and Danny found a carved stone. It wasn't a wasted night at all."

"But we still have no idea of where the flash of light I see at night might be coming from," she said.

"We will," Bracken assured her. "Come tomorrow, in daylight, we try the other entrance."

Danny slipped an arm around Kieran. "Cheer up, sis! There's one exceptionally fine thing about tonight."

"What's that?" she asked him.

"You *didn't* find another dead body!"

Friday, midmorning

"I'm sending you all the files I have," Egan said. "We've researched everyone on your island, and this is what we've come up with. They'll be in your email."

"Thank you. You've spoken with Brice today?" Craig asked.

"Early this morning. This is late for you, you know."

"Yeah, late night," Craig told him. He glanced at the old grandfather clock in Finn's office. It was nine forty-five. Not that late—certainly not when it was four by the time you got in bed.

"He's interested—now that he thinks the bank robbers were killed. He's at the autopsy as we speak," Egan informed him. "I'm surprised you're not there."

"I wanted to be on the island today," Craig said. He knew that, while he was speaking, Bracken was setting up at the entrance to the cave discovered by Kieran yesterday. "More crawling around," he added. "But last night, we found another carved stone—one in French. But we also found something brand-spanking-new. A flashlight."

"So, someone has been in there."

"Obviously we knew Frank had been exploring. But Kieran believes that flashlight might have been in a kitchen drawer. Anyway, I'll get it in to the lab so that we can check for prints."

"Won't prove anything—anyone in the house might have touched that light."

"It won't prove anything, but may give us a direction in which to look."

"Your dinner gave you nothing?" Egan asked.

"I don't know. All of our guests behaved as if they'd never been here before. They were pleasant to one another. No fireworks."

"Well, none of them has a record of any kind. I've also run searches on every member of the Believers. Parking tickets—that's about it. They are an educated group—each member has a college degree. I can't find anything questionable on any of them. It's been more interesting looking up your friends on the island."

"Oh?"

"Nothing of a severe nature. You'll see. Read the reports. They're just an interesting lot. I'll let you decide if any of it means anything."

Craig thanked him and told him about the night, and the day they had planned.

"Pay attention for a call from Dr. Hodges. He likes you. He's disappointed that you're not coming to the autopsy."

"He's a good man—he looks at all angles. He'll need a few hours with the corpses, I'm sure. But I'll be sure I speak with him as soon as he has some answers," Craig said.

"Yes, do that," Egan said.

They finished the conversation.

Finn came in as Craig was leaving the office.

"You're going into the caves today?" Finn asked.

"Yes."

"I should go with you." Finn said the words, but there was no conviction to them.

"Finn, don't worry about it. You don't need to be down in the caves."

"Right." Finn sighed and shook his head. "Is this all foolhardy? Should I be trying to create a resort out of an island that seems to be nothing but a massive graveyard, that may be…"

"May be what?" Craig asked, frowning.

"Evil," Finn said. "The whole thing may be evil." He let out another long breath. "I may wind up losing Elayne—she likes the house and the beach and the pool enough, but…"

He paused, and looked around as if he was afraid that someone might be listening.

There were just the two of them in the office.

"She hates the caves. Frank was my friend. It was just a week ago…and we still have to bury him."

"Finn, land isn't evil. The island isn't evil. And what you're doing is a good thing," Craig assured him.

"I hope so," Finn murmured. "Well, if you're done in here, I'm going to get back to my spreadsheets of estimates on the work that will need to be done—just to get up the extensions I'm planning."

"I'm out of here," Craig told him.

"If—if you find anything, you'll call me right away."

"You know that I will," Craig promised him.

On his way out, Craig pulled out his phone and went to his email. Just as Egan had promised, he'd received a large file.

There were reports on Finn Douglas, Elayne Anderson, Margie Appleby, John Smith, Jay Harding and Annie Green.

He skimmed them. There was nothing in there that he didn't know about Finn. His cousin had always been a good student; he had graduated from the Harvard School of Business, and worked on real estate development projects since.

Jay Harding and John Smith had also received degrees—both of them in social sciences and history. John Smith had once had a bench warrant out—failure to pay parking tickets.

Jay Harding had been arrested one time during a political protest.

Nothing hinted of violence.

He moved on to Margie's sheet. She had majored in hospitality at a university in Florida. Parking tickets. No arrests. She'd never been married; both parents had been killed in an automobile accident.

Elayne's sheet was more interesting. She had been

engaged to Sherman Meyers, the son of a wealthy New Yorker.

Meyers had died from a fall off a balcony during spring break at a hotel in Mexico.

Elayne had also been at the hotel. There had been no suggestion, however, that she had been with him when he'd gone over—the boys had been out doing some heavy drinking in Cancún the night before, the girls had been at an overnight spa.

He flipped through the pages again.

She'd grown up in the foster system. At eighteen, she'd aged out and taken a job as a stripper at a club in Atlantic City. She'd gone to school while working, and gotten a degree in design. It was while working on her degree that she'd met Sherman Meyers. After his death, she'd become a club hostess, working in the city. She had gone on an extended vacation to the Bahamas, and from there, called in to tender her resignation.

"Craig, you ready?"

"Yeah, yeah," he said, meeting Mike halfway up the stairs. "Just got some info from Egan."

"And?"

"Nothing that hints of criminal activity. The most interesting is our lovely Elayne."

"Oh?"

Craig passed his phone to Mike. Mike read the file on the screen.

"A bit…sad and slimy," he said. "She wasn't there when the fiancé died, so…"

"She worked hard to pick herself up in the world, so it seems. Still…"

"She bears watching."

"As she has from the beginning."

Danny descended the stairs. "You guys ready yet?"

"Yeah. We need to move. I'm just going to get Kieran," Craig said.

"You don't need to—she went out with Bracken."

"She did?"

"He's slipping in to assess the entry and the condition of the cave. Kieran won't go in until you get there," Danny said. "But she hasn't figured out what she saw the other night that glittered and drew her attention to the cave opening." He grinned. "She's really beating the bushes."

"All right, then, let's go."

"I'm ready," Mike said. "Oh, and speaking of gloves—"

"Were we speaking about gloves?" Danny asked.

"I've brought some," Mike said. "I mean, I've been ruining my manicure out there."

"You've never had a manicure," Craig told him.

"Yeah? Well, I've thought about it," Mike said.

They filed down the stairs and through the house. Evie was giving instructions in the kitchen to a young maid who was putting dishes into the cupboards. They all greeted her politely. "You'll be back for dinner?" she asked.

"Wouldn't miss it," Danny said cheerfully.

Evie actually smiled. "Good." She shivered. "You need to get out of those varmint-filled holes for a good meal."

When they went out the back door, Victor was working on the porch, hammering a plank that must have been loose.

"Off to work the caves again?" he asked.

"We'll find something eventually," Craig assured him.

"Eventually," Victor agreed.

"You're alone out here?" Craig asked him. "No bathing beauties today?"

"Haven't seen Margie or Elayne all day. Don't know what they do— I'll tell you, I couldn't stay in a house all day like that. I'd go stir crazy with boredom."

"I guess everyone has their thing," Craig murmured.

"Going a different way today?" Victor asked.

"Trying to make sure we see the whole place," Mike told him.

As they walked on across the patio and through the trees and bracken beyond, Danny glanced back several times and then noted, "He's still watching us."

"There's not much else to do," Craig said.

"Yeah—except make sure he doesn't hammer his hand," Mike said.

"Where do you think they are?" Danny asked.

"Who?"

"Elayne and Margie."

"In their rooms, I imagine," Mike said. "I try to keep an eye on the door to Finn's room—keep up with Elayne. But someone is always running in and out." He glanced at Craig. "I know you and Kieran don't want anyone in your room, but Finn wants his clean at all times."

"How much can they mess it up?" Craig asked.

Mike laughed. "Oh, I've seen into that sanctum. That woman has all manner of things going on all the time. Clothing thrown everywhere. Nail polish and makeup out. She wants a personal maid, that one. Oh, but she doesn't want Evie in her things. She made a point of telling Finn that he needed to get Evie to have a maid do her room—she didn't want Evie touching her belongings."

"Ouch," Danny said.

"There's obviously no love lost between Evie and Elayne," Craig said.

"Evie does like to think that she's queen of that roost," Danny said.

"Finn and Elayne have argued about Evie," Mike said.

"You've heard them?"

"I couldn't help it—Elayne can get loud when she's angry," Mike said.

They walked toward the crest of the cliffs. Halfway up the rough trail, Danny stopped. "Where the hell are we going?" he asked.

"Here—somewhere," Mike said.

"But… I don't see anything," Craig said.

"You can't see these openings—even when you're looking right at them," Mike said, frustrated.

"But Kieran said that they were halfway down," Danny told them.

They stood there assessing; Craig suddenly saw Kieran come out from behind a little thicket of bushes.

"You guys made it," she said. She was beaming broadly.

"Yes, and why are you so happy?" Craig asked her.

"I found it!" she exclaimed. He saw that Kieran had donned a pair of thin gloves. She was smiling ear to ear when she raised her hand, producing a chain and a pendant.

"A medal?" Craig asked. He didn't reach for the piece, but dug quickly into his pocket for an evidence bag. He wasn't sure that they'd find prints or anything that would help them, but they had to try.

"It's a St. Jude medallion," Kieran said. "It was what was glinting, caught in the bush, that made me see the entrance. It definitely means that someone was using this entrance to the caves and the tunnels."

With the medallion safely nestled just inside the evidence bag, Craig studied it. It wasn't encrusted with dirt; it was still gleaming.

Lost recently.

"St. Jude—patron saint of lost causes," Danny said.

"Frank would have liked such a medallion, I think," Kieran said. "Hunting for treasure, for the past…he was searching."

"It might have been Frank's," Mike said, looking at the piece, too.

"We'll find out. We can ask Margie," Danny said.

"We can ask her, certainly," Kieran said. "But…will she answer us? She's still in such deep mourning, and really, it has to be expected."

"Or Finn may know," Craig said. "If it was something he wore frequently and cared about, Finn will probably have noticed."

"Hey!"

The shout sounded like it was coming from the earth itself.

"Anyone else coming down here?"

It was Bracken.

"Yes, headed your way now!" Craig shouted back.

Kieran led the way to the cave entrance, showing them where it was behind the shrubbery, and how they needed to go low and crawl through.

"There's a drop," Bracken called up to them. "And, yes, critters! Think I've scared most of the rats away, but you should know."

Kieran looked at Craig and shrugged. "I'm wearing my boots," she assured him.

"I'll go down," Mike said. "Catch Kieran."

"Assuming I'll fall," Kieran said.

"You will fall!" Bracken shouted.

"There, you see?" Mike asked.

"Gotcha," Kieran said.

Craig watched as the others hunkered down at the entrance. Mike went nearly flat and crawled through. There was a soft thud.

"You were supposed to catch me!" he heard Mike tell Bracken.

"You're too big. I slowed your fall, buddy. That's the best I could do."

"Quit squabbling—I'm on my way!" Kieran said.

Kieran went down.

Down the rabbit hole, Craig thought. "I'll bring up the rear, come down right after Danny," he said.

He managed to roll, drop and land on his feet.

The others surrounded him; flashlights already blazing.

He was looking at Bracken. "This is it," Bracken said. "This is where Frank Landon was—before he died."

"How do you know that?" Craig asked.

Bracken swung his light around, down the tunnel.

"Follow me," he said.

They walked about fifty feet. They came to an area where dozens of rocks—small to large lay on the ground.

They were stained with dry, almost rusty-looking… blackened crimson.

They were covered with blood.

Kieran stared at the many boulders in the tunnel, wishing that she didn't feel as sick as she did.

Craig had gone up to report in to Egan that they had

found a location where they were certain Frank Landon had been killed. To confirm it, crime scene techs would have to come in; samples would have to be taken.

But none of them wanted to quit for the day.

They'd found where Frank had been. They still didn't know what Frank was searching for, or if he'd found anything—or just how deep he had gone into the cave.

But while the guys were waiting by the blood-stained rocks, she had to move away.

She played her light over the cave walls and the ground—making sure to stamp her feet so that little creatures would know she was coming, and figured she should search for more writing on the walls.

She didn't want to think about a man being stoned to death.

The bank robbers had most probably been stoned to death as well. That would suggest that whoever was doing the killing had been searching here before the bank robbers had ever come; they weren't after money and jewels, they were after something else.

The Ark?

Proof that aliens had visited in ancient times?

She paused the sweep of her flashlight, certain that she'd caught sight of a place where someone— not time—had etched something into the stone of the cave wall.

Foolishly, she didn't watch her footing.

This time, it wasn't a slanted shaft with a crude rock slide.

It was a hole—a hole by the side of the cave wall, and she fell right in.

She gasped with surprise, not even screaming. And

then she hit bottom and the breath was knocked right out of her.

She lay still for a minute, gasping for air. Then she tried to move, praying she hadn't broken a bone. She hadn't—she could move all her limbs.

"Kieran?"

She heard Danny's voice, as if from far, far away.

"Kieran! Where the hell are you?"

"Here! I'm… I'm okay."

"Here where?"

She heard footsteps as Danny, Bracken and Mike came running to find her.

"Where?" Danny shouted again.

She managed to sit up.

"Stop running!" she commanded. "You could fall, too. I'm… I'm in a hole again!"

"Dammit, Kieran, why were you wandering in farther?" Bracken asked with dismay.

"I was just looking at the walls!"

"You could have been killed," Bracken said. "Damn your gift for finding holes. Are you sure you're all right?"

"I'm fine, really!"

She was. She was bruised, she was certain. But she had been incredibly lucky. Maybe she had fallen so fast that she hadn't tensed; she didn't know.

"I'll get a spike for the floor and a rope down to you," Bracken promised. "I'll be down in a matter of minutes."

"It's okay. I'm not panicking."

She thought dryly that she was becoming experienced at unexpected descents.

"Damned writing," she murmured to herself. "There

probably is writing on the wall—writing that says, 'watch out for hole.'"

She had dropped her flashlight, naturally, but it hadn't gone out. She stood and fetched it off the ground, grimacing as she did so. She had done a number on her back. It would hurt the next few days.

She played the light around the space. It was a bigger cave, about eight feet across. Little archways, larger than either of the openings to the cave system they had found, seemed to surround the hole. It looked like it was a tunnel system below the one they'd been in.

Curious, she moved toward the closest archway, light streaming ahead of her.

As she stepped through the archway, she tripped.

And fell flat again.

She swore softly, and played the light around to see what she had tripped on.

And then she screamed. Again and again...

"Kieran!"

She heard Bracken calling to her. And she managed to stumble up and away.

She'd found another corpse.

This time...

A fresh one.

"Kieran!" she heard Danny shouting.

She bit down on her hand; she had to stop screaming. She stared at the corpse, moving away from it, back to where she had fallen from the tunnel above.

"I'm all right, I'm all right... Just get down here!"

She heard them working above, and then she heard a scream again. She thought she was losing her mind; the sound wasn't coming from her.

A woman came flying out of one of the archways, panicked and nearly knocking her over.

"Oh, my God, oh, my God, help me! Help me... help me!"

It was Elayne. Her eyes were wide with terror; she was shaking uncontrollably. "Help me, please, please... I've been terrified! I fell in, and I found her...oh, my God, I found her there...dead!"

A rope suddenly came flying down in front of them.

Craig landed easily on his feet, having descended the rope in a quick rappel. He glanced at Elayne, not showing his surprise at her being there, and then he reached for Kieran, staring at her searchingly, his eyes going over her in a quick appraisal.

Elayne flung herself on him, screaming hysterically again.

"Help me, help me, help me, oh, God, get me out of here!"

"Elayne, calm down, please, we're here. Kieran..."

Bracken came down the rope.

Kieran pointed to the archway. "She's—dead," she said quietly.

"Who's dead?" Craig demanded. "And Elayne, how the hell did you..."

"You all were exploring every day. This is *Finn's* island. I— I'll admit, the idea of crawling around caves doesn't really appeal to me, but I wanted to help! I wanted to find an archeological treasure. I... I found the opening, the tunnel, and I walked in and I fell and my flashlight broke and I touched her, I touched the corpse, and I screamed and no one heard me and I tried and tried to find my way out and...oh, God, she's dead!"

"Who's dead?"

Next to Elayne's hysteria, Kieran suddenly found herself in complete control. "It's Annie Green," she said quietly.

"And you're certain she's dead?" Craig asked.

"Yes," Kieran said, her voice quiet, calm and definitive. "She's dead. She's been stoned to death."

CHAPTER
FOURTEEN

The question of when to get a team to the island became moot. Egan—and the police, including Brice—made it out in record time. Kieran and Elayne had been lifted out of the cave-within-the-cave. Craig and Bracken climbed back up using the ropes. Elayne had remained hysterical; despite that, she was sticking to her story.

Forensics had taken the clothing she had been wearing—as well as Kieran's—and both women were at the house with Mike and Egan. They were keeping a close eye on Elayne. Kieran was being treated as a witness. It was obviously ridiculous to think that she could have gotten into the cave in time to stone a woman to death.

Large, bloody rocks were all around Annie Green.

Her death had not been an easily accomplished deed.

The body itself hadn't been touched—other than Kieran tripping over it—until Hodges arrived.

"You don't give me time to sew up one body before

bringing me another!" Hodges told Craig as he squatted down to examine the crime scene.

"Did you conclude that the bank robbers were stoned to death?" Craig asked.

"A definite possibility. Now, they've been buried for years, but the way the bones are broken—and with what you've found here—I'm going to say that it's a really sound possibility." He sat back on his haunches. "This young lady has been dead about two hours. The caves down here are quite cool, but even allowing for that, I'm going to say two to three hours, tops. She most probably died from one of the blows to her head—from the indent here…"

He paused, and flashed his light at a bloody place on the skull. "I believe the actual cause of death will prove to be blunt force trauma, but I'll know more when I perform the autopsy. Nothing about the body suggests how she got down here, but…"

His voice trailed. The stones used to kill her still lay around her. "I think you also have your murder weapon here," he said somberly.

"What was she doing out here?" Brice piped up from his spot standing to the side of the forensic crew, who were busy taking photographs, marking the stones and marking the spray of blood spatter.

"She wasn't staying on the island, was she?" Brice asked. "She was part of your dinner party?"

"She was," Craig said. "But I watched her get on a boat. And I watched that boat motor away."

"We'll need to interview everyone—the dinner guests, Finn's employees. Anyone at all who was on this island."

"Yes," Craig agreed.

"All right, I'm good to go," Hodges said. He rose and turned to his assistant. "Let's do our best to get her out of here easily."

"Special Agent Silverheels has the rigging set," Craig told them.

As the medical assistants and techs went to work, Brice turned to Craig.

"Thank you," he said.

"Of course, it's a joint investigation," Craig told him.

"No, I mean, beyond that. When we were first called out here for the Landon case, I would have sworn that a rich brat just got too full of himself and his abilities— and went off a cliff. You didn't accept that. We evidently have something far more sinister going on here." He was quiet for a moment. "That poor girl. How did she wind up back on the island?"

"She headed back to the city with all the guests— her employer, John Smith, and the two Believers, Jay Harding and a friend of his, Ben Garcia. The dinner was oddly civilized."

"You'd been hoping there might be fireworks?" Brice asked.

"I was hoping that one of them would say something that would trip them up."

"Well, now we know that Frank Landon was murdered, and now this poor girl…" Brice shook his head. "One of them has to know something," he added. "They all had to have gotten off the boat together in Brooklyn."

"Yes. We have people bringing them into the offices now."

"We're not doing any good here," Brice said. "Egan has Miss Anderson and your girlfriend up at the house, right?"

"He does."

"I'm going to question Miss Finnegan myself, of course."

"Feel free. But Kieran couldn't have done it, and there is no emotion in that statement, Detective. She was only down here alone a minute or two. What was done...it would have taken more time."

"And Miss Anderson?"

"I don't know. I do know that if she wasn't completely panicked and hysterical, she was damned good at pretending. She threw herself at me as if she'd been hurled out of a cannon. And the way that she was shaking...that kind of thing is hard to fake."

"Still, what the hell was she doing down here?" Brice asked.

Craig shrugged. "She claims that she wanted to find something herself. That she found the entry—Bracken already had supplies on the outside, and, we believe, of course, that this is where Frank had been searching before he was killed. Who knows? Maybe he had told her something about his explorations."

"Sounds like a fishy story to me."

"And it may be. But trust me, Egan won't let her hide anything."

"I still think we should be there."

The two carefully skirted around the techs who were still working the scene. Craig headed for the ropes, where the body was being hauled up.

As they waited, he looked around. So many caves. So many dark corridors.

So much that still needed to be searched. They would have more help now, with this second murder. Law enforcement agencies would see the need for manpower and taxpayer dollars spent.

So, why the hell would someone have killed Annie Green and left her body there to be discovered?

Had they been interrupted?

They had to have known that Craig and others were searching the caves.

There had to be more. Something he hadn't discovered yet.

And there had to be a place, some kind of a hidden enclave within the vast system of tunnels and caves.

Something that might be in plain sight.

That they had already walked by, time and time again.

It was a miserable and tense situation.

Mike and Richard Egan were acting as watchdogs overseeing Kieran, Elayne and Danny. Danny didn't have to be there; he'd been with the group, but he hadn't been in the deeper cave. He sadly reminded them that a young woman—with whom they had all just enjoyed a pleasant dinner—was dead.

Kieran knew—though she would soon be giving her official statement—she wasn't really suspected of anything. Not because Egan would overlook her, but because the time frame made it impossible for her to have done it.

Egan and Mike were being very pleasant. No real interrogation had started as yet, but Kieran gave her story to Egan. Finn, who had been in his office, was sitting with Elayne now.

There was going to be no problem getting her to talk. She hadn't shut up for a second.

"I just wanted to help! I just wanted to be the one who found something…the truth about poor Frank. Something…a Viking something. A pirate something… I just wanted to help. I thought I'd be fine. I thought everyone then would have to respect me, and understand what it was that you saw in me."

Finn kept soothing her.

Kieran wasn't sure what to think. Her mind kept slipping back to images of Annie Green, and she was shaken.

It wasn't that she hadn't seen a dead body before. It was just that she could remember the young woman's enthusiasm, how cute she had been when she'd smiled and flirted with Danny.

But what the hell had she been doing down there? How had she slipped back to the island after leaving it? Had she come alone and been surprised? Or had she come with her killer?

Evie bustled in to the White Room with coffee and pastries. The housekeeper hadn't shown at first, but when she had, she'd been in a dither—caught between the horror of a "fresh" body and police tramping through her house, not knowing whether to be in service mode, or escape mode.

Everyone gratefully took coffee from Evie, but no one felt like eating. Danny paced. Mike just sat—looking miserable.

Kieran found time to look at her phone; Craig had passed on the dossiers Egan had sent him.

She couldn't help but wonder about Elayne's dead fiancé, but was sure that it would be addressed when Elayne was questioned. And she couldn't help but wonder about Evie's treatment of Elayne; at the moment, when Evie made her sweeps through the room, offering more coffee, she almost shunned the petite woman.

Elayne didn't notice. Busy trying to calm her, Finn didn't, either.

Finally—thankfully!—Kieran heard the door opening, the cops talking briefly to new arrivals, and then Craig was back with Detective Teddy Brice.

She refrained from leaping up and into Craig's arms—it was not the thing to do at the moment. But she stood when the men entered, as did everyone else in the room.

Craig looked her way, and she gave him a nod. He was the ultimate professional, but he was also the love of her life. She wouldn't have him worried about her.

He spoke to Elayne and Finn. "I know that you've been speaking with my boss, Elayne, but I'm afraid you're going to have to answer questions that Detective Brice and I will have."

"Really, Craig?" Finn demanded, a protective arm around Elayne. "She's so upset! We've been waiting, but I'm thinking I need a doctor, something to calm her..."

"Shot of whiskey—soon as she's been questioned," Brice said.

"Seriously? She's been through hell," Finn said.

"And she could be under arrest or hauled in to the precinct," Brice said. "Miss Anderson, you were alone in a cave with a murdered woman."

"And terrified I'd be murdered myself," Elayne protested. She looked over at Kieran. "You were there! You were there, too!"

"Miss Finnegan will be questioned, too, I assure you," Brice said.

"But, but..."

"Arrested! Taken in!" Finn said indignantly.

"Finn, we have to speak with Elayne," Craig told him. "It's procedure."

Finn told him what he could do with procedure. The two officers looked as if they were about to move on him, but Craig walked over to his cousin and took him by the shoulders.

"A woman is dead, Finn. We have to question Elayne. She could help us. She could have seen or heard something. Please."

Finn nodded. "I think I need to call my attorney."

"You should do that," Brice said.

"No, no, stop!" Elayne said. "I'm sorry. If we get the attorney, they'll take me in. Please, Finn… I don't want to go to jail. Not even for a night. Please."

"I'd like to be with her," Finn said.

"It's all right, Finn, really. I have to—to cope," Elayne said.

"It will be Brice and me," Craig told Finn.

Finn didn't protest, but he didn't look happy.

"We'll use your office," Craig said.

The three left. Danny walked over to Finn. "It will be all right. Craig will be there."

Finn let out a breath. "Yeah, I know. But…"

Evie popped back into the room. "Can I get you something? Other than coffee?"

Finn shook his head and sat. He seemed to realize that he'd been rude. "No, no thank you, Evie."

Margie came into the room then; her face was pale. "I—I just woke up! I was resting…sleeping. I heard that…oh…so horrible," she said, shaking her head. "You found Miss Green…that sweet girl, Annie. Found her—dead."

"I'm afraid so," Kieran said.

For a moment, Margie looked as if she was going to faint. Egan hurried over to her. "Come, take a chair," he said.

Margie looked at him. "Thank you. And you are…?"

"Richard Egan, FBI," he told her. He smiled. "Craig's boss. You were with Frank Landon for years, right?"

Margie nodded, looking up at Egan. She had a wilted belle look about her that made Kieran think she was watching an audition for *A Streetcar Named Desire*.

Margie seemed to be relying on the kindness of strangers.

"You found Annie Green. So that would mean that Frank was…that Finn was right, that Frank was murdered!"

"Yes."

"And Craig and Mike are in there—questioning *Elayne*?" She sounded incredulous.

"Elayne was in the tunnels when Kieran crashed down and found the body," Egan explained.

Margie stared at Kieran. "They're not questioning you?"

Kieran smiled reassuringly. "They will be."

Margie turned to Finn then. "I'm so sorry," she said. "I doubted you."

"It's all right."

"Elayne didn't do it," Margie whispered. "You know that, right?"

"To be honest, we don't know anything," Egan told her. "We're hoping she can help us."

"She can't help you," Finn said. "She was scared to death down there. She's lucky she wasn't hurt or killed!"

"The thing is, Finn," Danny said, his tone gentle,

"questioning isn't always because law enforcement think that someone is guilty. It's because, if they ask the right questions, that someone might realize that they did see something...or heard something, or even smelled something. Right, sir?" he asked Egan.

"That's right," Egan said.

He leaned forward, talking to Finn. "Mr. Douglas, trust me. If there were real signs that Elayne had murdered Miss Green, we wouldn't be here. We'd be downtown, and she'd be facing arraignment. But we're just trying to find out anything that we can."

Kieran noted that he didn't say that he believed Elayne wasn't guilty.

He just said, basically, that they had no real evidence against her.

Kieran closed her eyes for a minute; she could still see, in her mind's eye, the dead woman.

Slumped on the ground, blood everywhere, rocks of different sizes all around her.

Could one person have done all that?

Kieran's phone rang; ridiculously, she jumped.

It was in her pocket, and she reached for it quickly, looking around apologetically. The ringer had been loud—intrusive—in the room.

"Excuse me," she said, rising, to take the call out in the great hall. But she had barely said hello before she heard, "Oh, God! Is it true, is it true? Annie?"

It was John Smith. It sounded as if he was crying.

"Mr. Smith, I'm so sorry..."

How had he heard?

"I was just called by the police! They say that they needed me, that they knew Annie was working for me. How could this have happened? She was on the boat with me. *I saw her get off the boat in Brooklyn.* How the hell did she wind up back there? In a cave—in a hole. Dead. Murdered!"

"I don't know, Mr. Smith. No one knows yet. But I'm so sorry. She was a beautiful and very sweet young woman. I have no idea—"

"You people caused this. She's dead because of you people!"

"Mr. Smith, you're the one who wanted to come out to the island," she reminded him quietly.

"I want to know what happened. I want you to rip up that wretched island until you find out who did this. The police, the FBI...who the hell do we need? Why can't anyone find anything? It's a bloody island!"

"I'm so sorry. Both agencies will have a much larger presence here—they will get to the truth, John." She hesitated. "Is there someone who can be with you... someone who can help you now?"

"There's a million people I can be with. That doesn't change the fact that she somehow wound up back on that island—and that she's dead!"

"No, I'm afraid it doesn't."

"And now, they're going to cut her all up. She'll go to the wretched morgue, and they'll slice and dice her and dissect her."

"She'll have to have an autopsy, yes," Kieran said.

"The cops suck—the FBI is even worse."

"I'm so sorry."

"Yeah, I'm sure you are!"

She didn't get to say anything more; he hung up.

Kieran let out a long breath. There was no sense in trying to call the man back and get him to calm down.

She wasn't sure what she could say anyway; she wasn't with him, and he was in no mood to talk to her.

But she didn't want to walk back into the White Room. Frankly, she wanted to head up to her room and crawl beneath the covers and wish that the day had never been.

The officer by the front door was looking at her.

She knew that she had to return to the others. At least Danny, Mike and Egan were in there.

She gave the officer at the door a grim smile and walked back in.

Egan glanced over at her, a question in his eyes.

"That was John Smith," she said.

"Oh?"

"Your office didn't call him and tell him that…that Annie Green is dead?"

"No. The police must have done so," he said.

"Imagine. So horrible, finding out from a phone call that a loved one is dead," Margie said. "At least…at least, with me, it was Finn. And he kept me from falling and…held me."

"Was Annie Green Mr. Smith's girlfriend?" Egan asked.

"Well… I assumed," Margie said. "Well, really, I don't know. But even if they weren't…um, sleeping together, they were close."

"Yes, of course," Egan said.

"I'm sure that John Smith cared about Annie very much. She was a really nice and interesting person," Danny said.

"You liked her," Margie said.

"Of course," Danny told her. "Didn't you?"

"Yes, but…never mind," Margie said. "I wish I'd

stayed asleep!" she cried suddenly. "I'm telling you, this island is cursed."

"Maybe it is," Finn whispered. "Maybe my father is right—he doesn't believe that I can make something good out of it."

"That's exactly what you still need to do," Kieran said.

"How? How in the hell do I do that, after all this?" Finn asked bleakly.

"You let us do our work," Egan said. "And we catch a killer—and put an end to what's apparently been going on here for a very long time."

Finn swallowed, looked down, and shook his head.

Everyone in the room fell silent.

They couldn't play at conversation.

They just waited.

Elayne Anderson was incredibly difficult to read. She was pretending to be strong—or pretending *to be pretending* to be strong.

She was excitable, tears stinging her eyes as she spoke, her limbs visibly shaking.

"Okay," Brice said. He had been doing the majority of the questioning; Craig had been observing. "Okay, Elayne. I think I understand... Craig and his group had been out exploring. You figured you wouldn't fall because you didn't intend to go anywhere near the top of the cliff. Furthermore, you hadn't really believed that Frank was murdered. I can see that. There might be incredible finds here on the island, hidden in those cliffs. So, you wanted to be a heroine...make the great discovery. I understand that, but...you went into the cave alone?"

"I didn't think that I'd ever do anything like that. I mean, I hate bugs! Especially spiders, and I knew there might be spiders. But I had a good flashlight. I just kept thinking how cool it would be if I found something, and everyone would say, 'Elayne? Elayne? Wow!' And when I got to the cave, it was bright daylight outside. When I slipped in, my light was so good I didn't feel afraid. I saw all of Special Agent Silverheels's equipment—I knew they'd be along soon. I thought I'd be standing there nonchalantly when they came down! Instead, I wandered in and walked over to the wall... I was down. And I cracked my light and it worked for a minute, and I saw... I saw... Oh!" She took a shuddering breath.

"What did you do after you saw the body?" Brice prompted.

"I stumbled away, and I screamed and no one heard me. I tried to climb back up to the hole, and I dropped my light and it broke and then I was desperately trying to find a way out in the dark when I heard someone... Kieran. I'd been down there in the darkness, knowing I was with a dead woman!"

"What time did you head out to the caves?"

"I'm not sure. I guess after breakfast. Margie was in a mood and didn't want to lie by the pool. She went back to her bedroom. It's just a week since Frank went out...a sad anniversary for her, and now...this. And Finn...he headed into his office. I guess I went out then."

If that was true, Craig reflected, she had left right before he and Mike and Danny left the house to meet up with Kieran and Bracken.

But Kieran had been combing the bushes.

And Bracken had already been in the caves. She had to have gotten there before Bracken and Kieran.

"You're sure it was right when Finn headed to his office?" Craig asked.

"I guess. I mean, I went out right after breakfast. You all weren't down yet."

Either she wasn't sure, or she realized she might have put herself in a trap.

"Elayne," he asked. "What happened to your fiancé—years ago?"

"What?" She knit her brow in a frown.

"You were engaged. Years ago," Brice said quietly.

"How do you know that?" she demanded.

"I am with the NYPD," Brice said.

"FBI, here," Craig said lightly.

"You—you pried...into my past?" Elayne demanded. "Oh, that's just cruel. My fiancé died—it was tragic and heartbreaking. We were young. He'd been with friends...they'd been drinking too much. How can you bring that up now—that's just too cruel!" She stared at them both, and then turned her anger on Craig. "You don't think I'm good enough! You looked up my whole past, and you don't think I'm good enough for your rich cousin. Well, Mr. Special Agent, I have news for you. I'm as good as anyone else. I know how to work, how to learn and most of all, I make Finn happy, and he makes me happy, and no one is better than anyone else!"

"We certainly didn't mean to imply that, Elayne. You did work hard. You got your degree. If you and Finn are happy, more power to you both," Craig said.

"Oh, oh!" she said, ignoring him. "You want to arrest me. You want to degrade me in front of Finn."

"Miss Anderson," Brice said, "that's hardly the case. You were, after all, in the caves—with a dead woman."

"I fell!" Elayne said.

"What did you hear, when you fell?" Craig asked.

"Hear?"

"Could you hear anything from above? Bracken or Kieran or the others above you? Rats scurrying around? Anything?" Brice asked.

Elayne shook her head. "I heard my heart pounding. I was terrified."

"You saw no one else down there, heard no one down there?" Craig asked.

"I was terrified!"

"Did you sense that anyone was down there with you? Were there any smells or odors?"

"Blood!" Elayne said. "I smelled the blood. And all I could hear was my own breathing—so, so loud, when I was afraid that the murderer might still be there. And my heart. And I'd screamed—and no one heard me. Then I thought that I needed to be quiet—and I was terrified that I'd already been heard, that someone might have been down there with me... Oh, it was terrible!"

Craig and Detective Brice were both silent. She stared at them.

"Should I have Finn get a lawyer for me? This is ridiculous...did you see her? How the hell can you possibly think that I could have done that?"

"We didn't accuse you," Craig said calmly.

"Oh, you didn't point at me and say, 'You! You, Elayne Anderson! You killed Annie Green.' No, you didn't do that. You hauled me in here. This is an interrogation. Well, guess what? I'm not an idiot. The point is, you have nothing on me. No evidence—because I didn't do anything. I fell, and I was terrified and that's it!"

Again, silence for a moment. Then Craig said, "Thank you, Elayne."

"That's it?" she asked.

"Of course," Brice said. "We were just hoping that you did know something, that you could help us."

"That's...it?" she repeated.

"Yes, that's it," Craig said. He smiled. "That's it. Thank you. When you head back in to be with Finn, will you ask Kieran to come in here?"

"Kieran?" she said.

"Yes," Brice said patiently. "We need to hope that she might have seen or heard something, had a sense of something. Because, of course, we know that someone besides the two of you had to have been down there. Although they were most probably gone before you got there—and that's why you are alive."

Elayne stood, shaking.

"I'll send Kieran in," she said.

When she was gone, Brice turned to Craig.

"What do you think?"

"Hard to tell," Craig said. "She got pretty defensive there. And the timing for when she went down in the cave is questionable. Her story might be true."

"What about the dead fiancé?"

"According to police reports, she wasn't with him at the time of his death."

"Convenient," Brice said.

"Well, there's this, too," Craig said. "We both saw the crime scene. There were a hell of a lot of boulders there. Heavy stones. I looked at her hands while she was speaking. Her hands are clean and nails weren't broken—she has a nice manicure."

"So," Brice murmured. "She might not have lifted all those stones."

"You're thinking she might have instructed someone else to do it?"

"Anything is possible," Brice said.

"Well, not anything," Craig murmured. "But there's still far too much that might be."

CHAPTER
FIFTEEN

"You're the psychologist," Craig said, staring at Kieran.

She stared back at him.

Glared, really, her gaze a question. He knew better. But he was frustrated.

"I'm a psychologist—not a mind reader. If you're asking me, yes, Elayne appeared to be absolutely hysterical. She was genuinely afraid."

"That's what I thought," Brice told Craig.

"Then again, she might have been really afraid—afraid that she was going to be caught."

Both men were quiet for a minute.

"Okay, so, we'll really question you," Craig said. "Tell us what happened from the beginning."

"I was waiting for you to keep exploring—you had gone outside to talk to Egan. Bracken, Danny and Mike were talking, and I thought I saw something on the wall. I moved toward it—and *wham*. I fell down a crevasse."

"And then?" Brice asked.

"I heard everyone coming, Danny calling out to me. I saw all the archways, and I went to one and went in and...tripped over Annie Green. I screamed—really screamed, raced back, stopped screaming—and heard a scream that wasn't me, but was Elayne. Next thing I knew, Craig, you were down, with me, and Elayne had thrown herself at you. And then you know what happened from there."

"Exactly where did Elayne come from?" Craig asked.

"The dark," Kieran said.

"Which archway?" Craig asked.

"I don't know... I think there were six. Six branches of the cave, going off into different directions."

Craig shook his head and dug into his pocket. He had Danny's maps. Rising, he spread them out on Finn's desk. Studying each, he said, "The first two show the aboveground caves. The third, this satellite image, shows a pattern of darkness beneath those. I thought it was just earth...now we know that there is a whole system beneath the main system. And the answers lie down there somewhere."

"So we'll start exploring again tomorrow," Kieran said. "We've got more manpower now—it may take a few days, but we should find what we're looking for—maybe not a treasure, but something."

"Should work that way," Brice muttered. "But we still don't know about those caves."

"Bracken knows what he's doing. He can't prevent a sudden cave-in, but when he's in the lead, we'll be fine," Craig said. "Although maybe Kieran should stay back," he added, turning to look at her. "I'm not sure that spelunking is your thing."

She just glared at Craig.

"Maybe we should bring Elayne in to the precinct," Brice said. "Hold her for twenty-four hours."

"I don't think that will work," Craig said.

"We have the authority—"

"Yes, but it would be a big mistake. Finn loves her, right or wrong. And he's a nice guy, but sharp as a tack. He'll have a million lawyers out in minutes flat. With the bodies, he can't prevent us from searching the island, but his lawyers could put all kinds of limitations on a search. I say we keep close watch on her for now—along with everyone else."

Brice sighed. "It's gotten late. How do we play this?"

"There are, what—six NYPD officers on the island now? And Egan has called in a few recruits. We need men at the entrances to the tunnels, and watching the house. The people in the house. We'll use our respective agencies, guarding through the night. Tomorrow, we start our search again," Craig said.

"I have another idea," Kieran said.

"What's that?"

"Watch those on the mainland. Get someone following John Smith and Jay Harding—and looking more deeply into the Believers."

"You're right. We'll get someone on it right away," Brice agreed.

Kieran stood up.

"What are you doing now?" Craig asked her.

"I'm going to go and help Evie. It is late, and no one has had anything to eat." She grimaced. "We can't call out for pizza."

"Good point," Craig said. "Dinner would be great."

Brice stood as well. "I want to stay on the island.

I'm imagining Egan will want to do so as well. I can crash on a sofa."

"You don't need to—there's enough room. And we can all get a decent night's sleep, since we'll have officers watching, and a new crew in the morning," Craig said.

"There goes our budget," Brice said. "I don't know how many men I can get the brass to commandeer for how long. Sometimes, we can't even summon the manpower to watch over witnesses before a big trial."

"Talk to Egan. See what the two of you can work out," Craig suggested. "I'll help with dinner."

"Please—don't," Kieran said. "I want to bond with Evie."

She left the office and headed back through the great hall to the White Room. As she passed by the stairway, she noticed Margie standing at the landing on the second floor, looking down at her.

"Are you all right?" Kieran asked her.

Margie shrugged. "As good as I can be. Two people—murdered. I suppose people are murdered every day. It's just that… Frank, and now that girl Annie."

"Yes, it's hard, and it's frightening," Kieran said. "I'm going to go see Evie, try to whip up something for the cops and us and everyone to eat. Would you like to help me?"

Margie just stared at her.

"Margie?"

"I'm not…um, Evie doesn't like me."

"I don't think she's fond of Elayne."

"No, but she doesn't like me. She tolerates you. You're with Craig. Besides, I'm sleepy, very sleepy."

"Okay, well, we'll have something thrown together for dinner, if you want to come back down in a bit."

"All right. I may just…sleep," Margie said. "I may take something and just sleep."

"Margie, you have to be careful—"

"I'm not going to overdose on sleeping pills," Margie said dryly. "But… I'd like to go to sleep, and stay asleep, for a good night."

"Okay. Please, be careful."

"I promise." Margie half-heartedly smiled, turned and headed to her room.

Kieran turned and saw the young officer standing at the door.

"I'd really love some dinner," he told her.

She smiled. "I'll do my best!"

She went into the White Room. Finn was still there, protectively holding Elayne. Danny was gone; Mike was standing by the door, talking quietly with Egan.

"I'm going to help Evie, get something going for dinner," she told them.

Just then, the housekeeper came through from the dining room. "I've already started a pot of stew," she said. "The meat is browning, but you may start chopping vegetables for me."

"Sure," Kieran said.

She followed Evie through the dining room and into the kitchen.

A massive pot was on the stove. Kieran hadn't thought herself hungry, but the smell of the meat keyed something inside of her.

The vegetables were already in a massive pile. Tons of potatoes, celery, onions and carrots.

Kieran set to the task, peeling and chopping. Evie stirred her meat mixture, and then turned to Kieran.

"I told you that woman was no good. I just wish that Finn would see it!"

"Evie, we don't know that she did anything," Kieran said.

"She was there, right? With a dead woman. Why else would she be there?"

"The medical examiner said that Annie Green had been dead several hours," Kieran said gently. "Elayne's story might well be true."

Evie sniffed. "The girl is trailer trash!"

Kieran kept working; she wasn't going to change Evie's mind.

When the vegetables were done and in the pot, she left Evie to stir her concoction and watch over it. Returning to the White Room, she discovered that Finn and Elayne were gone. Only Mike remained in the room. He'd found a chessboard and was playing a game against himself.

He looked up at her. "Egan is with Detective Brice and Craig, working out logistics for surveillance on the island." He shrugged. "Even murder doesn't change city budgets. But on the bright side, a lot of patrol officers are always looking for overtime."

"Danny went up to his room?"

"Some time back. He wanted to make sure that he called in and let Declan and Kevin know that you two are all right—surrounded by cops."

"I'm glad he thought of it."

"I'm sure you would have started getting phone calls," he said.

She nodded. "Dinner in about an hour," she told him.

"Great," Mike said. "Call me cold, but... I am hungry. Then again..."

"This is what you do," she said. "Can't do your best work on an empty stomach. Mike, do you mind if I go up to my room? I want to play around on my computer for the hour."

"Go ahead," he said.

Upstairs, she pulled out her computer, still wondering if anyone else had managed to go through it when she'd been out of the house.

She wasn't sure what she was looking for, but she started by searching Evie's name.

Evie didn't have any social media pages.

She tried for Victor Eider. Again, there was nothing.

She decided to try Jay Harding.

Jay Harding's name came up for dozens of pages. She began reading them. Most had to do with the history she already knew. A few had to do with the Believers.

On a registration page, she found a paragraph about joining.

"All are welcome! We are serious students of history, architecture and societies. We don't even ask that you accept our beliefs immediately, though we are called the Believers! We are a peaceful group, and our only limitations have to do with your respect for others in our group, and that, at all times, you keep an open mind."

A peaceful group?

She hesitated, but then pulled out her phone and called Jay Harding.

He answered immediately. "I heard the news! How horrible. I spoke to the cops. They wanted to know when I'd last seen Annie Green. She was with us, Kieran. She was with Ben and John Smith and me. And we all got off that boat Finn got for us at the docks in Brooklyn."

"After that?" Kieran asked.

"I already told the cops. We all went to hail taxis. I saw her get into a taxi."

"She didn't go with John Smith?"

"No. I thought they were a duo, too. But she didn't get in a taxi with John. Strange, huh, actually? I mean, I'd suggested that we all taxi together as far as Manhattan, but John said that he was tired, he'd prefer just getting his own to go straight home. Ben and I came in together, picked a block in between our apartments, and said good-night."

"Did you see her get into a taxi?"

"I saw her walk up to one."

"Thanks."

"Of course."

"I guess I'll never really see that island now," he said. "Oh, I'm sorry. That sounds horrible. And Annie seemed like such a lovely young woman. But…"

"I was also calling about your website."

"You still might really join?" he asked her.

"No, but I'm curious. Have you ever denied anyone membership?"

"Sure. I know you think I'm crazy, but I watch out for the crazies."

"What kind of crazy?"

"The kind who thinks that aliens are gods. Real gods—the kind who control the weather and life and death and all that kind of thing. I believe that there is other sentient life—in galaxies far, far away. Intelligent beings who know everything there is to know about string theory, black holes and time bending. I believe that they have been here. But they aren't gods. They are beings, similar to us. And my group is dedicated to historical research and scientific exploration. So we don't welcome anyone who is weirdly fanatical."

"Has anyone ever sounded...violent?"

"A few have been the postulating kind. Those who honor the gods will be rewarded, that kind of thing."

"Do you have a list of those people?"

"Um, I could put one together for you. Of course, I didn't meet them. I don't know these people. Some may have been kids, playing pranks."

"I'd really appreciate a list."

"Sure. And I'm so, so sorry to hear about Annie. Hey, by the way—am I a suspect?"

"I may even be a suspect," she told him. "Why? Can you help with anything else?"

"Nope. But there is a cop outside on the street. He's been there for hours now."

"He's watching over you, probably."

"Well, that's fine. I'll get you that list."

Another call was coming in before she could even hang up. It was Danny. "I may have something. Found something really cool. Where are you?"

"Next door."

"I should be FBI," he told her. "Where did I put my blue jacket...? Ah, there! Listen. Maybe nothing. Maybe something."

"What?"

"Give me ten minutes—then come over here, okay?"

"Danny!"

"Just ten minutes!"

"Okay." She hesitated. "You talked to Declan?"

"Yep."

"Good, thanks."

Danny laughed. "He was glad. And just so you know,

he said that it was a sad day when I was becoming more responsible than you!"

"Sad, indeed," Kieran said. She hung up, smiling. She turned back to her computer.

Craig was writing up an incident report, while Egan and Brice had been making calls when one of the uniformed officers came into the room.

"Excuse me, sirs, but I thought you'd want to know this right away. Our officer out the back said that he thinks he's seen someone up on the cliff. He was going to go up, but didn't want to leave his post and thought that you might want to get up there yourselves."

"You bet," Craig said, already up.

He started to head out when one of the bookcases caught his eye, and with a start, he realized there was another door in Finn's office. He hadn't seen it before, and he now knew why.

First, he hadn't been looking for a door, and it was covered by a bookshelf—except he saw now that the bookshelf was a door, just the kind of thing seen in an old horror movie. It was currently slightly ajar—no longer flush with the wall, and therefore, evident. He paused, annoyed that he hadn't noticed it and wondering at the same time if it would prove to mean anything.

He pushed it open.

It led to the enclosed back porch, and then out to the pool and patio and the path they would take to the top of the cliff.

"Go figure," Egan murmured.

"We didn't spend much time in the office before," Craig told Brice.

"Don't think it matters any," Brice said.

The pool and patio area were empty except for a uniformed officer. He was young, early twenties, and earnest. He seemed surprised to see the group pop out onto the porch from the previously hidden door.

"Sorry, I didn't know if I should run up, or…"

"You did the right thing. Do you still see him?"

Darkness had come in earnest. They still had something of a moon, but there was cloud cover. Craig strained to see, but the shadow of the cliff seemed to be all that was there. "I swear, I don't think he's one of ours," the officer said.

"Thanks, we're on our way," Craig said.

He walked quickly; neither Teddy Brice nor Richard Egan quite kept up with his pace. He hesitated, looking back, after he'd jogged around the pool to the rear of the patio, the trees and brush there—and the path.

"Go!" Egan told him.

Craig kicked up his pace; uphill wasn't easy, but adrenaline was with him. His muscles strained and he was panting, but he didn't really notice. Someone was on the cliff.

Bracken wouldn't have left the crime scene to wander the trails—not until the last tech had sailed away.

Unless someone had been beamed out of their rooms *Star Trek*–style, everyone was supposed to be in the house, *was* in the house.

He came closer and closer to the top of the ridge; shrubs and pines thinned out.

Then he paused, because he did see someone. A tall man, standing there, staring out.

"Hey!" Craig called.

The man turned.

It was John Smith.

He didn't run; he didn't move. He waited until Craig made his way to the crest of the cliff.

"What the hell are you doing?" Craig demanded.

"I had to come," Smith said simply.

"You had to come? How the hell did you get here?"

Smith just pointed down the cliff. There was a small motorboat offshore—a speedboat, a Donzi, Craig noted.

"You have your own boat?" Craig asked. "And you brought it in there—right in the middle of the rocks?"

Such an act was almost suicidal.

"I had to come," he said. "You wouldn't have let me. The cops wouldn't have let me. I saw the man downstairs, pacing in front of my building."

"And you walked right past him?"

"I went out the back."

Craig came closer. There were tears dampening the man's face.

"I loved her. I was an ass, so full of myself. But I loved her. I don't know… I don't know how she came to be here. I can't bear that…that she's dead." A loud sob escaped him. "I can't bear thinking about the way that she died."

By then, Egan and Brice had made their way up the trail. They stood single file on the narrow path, since there wasn't enough room for all the men at the space on the top.

"What the hell are you doing, man?" Brice demanded. "If you were about to jump—"

Smith swung on him with incredulity. "Jump? God, no! I just needed to be here, to look out on the water, to…try somehow to touch her, to understand, to believe…"

"If you want to believe, come to the morgue tomorrow. You can make the official identification—and speak to the medical examiner about when her body will be released," Brice said.

Smith stood there a minute. Then he said, "I had to come." He looked at them all as if they should understand perfectly. "I had to come. She died here. And I... I never let her know just how much she meant to me. I'm so afraid she came back here because of me, to find proof, to shine in my eyes."

Egan said calmly, "Or she might have come for herself, or another reason. We need to get off the cliff."

"I would never kill myself," John Smith said. "I just needed a moment..."

No, Craig thought. The man would never kill himself. He was too much of a narcissist.

"Well, you've had your moment," Egan said. "Let's get back down the cliff. We'll have someone see to your boat. And we'll get you back to your home via an escort."

When Smith hesitated, Brice said, "Let's go."

"Go—where?" Smith asked.

"Back to the house."

Smith lowered his head and nodded slowly.

Brice turned and started down the trail. Egan indicated that Smith should follow him. Once Smith was walking steadily downward, Craig looked to Egan. "You've got him?" Craig asked.

"Yes—what are you thinking?"

"Something I can't quite touch. I'll be a minute."

"Take care up here," Egan warned him.

Craig nodded, and peered out at the water, and then down at the rocks that looked like they'd been scattered below the cliffs, on the sand and out in the water by a giant hand.

The answer was so close he could touch it, he thought.

Annie Green. All the rocks by her.

She hadn't been killed by one person.

And neither had Frank Landon.

It looked as if it had been a true Biblical stoning... those who had condemned a man or woman to death carrying out the execution.

They weren't looking for one person, or even two people.

There had to be several involved.

And one had to have been part of the household.

Ten minutes were up.

Kieran walked over to Danny's room and tapped on the door.

He didn't answer.

"Danny!" she said, tapping again.

There was no reply. She opened his door and looked in.

Danny wasn't the neatest individual she had ever met, and his things were strewn around the room. She might have expected that. But she felt uneasy.

As she had felt sometimes in her room, as if someone had been in there when she had been gone, someone who left things carefully as they were, just ever so slightly askew.

"Where the hell did he go?" she muttered to herself.

She wasn't sure whether to wait or not, and decided to give him another five minutes before searching for him.

As she waited, she wandered the small hallway in

the attic. She was impatient, and her strides became longer and longer.

As she paced, she noticed that a door leading to one of the little rooms at the end of the hall was partially open. She knew that Evie had a room up in the attic, as did Victor.

She wandered to the room and looked in.

It wasn't a bedroom. It was more of a supply closet—but as large as the small bedrooms. There were shelves with linens, shelves with cleaning supplies and a stand filled with brooms and mops.

She started to leave when she noticed that there was another door at the side of the room. She frowned, curious. She should have been at the end of the attic, the end of the rooms, and the wall should have been the wall to the house.

She walked over to the door; it was ajar.

It led to a narrow winding staircase.

"Danny," she muttered.

She thought she saw light at the bottom. Danny must be down there; he had explored without her, and without anyone else.

She stared downward and realized what they had found. When the "employees" had been called "servants," the stairs had been the help's way of getting to and from their rooms. The winding staircase probably led to the second floor of the house, and then down to the first floor.

She looked around the room, searching the shelves for a flashlight. She found several in a box, with batteries nearby. Picking one up, she headed down the stairs.

"Danny?" she called softly.

He didn't reply.

She reached the landing on the second floor and tried the door to exit.

It was locked.

She kept stepping downward, certain that on the first floor the stairs would empty into the kitchen. She found a door, right on the bottom, one that should have led to the family room or the kitchen—maybe it had once opened onto the porch that had become the family room.

That door, too, was locked. She raised a hand to knock at it, but then didn't; maybe they weren't supposed to know about the stairs.

And the staircase kept descending.

She hadn't even thought about the house having a basement, which, of course, it naturally would—a foundation cut into the earth and the rock by the shore, something to keep the huge old mansion standing.

She kept going downward until she came to the last step; the place had the same smell as the caves. It wasn't a bad smell, it was a smell of earth and dampness and enclosure.

There was another door.

She tried the knob, and it opened.

She had, indeed, come to a basement. It was filled, as might be expected, with supplies. Woodworking tools, rakes, lawnmowers—pool supplies.

"Well," she murmured to herself, "I did say from the beginning that I needed a map not just for the caves, but for the house."

She saw another door to her side. And that door was cracked open just a bit.

Kieran hesitated, but then she saw something caught in the door's latch.

She moved forward and touched it, pulled it from the latch.

It was a piece of cloth—blue.

Like the jacket Danny had been wearing.

Kieran opened the door and shone her light into the darkness.

It was a tunnel.

Kieran was certain it had to be the way someone in that household had been slipping out, night after night, despite the fact that law enforcement officers had been living in the house.

Someone had slipped out and stoned Annie Green to death.

She needed to turn back, find Craig and Egan and Bracken and Mike and whatever cops she could, but as she turned to do so, she heard her name called.

"Kieran!"

It was Danny, and there was something about his voice.

He needed help.

"Please, Kieran!"

She paused again, wincing.

He wasn't far; he was just ahead. And he might be hurt. All she had to do was get to Danny, and get back to the stairwell...

Her brother was there, ahead in the darkness.

She had no choice.

Yes, she did. What if it wasn't even Danny's voice? What if he was being forced to cry out to her? Could he be forced to cry out to her?

If she rushed in, they could both be killed.

She pulled her cell phone from her pocket, but, as

she had half-expected, a large No Signal message immediately appeared.

Instead of heading into the tunnel, she raced her way back up the winding stairs, across the attic hallway and then down the main staircase. There was no one on the second landing; an officer was still standing guard, she could see him at the front door. She didn't go to him, but rushed into the office, thinking she'd find Craig.

Craig wasn't there, but Bracken was. He was studying maps laid out on the table.

"There's more to this. Obviously, the satellite image can't see beneath the beneath, if that makes any sense—" he began.

"Bracken, where's Craig?"

"He, Brice and Egan are out on the docks. Found John Smith on the island—brought himself in on a motorboat—fool is lucky he isn't dead."

"Smith," she murmured, shaking her head. "Bracken, you have to come with me. I'm afraid that my brother is in danger. We have to move very fast—please!"

"All right," he said.

"Just follow me."

He did; they ran back up the stairs and he followed her into the supply room and then to the door, and then down, down.

"Kieran, this is amazing. We should have torn the house apart first. Who would have figured though? This is fascinating, wonderful…"

"Danny disappeared into the tunnels," Kieran said. "I'm terrified for him."

"There's a tunnel…?"

"Here!" She opened the door to the tunnel from the house, splaying her light over it.

Without hesitating, Bracken said, "All right, let's go."

She listened; she couldn't hear anyone. But Bracken was with her now. She started hurrying forward. At this point, she thought, she was probably skirting the pool. The footing beneath her seemed solid.

She stayed away from the walls.

She had to stop, gasping. "I thought he was closer. I heard my brother. Bracken—"

She turned around. Bracken was staring at her.

He appeared to be confused.

Then he fell, flat to the earth in the tunnel.

CHAPTER
SIXTEEN

Craig stood on the dock and watched the little police patrol boat moving away, taking John Smith back to Brooklyn.

"Well, he's gone," Egan said.

"That's what we said about Annie Green," Brice murmured. "But there's a two-man team onboard—at least he'll get to the mainland."

"I'm going to go around and get his boat," Craig said.

"You don't have to do that," Egan told him. "We can get one of the officers to go for it."

"I'm actually pretty good with boats—and he has that thing up in the rocks. I'm also thinking it will help me figure out exactly how he got in—and how he landed there and got up the cliffs. There's no real path from the beach. Anything in that area is treacherous," Craig said. "Let Bracken, Mike and Kieran know what I'm doing," he said.

"It's night now, in earnest. Dark as hell," Egan warned.

"I've explored several times. I'm not going up the cliff again. I'm just going to try to figure out how the hell Smith did it."

"We could have asked him," Brice said. "But he could have lied."

"He seemed pretty broken up over Annie's death. It remains to be seen whether that was real or not," Egan noted.

"He might be a killer—or he might just be an idiot," Craig said. "Anyway, I'll get that boat around as quickly as possible, and then, I'm hungry as hell. I'll have some of whatever Kieran and Evie have concocted for dinner."

He left them. He heard Brice and Egan talking as he skirted the house. There were officers at the doors, front and back. No one would be going anywhere.

He headed to the cliff path, searching for another way to the top of the cliff—and to the second entrance into the caves.

Daylight would have been better.

But eventually, halfway to the cave entrance, he found a small break in the pines. Walking through it, he found more brush. Frustrated and ready to turn back, he noted that areas of the bushes had bent. Some had broken. He moved in that direction, and, beyond that little patch, he saw a clear path. It led down to the shore, he was certain.

The path would have made it easy for an intrepid boatman—as John Smith apparently was—to come to shore by way of that rocky eastern slope. Pull in, make use of one of the treacherous rocks to tie up, hurry up the cliff. Maybe the trail was even visible from the water.

Craig had moved halfway down the path, but he turned and hiked back upward again. Frank Landon's killers might have used this path to take his body from the caves where he was killed down to the shore below. If that was the case, there should be more broken brush and clues that a body had been dragged through. Maybe even blood.

He shone his light over the brush, searching.

Why hadn't the killers done the same thing with Annie Green's body? Why had they left her in the cave?

Most probably, they hadn't had time to dispose of the body.

Which meant that Elayne Anderson could have been one of the killers; she might have come screaming through the cave, acting hysterical, to ward Kieran off...to stop her accomplices from being discovered.

If Elayne was guilty, at least she wouldn't be getting off the island that night. The officers were covering the house, front to back.

But what if there was something they all had missed? Something basically in plain sight, so common they had missed it?

Could a person come and go through the windows? They weren't close to the ground, and Finn had seen to it during the renovations that he'd installed storm windows as well.

Craig suddenly froze.

A scream?

He thought he'd heard something. He paused. Now there was nothing. And yet...

What he had heard had been distant. As if had come from a long way away.

Or...

From right beneath his feet.

He turned, and started moving as quickly as he could back toward where he could get into the caves.

His phone buzzed.

It was Egan.

"We've got a problem," Egan told him.

Bracken was breathing. But he appeared to be knocked out.

Kieran felt for his pulse; he definitely had one, and it seemed to be working fine.

"Bracken!" Kieran shook him. He made some kind of a sound, but he didn't open his eyes.

Had he been drugged? She suddenly remembered talking to Margie about her sleeping pills.

Bracken wouldn't have taken pills.

Except that they might have been given to him in coffee, in water, in something.

She stood. Bracken was of no help, but it was obvious that—police on the island or not—the killers were still busy.

She had just come to that thought when she heard a scream—a long, terrified scream.

She shone her light just in time to hit Margie Appleby right in the eyes.

Margie gasped, stopping, bending over and drawing desperately for breath.

She looked like hell. Her hair was tangled; her clothing dirty.

"Margie!" Kieran said, hurrying over to her. "What happened? What the hell are you doing down here?"

"It was Elayne!" she said.

"Elayne...dragged you down here? How? She's with Finn."

"No, no, she's not with Finn. She came to me." She paused, staring at Kieran. "And now you're here. How are you here? Are you...did you come alone?"

"I'm alone right now. I'm looking for Danny."

"Danny? Why would your brother be here?"

"Never mind."

"How are you here?"

"The same way you are—the door from the supply room."

"Oh!" Margie seemed surprised.

"Margie—"

"Elayne, she begged me to come, she...she said that the treasure was in one of those archways, and if we didn't get there...come! Come with me, quick."

She grabbed Kieran's hand, enticing her to come along.

"Wait, Margie—have you known about this entrance all along?"

"Me? No, of course not!"

"How did Elayne know about it?"

Margie swallowed hard. "I guess... I guess... Elayne has always had her ways. Maybe she talked to Frank and he let her know what he was doing, what he'd found."

"Wouldn't he have told you?"

"He knew I hated him crawling around in the caves. I was afraid that he'd get hurt. Though I never even thought that he'd be...killed. I—I told you! Elayne has her ways."

Kieran tugged back, hard and determined; she was now far from the house, Bracken was on the ground and she was seeing no sign of Danny.

They were probably halfway to the area she had fallen in, if she was any judge of distance. The spot where Annie Green had been killed. "All right, that's it. Just where are we going?" Kieran demanded.

"Here!" Margie said.

Kieran shone her light around. They were in another cave. Rocks covered the earth here, large and small.

"Here? What's here?" Kieran asked.

A light flashed from one of the archways; Elayne came hurrying toward them, holding an electric lantern that lit the whole space as she entered.

"Don't believe a thing she says. Margie is just a bitch. Jealous—because Frank did talk to me."

"Never jealous of you," Margie said.

"Ladies, this is crazy. We have to get out of here. Agent Silverheels's been knocked out—he's out on the ground back there…"

She broke off.

For a moment, she was certain that her mind was going, that she was having a vision, or that she was in the middle of a bizarre nightmare.

Some *thing* was coming out of one of the archways.

Its eyes were brilliant…as if light poured from them.

It was hooded; its face was almost comically long, the mouth stretched out as if in an eternal scream. It was tall, the size of a man…

An alien. One of Frank Landon's *aliens*…

It was a costume, of course. But it was an excellent alien costume.

And the man beneath it was certainly a killer.

"Run!" Kieran said. "Go, go, go!"

She turned to run.

But Margie let out a high-pitched, terrified scream. Kieran stopped.

The woman was just standing there. And Elayne was just standing there. And the alien figure with the hood and cloak and pointed head and burning eyes pushed between them.

Margie started to laugh.

"Fooled you, huh?"

Kieran didn't reply at first; she just stared at the three.

"Yes, I guess you did." Kieran's mind was whirling as the pieces fell into place. "But you were with Frank a long time, so I heard."

"He was one hell of an investment," Margie said with a shrug. "Yes, I knew that Frank was working with Finn Douglas, and there were all kinds of rumors that the island was going to become a project for Finn and… like I said, sometimes investments take time. But that's the way it might be when you really want something."

"And all this time, the grieving, consoling and being afraid…and just now, it definitely sounded as if you hated one another," Kieran told her. "You're both really good actresses. Pity—you could have taken that talent to the stage." She was stalling for time.

Why? No one knew she was down here. Just Bracken Silverheels, and he was lying on the earth, out cold.

And still…it was natural to try to stall if someone wanted to kill you.

Elayne laughed. "I think we really have come to hate each other. But that's no matter. We have a goal, and I'm afraid…well, you wandered into this."

"Couldn't leave well enough alone," Margie said.

"How did you sneak away from Finn?" Kieran asked.

"Maybe he's involved," Elayne suggested.

"Good try. But I don't believe that. Not for a minute."

"You believed me today…when I was oh so scared," Elayne said.

"I believed you were scared, but in all truth, I thought that you might have been scared of being found out—of us not buying your story. And no one has bought it—this place will be crawling with cops by tomorrow. But seriously, how did you get away from Finn?"

"His evening warm milk," Elayne said.

"I did tell you that I had sleeping pills," Margie said smugly. "And you thought that I might injure myself! How sad, how sweet."

"So, who is the alien?" Kieran asked. "I mean, you two are here—right here, showing yourselves. Why is he in costume?"

"In honor, of course," Margie said. "In honor of those who came before."

Elayne moved forward slightly, winking at Kieran and whispering. "I'm just after the money the bank robbers hid. We know it's here somewhere."

The "alien" made some kind of an irritated, grunting sound.

"Oh, well, yes, I guess we have to get to it," Elayne said.

She stooped and picked up a rock.

Margie did the same.

And then the alien followed suit, picking up a very large boulder.

Craig made it to the cave opening, rolled in and staggered as he fell to the ground.

He listened; nothing.

But he was certain that he had heard a scream, and with what Egan had told him, he was almost positive that there were people in the caves—despite all the cops—and that, for the killers, things were unravelling.

That made them all the more dangerous.

He hurried through the part of the tunnel he'd come to know well.

The crime scene unit had been all through this area—collecting blood-spattered boulders.

He found the opening to the lower level of the caves and slid through it. The ropes that Bracken had set up were still in place.

The area below was marked up with numbers, tape and other paraphernalia left behind by the crime scene crew.

He heard something and paused. Not a scream again, but a shuffling sound.

Rats? Other creatures?

He looked around.

Six archways—which the hell one did he take?

Not the one where Annie Green had lain dead.

He wished that he'd seen when Elayne Anderson had come hurtling into the room. He wished he could even figure a trajectory…he could not.

If in doubt, Egan had once told him, go in a straight line.

Egan hadn't been referring to caves. But at the moment, it was all that came to mind. He started through the archway directly across from the drop. Even as he moved, he thought he heard a sound…a soft, swift sound, as if someone had accidentally scratched a watch or some other metal object against the cave wall.

He drew his gun, bringing it up under his flashlight, and moved very slowly, pausing just before the curve in that arch that would lead to a chamber in the caves—or another tunnel. He stepped out, gun aimed.

"Craig! Bloody hell, don't shoot! It's me!"

Danny was standing just inside the archway—holding a huge boulder over his head, ready to strike as well.

Danny dropped his boulder.

"What the hell are you doing here?" Craig demanded.

"I found an entrance to the caves from the house, and when I came down... I heard voices. I was trying to avoid whoever it was—they were chanting or something, and I sure as hell knew that it wasn't you and Mike or Bracken...if any of you chants, you don't do it on the job!"

"Did you scream?"

"Scream? No, no, that wasn't me...but..."

Craig felt something seem to freeze up in his veins.

"You didn't come down here with Kieran?"

"No! I was going to meet her in my room and tell her what I'd found, but I decided to head down the back hidden staircase in the house and follow it first. But... oh, God!"

Danny was suddenly ashen gray.

"I wouldn't have been in my room when Kieran came to look for me. But she didn't know where the door was...and even if she found it, she wouldn't have come down here alone—she'd have gone for you or Mike or Bracken...or Brice or Egan, right?" He paused, wide-eyed. "Oh, God. She could be down here."

"Which way did you come from?" Craig demanded.

"That's just it... I'm not sure. I was going to try to get out this way, and then go back to the house."

Craig grabbed him by the shoulders. "Danny, damn it! Which way did you come from?"

Danny shook himself free. "Hey! She's my sister! Don't you think…"

His voice trailed as he considered. "That way—that way. And listen, you can hear…you can hear voices!"

They began to move; slowly at first, throwing their lights along the cave walls. It was a maze. At one point, Craig thought they had gone in circles.

They could heard voices now—murmured at first, excited, angry.

Laughter.

"It sounds like it's…next to us," Danny whispered.

"Yes, but where…"

They moved again, looking for the closest opening.

They found an arch and slipped through it.

And then, they could hear voices clearly.

"You are condemned! Kieran Finnegan, the Gods of the Universe find you guilty of tampering with their most holy relics. You are condemned. As ancient holy judges of history have ordered, thus shall you face execution! Bow down that your suffering may be less!"

Craig couldn't be sure of the voice; he didn't know if it was masculine or feminine.

"Like hell, you idiot! I will fight you tooth and nail, and if I lose, well, this is a federal case, and you can face death yourself—as dictated by the laws of the United States of America!"

Those words were spoken by a voice he knew well. Kieran.

And she continued. "They will find you. The FBI and the police will find you, and you will pay, I promise you!"

"Where the hell are they?" Craig raged.

"There, another opening, down low… Craig there!" Danny said.

And Danny was right.

There was another low crack in the cave wall. Craig dropped low to the ground and rolled, followed by Danny.

They were down a corridor. Craig almost dropped his own light and ran, Danny's flashlight guiding him. But he forced himself to creep slowly toward the sound, where he could see faint light glowing ahead down the tunnel.

Then he saw them. Lit up by an electric lantern set on the ground.

He was in back of a tall person wearing a cloak. They held a huge boulder.

And there were Elayne and Margie, also holding large stones and heading toward Kieran.

But Kieran held her own rock—and she threw it with a vengeance.

It hit Margie hard in the hand; she screamed and dropped her rock. The cloaked creature raised his boulder, starting forward.

"Drop it! Now!" Craig roared out.

Margie and Elayne saw Craig at the same time, and they shrieked and started running.

The tall person in the cloak was still moving toward Kieran, quickly. From this angle, Craig could see that it wore a ridiculous alien mask.

"John Smith! Stop—or I will shoot!"

The alien swung around and came at him running, bellowing out something in a fury. He was nearly upon Craig with the boulder.

Craig squeezed the trigger, and shot the figure in the center of the chest.

The alien jerked and collapsed, and the mask fell away from his face.

It was John Smith.

Kieran came running toward Craig, skirting around the fallen man, rushing into his arms. He took a moment to hold her. Danny came in from behind him. He threw his arms around both Craig and Kieran.

Then Kieran pulled away.

"Craig, they're involved in this...both Elayne and Margie. They planned it all together. Margie managed to get close to Frank...she called him an investment. And she introduced Elayne to your cousin. But... John Smith. Bracken said that he was on a boat out of here."

"He was. He knocked out the captain and threw another officer overboard. Then he drove the boat back here, leaving it adrift once he'd landed. The coast guard got a distress signal the captain managed to get out— Smith didn't hit him hard enough to kill him. Egan let me know he was probably coming back here." He hunkered down by Smith, checking the man's pulse. There was none. He stood.

"Come on—we have to catch up with Margie and Elayne before they get back and maybe have a chance to take someone by surprise."

"They're not armed...except with stones," Kieran said.

"We've seen what they can do with those rocks," Danny said.

They started down the length of the tunnel—heading the direction in which Elayne and Margie had fled.

Craig took the lead with his gun still drawn, flashlight in the other hand, held tight to it.

"They've gotten away," Danny murmured.

They rounded a corner, and Craig's light played upon a trio.

Bracken Silverheels was still on the ground.

He was struggling to see against their lights, suddenly glaring into his face.

And Elayne and Margie were both on the ground as well.

"Bracken!"

Craig ran to the other agent.

Elayne was showing the first signs of a good whack to the jaw, as she was struggling to rise, held around the legs by one of Bracken's arms.

Margie had been knocked flat.

"How did you know?" Kieran whispered.

Bracken indicated Elayne. "This one…she gave me the coffee! And that one…well, she was just running with her, and so she looked like trouble to me."

CHAPTER
SEVENTEEN

Saturday, 7:00 a.m.

"I'm a rich guy. Rich guys get taken," Finn said, his tone dull.

He might not have believed them, that Elayne had been in on the plot that killed Frank, even when the place was flooded again with a crime scene team and more cops than ever before—had it not been for Elayne herself.

Handcuffed and headed for the dock, she had screamed vitriol at them all. And Margie had screamed at her—telling her to shut up.

Kieran reflected that Margie was right—they might have gotten away with much more, if Elayne hadn't been shouting that they were all the rich elite, continually preying upon others.

Detective Brice—who was standing next to Kieran and Danny when the women had been taken away, shook his head. "I guess she doesn't know the pay scale for NYPD cops. When I first started, I was constantly on overtime to pay for my ten-by-ten piece of an apartment."

"She did have a rough life," Kieran said.

But Craig shook his head. "We have friends who've been through worse, and they didn't become killers."

Now, Elayne and Margie were gone; Craig had given the arrest to Egan, who was taking them in. Craig would have to be cleared for the shooting of John Smith, but that would come. For the moment, Kieran knew that he wanted to stay on the island—to be close to Finn. And, so, while it was a ridiculous hour, Mike, Bracken, Danny, Craig and Kieran were sitting with Finn in the White Room, trying to make sense of it all.

"I slept with her," Finn said. "Every night. How did I not see?" He looked at Kieran and asked, "She said that Margie purposely hooked up with Frank—and made a point of seeing that Elayne and I were thrown together?" He shook his head. "She *murdered* Frank?"

"She had to have been in on it," Kieran said. "But, Finn, you weren't just blindsided. They were willing to put in a lot of time. They made a point of ingratiating themselves—very insidiously. You wouldn't have realized what was going on—it was all an 'investment,' as they told me. You needn't feel that there was some little thing you didn't notice."

"I was taken, completely taken," Finn said dully. "How could I have been so duped? Why didn't they murder me?"

"Finn, it was so well staged," Kieran said.

"I'm sure Brice will have more answers eventually," Mike said.

"The way I see it, they must have known John Smith for years—though why he was quick to ridicule Jay Harding... Honestly, I think greed was his real motive. The man coveted artifacts. I think he played off what he knew about the Believers and possibly pretended he thought aliens were gods who would come again and reward him. Finn, they were good. Really, really, good. Egan told me that the boat was hardly away from this dock when Smith clocked the captain and his mate."

"He had to have known he'd be caught," Finn said.

"They would have had a story planned for everything—and they might have made those stories ring true," Craig said. "He could have said the boat had hit the rocks or something of the sort—and that he'd barely escaped with his own life. And I think that they carried out some kind of a ceremony in the caves—honoring the alien gods that the Believers thought had come to Earth. That's why the alien costume. That's why Frank wrote the word *aliens* in the sand—they killed him in their alien garb. Elayne and Margie didn't intend to be found down there, but..." He paused, looking at Danny and Kieran. "Danny found the passage from the house. And Kieran followed her brother. They were going to have to get rid of Kieran—they didn't know yet that Danny was down there."

"They would have figured it out," Kieran said. "I didn't realize... I asked them if they'd seen Danny before I knew what was going on."

"Wow! Thanks, sis."

"Hey, I was worried sick about you."

"But..." Finn looked so lost. Kieran walked over to the chair where he was sitting and slipped her arm around him. "Listen, as Craig likes to point out, I'm a psychologist—and I didn't see how deep the problems were with any of them."

"That's the gift of people like that," Craig said. "The alien mask was nothing compared to the one John Smith wore every day of his life."

"I slept with Elayne—and didn't know that she was getting up night after night…"

"Probably not every night," Mike said, hoping to be helpful.

"And she whacked you with some powerful sleeping pills—every night," Bracken said. He lifted a hand. "I can attest to just how powerful."

"Why didn't they kill me?" Finn asked in a whisper.

"You were their ticket to the island," Craig said. "If something had happened to you, your father would have been found in deepest Africa—or wherever he is on safari or whatever—and brought back. The island would be closed down again."

"So, I'm alive because they needed me," Finn said bleakly.

"Yes," Bracken said.

It was morning, and no one in the house had slept. The police and more agents had been there through the night. Danny, Bracken, Craig and Kieran had given statements. A medical examiner—they didn't get Hodges this time—had come out for the body of John Smith. Another crime scene crew had come out.

Brice had properly arrested Elayne and Margie.

It had all taken time.

"I should just blow up this island," Finn said.

"The island doesn't create bad things, Finn," Craig said. "People come in good and bad."

"And," Kieran added, "you aren't just rich, Finn.

You're a good man. A really good man. And the thing is, this plot has been going on a long, long time. Change the way that the island is seen—and you'll stop the bad. Oh, wait! To be honest, if you open a resort, you'll still have a bad penny or two out here. Someone lifting a wallet. Someone skipping out on a bill. But you'll also provide an incredible little break for hundreds—thousands— of people. You're hurting—of course, you're hurting. Your best friend was killed, and you were betrayed by the woman who supposedly loved you. That's pretty bad—no one can say that it isn't. But you're stronger than that. You may be rich, but you're one of the kindest and most caring rich men out there. Keep using your money for good."

Finn almost smiled. "And I have family," he said quietly. "My cousin, who came out to help me."

"You have family," Craig assured him.

Finn frowned suddenly. "John Smith…he played an amazing game. He must have killed Annie Green, too, and he acted as if he was the most heartbroken man in the universe. I would have sworn that he really loved her!"

"Maybe he did. And maybe she crossed him," Mike suggested. "Working that closely with him, she would have either had to be in on it at some point, or she figured it out."

"Kieran, he was a psychopath?" Finn asked.

"Sociopath, I'd say."

"What?" Finn asked.

"A psychopath is a man like the serial killer Ted Bundy. He had no empathy for anyone at all—he and his desires were all that mattered. Absolute narcissist—and able to be absolutely charming and appear to care. John

Smith was a hell of a narcissist, thinking himself all-important—but I agree that he cared for Annie Green. And it did hurt him. So…"

Evie came into the room from the kitchen. "None of you has eaten since yesterday. The stew is even better now, it's been on warm for hours, and I…" She sighed, letting out a long breath. "Well, obviously, no one around here has been sleeping, so I've stirred, and kept it good, and…it's the least I can do."

Mike rose. "Nothing like a good stew for breakfast!"

Evie stood still for a minute, as if she wanted to say something to Finn. Maybe tell him that she had warned him about Elayne.

She apparently decided that it was not the time.

"Set places for yourself and Victor," Finn said. "Please, eat with us. I know Victor is up somewhere. He'd never sleep when all this was going on, when he was trying to help out here and there all night, I'm sure."

"Of course!" Evie said.

Kieran hopped up to help her. She started to follow Evie into the kitchen, and then she paused. "Finn, I found a medal by the bushes. I believe it belonged to Frank. I don't think that Craig will need it for any kind of evidence now. If you'd like to have it…"

"Yes, please," Finn said.

"I gave it to Egan, but I'll get it back," Craig assured his cousin.

Kieran went on in to the kitchen with Evie.

"I'll bring the stew out in the pot," Evie said. "If you would grab dishes…let's see, there will be eight of us. Dishes…silver…glasses. And I'll set out a big pitcher of iced tea. Or…do you think that the agents would like beer? I imagine that they're off duty now?"

"I think tea will be fine. Everyone is moving on adrenaline right now—when we've eaten, I imagine everyone is going to want to go to bed."

"Of course. I'm just so worried about Finn. Maybe he's going to need something to help him sleep."

"I'm pretty sure that the last thing he's going to want right now is something to make him sleep," Kieran said.

"Oh, maybe you're right," Evie said. "I told him. I could tell. I just didn't like her. And, from what I heard, at least John Smith was crazy. Crazy as a loon! Alien gods. That Elayne...she was just after the bank robbers' money."

"So it seems," Kieran murmured.

"Tell everyone it's ready. I'll go get Victor—he's just been sitting out back by the pool," Evie said. "He...well, he knows how upset Finn is... Victor is a wonderful man—just awkward."

Kieran didn't think that Victor was awkward, but Evie had her opinions and she wasn't going to change them.

Kieran went to the White Room and summoned the others to the dining room. As they gathered, everyone quietly filled bowels with stew, broke the bread and politely passed the tea around.

"Evie, this is wonderful," Danny said as they all sat to eat.

Evie beamed.

Finn turned to Craig. "You won't leave right away, will you?"

"No. It's—Saturday. Come Monday, I'll be on desk duty anyway, until paperwork comes through. I'm sure Egan will give me a day or two. Kieran..."

"My bosses are great. Unless there is something urgent at the office, I'm sure I'll be fine for a few days off."

"Mine may make me work," Danny said glumly. Then he brightened. "Finn, we should talk. I could do some terrific history lessons out here, once you're up and going."

"Do you think anyone will want to come out here?" Finn asked.

"Yes. We're New Yorkers, and New Yorkers are tough," Kieran said. "People have taken offices in the new World Trade Center Complex. They dine at restaurants where Mafia dons were gunned down. We don't stay down around here—we get back up."

Finn smiled at her. "Thanks," he said. "You're right."

"I'd like to stay on awhile, Finn, if I may," Bracken interjected. "The cave system is fascinating to me, and it would be good to get it properly mapped. I'd like to bring in some other folks, too."

"More FBI?" Finn asked.

Bracken shook his head. "I have friends I've done cave dives with—this isn't a cave dive, but a cave dive is even more complex. Rock climbing friends—and friends with whom I've done explorations in caves in Mexico and various places."

"Of course," Finn said. "Maybe all the treasures will cease to elude us all." He shook his head. "To think of it…do you think that John Smith killed the bank robbers?"

"We don't know that. Maybe once Elayne and Margie start talking, we will. In fact, at some point, I intend to have a talk with Elayne and Margie myself. We didn't get much out of them last night—and, maybe not Margie, but Elayne will eventually say whatever we want to hear. She'll be the one who is going to want a deal. Egan called me while you were helping set up the food, Kieran," Craig said, turning to her. "They both clammed up. The detectives deemed it best to let them spend a night in jail awaiting arraignment. Then they'll try talking. Of course, they both said that they wanted attorneys."

"They won't be getting any help from me," Finn said quietly.

"They do need to talk," Mike said. "But I know one thing—they didn't find the bank robbers' haul."

"Because?" Danny asked.

"If they had, Elayne would have been long gone with her riches."

Evie apparently couldn't stand it any longer.

"Oh, Finn! I did try to tell you!"

"Evie," Victor Eider murmured.

"Victor, it's true."

"Evie, please, it doesn't help!" Victor said.

"It's all right. Evie was right," Finn said.

Danny hopped in immediately. "I guess I wouldn't make much of a cop. I thought it was going to be Jay Harding—with his Believers!"

Kieran almost spoke up. But she didn't.

Jay had told her about people he hadn't let in. He was getting her a list.

A list of people who were fanatics.

Craig might have been reading her mind. "Harding and his group may have believed some things that stretched credulity, but John Smith is a fanatic. The alien gods were his religion—and while religions should be wonderful and teach us the best of how to behave, any kind of fanatic becomes dangerous."

Everyone was silent after those words.

Danny filled the void, loudly yawning. "Wow. It's daytime. I feel like I have jetlag, except that I haven't been anywhere. I'm for bed."

"We should all try to get some sleep," Finn said. Seeming stronger, he stood. "I will see you all when I see you all."

"Finn, would you like something—" Evie began.

"No!" he said sharply. Then, being Finn, he quickly apologized. "No, thank you, Evie. I'd like to sleep—or not sleep—on my own."

The others rose as well. "We can talk more, work on things, when everyone has had some rest. This will…it will take time," Craig told Finn.

Finn nodded and impulsively hugged Craig. Craig seemed surprised for a moment, and then he hugged his cousin back.

Everyone bid everyone good-night.

When Kieran and Craig reached their room, Craig set his holster on the bedside table, took off his shoes and crashed down on the bed.

Kieran opened her computer.

"What are you doing?" he asked her.

"I spoke to Jay Harding before. He had told me that yes, the Believers actually turned people down—for being fanatics."

"Well, we found the fanatic."

"Still…"

He rose and came to stand behind her, slipping his arms around her.

"If you're restless, looking for a way to feel sleepy, I know a great one!"

She smiled, but checked her email. Jay hadn't gotten back to her yet.

"You know," she murmured, "something else bothers me. I do believe that John Smith loved Annie Green. And yet—he stoned her to death!"

"Fanatics—he was probably crying as he did it, but…"

"Yes, maybe," she murmured.

"Anything from Jay?"

"No. Not yet. He was going back through all of his applications and queries. I guess it might have taken some time, and it was late when I talked to him."

She turned into Craig's arms. "I guess at this point, another five minutes won't matter."

"Five minutes! Oh, ye of little faith!"

She laughed, and he pulled her out of the chair and into his arms.

His kiss was hot, wet and deep. They were quickly discarding their clothing and his lips fell everywhere on her flesh…still provocatively hot, wet and very deep.

Later, she rolled against him.

"Five minutes, huh?" he whispered.

And she curled against him, so sated, and so happy to be in his arms.

Saturday, 4:00 p.m.

Kieran was still sleeping.

Craig rose silently and headed to shower and get dressed.

When he came out of the tiny bathroom, she was still asleep. He walked over and looked down at her, and thought that he had to be one of the luckiest men in the world. Yes, she was headstrong—and could worry the hell out of him. But her determination to do the right thing at all times, to move forward…even her remarkable aptitude for diving into any situation…were all part of why he loved her so much. And, looking down at her, dark red hair splayed over the pillows as she slept, beautiful form half curled in the covers and half not, he smiled. She was so tempting as she lay there…

The better part of him insisted that he let her sleep.

Going down the stairs, he checked his phone for messages.

Both Brice and Egan had written him.

No news yet; the women were both meeting with their court-appointed attorneys.

If anyone was up yet, he thought, it would be Evie. If she wasn't up yet, he'd figure out how to make himself some coffee—not a hard task, but he hoped to find a small pot and not have to deal with making a giant carafe, which, he was sure, Evie often did.

But it wouldn't be a difficulty; Evie was up. She had just made coffee.

"You couldn't sleep?" he asked her.

"I'm worried about Finn."

"Don't be—he's stronger than he looks at times."

Bracken walked into the kitchen. "Anything from Egan or Brice?" Bracken asked.

"Nothing new—Elayne and Margie have both clammed up, waiting for their lawyers," he told Bracken. "So—"

"I'm going back to the caves."

"All right. I'm going with you."

"Sounds like a fine plan," Evie said. "But aren't the

tunnels still filled with all kinds of stuff left by the crime scene people?"

"Yes, and no—some tape, maybe. But they finished with what they needed to do." He turned to Evie. "Didn't you and Victor know about the door from the basement?"

Evie paused, thoughtfully. "I suppose… I mean, yes. I opened it one day, but it just led to a black hole!" She shivered. "I wasn't going into it! In fact, I never go to the basement, unless I absolutely have to. We haven't been here that long, you know. Victor and me. We were here a few days when Finn first wanted to get out here and start planning—then Victor and I went back home to pack up to stay out here awhile. But of course, you know that." She hesitated. "We weren't here when Frank was killed," she said softly. "I wish we had been. My poor Finn." Her face hardened. "But of course, he had his Elayne then. And I told him. I warned him!"

"We all know that, Evie," Craig said.

Bracken finished his coffee. "Well?" he asked, turning to Craig.

"I'm ready," Craig assured him.

"Don't you want something to eat?" Evie asked.

"I'm still full from the stew!" Bracken told her.

Evie smiled.

"Let's go through the basement entrance," Bracken suggested. "Follow everything that happened last night."

"Right. There has to be some kind of stash there—where John Smith would have been stowing his alien gear. He came by his own small boat, concealed it on the shore—and really had his whole thing planned out and going smoothly—at first."

"There should be a key to the door from this floor," Evie told him. "Not sure where… Wait! Oh, yes, it's in the drawer. I'll get it for you."

She did. Soon, Bracken and Craig were moving through the tunnel beneath the house.

"When the hell do you think this was dug?"

"Well, not until the house was built," Craig said. "I guess…whichever Douglas built it back then, he or someone right after him had it dug. They probably discovered some kind of natural formation when they were doing the foundations for the house."

"Probably," Bracken agreed.

They traveled deeper into the system.

Bracken paused at one point. "Right there. That's where the pills got me. I'd been feeling tired, and suddenly just couldn't go on."

"You probably should have gone to the hospital—God knows what they dosed you with."

"I was out like a light. I just fell. It was pretty powerful." Bracken was quiet for a minute, playing his light over the walls as they went along. "I wonder if she thought she gave me enough to kill me."

"She might not have estimated your size right," Craig said. "Then again, she didn't know you were coming out into the tunnels—she might have just wanted to make sure you were out for the night so that she could slip by you."

"Maybe, but I didn't need a hospital. Once I started to come to…" He paused smiling. "Right when the little piece of work was about to race by me!"

"There were cops all over—we would have gotten them."

"Probably. But I was really happy to get them myself."

Craig agreed. They had come to the place where he had met up with John Smith.

There was still blood on the ground.

"Okay, Danny and I came in through the other entrance. And I actually think that I can find my way back, but...there are other archways. And they wouldn't have used a tunnel that you walked through."

"Right. They would have found a little niche. You check right—I'll go left. And keep calling out to one another. It was really remarkably easy for John Smith to get on this island. I don't think we know nearly all of it yet."

Craig agreed. Bracken went one way, he went the other, checking out the tunnels.

"Anything?" Bracken called.

The cave made an eerie echo out of his voice.

"Nothing yet!" Craig called back.

He was very careful to stay in the center of each path. They were in the caves-beneath-the-caves already, but he didn't trust anything here.

He saw a smaller opening. Hunkering down, he saw that it could fit a body.

He crawled in.

And he called out. "Bracken!"

His voice bounced around.

"Yeah!"

"I've got something!" he called.

"Where?"

"Follow my voice. I'll keep talking. Or, I could sing. Never mind. I'll keep talking. I have something here...capes. And more of those ridiculous masks. Alien masks...they're made out of plastic. I'm betting you could find these about anywhere."

"I hear you. Where are you?"

"Look down. Very small archway."

Bracken dropped down beside him. With two lights in the little niche within the caves, the small area was clearly visible.

"Damn...there are a number of robes here. It looks like a cult was busy. One, two, three...four. Masks... there are more of these, too."

Craig sat back.

"Because we didn't get them all!" he said. He looked at Bracken. "We have to get out of here—fast. We have to get back to the house."

Craig was gone when Kieran woke; he never seemed to need much sleep.

Rising, she first checked her email.

Still nothing from Jay Harding.

She decided on a long, deliciously hot shower. Then she dressed—jeans and her boots, just in case.

Downstairs, she found Finn in the dining room, just finishing his coffee. Mike was there as well, also drinking coffee and studying his emails.

"Good morning," Kieran said. She looked at Finn. "Are you doing all right?"

"I'm fine, but... I need to walk, or something, I'm restless."

"If you want to walk, I'll go with you," Kieran volunteered.

"That would be nice," Finn said.

"Mike, do you want to come with us?" she asked. He

looked up from his email. "Is there something new?" she asked him.

"No, sorry. Everything is on hold," he said. "Neither Elayne nor Margie will talk to anyone until they've talked to their attorneys, and it's the weekend."

"Craig is—out?" she asked.

"Yes, sorry again! He texted me a bit ago, asked me to hold down the fort here, and so... I'm holding down the fort here, for whatever that's worth. Craig went with Bracken. They're back in the caves."

Danny wandered on in then. "Coffee!" he said. Then he quickly looked at Finn. "You okay?"

"Yeah," Finn said. "I'm okay."

"We're going to go for a walk," Kieran said. "Want to come?" She hoped that her look conveyed the fact that she wanted him to join them.

"Uh, sure! I'll just slurp down some coffee and be ready," he promised.

A few minutes later, they were outside. They went out by the back, and Finn paused to look at the pool. "The place is really beautiful, right?" he asked. "I'm going to let Bracken tear this place apart—as far as the caves go. I can hire more people. We can clear it all out."

"That sounds great," Kieran said.

"You never used the pool," Finn said.

"I did!" Danny assured him. "It is beautiful."

"I'm going to really enlarge it—I want a wading pool for young children. And we'll have a kiosk—love kids, but little ones... I want to make sure that we have a good brand of those pool diapers for the really little ones."

"Now, there's a plan, my man!" Danny said.

They left the pool area and started to climb.

"Hiking is great—and didn't Frank say you should

have horses or mules or something?" Danny asked Finn, panting slightly.

"Well, he said mules because of the landscape. I'm thinking horses—and rides that go around the island, and not up anything!"

Finn paused. Where they stood, they were nearly halfway up.

Kieran looked around. The sun was just beginning to lower in the sky, casting beautiful glows everywhere; shades of yellow and pink and mauve fell over the pines and the brush and rugged landscape. They climbed a bit higher, pausing near the cave entrance.

"I'm going to get down in there myself," Finn said. "It's time that I do it."

"Now?" Danny asked.

"No. I guess not. But I will."

Finn started walking again. They followed, nearing the great cliff that stood high over all—including the treacherous and rocky shoreline beneath.

"The view here…it's spectacular. And, yet, so dangerous!" Finn said.

Kieran's phone vibrated in her pocket. She drew it out, quickly looking to see if Craig had called her. The notice wasn't for a call.

It was a text message from Jay Harding.

Looked up people, sending you a list. But someone who wrote in sounding crazy was a Douglas. They signed their name as F. Douglas. Can't be Mr. Finn Douglas, but…thought I should let you know!

Kieran tried not to react; Finn was standing at the exact precipice of the cliff.

"Come here!" he told her. "You, too, Danny. Be careful, of course, but…this is part of what brought me here—this absolutely spectacular view!"

"Yeah! The views are amazing," Danny said, heading up to join Finn.

"No!" Kieran cried, racing after her brother. "Stop!"

And then she realized that she was standing there, and Danny was standing there…and jagged rocks were below, with the waves washing over them, whispering of death.

If it quacked like a duck, walked like a duck, it was a duck.

"Who the hell else?" Craig demanded, cursing beneath his breath. He wouldn't get a signal until he was out of the cave. "I couldn't accept it. I don't accept it. Finn has always behaved decently—generous with his giving… He's polite to everyone always, especially servers in a restaurant, even if things are going to hell. My aunt Deedee was the sweetest thing… Finn was always like her."

"Then maybe he isn't a duck!" Bracken said.

They finally burst out of the cave opening—the one that was halfway up the cliff.

"Why didn't I see it? I didn't want to see it—that's the reason. I thought I knew Finn. But who else could it have been? It was Margie, Elayne and Finn on the island the night that Frank was killed. And the two women aren't giving him up because they still believe that he'll do something, and he'll come to their aid. Of course, he couldn't have done so right away—we would have been suspicious."

"Craig, we know that others can get on the island."

"Finn must have known about the basement and the way through. And that may be why he had Evie and Victor go away—Frank was supposedly helping him with the island plans, but he knew that Frank was exploring, getting too close. Ah, hell, I could be wrong, but how the hell do we take the chance?"

"We don't take chances. We get to Kieran quickly, and we get to Finn," Bracken said.

Craig called Mike. He answered immediately.

"You found the treasure!" Mike said.

"No, no…where are Kieran and Danny?"

"They went for a walk with Finn."

"What?"

"They went for a walk. You know Kieran—she's trying to do anything to make Finn better."

"Mike, get after them. Get after them right away. Where are Evie and Victor?"

"Evie is working in the kitchen. Victor is out back. I'm just sitting in the White Room—holding down the fort."

"Leave the damned fort—go after Danny and Kieran. And," he paused, gritted his teeth hard. "And watch out for Finn."

"Finn?"

"There were alien outfits in the cave…a bunch of them. Finn… Just get going, circle the island until you find them! I don't know anything, except that something is still going on. And…and Finn just might be in on it."

"Danny!"

Kieran reached her brother. Finn was dangerously close to the edge, beckoning to them. "Isn't it beautiful?" he asked.

Kieran caught Danny's arm and pulled him back.

"Beautiful," Kieran agreed. "Sorry, I'm a little bit afraid of heights."

"I found Frank down there," Finn said.

"Danny, come on, get back!" Kieran said.

"Kieran, what's the matter with you? You were never afraid of heights. And I'm sure as all hell not afraid of heights!" Danny said.

Finn was frowning as he looked at her. "Hey, it's okay!" he said. Then he paused, staring past her.

Kieran quickly turned.

They weren't alone up on the precipice—there were two people there, smiling at them.

Victor and Evie.

Victor was wielding a gun.

"Victor. What the hell are you doing?" Finn demanded. "Why do you have that gun?"

"Because you're going to jump," Evie said.

"What?" Finn demanded. He was still confused.

Kieran wasn't surprised—she simply wanted to kick herself.

"They want us to jump off the cliff, down to the rocks," she said. "One of them used your name in an email to Jay Harding."

"That asshole!" Victor said. "The man has no guts—and no real belief. He said that I was a fanatic, and that I didn't understand the true philosophy of his group. He didn't understand! We're the chosen ones...we are to find the Ark of the Covenant, for the gods, and when we do, they will return. They are due the glory—we are but ants on this earth. There was no comprehension there at all—none! The gods have been protecting the island for decades and decades, *we* have protected the island, from the Douglas family…from all."

"I really do care about you, Finn, dear. We didn't want it to come to this," Evie said.

"Come to this? Are you crazy? I'm not going to jump!" Finn said.

"And you won't get away with it," Danny said. "The cops will know right away."

"They would…except that they'll never find us," Victor said. "Even if they bring in an army. But they won't. They'll bring old Jamie Douglas back from wherever he is, and he'll see to it that the island is shut up again, tighter than a drum."

"No," Kieran said. "Craig will find you. Mike and Bracken are still on the island. And they will hunt you down until they find you," she promised calmly.

Her heart was actually thundering. Die by a bullet— or by the rocks? Or be stung by a bullet, and fall…down upon the deadly edges of the rocks below?

"We just find them first," Evie said, giggling. "They sure don't think that the poor help will be after them with guns."

"I don't get it," Kieran said. "The two of you…and you got John Smith into this and Margie and…well, Elayne wasn't a believer. I get it. She and Margie were friends. Margie found Elayne and got her involved. But…how did you get John Smith into this?"

"Oh, silly girl—John Smith found us. He wanted in the worst way to get to the island."

"We made him prove himself, long ago. John is a true believer—not a fake like Jay Harding. Jay makes money off his articles and books and thinks he believes in our true gods. But John! He knew. And he proved himself."

"You were here when the bank robbers were killed—ten years ago?" Kieran asked.

"I don't believe this," Finn muttered.

"We worked for Jamie, and then Finn," Victor explained. "Of course, we knew the old bastard thought the island was cursed. Nothing to do with curses. We were appalled. Bank robbers, here, hiding their stash... here! On this sacred ground. John had just come to us—we were beginning to understand the caves and the system. And...the bank robbers had to die. Biblically. See, what you don't get is this—the Ark of the Covenant came out of Egypt with Moses—and the 'god' he talked to on the Mount was a true god, an alien. The alien way of death was taught to the ancient Hebrews. Stoning. The bank robbers had to be stoned to death."

"And Frank?" Kieran asked.

"Frank was defiling sacred ground," Evie said.

"And Margie and Elayne...they helped you stone Frank to death."

Evie gave them one of her sweet smiles. "Didn't even blink," she said. "You must understand. Margie came to know a great deal of truth through me—through our family. Victor met her on the mainland years ago at an NYU lecture on outer space and the possibility of worm holes. Great connection, but... All right, enough about that. Now, if you three will kindly step over the edge..."

"I don't get it!" Kieran said.

She was buying time. How had she found herself in this position again?

She was stalling, she knew, because that's what one did to survive.

And there was always hope. Craig was somewhere, maybe nearby...

She had her phone; all she had to do was reach him.

She tried not to be noticed as she slipped her hand toward her back pocket.

"John Smith really loved Annie Green. I could swear it," Kieran said. "How did you get John to help you kill Annie?"

Victor sighed, waving the gun around. "You really don't get it, do you? I am the high priest. I watch over this domain. John was a believer. My obedient servant. I told him that she kept getting into things. He followed her when she came back here. Poor, sad Annie! She thought, I suppose, that she could surprise John with some wonderful gift or piece of knowledge. I think she suspected something was not quite as it seemed. But you see, there's a true believer."

Kieran inched her phone out of her jeans as Victor went on, "I told John that she was coming too close. I told him that the gods commanded that she die. He did it. He cried like a baby—but he obeyed." His eyes snapped to her. "Hands where I can see them!"

Kieran quickly brought her hand back in front of her. She hadn't managed to pull out her phone, much less dial Craig.

Only Victor held a gun. Kieran thought, if she rushed him, at least Danny and Finn might survive.

She edged toward Victor, tugging at Danny so that he stayed close to her. Finn did the same.

"Stop!" Victor commanded. "You must go over the cliff—onto the stones!"

"Help me understand," Kieran said. "Do the gods speak to you? How did you come to know about this place?"

Victor let out an impatient sigh. "My great-great-great or whatever grandfather. Anthony Eider!"

They all just looked at him.

"You never heard of Anthony Eider?" Victor demanded.

"No, I'm afraid not," Kieran said politely.

"He was one of the greatest blockade runners to ever tear up and down the coast! He was marooned here, after a sea battle, and he survived a prisoner of war camp. He left letters behind, wonderful letters about the island. And survival."

"He must have been quite a man," Kieran said.

She paused.

Behind Victor Eider and Evie Summers, Craig was coming up the cliff, and Bracken was behind him and both men had their guns out and...

She didn't need to say any more, stall anymore.

Craig's voice rang out. "FBI! Drop it, Victor, drop it now!"

Naturally, Victor and Evie swung around.

Victor stared at Craig, and he dropped his gun. "Some people," he said, "are willing to die for their beliefs! And the gods are stronger than all of us. In dying, we are martyrs, raised to their Elysian Fields in the greatest of galaxies! Evie?" he said.

Evie looked at him and nodded.

Kieran grabbed Danny and shouted to Finn.

"Down!" she shouted.

The three of them dove to the ground just in time.

Victor and Evie made a mad dash to the cliff, running over the three of them.

To the cliff edge...
And then over it.
Down to the rocks below.

EPILOGUE

Saturday, a week later

"Eureka!" Danny cried.

They were back in the caves for the first time since Victor and Evie had gone over the cliffs.

For a week, they'd gotten Finn off the island; he had taken up residence in Craig's apartment. While Craig and Kieran had been living in her apartment but planning to move to Craig's much larger and nicer one, they had finally done so. That way, they had their private spaces, and Finn could have his own room—and yet be around people. Kieran had managed to get back to work for Drs. Fuller and Miro for the week, and Craig and Mike had questioned Margie Appleby and Elayne Anderson—who were by then talking away.

With Evie and Victor gone, they had no more bargaining power.

But when Saturday had rolled around, Finn was

ready to go back to Douglas Island. And they were all packed and supplied. Bracken had pulled together a group of six men experienced in caves and tunnels. By the time they returned, crevice holes had been closed with heavy screens, and much of the tunnel system that they had already explored had become easy to traverse.

Kieran believed that Frank had been close to a discovery when he was killed.

Close to exactly what, she didn't know, but she'd found one of the little crevices within a tunnel on the lower level near the rocks—now gone—that had been splattered with Frank's blood. She'd found more strange symbols on the wall, and she and Danny had gone to work there.

As they dug, Danny hit something.

Craig and Bracken came in, and they all set to digging together.

"We're going to find another stone that says 'park horse here,'" Danny said, sighing.

"No, no," Craig said, "it's something else…listen. The sound is different from when we hit stone…it's…"

"I think it's some kind of a trunk," Bracken said.

"The Ark of the Covenant?" Danny said incredulously.

"No, I don't think so…it's wood, and the latches look like…iron? I'm not sure."

"Let's get her out!" Craig said.

They cleared all the dirt from the top and sides and heaved the chest out of the earth. And then they all fell back and paused for a minute.

"Is it a pirate chest?" Kieran asked.

"No…older, I think," Bracken said. He turned to Finn. "You do the honors."

"There's some kind of an old lock on it," Finn said.

"*Old* being the key word," Craig said. "I hope this doesn't ruin history, but…"

He simply kicked the lock with his heel. It sprang open.

And Finn opened the lid. He stared into the chest. "I… Wow," he said softly.

"Let's not touch the things in it—let's get it to a museum," Craig suggested.

"Yes, but…may we look?" Danny asked.

"Of course!" Finn said. "Oh, my God, this stuff is… ancient."

Kieran looked in the chest. There were chalices—jewel encrusted—and beautiful crosses, medallions and more. She looked up at Bracken and Craig. "No, we didn't find the Ark of the Covenant, but I do believe we might have discovered a trunk of relics that the Norse traders brought here on behalf of the Knights Templar. It could be."

"I think you're right," Danny said. He looked around and said, "And I'm almost-kind-of-a-little-bit like a historian!"

"Let's get it out of the cave," Finn said. "And let's celebrate."

That meant that they all cleaned up, left the island and went into Finnegan's Pub on Broadway. An Irish band was playing. It was the perfect place to celebrate.

Declan and Kevin joined them, and Declan's fiancée, Mary Kathleen.

They invited Jay Harding and Ben Garcia and the Believers as well.

Egan might have already been considered a regular, Mike was always with them—and Teddy Brice had come.

A reporter came in, and Finn kindly gave an interview.

He was approached by others, and promised to appear in interviews for national television.

Finn was, as always, gracious to everyone.

"And to think," Craig whispered to Kieran. "At the end, for a minute there, I'd pinned him for being the one about to kill you."

"Don't feel bad—when I got the info from Jay Harding, I was ready to name him as well."

Kieran wasn't sure if Finn knew they'd been whispering about him.

But he smiled, and he lifted his beer mug.

"To family!" he said.

Declan, who had been dividing his time between their table and the bar, lifted a glass of soda water. "To family, indeed!"

"Finnegan's Pub and family!" Danny cried.

The night wore on.

When they finally returned to Craig's place that night, they were alone.

Finn was heading home to the island. He was determined to get back to work. Bracken had taken a leave; he'd be staying on the island, too, while he kept searching the caves. Which was good because they didn't think Finn should be on his own just yet.

On entering their apartment, Craig closed and locked the door. Then he turned. Kieran had barely had a chance to step in, but he swept her into his arms.

"To family...to love!" he whispered.

She smiled. "To family, and to love," she agreed.

"And to the fact that we have way more than five minutes, or fifteen minutes or..."

She smiled, rising on her toes to kiss his lips.

"In truth, my love, we have forever."

"Forever? Even I may not last that long."

"I rather meant that you have me forever. As to the rest, well, we do have Sunday," she said.

"Forever with you? Yes, that works. And Sunday… that will work, and I will take it!" he told her, and being Craig, he dramatically made a big show of sweeping her off the floor and into his arms and into his bedroom.

They did have the night.

And, Kieran thought, yes…

Forever.

* * * * *

*Keep reading for a special sneak peek at the next
thrilling story in the New York Confidential series,
where Kieran Finnegan and Craig Frasier will have
to untangle a web of deceit, privilege and greed when
their manhunt for an escaped serial killer brings
them right to the doorstep of Finnegan's Pub.*

The Final Deception

by New York Times *bestselling author*
Heather Graham,
available March 31, 2020, from MIRA Books.

PROLOGUE

PROLOGUE

Craig Frasier breathed it in before he could stop himself—the bloodcurdling scent of burning flesh.

Human flesh.

Flames still skittered over the body—an accelerant had been used. As he stood there in the small dark alley, he heard others rushing in: Mike, his partner, and patrol officers. He heard the sirens. The fire department was coming.

But there was no saving this victim.

Craig was already tamping the fire out—an extinguisher would make the work of the medical examiner more difficult.

But he knew what the medical examiner would find.

The victim had been strangled, then the tongue had been cut out. And then the eyes had been gouged out. Death had occurred, mercifully, before the fire had been set.

The corpses haunted his dreams. Burnt shells, some

flesh and soft tissue remaining, charred and clinging to the bones, mummy-like. The mouth in the blackened skull was agape, and those empty, soulless eye sockets seemed to be staring up, as if they could still see, as if they stared at him in reproach…

Why hadn't they caught the killer sooner?

He heard a rustling sound. Looking across the alley, Craig saw a shadow moving. Leaving the corpse to the others, he took off like a bullet. He pursued the moving shadow at a run, running and running for blocks.

He reached an apartment on Madison, with a coffee shop and dress store on the first floor, just as the gate at the street entry to the residential units above had been closing. He caught the gate and reached the elevator in time to see what floor it stopped on. He followed.

And again, as he arrived, a door was just closing; he didn't let it close.

And there he was, the Fireman, still smelling of gasoline, ready to sit down to a lovely dinner with his family. About to say a prayer before the meal. Just a husband and a father, and a man who looked at Craig and calmly said, "So, my work is over. But I have obeyed the commandments given me, and I will go with you."

Why did you take so long? The corpse again! In Craig's dreams, the corpse was back, animated, flying at him like a ghostly banshee, issuing a silent scream.

Craig opened his eyes.

He didn't awake screaming or startled. He didn't jerk up. It was almost as if he'd always known it was a dream, reliving the day the Fireman had gone down.

He'd had the dream several times before. But now, it seemed as though it had been a long time. Weeks. He'd thought he'd ceased experiencing it altogether. He'd been doing all the right things, quietly seeing a bureau shrink a few times. He hadn't told Kieran Finnegan, his fiancée, about his recurring nightmare, and while she was a criminal psychologist working with two of the city's finest criminal psychiatrists, he'd made a point of not telling her or her bosses.

He'd thought he'd settled it on his own. It was a little strange and sometimes intimidating being in love with someone who studied the human psyche, and he hadn't wanted Kieran worried about him or trying to analyze him.

Why the hell had the dream come back?

He felt Kieran shift against him. He pulled her into his arms and she rolled, crystal eyes opening wide when she realized that he was awake.

And aroused. Kieran's tangle of auburn hair was a wild mass around her face, emphasizing her eyes and the quick smile that came to her lips.

"Ah!" she murmured, feeling his arousal against her.

"Your fault!" he accused.

"Well, thankfully," she murmured. And then, "What time is it?" she asked with a soft whisper.

He laughed. "Quickie time, or time for a quickie," he said.

Her smile deepened, and there was something so sensual about it that it never failed to increase whatever he had begun to feel.

In her arms, in the liquid burn of kisses strategically placed here and there, in the swift and intense blaze of arching and writhing and thrusting, all else faded.

After, Craig headed for the shower. He was an FBI agent in the Criminal Division of New York City's branch of the FBI. He could be satisfied in having brought down several killers. But there would be more; a sad fact of the world and humanity. He was blessed to have his job, his vocation, and it was time to go to work.

He shoved the dream to the back of his mind.

Whatever his day held, he'd already seen the worst that this world could offer.

Little did he know.

CHAPTER
ONE

Two months later

"Thou shall not suffer a witch to live!" Raoul Nicholson said. His voice was low, but passionate. He stared at Kieran Finnegan with eyes that pleaded for understanding.

Kieran sat in a chair across from Nicholson, her hands folded on the simple metal desk between them.

Nicholson was handcuffed—and chained to pegs at the foot of his side of the table.

The man's attorney, Cliff Watkins, had chosen not to sit. He stood, hands folded behind his back, behind Nicholson. He'd assured Kieran he was there just to protect his client—though protecting him seemed a futile effort at times.

She liked Watkins. He was clean-shaven and bald, somewhere in his early to midforties, lean and wiry and calm. Despite his client, he wasn't a grandstander.

His firm had taken on the case pro bono, and he was doing his best to see that the man was treated fairly and locked away in the right place.

Trying for an innocent plea of any kind didn't seem to be his game.

Good. Nicholson could never be deemed innocent.

Watkins didn't seem to be concerned with safety issues. He'd shrugged when they'd chained Nicholson down. He'd known a protest would be foolhardy, and for the record alone.

Kieran wasn't sure the security measures were necessary. She didn't believe Nicholson was a threat to her because he didn't believe that *she* was a witch.

Or was it all a ruse for an insanity plea?

She started to speak, but before she could, he was pleading with her again. "Don't you understand? The world is a disaster because no one adheres to the commandments. Those I executed, they weren't men and women. You must believe me. I killed witches. I helped rid the world of monsters. You must obey the commandments. 'Thou shall not suffer a witch to live!'"

"What about 'Thou shall not murder?'" Kieran asked quietly.

"It refers to *people*!" Nicholson told her, distressed and shaking his head. "You don't understand what I'm trying to tell you. They were *witches*. Satan's minions."

Nicholson had brutally murdered five people—two prostitutes, a senior at NYU, a fashion designer and an accountant. Before they had been murdered—the investigations into their deaths had proved—he had delivered each one of them a simple message.

I know what you are; you are going to die.

The bodies had been found across the city—one

downtown, one in the West Village, one in Hell's Kitchen and two in Midtown.

They had been burned, leaving very little to be discovered by the medical examiner. But even with the use of an accelerant, there had been enough left behind for the ME to report that, in each case, the eyes and tongue had been removed. That information, however, had been kept from the public.

The press had given him the moniker the Fireman.

Once in captivity, Nicholson had never denied his guilt. He had been on a mission. And in the eyes of His Maker, he had done what needed to be done. He was happy to be a martyr. His reward would come to him, and he would be judged by "He Who Mattered," or his "Higher Power." What happened in earthly courts didn't matter to him.

Nicholson had a wife, Amy, and two children, Thomas and John; the first had graduated from NYU, and John was now studying at Princeton. He owned a furniture repair shop in the Village and had a rent-controlled apartment.

His wife was, understandably, devasted. Crying 24/7. They had been a religious family, yes. But she'd had no idea of her husband's homicidal desire to cure the world of witchcraft. Or *so she claimed.*

His pastor, Reverend Axel Cunningham, had been similarly stunned, or *so he claimed*, as well. As had his coworkers at the furniture shop. And according to everyone at Annie's Sunrise, where Nicholson stopped every morning for a donut and a latte, he was always kind and courteous and polite. Annie Sullivan, who owned the place, was heartbroken, claiming that he was one of the nicest customers who came in, courteous to everyone around him and making people smile as they started out their day.

To everyone, he was just a wonderful person. If he hadn't admitted his guilt, they would have all said it couldn't be so. Even his attorney said he'd never met such a sincere man.

Nicholson was a thin man, but lean muscled, forty-eight years old, with a full beard and mustache and long, wild brown hair.

"I'm sorry, Mr. Nicholson, that you perceived these people to be witches, but they were young men and women. I'm trying to understand why you thought they were witches—and why that allowed you to kill. They weren't broomstick-riding crones... I'm not making fun of you. I'm trying to understand you."

And determine if you're lying! she thought silently.

He leaned forward, as if he felt he had found a friend—one who really might not just understand him but agree the witches needed to die.

"You must listen to me." He paused to sniff suddenly. "They're not even silly people who practice sanctioned 'Wicca' religions. Witches don't dance beneath the moon in the forest, naked, bowing to their horned god there. They are devious. They wear beautiful shells, and that's how they manipulate men—and women—and cause them to do hurtful things. I heard the voice that told me who they were and what must be done."

"A voice? God's voice?"

"Perhaps it was God's voice. Perhaps He sent Gabriel or another angel. We all see God differently, but, yes, if you like, God's voice. But the point is, I knew what must be done. And as hard as it was, I did it. I was told to be merciful—one does not retrieve a soul by cruelty. I offered them a chance to repent, and I strangled them as quickly as I could. Then I cut out their eyes and tongues so they would no longer see the devil as they made their way to purgatory, no longer be able to answer his call. And if I am to die for the good I've attempted to bestow upon the world, so be it. I have done as I was commanded."

Watkins spoke up. "You're not going to die, Raoul."

"If there are federal charges, I could be sentenced to death," Nicholson said.

"No, Mr. Nicholson, what we're trying to determine here is just what charges they wish to pursue," Kieran told him quietly. She looked over at the man's attorney. Watkins met her gaze with steady brown eyes that said, *"The man is sick. Whether he admits it or not, he's not playing with a full deck."*

"The laws of man must be used as man chooses," Nicholson said. "I will answer in the flesh, as such laws command. I only killed witches. I killed nothing but evil."

"You killed people with family and friends and long lives ahead of them," Kieran said.

"The voice was very clear on who must be killed and when. You can't imagine what havoc they might have done to the world. There are more out there, of course. They are the Devil's disciples—and you must be afraid, Miss Finnegan, you must be very afraid."

"Mr. Nicholson, I beg you, watch your words!" Watkins warned.

Kieran was startled. She hadn't expected to be on his list. She hadn't even expected to be here.

In a case this serious, her employers, Drs. Fuller and Miro, usually did the interviews, and several of them, for the police or the FBI. They were psychiatrists. She was on their staff as a psychologist and most often worked when therapy was ordered by the court or the effect of that therapy was to be determined.

But because of the circumstances of this case, they had both already spoken with the accused. And they wanted Kieran's opinion of his mental state, as well. If he was a liar, he was a good one, a passionate one.

"I'm in danger?" she asked, keeping her voice even and low. Was he a threat to her?

"Witches—slaves of Satan! I fear for you greatly. You don't know the danger they present. You can't imagine what they might do to you! You are in no danger from me—you're a good person. Anyone can see that. But you also must believe that evil is out there. I barely began to rid the world of a tiny portion of the evil."

"Mr. Nicholson, I really want to see all this, see what you're seeing. But your victims... I just can't see what harm they caused anyone."

Nicholson sighed softly. "You don't see, but you will. The young woman I last freed... If they haven't discovered it yet, she was spreading a deadly disease. Satan commanded her to spread it as far as she could. The man...second, third... I don't remember...he killed his father. Satan told him to do so. They were all obeying *their* Higher Power, Satan. I was charged to stop them!"

Kieran sat back. She didn't know if it was true or not. Could the burned body have allowed the medical examiner to test for infectious diseases? If that had been the case, she didn't know about it.

"How did you know these things about your victims?" she asked.

"The voice told me, of course." He leaned forward

again. "You must watch out for evil people—the true murderers, true spawns of Satan. You see, I am afraid. Afraid for you. Not from the voice I hear—the voice likes you, it commanded me to be honest with you—but danger lurks from Satan."

Well, at least he thought she was good. And he was talking to her, talking more than when he had been interviewed by her bosses.

Back against the wall, Cliff Watkins sighed as if with great patience.

"Mr. Nicholson, how did the voice—telling you to kill—come to you?"

"Different ways. Sometimes in a crowd, I'd hear the whisper. But you know New York. No one near me was talking to me. Once, through my cell phone. Once, I saw the name in the paper, and I knew. And when I dreamed that night, the voice came to me in the dream, showing me what I must do."

He seemed so positive, so certain.

She jotted down some notes. There were fine lines to be drawn between someone who was incompetent to stand trial and someone who was legally insane.

She was glad all she had to do was report on her findings, give her opinion on his mental state.

"Thank you for talking to me, Mr. Nicholson," she told him, nodding to the guard who stood by the cell door. He opened it for her; another guard waited to escort her out.

Cliff Watkins followed.

"He's sick, can't you see? We can take a deal on this and get him into a facility from which he can't escape, where he'll be given the help he needs. Please, I hope you see the truth of the man."

She smiled; she wasn't sure what she saw yet.

David Berkowitz, the Son of Sam killer, had heard voices ordering him to kill.

And, in the 1970s, in Southern California, Herbert Mullin had killed because a voice told him that an earthquake was imminent if he didn't offer blood sacrifices to the earth. Anthony Sowell, the Cleveland Strangler, had killed because a ghost had ordered him to do so.

And there were so many more killers who had somehow justified their actions.

He wanted her to see the truth.

What was the truth?

She exited the prison. Dr. Fuller was waiting for her, ready to head from Rikers Island back to the mainland. They could discuss it all as he drove over the Francis R. Buono Memorial Bridge to Queens and, from there, down to Lower Manhattan. It was, in the city, a long trip in heavy traffic; they would have plenty of time to discuss their thoughts and findings.

One way or another, Nicholson would be locked up for a very long time. Hopefully, as far as Kieran was concerned, for life.

"I don't think he's lying. I think he believes every word he says," Kieran told Dr. Fuller. "It's hard to judge, but…" She pulled out her phone and the notes she had written after studying all she could about the man's life. "He was an avid churchgoer, and his church, Unitarian, is truly fundamentalist. He never danced, celebrated a birthday or did anything that was slightly fun—from what I can tell—much less indulge in drugs or alcohol or any other vices."

They continued to talk, and the drive went more quickly than Kieran had imagined it might.

"I just wish I could be sure," Kieran said.

Fuller cast a sideways glance and smiled. "Don't we all. Why do you think Dr. Miro and I had you talk to him, as well?" Dr. Fuller was an older man with classic Hollywood movie-star good looks, though he was one of the most humble people Kieran had ever met.

They had made it all the way down to Lower Manhattan, Kieran realized. Dr. Fuller was going to pull over for her to get out soon, and they couldn't tarry long on Broadway.

"Write it all up for me, and we'll give it to the prosecutors. They'll have to make the decision on just how to proceed," he told her. He stopped the car.

"Did you want to park somewhere, grab something to eat?" she asked him. Her family owned the pub where they had stopped: Finnegan's on Broadway. Kieran loved her work with the doctors; she also loved her three brothers and the pub. Her bosses were both known to accept a free dinner now and then, and both were classy enough to tip the waitstaff well.

It was early, barely 4:00 pm, but it was Friday evening, and the pub would be entering into cocktail hour, a crazy time.

"Thanks, but I have a romantic dinner tonight with the wife!" he told her, smiling. And then he frowned. "Oh, you should see the look you're giving me!" he told her. "Kieran, shake it off. It's the weekend. We deal with horrible things all the time. You'll have to quit thinking about it. I'm sure Craig is waiting for you or will be here soon—and your brother has made sure there's a great Irish band playing tonight, especially since it's Friday night. Nicholson is off the streets—that's what is most important. Get in there. And enjoy your family, your beau and your life!"

She saluted him. "Yes, sir!" He grinned as she slid out of the car. She did have to shake off her time with Nicholson and she knew it.

Her "beau," as Dr. Fuller had called him, was stepping out onto the sidewalk, obviously looking for her, just as she started for the door of Finnegan's.

"Hey!" she said cheerfully. Maybe too cheerfully.

Craig took a step toward her and pulled her firmly into his arms. It was good; the warmth of him, the strength of him, all coming into her after…after Nicholson.

"Craig, I…" Her voice trailed off.

"I know," he said softly. "Don't forget," he added, his voice husky, "I was on the task force that brought him down."

For a moment, they stood there, taking strength and comfort from each other, and then they went in.

Kieran's oldest brother, Declan, had brought in a great Irish band—the Boys of Shannon. They were playing and the pub was in full swing. Declan, behind the bar, waved her way. There was a little concern in her brother's eyes. She smiled and waved in turn.

Then she saw her other brothers, Danny and Kevin, running around helping. They were apparently short on staff this night.

"Looks like I'd better pitch in for a few minutes," she told Craig.

"Sure."

She served Guinness and Smithwick's and all the pub's specialties: shepherd's pie, corned beef and cabbage, pot pies and more. And the music touched her—guitars, drums, violin and keyboard. The night went on. She chatted and laughed. Danny and Kevin wound up sitting with Craig while she ran a bit ragged. Then she announced they were leaving. It wasn't even eight, but her brothers could take over; she'd done her bit.

"Hey!" her brother Danny—onetime bad-boy, petty thief turned historian and New York City tour guide—called to her, grinning. "You're going to miss the band coming back on."

"Maybe we'll come back—I need a breather after work. And work!" she said, letting him know she'd been the one running while Declan had been behind the bar—and he and Kevin had been sitting, entertaining Craig.

"Hey, I have a tour first thing in the morning!" Danny cried.

She shrugged, taking Craig's arm and waving goodbye.

Wincing, Danny stood, assuring one of their regulars he'd be happy to get him another soda with lime.

"Do come back!" her twin, Kevin, called. "Be social!"

"Sure!"

The pub would still be open for hours—until 2:00 a.m. on a Friday night—but she wanted time with Craig. By the time they headed out, she thought she had put her day—and Raoul Nicholson—into perspective.

Though Craig had a bureau car, they walked from the pub. It was merely six blocks to their new home. They'd moved a lot in the last few years—his place, her place, a place together—but now they were in a new condo and she loved it. Loved that it was theirs and they had chosen it together.

Upstairs, she showered quickly, loving as well that while the previous owner had kept the architectural integrity of the place, he'd installed a new master bathroom with a seriously fine shower nozzle. It seemed to wash the feeling of the day away. Maybe she made it do so in her mind. She stepped out of the bathroom in a thick terry robe, walked over to the windows and peeked out into the night. The apartment stretched from side to side of the building, so from the living area with its high ceilings they could look out at the skyline, just as they could from their bedroom, which was in an open loft space up a flight of stairs.

Stars were visible, and they were beautiful in the night sky. She heard Craig come in, and she smiled. It was Friday night; it was early. They had hours together here in the new home they loved like a pair of children excited over a new treehouse.

She nearly said something about Nicholson, but she didn't.

Until he touched her, she hadn't realized Craig was right behind her.

She didn't speak. He lifted her hair, kissing the nape of her neck. She turned to him and the kiss came to her lips, and his hands were on her, teasing on the tie of the terry robe.

Soon it was gone, and his clothing was strewn everywhere. His lips were liquid and afire on her flesh, they became a tangle of limbs on the bed, and they made love.

They lay comfortably together. And for a very long time, they still didn't speak. But then the day began to gnaw at the back of her mind. She was hesitant; she knew Craig had been on the case and he'd seen the results of the killer's work.

"What?" he asked her. "Come on—something is weighing on your mind."

"They sent me to interview Raoul Nicholson today," she said.

She felt him stiffen. "I thought Fuller or Miro did the interviewing on someone like Nicholson."

"They both spoke with him. Then they asked me to, as well."

"He has to be a madman."

"Or speaking the truth—just as he sees it. Or he's creating an unbelievably good con."

He rose on an elbow and looked down at her. "And?"

She shivered slightly; he held her closer. "I don't know—there's something about him. I've heard no one had any idea he was a killer, no one believed the Fireman might have been him—not his wife, coworkers, casual friends at the coffee shop he stopped by each morning. And yet…"

"And yet?"

"There's something about him. He doesn't seem delusional on the surface. But the way he speaks is…too passionate. The voice made him do it. The voice of God, in his mind. And those he killed were diseased—or about to kill the innocent. Well, you know his story. I guess the world knows his story. He's been written up in every major media outlet in the country, if not the world. The Fireman—apprehended." She grimaced at him. "At least you made the Bureau look great."

"Yeah—because he immediately admitted his guilt, and they finally managed to match a fingerprint at a crime scene," Craig said. "Otherwise… I'm not sure how my opening the door to his home would stand up."

"You said the door was open."

"It was," Craig said with a shrug. "Anyway, what will you say at trial?"

"That he needs to be locked up—and never let out."

"But…is he competent to sit at trial?"

"Yes, I believe he's cognizant to what's going on around him. He's just living in an alternate world. Or as I said, it's possible he's creating the best crazed persona possible to get into a hospital rather than a maximum-security prison—where he would be held without a chance for parole."

"It will be a while before we get to it," Craig said. He remained on his elbow, observing her carefully. He added quietly, "Life—and crime—will go on. But, aside from all that, we've got to…"

"To what?" she asked. They were personally involved with several cases. She knew people led normal lives by stepping back when they weren't working, but she and Craig had met because of a string of diamond heists in the city when they'd both wound up a little too personally involved. They didn't ask each other to forget friends, family—or even the problems of those who frequented Finnegan's on Broadway.

This one, though…

"Step back," he finished.

Yeah, she needed to step back.

She couldn't help but wonder, though, if his thought hadn't been for them both. She'd seen pictures of the victims. He'd seen the real deal.

"We have a wedding we keep putting off planning. People to see, places to go," he reminded her. He was right. "We've been together years. Your brothers are starting to look at me as if they question my intentions."

Kieran grinned and ran a teasing finger down his chest. "I'm sure many a night when we leave the pub, they're well aware of our intentions."

He smiled at that and drew her closer. "So, the wedding."

"Want to run away to Vegas?"

"I'm not into being hated the rest of my life."

"Well, your intentions will have been honorable, at the very least!"

"Seriously, it is absolutely foolish to even consider having the reception anywhere but the pub," Craig said, rolling on an elbow to smile at Kieran. "You would break your brothers' hearts—not to mention those of your regulars, who must, of course, be invited." He grinned. "We should head back over tonight, let them know we still haven't figured out a date, but there's no question about the reception. Make them happy. And Danny can give us his latest historical discovery and we can see what Kevin is up to—it is a Friday night, and it's still early. We should be free and clear."

"Sounds good. Maybe. Maybe not—let me mull on that!"

Kieran stretched and rose and walked to the window, just slightly opening the drapes. Their loft was on Reed Street, once part of an industrial complex, a massive tailoring shop, converted to apartments, and now apartment/condos. There were large, plate glass windows that looked over the street. Downstairs, the living area offered high ceilings and more intricate little architectural details. The apartment was perfect. She liked their neighbors. New York was amazing, and while she had traveled many places, she still found her native city to be one of the most diverse, historical and fascinating places she had ever seen. The view out the window was always intriguing. They had something of a neighborhood; she saw the same people in the little deli down the street all the time.

Life was good. Forget Nicholson.

She was determined to do so. The night itself commanded she do so—it was beautiful. She turned to look back at Craig and a real smile came to her lips.

Even after several years and many a strange adventure along the way, she still adored Craig. Her smile became an amused grin as she observed him with a trace of amusement as he lay stretched out over the bed.

"What?" he demanded, brows becoming an arch.

"You look like a pullout poster."

"What?" he demanded indignantly, starting to rise.

"Not an insult. You look…great," she said, and her smile became a laugh. "You just look like a pullout, a pinup, you know? All you need is a come-hither look on your face."

He was long and wire muscled and bronze against the sheets—and still naked. Of course, part of his physique was demanded by his job. She knew enough of his friends and coworkers to know that FBI agents did tend to come in athletic and fit—very fit. Naturally, they had to go through the academy and keep up for their work.

"You want a come-hither look?" he teased. He wiggled his eyebrows. She wasn't sure the look was really all that come-hither, but then, again, the way he was stretched out…

Come-hither enough!

She paused to adjust the drapes, and as she did so, she noticed that in seconds the weather had changed. Dark clouds covered what had been a striking star-lit sky. She shivered suddenly; it felt ridiculously like an omen or a foreboding.

It was just rain.

She made sure the curtain was back in place and turned toward the bed. She flew at it, flinging herself onto his naked body.

He gasped, groaned, caught her, held her above himself and laughed.

"My come-hither was okay, then?"

"No, it sucked!"

"Ah, I see. But you're coming to me anyway, right?"

"As you pointed out, it's Friday night, and neither of us have work, and I already helped out at the pub, so we can head over when we feel like it—or not—*and so* we have a chance here for sex, which, since we live together, we should be having far more often, while we're both physically here and awake! The come-hither look we'll have to work on."

"I'm crushed."

"You are not. You're overconfident, if anything. You're certain your look is completely seductive and compelling."

"I don't know about that. Crushed. I am crushed. You're lying on top of me, crushing me."

She grinned and didn't budge for a minute, then she pushed up against his chest and straddled him. "The big bad agent-guy can't handle it, huh?"

"Oh, he can handle it, all right." Calmly, he folded his arms behind his head. "Part of any investigation is to see just how far and where the other party is willing to go."

"Far!" she warned. She eased herself around in a slow and sinuous motion, and then eased slowly down on his arousal, drawing a groan and tremor from him.

She began to move.

He caught her arms, pulling her down to him, not losing a beat. "Big bad agent, eh?" And with a fluid motion, he rolled the two of them together, drawing her beneath him, and then their eyes locked, and their bodies moved.

Replete at last, they lay together, damp and shimmering, holding each other still.

Craig's phone rang.

Kieran groaned softly.

Craig hesitated; on the fourth ring, he rolled over, found his phone on the bedside table and answered it.

He listened; she watched the tension come into his face.

"What is it?" Kieran asked.

"Um, not sure yet. Just a crime scene that I must get to. Kieran, I'm sorry—"

"In for a penny, in for a pound," she told him, and reminded him, "Sometimes it's me. You put up with my crazy family and an entire Irish pub. And still…"

"And we wake up together," he said.

"And go to bed at night together. Sometimes." She laughed softly. "It's okay. Go—go! Get to your crime scene."

He gave her a grim smile and rolled to the edge of the bed to rise, and then padded into the bathroom. "I'll be there. I'm just not sure how late."

"It's a pub. It's open late. Especially on a Friday night. Oh, and I'm tight with the owners. It will be fine."

She lay back down, thinking she could just go to sleep, relax for the night, if she wanted.

But she didn't want to be alone right now, though she would never say so to Craig.

She wasn't usually so unnerved—she'd spoken to murderers before, along with rapists, child abusers and occasionally those who really might find a way to go straight.

She'd get up—and first go over her notes, because it was necessary. Then she'd head to the pub. She might not be needed to wait on any of the tables, but Declan was always there when she needed him. While she and

Danny and Kevin had "day" jobs—they all headed to the pub when they were off, or when they wanted to be with the family, or when they were simply at loose ends.

Craig came back into the room after what must have been a two-minute shower, buttoning his tailored shirt as he emerged. His Glock and holster were already at the small of his back.

He barely finished buttoning his shirt before he reached for his jacket.

He strode to the bed and hesitated, unusually tense. He was accustomed to his work; he dealt with it well.

"I'll keep in touch," he promised. "And I'll see you as soon as I can get there."

Then he was gone. She lay there, contemplating the darkened sky. To her, it seemed there was something else about it.

A whisper of warning.

She shook off the thought, rose, showered and dressed. Later, she would realize just how dark and foreboding the night and the coming days would prove to be.

Kieran and Craig will have to be smarter and bolder than ever before, because this time it's personal and they have everything to lose.
Don't miss it!

The Final Deception

by Heather Graham,
available March 31, 2020, from MIRA Books.

**The fifth and final novel in the
New York Confidential series by
long-established *New York Times*
bestselling romantic suspense author**

HEATHER GRAHAM

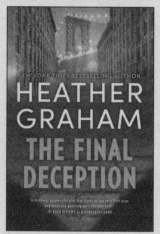

Criminal psychologist
Kieran Finnegan and
FBI agent Craig Frasier
face their most chilling
challenge yet. When a
serial killer escapes from
prison, murders in his
gruesome style begin again
right away. Kieran has
an unnerving connection
to the killer, having
counseled him prior to his
incarceration. As the threat
looms ever closer, Craig is suspicious that there's
more to the case than an escaped convict, and the pair
will dig deep to discover if someone else is following
in the killer's footsteps.

Coming soon from MIRA books.